W9-BWK-021

CATCHING UP

"You're beautiful," he murmured. "More beautiful than I remembered." His gaze lowered to her breasts. "I don't recall you being so well-endowed, either. The years have been kind to you."

"I was but seventeen when we married. Women do mature and change over the years. You've changed, too."

His gaze returned to her face. "How so?"

She hesitated a moment, then said, "You're harder, colder, more in control of yourself. You've matured, too. Your body is, . . ."

She turned her gaze away, but Sam would have none of it. He lifted her chin and lowered his head. A startled cry slipped past her throat when his lips came down on hers.

The first touch of his mouth was feather light, a mere whisper of sensation against her lips. Her breath caught. Then he deepened the kiss, sliding his mouth back and forth against hers. The sweet, titillating friction tilted her world. What happened next totally undid her. Suddenly Sam's lips became hard, demanding, his tongue a dagger that probed ruthlessly into her mouth. Seeking, searching, as if starved for the taste of her.

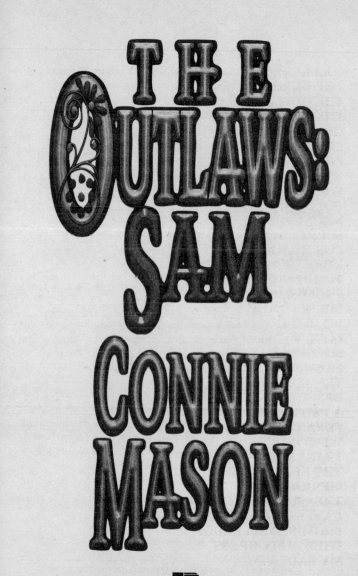

THE OUTLAWS: SAM

CONNIE MASON

LEISURE BOOKS   NEW YORK CITY

A LEISURE BOOK®

May 2001

Published by

Dorchester Publishing Co., Inc.
276 Fifth Avenue
New York, NY 10001

ISBN 0-8439-4865-5

Printed in the United States of America.

Visit us on the web at www.dorchesterpub.com.

Chapter One

Denison, Texas, 1868

He opened his eyes one at a time, slowly, carefully. His head pounded and his mouth tasted like the inside of an outhouse. Sam Gentry knew without a doubt he had the granddaddy of all hangovers. Even more disheartening was the fact that he was in jail and had no idea how he got there.

Had the posse caught up with him? Had the sheriff of Denison, Texas, seen his picture on that blasted Wanted poster that proclaimed to all the world that the Gentry brothers were outlaws? The last thing he remembered was sitting down at the poker table in a saloon whose name he couldn't remember and betting the last of his money on a winning hand. The pot had been substantial and he'd bought a around of drinks for everyone at the table. He searched his memory for more information and came up blank. He choked out a groan. What in the hell had happened?

"You finally woke up. I was beginning to worry."

The gruff voice sent pain shooting through Sam's head. He turned slowly. His bleary eyes focused with some difficulty on a man who looked vaguely familiar. He was sitting on the floor, his back braced against the wall. He was older than Sam by many years. His faded red hair was streaked with gray, and his leathery complexion had the look of a man who'd spent his life outdoors.

"Do I know you?" Sam didn't recognize his own voice, which came out raspy and grating.

The man chuckled. "You sure as hell ought to. I'm Rusty Ramsey from the B&G Ranch. How much do you remember about last night?"

"Damn little."

"You're one helluva fighter, Sam."

"You know my name?"

"You mentioned it last night. In Texas nobody asks for last names. It ain't healthy, if you know what I mean."

Sam knew exactly what he meant.

"You won a heap of money at the poker table last night and bought everyone a round of drinks. I reckon you decided you needed a few more, 'cause you sure hung a good one on."

"I remember that much. But that doesn't explain why

I feel like I've been run over by a hay wagon. Why did you say I was a good fighter?"

"The fight's the reason we're both cooling our heels in jail. I reckon Sheriff Hale will show up soon to turn us loose."

Sam sat up slowly. Very slowly. "Tell me about the fight, Rusty. I can't believe I'd do anything that would land me in jail. I've been trying to stay out of jail since I left Dodge a few weeks ago."

"So you're from up Kansas way," Rusty said. "Thought I recognized that Kansas twang. I take it you don't recall the boys from the Cramer spread picking a fight with me."

Sam shook his head and was immediately sorry.

"They were goading me about their boss's upcoming marriage to the owner of the B&G. Said I was too old to continue on as foreman, that I'd be out of a job after Taylor Cramer took over. I took exception to being called old." He wiggled his jaw back and forth. "I reckon it was foolish of me to take on two men younger than myself by several years, but they made me mad. I didn't ask for your help, and you didn't ask if I wanted it, but I sure as hell appreciated it when you threw yourself into the fight."

"No wonder I feel like I've been battered. I can usually hold my own in a fight, but I'm not usually drunk when I'm doing it. Did we win?"

Rusty grinned. "We weren't losing. The sheriff broke it up before anyone was seriously hurt."

"Are the Cramer hands in jail?"

"No. Sheriff Hale learned that I started the fight and let the Cramer hands go. Don't worry, we'll be out of here soon. I need to get back to the ranch. The boss lady depends on me."

Sam gave a shudder of relief. He was to be set free, so obviously the sheriff hadn't seen the Wanted poster. "A woman owns the B&G?"

"Yep. Her uncle up and died a couple of months ago and left it to her. A pity, too. She wasn't born to ranching and don't know beans about it. But I gotta hand it to her. She's learning fast and she ain't afeared of hard work."

The sound of squeaking door hinges sent renewed pain shooting behind Sam's eyes. He blinked, and the tall, solid form of the sheriff came into focus.

"You boys ready to leave?"

Rusty dragged himself to his feet. "I reckon we are, Sheriff."

The sheriff fit the key in the lock and swung open the door. "You're both free to go. You know better than to pick a fight, Rusty. And you, young fella," he said, fixing Sam with a stern look, "you're a stranger in town, aren't you?" Sam nodded. "If you plan on sticking around, you should know I don't condone fighting in public places. Denison is a peaceful town, and I aim to keep it that way."

"Sam won't give you any more trouble, Sheriff," Rusty promised.

Sam rose unsteadily, anxious to leave the jail. He followed Rusty out the door, squinting into the brilliant daylight.

"You look awful," Rusty said.

"You don't look so good yourself."

"What are you gonna do? You got business in town or something?"

Sam rubbed the dark stubble growing on his chin. "I'm just riding through."

Rusty slapped him on the back. "I like you, son. If you're looking for work, I can offer you a job on the B&G. We can use another hand or two."

"What about your boss? Won't she have something to say about it?"

"She leaves the hiring and firing to me. She's got enough to do taking care of her son. Cute little tyke named Andy."

Sam seriously considered taking Rusty up on his offer. He'd always preferred ranching to farming, and a ranch sounded like a good place to lay low for a while. And he doubted that those Wanted posters he so feared had reached this far south yet. Denison was a small town; he felt reasonably safe here.

"Maybe I'll take you up on that offer, Rusty. I need a job and a place to light for a while. At least until your boss marries that Cramer fellow and we're booted out."

"He won't fire all the hands, just me and a couple others. Me and Cramer had a little run-in a while back. That was before Hob Bigelow, Lacey's uncle, died. Come on, Sam, forget that bastard. Let's get our horses from the livery and ride out to the ranch. I'll introduce you to the boss lady and show you the ropes. You know anything about ranching?"

"A little. My people were farmers, but I can ride and rope with the best of them."

"You'll do."

Sam and Rusty headed out of town. Sam was happy to see the last of Denison. He'd tried to avoid towns since shaking the posse a few weeks ago, but he'd run low on provisions and money. He had stopped at Den-

13

ison to find a poker game. He'd always played a good hand of poker, not as good as Jess, but better than Rafe. He'd used the last of his money to bet on an inside straight and won, but Lord only knew what he did with the money. From the size of his head, he suspected he had squandered it all on booze.

Sam needed a drink. His head felt ready to burst, and riding made it worse. A cup of strong coffee would be mighty welcome now. Sam's mind wandered back to Kansas, to the day he and his brothers were falsely accused of bank robbery. They hadn't had time to consider whether running away was a good idea, not with a posse of hotheaded men with hanging on their minds breathing down their necks.

During the past few weeks Sam had often wondered if they would have been able to prove their innocence had they not run. He seriously doubted that the posse would have let them live long enough to face a judge and jury. The Gentry brothers had been Southern sympathizers in a Yankee state, and the people of Dodge never let them forget it. They hadn't even allowed Jess, a dedicated doctor, to practice medicine after the war. They had shunned his services in droves, and Jess was forced to take down his shingle.

Rafe had tried hard to make a go of the farm, but the last drought had all but wiped them out. And asking for a bank loan had started all the trouble with the law.

"I'll bet you're hungry," Rusty said, reining in beside Sam.

"Nope, but I can sure use a drink," Sam answered. "You don't have a bottle on you, do you?"

"Nope. I ain't a drinker. I hope you're not one either,

'cause the boss don't cotton to drinking men working for her."

"I don't usually drink to excess, though I do like a drink now and again. Last night was an exception. I've had a . . . bit of hard luck recently. I reckon I let it get me down and reacted by getting drunk. It won't happen again, though a drink would settle my stomach right now."

"The ranch is just up ahead. A cup of Luke's coffee and some of his hot biscuits should perk you up."

Shading his eyes against the brilliant rays of the sun, Sam spied the ranch. Squat and rambling, it sat on a low rise surrounded by numerous outbuildings and scraggly trees. In the distance, he could see cattle grazing on the range, and the yard and paddock were a beehive of activity.

"Looks like a prosperous spread," Sam said.

"Looks can be deceiving," Rusty answered. "Miz Lacey is having the devil's own time keeping the ranch. Several years of back taxes are due shortly, and she hasn't the cash to pay them. I swear she's marrying Taylor Cramer for his money. She and little Andy ain't got nowhere else to go."

Lacey!

The name produced a tangle of painful memories that Sam had tried hard to forget. Not even his brothers knew about Lacey, and he intended to keep it that way. He could hardly stand thinking about her himself. But this Lacey couldn't be the same Lacey who had cold-bloodedly betrayed him. The woman who had sent him to a sure death. But he had fooled her and escaped. He shook his head clear of unwelcome thoughts. As far as he knew—though he hadn't bothered to find out—Lacey Peters was still living in Pennsylvania.

"I assume your boss is a widow."

"Yep. Her husband died in the war. Then her pa died. After the war, she and her son came to live with Hob Bigelow, her mother's brother. Old Hob renamed the ranch to include the initial of Miz Lacey's last name."

"Hob Bigelow must have been a poor businessman," Sam mused, already putting Lacey Peters behind him where she belonged.

"Hob did his best, but he lost a bundle supporting the Rebel cause during the war. Never did recoup his losses. He died a mite sooner than he thought and left Miz Lacey with a heap of bills she had no idea existed, including five years of back taxes."

"And you think she's marrying Taylor Cramer for his money?"

"Can't think of no other reason. That man wanted to get his hands on the ranch before old Hob died, but Hob wouldn't sell. He didn't trust Cramer, and neither do I."

"Maybe Miz Lacey loves Cramer."

Rusty gave a bark of laughter. "Ha! That ain't likely. I'd be the first to admit her boy needs a pa, but Cramer ain't that man. He don't even like little Andy."

They rode through the gate. Rusty directed him toward the paddock. "You don't look in any condition to meet Miz Lacey today." He dismounted. "Leave your horse; one of the hands will take care of him. I'll take you to the cookhouse first, and you can sample some of Luke's coffee. If you survive that, you can survive anything. Then I suggest that you clean up, find yourself an empty bunk in the bunkhouse, and sleep off your hangover. You'll find the bunkhouse over yonder." He pointed to a long, low building a stone's throw from the cookhouse.

"I reckon I do look pretty rough. Don't want to scare the boss lady." Sam shouldered his saddlebags and started off toward the cookhouse. "Are you coming?"

"Not right now. I want to check on the hands first. Don't want any of them shirking their duty. I'll see you later."

The cook wasn't in the cookhouse, so Sam found a tin cup and helped himself to the coffee sitting on a back burner. It was thick and black, and he gulped it down in one long swallow. It burned clear down to his stomach, but it did help settle it. The thought of food was revolting, so he headed over to the bunkhouse. He stopped at the pump and pulled off his shirt. Then he bent over and pumped cold water over his aching head.

Lacey stepped out the back door, shaded her eyes against the glare of the sun and walked briskly to the henhouse to gather eggs. Dust swirled around her booted feet and along the hem of her split skirt. We need rain, she thought as she gazed out over the brown prairie grass. She worried excessively about the cattle during this dry time of year, but fortunately there was a stream on the property that rarely ran dry due to the underground spring feeding it. Other ranchers weren't as lucky in that respect.

Lacey had nearly reached the henhouse when she caught sight of a man washing up at the pump. His back was to her, but she would have sworn no hired hand on the B&G matched his description. He was magnificent, like no other cowhand she'd seen. His hips were narrow, his back broad and his shoulders wide. When he bent over to dunk his head beneath the pump, her gaze lingered on the taut mounds of his buttocks.

Her breath hitched.

Even though she couldn't see his face, something about the man was familiar. Too familiar for comfort. A shiver slid down her spine as memories assailed her. Her thoughts were so painful she forced them away. Then she realized she was staring at the man's backside and deliberately looked elsewhere. What would he think of her if he caught her watching him?

Shaking inappropriate thoughts and unwelcome memories from her mind, she proceeded to the henhouse. But Lacey's wayward thoughts still lingered on the man she had once loved. The dark-haired stranger reminded her of him, and the war, and how her life had changed because of it. A Rebel had walked into her life and left her a little wiser, a little older, a little bruised. But she had Andy, and she couldn't regret a moment of the experience.

Chapter Two

Sam slept the entire day and through the night. The following morning Rusty took him in hand, introducing him to Luke, the B&G cook, and the ten hands who worked the ranch. Most were young men ranging in age from seventeen to just under thirty. Sam fell somewhere in the middle.

After a satisfying breakfast, Rusty took Sam to meet Miz Lacey.

"She's usually in her office going over accounts at this time of day. I'm sure she won't have any objections about me hiring you on, for that's my jurisdiction, but you need to meet her anyway."

Sam squared his shoulders. "So let's go meet your Miz Lacey. By the way, what does this paragon look like?"

"Like an angel. Small and blond with unusual greenish gold eyes and a smile that could light up the world. The boys would do anything for her, but they don't think much of her intended husband."

Sam fell silent. Small and blond with greenish gold eyes could describe the Lacey he had fallen in love with during the hellish war between the states. But that Lacey was a Yankee and to his knowledge was still living in Pennsylvania.

Rita, the cook/housekeeper, let them in the back door. She smiled at Rusty. "The señora is in her office. You know the way."

The house, Sam noted as he passed through the kitchen and parlor and down the hallway, was neat, clean and well kept. The furniture was functional, not fancy, apparently built for hard wear. Rag throw rugs were scattered over polished hardwood floors, and the curtains were drawn back to allow the breeze to pass through the open windows.

"This is Miz Lacey's office," Rusty said, pausing before a closed door.

Rusty rapped lightly, and moments later a feminine voice bade them enter. Rusty opened the door and walked inside. Sam followed close on his heels.

"Howdy, Miz Lacey," Rusty greeted. "I hired on a new hand. Thought you'd like to meet him. Say howdy to Miz Lacey, Sam."

Sam stepped forward, and found himself entangled in his worst nightmare. Miz Lacey was Lacey Peters! The one woman he had every reason to hate. The woman who evoked memories he'd fought hard to bury all these years. Now here she was, his nemesis, his nightmare, looking more beautiful than he remembered. Fate had dealt him a devastating blow.

Lacey stared at Sam Gentry as if he were a ghost come back to haunt her. Her face paled and her hands shook as she clutched the edge of the desk. Sam Gentry! Alive! Not dead and buried all those years ago like she'd been led to believe. He stood before her larger than life, a bit older but more handsome than she remembered. She couldn't believe it. Alive! And he was staring at her with more venom than she deserved.

Why hadn't he gotten in touch with her after the war? Her heart sank. She knew why, but he was wrong. She'd had nothing to do with her father's decision to trade him to the Yankees for her brother.

"Are you all right, Miz Lacey?" Rusty asked. "You look kind of peaked all of a sudden."

Lacey heard Rusty's voice as if it were coming from a great distance. She knew she had to answer but couldn't seem to make her mouth work. She realized her face was as white as a sheet, but she had just received the greatest shock of her life. She collected her tattered nerves, swallowed hard and said, "Anyone you hire on is fine with me, Rusty. You're the expert here. But if you don't mind, I'd like a few words alone with Sam."

If Rusty found anything unusual about Lacey's request, he made no mention of it. "Sure thing, Miz Lacey. Meet me at the corral when you're finished here, Sam."

Sam and Lacey continued to stare at one another long after Rusty left. Lacey was the first to break the weighted silence. "You let me go on thinking you were dead all these years! Why?"

Sam searched for his tongue and finally found it, along with his anger. "You damn well know why! Did you think I would return to you after you betrayed me?"

"I had nothing to do with that."

Bitterness colored his words. "Tell it to someone who will believe you."

"I begged Captain Wiltshire to tell me what happened to you. All he'd say was that you'd been taken to a ship to be transported north to prison. I wrote to Washington, but they had no record of you ever being in one of their prisons. I was told that you had probably died before you arrived at the prison, given the condition of the prison ships. I didn't want to believe you were dead, but everything I'd been told pointed in that direction."

"Captain Wiltshire!" Sam spat. "Wasn't he that blond Yankee who came for me after you betrayed me? Did you take up with him after he carted me away?" He gave a bark of laughter. "You didn't really think he would trade me for your brother, did you?"

A pained look crossed Lacey's face. "I didn't know it then, but my brother had already died at Andersonville. Something Captain Wiltshire neglected to tell us."

His voice held a biting edge. "So your betrayal was for nothing. Well, you needn't have worried. I never reached the prison. It's true that a Yankee patrol escorted me to the prison ship, but they were set upon by Rebel forces and I was set free. I survived the rest of the war without a scratch."

"Why didn't you tell me you were alive? I'm your *wife!* I had a right to know."

"You had no rights where I was concerned. You lost them the day the Yankees came for me."

"Why are you here? How did you find me?"

"I'm here by accident; I had no idea I'd find you here. In fact, I never even think about you. It's like you never existed."

Lacey looked stricken, but she immediately recovered. "Did you end our marriage? Have you taken another wife?"

"I saw no reason to end our marriage, since I had no desire to remarry . . . ever. You taught me that women were untrustworthy. I was young and foolish when we met. The war, the threat of sudden death, does strange things to men. Our marriage should never have happened. Over the years I managed to forget I had a wife. I understand you're to be married soon, so I suspect I'm not the only one who forgot our marriage."

Lacey's chin quivered, but she wouldn't give in to her anger. "I thought you were dead. I waited six years for you to return to me. What else was I to think?"

"Nice try, Lacey, but it won't work. How many lovers have you taken since that day we parted? I understand you have a son."

"Leave Andy out of this. He has nothing to do with you and me."

"Who's the boy's father? Is it Wiltshire? Why wouldn't he marry you? Oh, that's right, you were already married. Whose name does the boy carry?"

"Mama, Mama! Rita made sugar cookies. Can I have one?"

The lad who burst into the room was the image of Lacey. Right down to his blond ringlets and pert nose. Only his eyes were different. They were a clear, guileless blue. Sam knew immediately the boy wasn't his, for the Gentry men were all dark-haired and dark-eyed. Obviously the lad belonged to the blond Captain Wiltshire, just like he'd suspected.

Sam watched dispassionately as Lacey held out her arms and Andy ran into them.

"Can I, Mama? I promise to eat all my lunch."

"Of course, Andy. Run along now. Tell Rita you can have a cookie. But only one."

Andy beamed at her. Then he noticed Sam for the first time. "You're new here, aren't you, mister?"

The boy was so appealing Sam couldn't stop the smile that sprang to his lips. "I just hired on. My name's Sam. What's your name?"

"Andy."

"Andy what? You have a last name, don't you?"

"Sam . . ." The warning came from Lacey, but was promptly ignored.

"Andy Gentry," the boy said. "My papa's dead. He died in the war. Mama said he was a hero."

Sam stared at Lacey, his expression fierce. "She did, did she? How old are you?"

Andy puffed out his chest. "Five. Almost a man. Man enough to take care of Mama, anyway."

"Run along, love," Lacey said. "Mr. . . . er . . . Sam and I need to talk."

"I'll see you around, Sam," Andy called over his shoulder as he flew out the door.

"You gave him my last name!" Sam hissed. "He's the picture of Wiltshire. Why does your bastard bear my name?"

"I don't owe you any explanations," Lacey blasted.

"What do you intend to do about our marriage? Will you apply for a divorce or shall I?"

The stubborn streak in Sam spoke before his saner self thought his answer through. "I'm not going to do a damn thing."

Anger made him want to hurt Lacey. If throwing a monkey wrench into her wedding plans hurt her, then so be it. Let her suffer as he had suffered. He had married her because he'd loved her. She had found him in a field littered with bodies after a battle in Pennsylvania. His leg had been broken by a minnie ball and she'd taken him in and healed him, hiding him from the Yankees.

They had fallen in love . . . or rather, *he* had fallen in love. Her father had caught them making love one night and dragged the preacher out of bed to marry them. Sam was nearly recovered when the Yankees came for him. Tom Peters, Lacey's father, led him to believe that Lacey had betrayed him, and Sam had no reason to doubt him. He was told she had done it to save her brother. Captain Wiltshire had informed them that Ron Peters was being held in a Southern prison and so ill he might die. Sam was sure that Lacey had offered Sam as a trade for her brother.

Lacey paled. "What did you say?"

"You're not getting out of this marriage that easily. Does your intended know your son is a bastard? Have you told him anything about your background?"

"Damn you," Lacey hissed. "Taylor Cramer knows I'm a widow. Andy's birth was legal in every way."

"But you're not a widow, are you? And Andy isn't mine." He paused, suddenly appalled by what Lacey had done. "How dare you give your son my last name!"

"What other choice did I have? I was your wife; I bear your name."

"Wife, bah! Do you know how betrayed I felt when the Yankees came for me? Do you have any idea the anguish you put me through? I loved you, dammit! It sickens me to think how young and foolish I was back then."

"I wasn't even there when Captain Wiltshire came for you. It wasn't my doing. Do you know how I felt when you showed up alive and well today? My first reaction was shock. Then anger took over when I remembered all the years you let me think you were dead."

"You were dead to me; why shouldn't I be dead to you?"

A frisson of guilt passed through Sam, but he pushed it aside. What Lacey had done to him was unforgivable. He shouldn't feel any remorse for having let her believe he was dead. Obviously she hadn't grieved too long. Her son Andy was proof that she hadn't waited to take a lover.

"Surely you don't intend to stay here," Lacey said. "I'm to be married in a few weeks."

Sam sent her a mocking smile. "I don't think so."

"Sam, please. If you ever cared for me you'd . . ."

His dark eyes narrowed and his face hardened. "The young man who loved you no longer exists. Sorry, Lacey; there will be no marriage. Do you want to tell Cramer or shall I?"

Lacey gulped back a cutting reply. She didn't know this Sam and had no idea what he was capable of. The Sam she'd once loved was kind and loving and sweet. This Sam was hard and cold and unfeeling. Why did he have to return from the dead?

"I'll tell him, in my own good time. But he won't take this lying down. He wants to marry me, and . . . and . . . I want to marry him."

Dark, glittering eyes searched her face. "You don't sound all that convinced. This ought to prove interesting. It's your turn to hurt for a while."

Sam didn't know what hurting was, Lacey thought. She'd been devastated to learn that her father had betrayed Sam. When no one could tell her what had happened to Sam, and she thought that he had died in a prison camp, she'd felt as if her life had ended. Knowing that Sam had gone to his death believing she had betrayed him had nearly killed her. Then she learned that she was pregnant, and her son had given her a reason to go on.

Now Sam had turned up in her life again, but it wasn't the Sam she had loved. She knew intuitively that this vindictive man wouldn't listen to her explanation, so she didn't give him one. She wanted him gone, before painful memories made her recall all the things she had loved about Sam Gentry.

"I can fire you," Lacey charged. "I don't have to hire you on. I own the B&G and can fire and hire whomever I please."

"You can't fire me, Lacey. I'm your husband. You may own the B&G, but I own you. May I assume you still have our marriage license?"

"You may assume whatever you like."

"Of course you'd still have it. It's the only way you can prove Andy's legitimacy, even though I'm not the boy's father."

Lacey hesitated. Now would be a good time to tell Sam that Andy was his son, but a voice inside her told her it would be unwise to divulge that information. She had no idea if Sam would react favorably toward his son. If he believed her, he might try to take Andy from her, but she seriously doubted that he would believe her.

Lacey decided to take a reasonable approach. "It would be best for both of us if you left and let me quietly pursue a divorce."

Sam mulled over Lacey's request and rejected it out of hand. He didn't want a divorce, but it wasn't because he still felt emotionally bound to Lacey. Far from it. He felt nothing but contempt for her.

"Sorry, Lacey. I'm not going anywhere. I'm going to stick around for a bit." He headed toward the door. "I'll see you tonight at supper."

"What!"

His tone made a mockery of his words. "I think it's time I got to know my son, don't you?"

"Damn you, Sam Gentry! If you hurt Andy I'll never forgive you."

Sam closed the door behind her tirade and leaned against it. Seeing Lacey after all these years had taken a toll on him. She had changed from an innocent young girl to a beautiful, mature woman. Childbirth had enhanced her figure; rounded curves fulfilled the promise of her youthful, immature figure. Her blond hair hadn't darkened, but remained the color of ripe wheat, and her eyes were still the entrancing hazel he remembered. He could easily look back and see how he had come to love her.

Pushing himself away from the door, Sam left the house and headed for the corral. Rusty was waiting for him.

Rusty eyed Sam narrowly. "You and Miz Lacey must

have had a lot to talk about. Ain't never known her to talk to one of the new hands so long. Are you staying or ain't you?"

"I'm staying."

That brief answer didn't seem to appease Rusty's curiosity. "What did you and Miz Lacey talk about?"

"This and that. What do you have for me to do today, Rusty?"

Rusty must have realized he was getting nothing more from Sam. "Keep your secrets, Sam. We can use you in the north pasture. The herd needs to be moved to a field with better grazing. If this drought doesn't end soon, our cows are gonna start dropping like flies. Saddle your horse and meet me by the fence. I'll take you out there myself."

While Sam was saddling his horse, Andy peeped into the corral, saw Sam and hurried up to join him.

"Did Rusty hire you on?"

Sam sent the boy a cursory glance. "Yep. I'm headed out to the north pasture now."

"You'll like it here. Everybody likes Mama and Rusty. Where you from, Sam?"

The boy was a friendly sort, Sam gave him that much. "Up around Kansas way."

"Me and Mama moved here with Uncle Hob after Grandpa died. We used to live in Pennsylvania. Did I tell you my daddy died in the war?"

"Yep. I hear you're gonna have another daddy soon," Sam couldn't help asking.

Sam almost burst out laughing at the face Andy made.

"Mean old Cramer will *never* be my daddy," Andy said with a vehemence that immediately sobered Sam.

"He wasn't even in the war. He doesn't like me and I don't like him."

"Have you told your mother how you feel?"

Andy nodded glumly. "She said I'm imagining things. She says we need mean old Cramer to save the ranch." His young face puckered, as if he wanted to cry. "I don't care about the ranch. I don't want Mama to marry that mean man."

An unwanted pang of compassion touched Sam's heart. He had to admit the little tyke was appealing. He couldn't help the circumstances of his birth. He was innocent of his mother's misdeeds. Sam's compassion, however, didn't extend to accepting Andy as his son, regardless of the fact that the boy bore the Gentry name.

Sam mounted his horse. "I gotta go now, Andy. We'll talk about this later, if you'd like."

Andy beamed up at him. "Yes, sir! Rusty don't mind if I talk to him, but he's always so busy. I'll see you later."

Sam worked his butt off that day. He couldn't recall when he'd been so tired. Farming was hard work, but ranching was no child's play. He'd met some of the hands and found them all to be congenial fellows. When they had gathered together to eat the lunch Luke brought them, Sam listened to the talk and concluded that most of the hands intensely disliked Taylor Cramer. As he washed up at the pump, he recalled bits and pieces of the conversation.

"Miz Lacey is too good for Cramer," a young man named Bart said.

A hand known as Lefty for the obvious reason added

his opinion. "I don't plan on sticking around after she marries Cramer."

Several grunts of agreement followed. Sam decided to find out what the hands had against Cramer.

"Why do you all dislike Cramer?" he drawled, pretending only slight interest.

"For starters, he don't like Andy," Lefty explained.

"You got that right, Lefty," young Bart agreed. "Andy gets in the way sometimes, but he's a friendly little fellow. I don't mind his questions. Cramer seems to resent the kid. Don't know why Miz Lacey can't see it."

"We all know why," Lefty injected. "He's rich, and Miz Lacey needs money to save the ranch. I think Cramer has some private agenda, too. He's wanted the ranch for a good long time."

"Why doesn't the boss apply for a loan?" Sam ventured.

"She's a woman. Banks don't loan money to women," Lefty elaborated.

Sam had gotten more from that conversation than he wanted. He shouldn't care what happened to Lacey, or what went on in her life, but hearing the hands complain about Cramer got his dander up and made him more than a little curious about the man Lacey intended to marry.

Sam finished up at the pump and saw Rusty headed in his direction. "I'll walk with you to the cookhouse, Sam," Rusty said. "Luke's serving up his special stew tonight."

"I'm taking supper at the big house tonight," Sam answered.

Rusty stopped in his tracks. "You what? Did I hear right, son? Did you say you were having supper with Miz Lacey and Andy?"

31

"You heard right, Rusty."

Rusty removed his hat and scratched his head. "What's going on, Sam? That don't sound like Miz Lacey. Are you sure she asked you for supper?"

"Yep. I'm heading up there as soon as I change."

Rusty grinned. "Well, don't that beat all. Miz Lacey must have taken a shine to you. I haven't seen her interested in a man since she came to live with Hob Bigelow."

"She must have been interested enough in Taylor Cramer to agree to marry him."

Rusty crammed his hat back on his head. "Yeah, well, I ain't so sure about that. Watch your manners up there. Miz Lacey is a lady."

Sam rolled his eyes. He knew Lacey better than anyone. She was a lady, all right; a lady without a heart.

Lacey paced restlessly, pausing every so often to look out the window. Sam wouldn't really come, would he? Inviting himself for supper took nerve, but this new Sam had nerve in abundance. What would Rusty and the hands think? She'd never invited a ranch hand to take a meal at the big house before. To her knowledge, neither had Uncle Hob, except for Rusty, and he was more of a friend than a foreman.

Perhaps she should feed Andy first. Get him out of the way so Sam wouldn't hurt him. Yes, that's what she'd do. She started toward the kitchen. Rita met her in the doorway.

"Señor Sam is here, Señora. He came in the back door. Shall I show him to the parlor?"

Sam pushed past the rotund little woman, which was no easy feat. "Don't bother, Rita. I'm already here."

"Sí, Señor. Supper is ready. I'll call Andy."

"Here I am, Rita," Andy said, darting into the room. "I hope we have chocolate cake for dessert."

"Sí, it is what you ordered, is it not?"

"You spoil him, Rita," Lacey said, smiling.

"Take your mother's other arm, Andy; we'll both take her in to supper."

Eyes shining, Andy offered his arm to Lacey.

"Are you eating with us, Sam?"

"Do you mind?"

He sent Lacey a wary look. "Not if Mama don't mind."

Lacey turned in silent fury. There was little she could say with Andy around.

They reached the dining room and Lacey seated herself at the head of the table, settling her skirts around her. Sam slid into the chair on her left and Andy sat in his usual spot on her right. Rita entered almost immediately with platters of roast beef, browned potatoes, peas, mixed greens and fresh bread.

They ate in silence. Lacey toyed with her food, refraining from starting a conversation for fear of what Sam would say in front of Andy.

"I'm done, Mama," Andy said, showing Lacey his empty plate. "Can I have my cake now?"

Rita entered as if on cue with three thick portions of dark chocolate cake.

"Chocolate cake is one of my favorites, Andy," Sam said, eyeing the cake with appreciation.

Lacey said nothing. Each time Sam spoke to Andy, her heart broke a little. Andy needed a father, but Sam didn't fit the bill. There was too much anger inside him.

All she wanted was to get Sam out of her life before he spoiled things for her and Taylor.

Taylor! She had yet to tell him that her husband was alive, and she didn't look forward to it. Then again, perhaps Taylor could help her obtain a speedy divorce.

Andy yawned hugely and set down his fork. "I'm full, Mama."

"You're tired, too, honey. Go on up and get ready for bed. I'll come up later and tuck you in."

Andy slid down from his chair. He planted a wet kiss on Lacey's mouth, then ran over to Sam. "Put your head down a minute, Sam," he said shyly.

Lacey groaned when she became aware of Andy's intention and tried to head it off. "Don't bother Sam, honey."

But Sam had already lowered his head. Lacey could tell by his puzzled look that he had no idea what Andy intended. He appeared startled when Andy stood on his toes and placed a smacking kiss on his cheek.

"G'night, Sam. I'm glad Mama invited you to supper. It's better than when mean old Cramer eats with us. He always tells me to mind my manners."

"I think your manners are just fine, Andy. Good night."

Andy skipped from the room.

"Thank you for not saying anything to hurt Andy," Lacey said grudgingly.

"I'm no monster, Lacey. Andy has nothing to do with you and me. He's caught in the middle. He dislikes your Taylor Cramer, you know."

"I know, but he's only a child. He'd dislike anyone he thought was stealing his mama."

"He doesn't appear to dislike *me*."

"He thinks of you as a ranch hand. Andy befriends all the hands. Ask anyone. He has no reason to be jealous of you."

"I think you're wrong, Lacey. But Andy isn't my responsibility, is he? I have no reason to see to his happiness. Fortunately for Andy, I have no intention of divorcing you, so the lad doesn't have to worry about Taylor now, does he?"

Lacey had just about all she could take from Sam. In six years Sam had gone from a sweet young man to an arrogant tyrant. She rose with as much dignity as she could muster and slapped her napkin down on the table. "It's time—"

"Would you like coffee in the parlor, Señora?"

Rita stood in the doorway, an expectant look on her around face.

"No, I—"

"Coffee sounds wonderful," Sam interjected before Lacey could finish her reply. "The parlor is fine."

"How dare you!" Lacey hissed once Rita left. "This is *my* home."

"And I'm your husband," Sam drawled, grasping Lacey's elbow and drawing her into the parlor.

He stopped before the sofa, but instead of letting her sit, he gripped her upper arm with his other hand and drew her against him. A frisson of fear slid down Lacey's spine. He was staring into her eyes, his face so close she could feel his breath ripple across her cheek. She blinked, breaking contact, but when she opened her eyes again, he was still staring at her.

"What? What is it?"

"You're beautiful," he murmured. "More beautiful than I remembered." His gaze lowered to her breasts. "I

35

don't recall you being so well endowed, either. The years have been kind to you."

"I was but seventeen when we married. Women do mature and change over the years. You've changed, too."

His gaze returned to her face. "How so?"

She hesitated a moment then said, "You're harder, colder, more in control of yourself. You've matured, too. Your body is . . . " Her words fell off, unable to force compliments past her lips. And they would be compliments, for Sam's body was now a man's body. In youth he had been lean and lithe, now he was muscular and magnificent.

She turned her gaze away, but Sam would have none of it. He lifted her chin and lowered his head. A startled cry slipped past her throat when his lips touched hers. Oh, God, she couldn't stand this. Not again. Not when she'd learned to live without Sam. Allowing him to hurt her again would destroy her.

The first touch of his mouth was feather light, a mere whisper of sensation against her lips. Her breath caught. Then he deepened the kiss, sliding his mouth back and fourth against hers. The sweet, titillating friction tilted her world. What happened next totally undid her. Suddenly Sam's lips became hard, demanding, his tongue a dagger that probed ruthlessly into her mouth. Seeking, searching, as if starved for the taste of her.

She melted into the kiss, giving him what he sought, her mouth and body softening beneath his touch. Then she heard him groan and was abruptly jarred back to reality. Pushing against his chest, she broke away, staring at him in horror.

"Why are you doing this to me? You hate me."

"I wanted to see if you remembered how it once was between us . . . if the passion between us still existed."

Lacey scrubbed her mouth with the back of her hand. Her voice was bitter with resentment. "And what did you learn?"

Sam gave her a mocking smile. "I felt nothing. There's nothing between us. You killed the passion we once shared when you betrayed me."

Lacey stared at him, her eyes bright with tears she refused to shed.

One trembling word tumbled from her lips. "Liar."

Chapter Three

Sam's fierce frown betrayed his anger. His eyes narrowed into slits, and a muscle twitched along the strong line of his jaw.

"I'm not a liar," he growled, pushing her away. "You killed the love I once felt for you. You're nothing to me."

"I'm glad!" Lacey said with equal venom. "The feeling is mutual."

Whirling on his heel, Sam slammed out of the house. He couldn't recall when he'd been so damn angry, except for maybe that day when Lacey had betrayed him to the Yankees. Why in the hell did he have to kiss her? What exactly did he hope to gain?

He ran his tongue over his lips, tasting her essence on them. He could still feel her soft mouth moving beneath his, still feel her body melting into him. He shook the stirring memory from his head. What in the hell was wrong with him? By the war's end he'd been so sure he had banished Lacey from his mind and heart that he'd never mentioned her to his brothers. Fate must be conspiring against him, bringing Lacey into his life at the worst possible time.

What would Lacey say if she knew he was wanted by the law? Would she turn him in, hoping he'd hang so she could marry Cramer? Didn't she realize that Andy would be miserable if she married Cramer? Did the ranch mean more to her than her own son's happiness?

The moment Sam entered the bunkhouse, a hush fell over the room. He called out a greeting, ignoring the inquiring glances directed at him. Sam knew the men were curious about his relationship with Lacey, but he wasn't about to reveal the truth . . . yet. He didn't even know himself what he was going to do or how this would play out. He was still too stunned at finding Lacey in Texas to think this through.

"We're having a friendly game of poker," Lefty said. "Shall I deal you in?"

"Why not?" Sam answered, settling in the empty chair Rusty pulled out with his foot.

Sam lost the first hand and won the next two. Dimly he wondered how long it would be before someone brought up his invitation to eat supper with Lacey and Andy.

He didn't have long to wait. "You missed a mighty good supper," Rusty said. "Luke's beef stew is the best I've tasted. Even better than Rita's."

Sam merely grunted.

Rusty cleared his throat. "I don't mean to pry, but I'd swear you and Miz Lacey met before today. Thinking back on it, you both seemed shocked to see one another."

The card game came to an abrupt halt. All attention was centered on Sam and his answer to Rusty's question. Sam realized he had to say something to satisfy their curiosity without telling the whole truth. He wasn't prepared to do that yet.

"Lacey and I knew one another a long time ago."

A weighted silence followed his announcement.

"Did you know Miz Lacey's husband?" Lefty asked.

"Yeah, I reckon you could say that."

When nothing more was forthcoming, the card game continued, but it didn't stop the speculative glances aimed in his direction the rest of the evening.

After the game folded, Sam found his bunk. Sleep eluded him. He was plagued by thoughts of Lacey. Lacey had been right. He had been lying when he said he'd felt nothing when he'd kissed her. He'd felt and tasted and remembered . . . too damn much. She had been a virgin the first time they made love. Sweet, untouched and innocently passionate. He recalled their stolen kisses, their frantic groping, before they finally indulged their youthful lust for one another.

Once they had made love, they couldn't seem to get enough of one another and had become incautious. One night Tom Peters had walked in on them while they were making love, and a shotgun wedding immediately followed. Not that Sam regretted their marriage—not at first, anyway. He had been so in love he had welcomed the wedding. Sam knew that old man Peters wasn't thrilled about having a Rebel for a son-in-law, but the thought of Lacey bearing a child out of wedlock was even more repugnant to him.

Then Lacey had betrayed him. She hadn't even stuck around to see the result of her betrayal. She had absented herself that whole day.

Before sleep finally claimed him, Sam relived the kiss he and Lacey had shared tonight. He drifted off to oblivion recalling how deliciously soft and sensuously lush her body had felt against his.

The following days were too busy for Sam to have any thoughts save for those connected with his work. It was branding time, and the work was hot, dirty and exhausting. But Sam discovered something about himself during those hectic few days. He liked ranching. He could understand Lacey's determination to save the ranch. What he couldn't excuse was her method of saving it. He hadn't met anyone yet who liked Taylor Cramer.

The branding was finally over. The ranch hands quit work early that day, grateful for a few hours of free time before supper. Sam was as eager as anyone else to collapse on his bunk and relax—until he saw a horse tied to the hitching post outside the big house and changed his mind. He knew intuitively that the infamous Taylor Cramer had come calling. Exhaustion departed, replaced by a sudden determination to meet the man Lacey had chosen for a husband. He couldn't wait to disabuse Cramer of the notion that he and Lacey would marry.

Sam stopped briefly at the pump to wash up before

heading up to the house. He entered through the back door without knocking, startling Rita.

"Señor Sam, I did not hear you knock."

"I didn't knock, Rita. Where's Lacey?"

"But, Señor, you cannot come into the house whenever you please. Even Señor Rusty knocks. Señora Lacey has set strict rules for the hands."

"I don't give a damn what Lacey wants, Rita. Is she in the parlor with Cramer?"

"Sí, Señor. Wait here. I'll tell her you wish to speak with her."

"I'll announce myself."

For some reason the thought of Lacey alone with Cramer disturbed him. What in the hell was wrong with him?

Sam strode down the hallway separating the kitchen from the parlor and stopped dead in his tracks when he saw Andy flying toward him. He snagged Andy around the waist, halting his flight.

"Whoa, there, what's the hurry?"

"He's here," Andy said, arms and legs flailing.

"Who's here?"

"Mean old Cramer. I heard him tell Mama that she should send me away to school. I hate him! Why does Mama want to send me away? I've been a good boy." He hung his head, sniffed and mumbled, "Most of the time anyway."

Sam set Andy on his feet. "Why don't you go see what Rusty's up to? I want to talk to your mother."

Andy sent Sam a look so filled with hope that Sam had to look away. "Will you try to change Mama's mind about sending me away? I want to stay here."

"I'll do my best, son."

Andy grasped his hand and gave it a squeeze. "I like you Sam. Do you want to be my pa?"

Sam had no answer to that. "Go on, Andy. Leave your mother to me."

Andy scooted off, his steps decidedly lighter as he brushed a tear from his eye.

Sam watched him leave, his hands clutched into fists at his sides. What in the hell had happened to make Lacey an uncaring mother? He found it difficult to believe that she'd send her own son away to save the ranch. Had she no compassion? No heart?

Sam heard voices coming from the parlor. Firming his resolve, he barged into the room, startling the two occupants.

A man spun around to confront him. "What's the meaning of this? Who are you?"

Sam studied Taylor Cramer and disliked him on sight. He was handsome enough, he supposed, but something about his appearance rubbed Sam the wrong way. He was of medium height, blond and slim. A thin mustache rode his upper lip, and his face was not displeasing, until one looked into his eyes. They were a cold, almost colorless gray, exuding no warmth, no emotion. Andy had been right in calling Cramer mean. Those dead eyes gave mute testimony to the meanness inside him. Sam had met men like Cramer before, and looked upon them with contempt.

"Sam! What are you doing here?" Lacey exclaimed, echoing Cramer's words. "I told you I'd take care of this."

Cramer regarded Lacey with cool disdain. His voice was soft, but his inflection held a note of authority. "Perhaps you'd better explain, my dear."

Sam waited to see what Lacey would say.

"This is hard, Taylor," Lacey began. "I never would have agreed to marry you had I known."

Taylor darted Sam a look that would have quelled a lesser man. "Go on, Lacey."

Lacey made a nervous gesture. "I told you I had been married before, and that my husband died in the war."

"I knew that," Cramer said. "What does your previous marriage have to do with this ranch hand barging into your home?"

Sam lost all semblance of patience. The sooner Cramer knew the truth, the sooner the bastard would leave Lacey and Andy alone.

"I assume you're Taylor Cramer," Sam said, sending Cramer a look that spoke fluently of his contempt. "It's time I introduced myself. I'm Sam Gentry, Lacey's husband. Forgive me if I don't shake hands. I find meeting my wife's fiancé rather awkward."

Cramer's face turned a vivid red. "What?" He rounded viciously on Lacey. "Tell me it isn't true, Lacey. Tell me this bastard's lying."

Sam almost felt sorry for Lacey, but hardened his heart.

"I . . . I didn't know Sam was alive," Lacey explained. "He never once attempted to contact me in all the years since his presumed death. I believed I was a widow. No one I contacted told me otherwise. Everything I was told led me to believe Sam had died in the war."

Cramer's eyes narrowed. "Sam Gentry," he said with bitter emphasis. "Why did you show up now? You've had years to let Lacey know you're alive. I understand none of this."

Lacey remained mute, so Sam jumped into the void.

"You're not expected to understand. I'm Lacey's husband, that's all you need to know. There will be no marriage. Not now, not ever."

"We'll see about that!" Cramer sputtered. "You can't just show up now and claim your wife. I'll not have you ruin my plans."

"I seem to have done just that," Sam drawled. It felt damn good to thwart Lacey and her intended.

Cramer grasped Lacey's upper arms and spun her around to face him. Sam emitted a low growl and prepared to tear Cramer limb from limb. Then Cramer spoke, and Sam forced himself to delay long enough to hear Lacey's answer to Cramer's question.

"Do you still want to marry me, my dear?"

Sam could see Lacey's throat working, and his patience fled.

"Dammit, Lacey! Tell the man what he wants to know."

Lacey hated the way Sam was bullying her. How dare he interfere in her life now? Had he wanted her, all he had to do was return to her after the war and claim her and their son. She owed him nothing. Not a blasted thing.

She glared at Sam but directed her words to Cramer. "Of course I still want to marry you, Taylor."

Sam muttered a curse beneath his breath. Lacey reeled beneath the heat of his anger and wished the words back. She feared that this Sam, the Sam she barely knew, would react violently.

Cramer sent Sam a smug smile. "That's all I needed to know, my dear. Leave everything to me. Sam Gentry abandoned you. The law will take that into consideration. I foresee a swift end to your unwanted marriage."

Frustrated beyond endurance, Sam grit his teeth. "There will be no divorce. I suggest you leave, Cramer. Don't bother my wife and . . . son again."

Lacey went still. She couldn't believe her ears. Sam had just claimed Andy! What did it mean? Had he finally noticed the resemblance between Andy and himself? Had he looked beyond the blond hair and blue eyes and recognized his own image?

Cramer picked up his hat and shoved it down on his head. "You haven't heard the last from me, Gentry. As for you, Lacey, I'll get right to work on freeing you from this bastard. I'll be back."

The moment Cramer slammed out the door, Lacey rounded on Sam, her eyes blazing fury. "Damn you, Sam Gentry! You've ruined everything! Why didn't you stay dead?"

"I never was dead," Sam hissed. "I can't believe you want to marry that unfeeling bastard."

"Unfeeling! You know nothing about Taylor, how can you call him unfeeling?"

"I spoke with Andy. When he saw Cramer he rushed out of the house as if the devil was on his heels. He hates Cramer. Did you ever wonder why?"

Lacey's jaw firmed. "I know why. He's jealous."

"Jealousy has nothing to do with it. Andy thinks you're going to send him to school after you and Cramer marry."

Lacey flushed. "He must have heard us talking. Taylor thinks a boarding school will be good for Andy, but I'm not convinced. He's far too young to send away. Andy should have listened to the rest of the conversation before jumping to conclusions. Why should you care? Andy is nothing to you."

"I'd care about any child who hates and fears the man his mother plans to marry."

"Andy and I need Taylor. I've done my best since Uncle Hob died, but I'm not knowledgeable enough to run a ranch. Taylor is, and he has the means to make our lives easier." She stared him in the eye and said, "Andy needs a father."

"You've managed to convince yourself, but not me. There will be no divorce. It's time you learned you can't have everything your way. Think of your son for a change."

"Andy is my reason for living!" Lacey all but screamed. "Father died, you were gone, I had no one but Andy. Uncle Hob literally saved us both when he asked us to make our home with him in Texas. He loved this ranch. It was his dream come true. The least I can do is save his dream."

"You owe me a helluva lot more than that. Betrayal isn't a pretty word."

"Tell me truthfully, Sam. What can you give me and Andy? Do you have the money to save the ranch? Do you have a home? Property? What can you promise us?" She shook her head. "Nothing, I suspect. Something brought you to Texas. Dare I ask what?"

Sam wasn't in a position to answer most of those questions. How could he tell Lacey he was an outlaw, though wrongly accused? He had nothing. No home. No property. Very little money. But he wasn't going to let her off the hook that easily. She had to pay for betraying him. Besides, preventing the marriage between Lacey and Taylor would benefit Andy.

"You're right. I have neither home nor property," he

confirmed, "but I have a wife that has both. Now if you'll excuse me, I've had a long day."

He turned his back on Lacey, which was the wrong thing to do. She flew at him, pounding his back with her fists and sobbing her frustration.

"Why are you doing this to me?"

Sam spun around, grasped her arms and pulled her against him. "You know why."

Her fury was palpable. He imprisoned her against him and stared into the smoldering depths of her beautiful eyes. What he saw there set him back on his heels. He recognized despair, and hopelessness, and something else. Something startling and confusing. He saw need. Need for him, Sam, not Cramer. Something snapped inside him, opening a floodgate of emotions.

A groan rumbled in his chest as he lowered his head and captured her lips. She went still in his arms, her body stiffening. Her eyes widened, then closed when he deepened the kiss, parting her lips with his tongue. Her taste, her scent, the way she suddenly melted against him, all these and more dragged forth long-forgotten memories, a long-forgotten love.

Lacey couldn't resist the lure of Sam's soft lips. This was the man she'd once loved beyond all reason. This was Andy's father. She whimpered a protest when his hands slid up her back and around to her breasts, cupping their fullness. She sighed into his mouth when his fingers teased her nipples.

"Why did you betray me, Lacey?" Sam whispered against her lips.

The bubble burst. Lacey attempted to free herself from the circle of Sam's arms, which suddenly felt hard and unyielding. "I didn't."

His arms tightened. "Who is Andy's father?"

Lacey gazed up at him, controlling with difficulty the panic rising inside her. Did he suspect? "You tell me."

He shoved her away. "Don't play games with me. You'd like me to think he's mine, wouldn't you?"

Lacey wiped her lips with the back of her hand. "That's the last thing I want you to believe. You'd better leave. I need to find Andy and give him his supper."

"I'll find him for you," Sam said after a lengthy pause. He started toward the door.

A disturbing thought came to Lacey. "Sam, wait!"

Sam turned slowly, his dark brows raised in question.

"Do Rusty and the ranch hands know? About us, I mean."

"Not yet, but I doubt they can be kept in the dark for long."

Then he was gone, leaving Lacey confused and shaken.

What had gotten into her? All Sam did was touch her and she was lost. She prayed he'd never discover just how powerfully drawn to him she was. Their lives could have been so different if only he believed in her innocence.

What had happened to Sam during the years they were apart? she wondered. She knew he had brothers, because he'd mentioned them often. There was a farm in Kansas, too. But Sam had as much as admitted that he had nothing—no money, no home and no property. There was a mystery here she wasn't even close to solving. Something had happened to bring Sam to Texas. Something she was probably better off not knowing.

Sam couldn't get Cramer off his mind. The following days were filled with work, work and more work. And

Andy. The lad seemed to enjoy following him around, and Sam had no idea why. Andy didn't appear attached to any of the other hands that way. Not even Rusty, who doted on the boy. Sam had to admit the lad was engaging, and bright as hell. In fact, Sam was growing more than a little fond of the boy, and he wasn't sure that was a good idea.

Cramer hadn't returned to the ranch, and Sam figured the man was a coward but he wasn't about to sell the scoundrel short. That thought brought another. The relationship between Cramer and Lacey didn't appear at all warm or loving. Cramer seemed more interested in the ranch than he was in Lacey, and for some reason that bothered Sam.

Tonight Sam had taken supper with the boys in the cookhouse and was walking back to the bunkhouse with Rusty when he saw Cramer's horse tied to the hitching post, swishing flies with his tail.

"Excuse me, Rusty, but I need to see Lacey about something."

Rusty grabbed his arm. "Hold up, Sam. Is there something I should know about you and Miz Lacey?"

"Not yet, Rusty. You'll be the first to know if there is."

"I ain't sure what's going on here, but I don't want to see Miz Lacey hurt."

Sam spun around to confront Rusty. "You think *I'll* hurt her and Cramer won't?"

"I don't know what to think. I was upset to learn that Miz Lacey was going to marry Cramer, but I'm not sure you're the one for her."

"Set your mind at ease, Rusty. Almost anyone would be better for Lacey than Cramer." He pulled free of Rusty's grip. "I'll see you back at the bunkhouse."

Sam's mounting anger matched the storm clouds roiling overhead. If Cramer didn't back off, he'd be damn sorry. Sam was so emerged in his dark thoughts that he failed to see Andy skip up to him.

"Hey, Sam, slow down."

Sam turned and waited for Andy to catch up to him. "What are you doing outside? It's going to storm soon."

"I sneaked out," Andy whispered. *"He's* here again."

"I know. I was just heading for the house to have a little talk with him."

Andy beamed. "I sure do like you, Sam."

"I like you too, Andy," Sam heard himself saying. "Tell you what. Why don't you sneak back up to your room before your mama comes looking for you?"

By the time Sam reached the house, he was mad enough to toss Cramer out on his ear. The parlor was ablaze with light, but Sam circled around to the back and entered through the back door. Rita was preparing supper.

"Don't scold," Sam said as Rita opened her mouth to reprimand him. "There's something you should know, but I'm trusting you to keep it between the two of us until the time is right to tell everyone."

Rita's brow furrowed, but she said nothing, apparently waiting for Sam to continue.

Sam hoped telling Rita was the right thing to do, since he saw no help for it. She deserved an explanation for his barging into the house without an invitation.

"It's a long story, Rita, but you should know that Lacey and I are married. We've been husband and wife for six years."

Sam could tell by her stunned expression that she didn't believe him.

"It's true, Rita," Sam said. "My name is Sam Gentry."

"But . . . but, Señor Sam, Señora Lacey is going to marry Señor Cramer. Her husband died in the war."

"As you can see, I'm very much alive. We . . . we lost track of one another and she believed me dead. Now that I've found her, there will be no question of Lacey marrying Cramer. Are Cramer and Lacey in the parlor?"

"Sí, Señor, I will tell her you're here."

"Don't bother. I'll tell her myself."

Lacey sat on the edge of the sofa, hands tightly folded, listening to Taylor as he paced back and forth in front of her, ranting and raving.

"How could you have done this to us, Lacey?" Cramer blasted. "We were to be married in two weeks. Now it will have to be put off until I can send Sam Gentry packing." He stopped in front of her and pulled her into his arms. "It's what you want, isn't it? You don't want to stay married to that penniless cowboy, do you?"

"Of course not," Lacey said without hesitation. She wanted Andy's future to be secure, and Taylor could provide what Andy needed. A home, security, money to give him an education.

Cramer's smile held no warmth. An unexplainable chill slithered down Lacey's back. "Good," Cramer said. "I hoped you'd say that. Leave everything to me, my dear. One way or another, Sam Gentry will be out of your life. I won't let him interfere with my plans for the ranch." He paused, as if aware of what he had carelessly revealed. "Forgive me, my dear, I meant our wedding plans."

Sam entered the parlor in time to hear Lacey say, "What do you intend to do about Sam?"

"Leave the details to me, Lacey. I know exactly how to get rid of Sam Gentry."

Before Lacey could gather her wits, Cramer's arms tightened around her. Then he lowered his head and kissed her. Lacey had been kissed by Cramer before, but this time she felt repelled by his hard lips and probing tongue. Nor did she remember his taste and scent being so repulsive. She felt his hard fingers crushing her breasts moments before all hell broke loose.

A roar filled her ears as Sam came hurtling out of nowhere. Cramer was torn away from her and backed up against the nearest wall.

"I warned you once about bothering Lacey," Sam snarled. He pulled his arm back, his hand fisted, ready to let it fly into Cramer's face.

Lacey grabbed his arm. "Please, Sam, don't do it." She knew Cramer's vindictive nature and didn't want his anger directed at Sam.

Sam hesitated, then shoved Cramer away. "Get out, Cramer, before I really lose my temper. You can thank Lacey this time for saving you, but I promise I won't be so lenient the next time."

Cramer slithered away, eyeing Sam with loathing. "I won't forget this, Gentry."

"I'm counting on you remembering," Sam barked through gritted teeth. "And just to make sure you won't bother *my* wife again, I'm moving into the big house . . . into Lacey's bed."

Lacey couldn't believe this was happening. Just when her life had gotten back on track, Sam had shown up and ruined everything. He intended to move in with her and share her bed, did he? Well, she'd have something to say about that!

"You'd better leave, Taylor," she advised. "I can handle Sam."

"He's a savage. I don't trust him with my future wife. Stay away from him, Lacey. Sam Gentry is trouble."

"I want nothing to do with Sam," Lacey averred. "I can't wait until he's out of my life."

"I'll see what I can do to make your wish come true," Cramer said, slamming his hat down on his head. "I'll be in touch, my dear."

Lacey confronted Sam the moment the door shut behind Cramer. "Do you have to settle everything with your fists? What kind of man have you become?"

"You don't want to know," Sam muttered, rubbing his knuckles.

Never had Sam wanted to hit a man more. But Lacey was right. The one thing Sam needed to avoid was the law, and he knew intuitively that Cramer was the kind of man who wouldn't hesitate to bring the law down on him if Sam had hit him.

"You had no business telling Taylor you were going to share my home and my bed."

"I meant every word," Sam growled. "I'm your husband. It's time the hands were told."

"You abandoned me!"

"You betrayed me!"

"You don't even like me."

"I thought the feeling was mutual."

Suddenly Sam's eyes darkened and his anger renewed itself. "You kissed Cramer."

Lacey's shoulders firmed. "He kissed *me*. There's a difference."

"Did you enjoy it?"

Her mouth thinned. She had no intention of telling Sam that she'd hated Taylor's kiss. "That's none of your business. I *am* going to marry Taylor. Engaged couples do kiss."

Sam's temper ignited. Grasping Lacey's upper arms, he dragged her against him, his fingers digging into her soft flesh. "What else have you done with Cramer? Is he one of your legion of lovers?"

Lacey exploded. She pushed away from him and dealt him a stinging blow to his face. Sam was the one who had abandoned her, the one who refused to listen to her explanation. How dare he accuse her of promiscuity when he'd probably bedded more women than he could count.

Sam reeled backward, his hand flying to his cheek. She'd struck him! No woman had ever done that to him before. Women liked him. He'd never had problems finding willing women for his bed. Even Lacey had come to him willingly.

He took a menacing step forward. She stood her ground, her chin still jutting forward. He'd never known her to be pugnacious, and he felt a grudging respect for her courage. Nothing he did or said seemed to intimidate her.

"Don't ever do that again," he warned. His voice held a note of controlled fury.

"You don't frighten me, Sam Gentry."

"Frightening you was never my intention. Making you pay for betraying me is."

"The war was over a long time ago."

"The war between you and me never ended. Expect me to move in and share your bed very soon."

His wolfish grin offered Lacey scant comfort. Having

Sam show up at the ranch after all these years had been a stunning blow. Having him live in the same house with her and Andy could only lead to disaster. Sam had broken her heart once; she couldn't survive having it broken a second time.

"Sam, think about this before you do anything rash. What about Andy? What is he to think?"

"Andy likes me. I don't suppose he'll think anything about it."

"He's bound to learn that we're married, and . . . well, he'll assume you're his father. Are you prepared to explain to him why you've been absent all these years?"

"I'll think of something," Sam replied, not at all sure he was ready or willing to claim a child not of his own blood.

"Hurt him and I swear I'll kill you," Lacey gritted out.

The threat didn't bother Sam at all. Lacey couldn't hurt a flea, even if she wanted to. But nevertheless, he heeded the warning and filed it away.

Chapter Four

During the following days Sam was so busy that he found no time to move into the ranch house. As for sharing Lacey's bed, he'd said it to taunt her, and her vigorous protest didn't surprise him. Especially if Cramer was her lover. That thought made him want to spew out his guts.

Sam was walking to the bunkhouse after an exhausting day in the saddle when he spied Lacey walking across the yard. It was washday, and she was headed toward a clothesline stretched between two trees, where dry clothes were blowing in the breeze.

Sam watched her long, graceful strides, admiring the

Connie Mason

way her skirts outlined her shapely legs and clung to her hips and thighs. He knew from experience that there was a lot of passion packed into her neat little form. From the first, Lacey had been hot and eager for him. His heated gaze settled on her breasts. They no longer resembled the small mounds he remembered. They were full and temptingly round, exactly how he liked them. Her waist was slim, her hips gently curved, and her face had grown even more beautiful, if that was possible.

His steps took him in her direction without conscious thought. In fact, he was surprised when he found himself standing beside her. She gave him a cursory glance and promptly ignored him as she continued plucking clothespins and clothes from the line.

"I haven't seen your lover around lately," Sam said. "Let's hope he took my warning to heart and gave up on you."

Lacey merely glared at him.

"Where's Andy? I haven't seen him around. He isn't ill, is he?"

"A cold and fever, nothing serious. I've had a devil of a time keeping him in bed."

"Tell him I'll look in on him after I clean up."

"That's not necessary."

Sam's jaw firmed. "Just tell him."

"Why? Why do you care? Andy is . . . nothing . . . to you." Lacey nearly choked on her words. Lies didn't came easily to her. But Sam didn't deserve a son like Andy. The only reason he'd stuck around this long was to punish her for something that happened long ago, something for which she was blameless.

"Andy is innocent of any wrongdoing," Sam replied.

58

"I like the tyke. It's his mother I hold responsible for . . . what happened in the past."

"Why are you still holding this grudge against me? You never went to prison. You escaped and went through the war without a scratch."

"Just because I lived doesn't right a wrong. Love isn't supposed to hurt. Your betrayal hurt me beyond repair. Now it's your turn to hurt."

His words served only to enrage her. "You think I didn't hurt when I was told you were dead?"

"That's exactly what I think. Andy is living proof that you didn't mourn very long. Don't tell me you were vulnerable and Wiltshire took advantage of you. That's a bunch of bull."

Lacey gave him a defiant glare. "I won't tell you anything of the sort, because it wouldn't be true."

"I suspected as much," Sam bit out.

Why were men so dense? Lacey wondered. Sam hadn't an inkling what her answer meant. Captain Wiltshire hadn't taken advantage of her. She'd only seen him a time or two after Sam was taken away, and then only on a professional level. Had he been even remotely interested in her, nothing would have come of it, for she wasn't interested in him. She'd been too distraught over Sam's alleged death to look at another man with romantic intent. And in six years she still hadn't found a man she could love like she'd loved Sam.

With tangled emotions, Lacey watched Sam walk away. Suddenly her whole life was crumbling around her. She still had a ranch to run and little hard cash to see her through until the cattle were driven to the railhead. She was so desperate for money she considered taking them to market before winter. She'd thought marrying Taylor would solve her problems, but then Sam had shown up and ruined everything.

An hour after he left Lacey by the clothesline, Sam returned to the house to visit Andy. He hadn't lied about his feelings for the lad. He *did* like Andy, even though he'd tried not to. He recalled wishing for a son just like Andy a long time ago. But he and Lacey hadn't been intimate enough times to produce a child. He could count on the fingers of one hand the times they had made love. Three, four times at the most. Hardly enough time to plant his seed in her.

Sam entered through the back door. This time Rita merely smiled at him and motioned him inside.

"Señora Lacey is in the parlor."

"I've come to see Andy. How is he?"

"Much better. I do not think we will be able to keep him in bed much longer."

"Point me to his room," Sam said.

"Up the stairs, Señor Sam. First door on the right. His door is open; you will be able to see him."

"Much obliged, Rita."

Sam hurried off, hoping to avoid Lacey. He didn't know if he could survive another confrontation with her. Every time their paths crossed he remembered . . . and wanted. He was finally willing to admit that he wanted her in his bed. He wanted her under him, over him, wanted to toss up her skirts and thrust himself inside her. He wanted to hear her scream his name as she climaxed.

Sam paused on the upstairs landing in an effort to control his body's response to his erotic fantasies about Lacey. It wouldn't do for Andy to see him with the front of his trousers stretched out. He adjusted his denims, took several deep breaths and continued down the hall. The door to Andy's room stood open and he walked inside. Andy was staring out the window, his expression wistful. He saw Sam and gave a whoop of joy.

"Sam! Sam! I was hoping you'd come."

Sam settled on the edge of the bed. "I didn't know you were sick, Andy. I've been a mite busy lately."

"I know. Everyone has been busy lately. How did you know I was sick?"

"I spoke with your mother earlier. She said you've been under the weather."

"I can get out of bed tomorrow. Mama said I can."

"Your mama said you can get out of bed if your fever is gone tomorrow," Lacey said from the doorway.

"Mama! Sam came to visit me. He didn't know I was sick."

"So I see," Lacey said coolly.

"Tell you what," Sam said, surprising himself. "If you're well enough tomorrow to get out of bed, I'll take you for a ride on Galahad. Tomorrow's Sunday. All the hands except those guarding the herd are going into town tonight, and Sundays are pretty dead around here."

Andy's eyes glowed with excitement. "Is Galahad your horse? I'd like that. It's all right, isn't it, Mama?"

"We'll see," Lacey hedged. She turned her attention to Sam. "Aren't you going into town to carouse with the others?"

"Nope. There's nothing much in town that interests me."

"I find that hard to believe," she said with a hint of sarcasm.

Sam's eyes narrowed. "Are you trying to get rid of me?"

Sam could tell that Lacey wanted to spit out a harsh reply and held her tongue because of Andy. He rose and smiled down at Andy. "If we're going riding tomorrow, I suggest you get all the rest you can today. I'll come for you around ten tomorrow morning. Does that sound about right to you?"

"That sounds just fine to me, Sam. I'll be ready."

Lacey sent Sam a potent glare. "I'd like a word with you before you leave."

"Whatever you say," Sam answered.

He followed her out the door, admiring the sway of her hips beneath her split leather skirt. Unfortunately, his arousal returned just as she turned around to face him. Her gaze slithered downward. He heard her gasp before her gaze flew upward, settling disconcertingly on his face.

Sam chuckled. "You're not surprised, are you? You're a beautiful woman, Lacey. You've gotten even more beautiful during the six years we've been apart. I won't deny that you tempt and arouse me, for it's obvious. I'm a man who enjoys women, and you're all woman." He closed the gap between them. "More importantly, you're my wife."

Lacey retreated until her back was pressed against the wall. "Do you enjoy taunting me?"

"Actually, no." His words surprised the hell out of him, and scared him even more. Hadn't that been his purpose in staying on at the B&G? "What I would really enjoy is making love to you. Surely you haven't forgotten how good it was between us."

"I've forgotten everything about you."

"Like hell," he growled. "It's long past the time for everyone to know about our relationship. I'll move my things from the bunkhouse tomorrow, after Andy and I return from our ride."

Lacey's panic was palpable. "No! You can't do that."

Sam's answer was to snag her around the waist and pull her close. Her soft breasts flattened against him, making him aware of every luscious curve. His arms tightened, bringing her even closer. Her eyes widened and he smiled, for he knew she could feel his erection prodding between her legs.

"I want you, Lacey," he whispered against her lips. "That has never changed despite our years apart and your betrayal. I didn't realize how much I still wanted you until I saw you again."

"It's too late," Lacey hissed. "You let me believe you were dead. I can't forgive you for that. We can never have a meaningful relationship. Let me go, Sam. It was over for us years ago."

Sam was quick to respond. "Who said anything about a meaningful relationship? You misunderstand. I'm not going to divorce you, so we may as well make the best of the situation. I can tell you want me. Your lips and body tell me all I need to know. You're a passionate woman, Lacey," Sam continued. "I haven't forgotten that about you. Since Cramer is out of the picture, why not share your passion with me?"

"That does it, Sam Gentry!" Lacey cried. She raised her arm to strike him, but this time Sam was too fast for her. He caught her wrist. Then he scooped her into his arms and carried her down the hallway until he found another door.

Sam shoved the door open with his foot and stepped

into the room. He smiled when he saw how well he'd chosen. The bedroom definitely belonged to a woman, probably Lacey. He slammed the door shut with his foot and carried Lacey to the bed. He dropped her, watched her bounce, then flung himself on top of her.

Lacey's words were tinged with fear. "What are you going to do?"

"Prove something to both of us," Sam bit out.

"Get off of me!"

"I will, in time. Tell me you don't want me."

Her chin lifted pugnaciously. "I don't want you."

"Tell me after I kiss you."

His mouth came down hard on hers. His kiss was not gentle, nor was it particularly brutal. It was very persuasive, utterly demanding. Lacey thought she had survived the worst of it quite nicely until he prodded her lips apart and thrust his tongue past her teeth. He kissed her so thoroughly that she felt a compelling need to kiss him back. She fought it as long as she could; then her mouth softened beneath his.

Sam lifted his head and smiled down at her. "Tell me."

Gathering her scattered wits about her, Lacey cried, "I don't want you!"

Lacey was forced to endure another assault upon her senses as his mouth returned to feast on hers. Then his hands covered her breasts and she lost the ability to think. Lacey had no idea that Sam had worked her buttons free until she felt his fingers tweak a bare nipple.

"Remember how it was between us, Lacey? We couldn't keep our hands off of one another. The few times we were together weren't nearly enough. I hadn't satisfied my lust for you before I was taken away. We have all the time in the world now to explore our unsated passion."

"You can't mean that," Lacey whispered. "You can't mean for us to stay together."

Sam appeared too interested in her breasts and puckered nipples to answer. She watched in trepidation as he licked and nipped at them. She bit out a gasp when he took one aroused tip into his mouth and suckled her.

"You always did like it when I sucked your nipples," he said, raising his head and grinning down at her. "You liked it when I did this, too."

Lacey tried to stop his hand from crawling beneath her skirts, but she wasn't fast enough. She felt the pressure of his fingers between her thighs, inching upward, close, so close. No one had touched her intimately since Sam. Holding her breath, she anticipated his fingers there, where she was slick and needy. She nearly screamed when the delicious pressure ceased.

"Shall I stop, Lacey?"

"Yes! No! Oh, please!"

Her back was bowed, her breathing now painful gasps. "I know what you want, Lacey," Sam said as his fingers continued exploring the intimate flesh between her thighs. One finger pushed inside her, and she arched violently. He began to stroke, in and out, his rhythm increasing until she was nearly mad with the need to end it. Then it came, from somewhere deep inside her, the explosion that turned her body into a raging inferno. Seized by euphoria, she rode the cresting waves until they finally ebbed and she lay limp and sated.

"Like that, did you?" Sam asked.

"I . . . I . . . damn you, Sam Gentry! You had no right."

"I'm the only man who has a right."

He pushed himself away from her. Her gaze drifted down his body, noting with alarm that he was still hard, still fully aroused. She feared that he would . . .

"Don't worry," he said, following the direction of her gaze. "I'm not going to ravish you. When we come together it will be because you want me. And believe me, wife, I'm going to make damn sure you want me. Have Andy ready when I come for him tomorrow," he threw over his shoulder as he headed out the door.

Lacey was so angry she grabbed the pitcher from the nightstand and hurled it at him. It would have hit its mark had he not closed the door. The pitcher struck the door and shattered. Even though it had missed Sam, Lacey felt better for having thrown it.

Lacey couldn't believe what had just happened. Sam's touch had set her afire. Why had he done it? She knew he hadn't gained any satisfaction from the encounter. He was still hard when he'd left her. She feared that this time Sam meant what he had said. He was going to tell everyone they were married and move in with her. How could she endure it?

Sam arrived for Andy at precisely ten o'clock the following morning. Galahad pranced beneath him as Andy ran out of the house to meet him, his eyes shining with excitement.

"You didn't forget!" Andy squealed.

Sam dismounted. "Did you think I would?"

"Maybe. Mama said not to expect too much from you."

Sam lifted Andy into the saddle, then swung up behind him. Lacey had no right to discredit him to Andy.

He knew she believed he had abandoned her, and perhaps he had, but he'd had good reason. He'd had no desire to return to a wife who had betrayed him.

"Can we go fast?" Andy asked. "Sometimes Rusty takes me for rides, but his horse goes so slow."

"Take care of Andy," Lacey called from the porch.

Sam glanced over his shoulder. He hadn't known Lacey was there. "Don't worry. I'll treat him as if he were my own."

Then he galloped off in a clatter of hoofs. He didn't hear Lacey whisper, "He *is* yours."

"This is fun," Andy said, laughing. "Being sick isn't fun at all. Where are we going?"

"See those hills in front of us?" Andy nodded. "There's a place up there where cool water trickles between two rocks into a pool. We'll rest there awhile and return to the house in time for lunch."

Sam pulled Andy's warm body close against him. The boy felt good in his arms. Maybe he should give Lacey her divorce, find a woman and start a family of his own. Then he thought of Andy, and how miserable he'd be with Cramer for a stepfather. He wished he had money to give Lacey so she could save the ranch and not have to take up with men like Cramer, but he had nothing. Not even his good name. He was still an outlaw, still on the run from the law.

They reached the spot Sam had pointed out. Sam reined in, dismounted and lifted Andy from the saddle. The boy immediately ran to the small pool and quenched his thirst.

"It's just like you said," Andy said, beaming. "Do you ever lie, Sam?"

Sam was taken aback by Andy's innocent question. "Not if I can help it."

"Will you answer truthfully if I ask you a question?"

"Fire away." What kind of questions could a five-year-old ask?

"Do you like Mama?"

Sam shifted uncomfortably. Andy's question was a loaded one. Sam thought it out carefully before replying. "Why do you ask?"

"I was just wondering." He sent Sam a guarded look. "I wish you could be my new papa instead of mean old Cramer."

Sam went down on one knee before the lad. "Would you really like me to be your papa?"

Andy beamed and threw his arms around Sam's neck. "You bet! Do you think Mama would let you marry her?"

Sam decided that now was as good a time as any to tell Andy the truth. Especially if he moved into the house today like he intended.

"You might find this hard to understand, Andy, but your mama and I are already married. We've been married for six years."

Andy's eyes grew huge. It took a long time for it to sink in, but when it did, Andy appeared more confused than ever. "Are you my papa? Mama said my father died in the war."

Sam's fingers tightened on Andy's shoulders. He didn't want to lie, but neither did he want to hurt the boy. God, this was difficult. "I'll be your pa if you want me to be," he said after a weighted pause. It was the best he could offer without lying or hurting Andy. Lacey would probably be livid at what he'd done, but he didn't care. His own flesh and blood or not, Sam wasn't about to relinquish custody of Andy to Cramer.

Andy suddenly turned shy. "Can I call you Papa?"

A lump formed in Sam's throat. "If you'd like."

"I'd like that very much, Sa . . . Papa." Andy still didn't seem satisfied. "If you and Mama are married, why are you living in the bunkhouse?"

"I won't be for long. I'm moving in with you and your mother tonight. I'm going to help her run the ranch. She's doing a pretty good job, but she doesn't know a whole lot about ranching." Neither did he, but he'd bet he knew more than she did.

Sam stretched up to his full height. "We should be starting back. You must be hungry."

Andy seemed reluctant to leave. "Can I ask you one more question?"

Sam hesitated. Andy was too astute for his own good. Nevertheless, he owed it to the boy to provide answers to his questions.

"How long are you gonna stay with us?"

Sam went weak in the knees. Truth to tell, he didn't know the answer to that himself. If the law ran him to ground, he might be leaving real quick. He wasn't even sure he wanted to stick around for an extended period. Too much pain and heartache lay between him and Lacey. Could he learn to forgive her? Could she forgive him? How set was she on marrying Cramer? Too many questions, so few answers.

Andy was still waiting for Sam's answer. "Let's just take it one day at a time, son. I'm not going anywhere in the foreseeable future."

Andy brightened perceptibly. "I reckon that means forever. I'm ready to go home now . . . Papa."

* * *

Lacey was waiting for them on the porch. "It's about time," she said, snatching Andy from the saddle. "Go on inside, honey, Rita has your lunch ready. I'll join you in a moment."

Andy ran off, paused at the door, then turned and waved at Sam. " 'Bye, Papa. I'll see you tonight."

The color drained from Lacey's face, and she clutched the porch railing to steady herself. She felt as if she'd been punched in the gut.

"What did Andy mean? You didn't... You wouldn't ... Oh, God, I'm going to be sick."

Sam leaped from the saddle and helped Lacey over to the rocker swaying back and forth in the breeze on the porch.

Then Lacey lit into him. "Why? Why did you hurt him? Andy has always wanted a father. It will kill him when you leave."

"I told Andy that you and I were married. He figured out the rest himself. I didn't tell him I was his father. I merely said I'd *be* his father if that was what he wanted."

"He's only five years old! He isn't mature enough to recognize deception. I'll never forgive you for this, Sam."

"What's Papa done, Mama?"

Lacey stared at her son. "Andy, how long have you been standing there?"

"Not long. Rita is waiting lunch for you. Are you coming?"

Lacey rose unsteadily. "Yes, certainly."

"Are you coming, Papa?"

"No, he's not!" Lacey said before Sam had a chance to answer.

70

Sam sent Lacey a speaking look. "You and your mother go eat your lunch. I'll see you both later."

"Promise?" Andy said.

"Promise," Sam answered.

He made a hasty retreat before Andy could come up with anymore questions.

Sam was walking his horse to the corral when a cowboy rode hell for leather into the yard. It was Amos. He and four hands were riding guard on the herd this weekend. Amos reined in sharply before Sam. Sam knew immediately that trouble was afoot.

"What happened?" Sam asked.

"Rustlers in the north pasture," Amos ground out. "I came for reinforcements. Are you the only one here?"

"The boys went to town last night and haven't returned," Sam said. He checked his guns. "Let's go."

They rode at full gallop. Sam heard shots before they reached the herd. The ground shook beneath him. The cattle had bolted.

"Stampede!" Amos shouted over the din.

Sam rode into the midst of the stampeding herd, joining Amos and the other cowboys who were trying to head them off. From the corner of his eye he saw several men with neckerchiefs covering the lower half of their faces cutting cows out of the herd and driving them off. Sam turned his horse and rode off to intercept them.

He had nearly caught up to them when one of the rustlers turned in the saddle, raised his gun and took aim at Sam. Sam clearly heard him say, "Good-bye and good riddance, Gentry." Then the rustler fired. The bullet came too close for comfort. Sam drew his own weapon, but it was too late. The rustler's second shot whizzed past so close it dug a deep groove in the side of Sam's head.

Sam reeled in the saddle but managed to keep his seat. His hand flew to his head and came away covered with blood. He knew he was bleeding profusely, for head wounds were notorious bleeders. He also knew he was perilously close to losing consciousness. Turning Galahad, he headed back to the ranch.

By the time Galahad carried him back to the ranch, Sam was weaving back and forth in the saddle. Galahad halted at the corral gate. Rusty, who had just returned from town, saw him and ran over to see what was wrong.

Barely conscious, Sam lurched sideways and slid from the saddle before Rusty reached him. Blackness engulfed him and he knew no more.

Sam awakened in pain. His head hurt like the very devil, and his whole body felt as if he'd been beaten. He opened his eyes slowly. Once everything came into focus, he realized he wasn't in his bunk in the bunkhouse. The room was cheerful, the bed beneath him soft, and the sheets sweet-smelling.

The pain in Sam's head was unrelenting. He groaned and explored his head with his hand. His fingers encountered a thick bandage.

"You're awake."

The voice was softly feminine and soothing, putting him immediately at ease despite the grinding pain. Then Lacey came into his view.

"Lacey." His voice sounded rusty; his throat felt raw. "Water."

Lacey reacted quickly. She poured water from a pitcher into a cup, gently lifted his head and held the cup to his lips. Sam drank greedily, then lay back against the pillow.

"Where am I?"

"In my spare bedroom."

Sam tried to grin but could only manage a weak grimace. "I'd prefer to be in *your* room, in *your* bed."

Lacey ignored him. "Can you tell me what happened?"

"Rustlers. Amos rode in to get reinforcements, but the boys hadn't returned from town yet. I rode out to help. Were any of the others hurt?"

"No, just you. The raid doesn't make sense. Rusty reported that the rustlers didn't even take the cattle they had made off with. The hands found them grazing not far away from the main herd. Rusty doesn't know what to make of it."

Sam shot her a speculative look. "The man who shot me knew exactly who he was aiming at. If what you say is true, I believe I was targeted as the victim. The rustlers didn't want the cattle; they wanted me . . . dead," he added.

Lacey's eyes widened. "Why?"

"You tell me," Sam bit out.

"Me? What makes you think I know anything about this?"

"I distinctly heard you tell your lover you wanted me out of your life. And Cramer promised to see the deed done. Killing is permanent and quite effective, I might add."

Lacey recoiled as if she'd been struck. "I may want you out of my life but not in the way you think. I would never . . . How could you even think such a thing?"

"Easy," Sam said. "Your lover was simply carrying out your wishes."

73

"You're delusional," Lacey insisted. "Try to rest. Rita will bring some broth up to you soon." She turned to leave.

"Wait! Who bandaged me?"

"I did."

"How did I get up to the house?"

"Rusty and a couple of the boys carried you. Anything else?"

Sam closed his eyes. He had much to think about, but his head hurt too badly for him to concentrate. "No."

Lacey closed the door behind her and leaned against it until the anger left her. How could Sam think she had anything to do with the shooting? His unfounded accusation gave her a clear picture of exactly what he thought of her. He might want her sexually, but she meant nothing to him as a person. The world was filled with men like Sam. She was more determined than ever to keep her heart out of Sam's reach.

Lacey left the house and strode with grim purpose to the corral. Sam had made a serious accusation, and she felt compelled to learn the truth for herself.

"Going somewhere, Miz Lacey?"

Lacey was startled to find Rusty beside her. "I'm going on an errand, Rusty. Would you have one of the hands saddle Ladybird for me?"

"I wouldn't ride out alone if I were you," Rusty advised. "Those rustlers could still be around. How is Sam?"

"He's conscious and in no danger of dying. He was lucky; the bullet only grazed him. You can visit him later. Now, about my horse . . ."

"Sure thing, Miz Lacey. I'll go with you."

"You're needed here, Rusty. I'm not going far. Just over to the Cramer spread."

Rusty frowned. "You gonna visit Mr. Cramer?"

"Yes, it's business."

A few minutes later Lacey rode off. She knew Rusty hadn't liked her going alone, but that couldn't be helped. She had something to do, and only she could do it. She didn't want to believe that Taylor had tried to kill Sam, and wouldn't believe it unless she heard Taylor admit to the crime.

Chapter Five

Lacey rode up to Taylor Cramer's spacious ranch house and dismounted. She had visited the ranch before but never alone. Usually Andy was with her, but this time she'd left him home, and the thought of being alone with Taylor in his home made her uncomfortable. She knew she was being foolish; Taylor would never hurt her. He loved her. He'd told her so many times. That was one of the reasons she had agreed to marry him. Even if she couldn't love him like he deserved, she intended to be a good wife to him.

Lacey hitched her horse to the post, suddenly aware that she was being watched. Glancing over her shoulder, she saw that several of Cramer's hands had stopped their work to stare at her. Their knowing looks did nothing to reinforce her courage. Only the thought of Sam being shot at kept her from turning around and riding home as fast as Ladybird could carry her.

Lacey started up the porch steps. Suddenly the front door swung open.

"Lacey! I do believe this is the first time you've come to my home without your br . . . er . . . son." Taylor held the door open. "Come in, come in. I'm pleased you care enough about me to disobey Gentry's orders. I knew you would find a way to see me. Has Gentry left?"

Lacey stepped inside. She jumped when the door slammed behind her. What was wrong with her? Surely she didn't believe Sam's unfounded accusation. Taylor wasn't the kind of man to take another's life. She knew he could be ruthless in his business dealings, but killing was an entirely different matter. Only a fraction of an inch had separated Sam from sudden death. Furthermore, she didn't like being accused of conspiring with Taylor to take Sam's life. She needed to know the truth, and Taylor was the only one who could provide it.

Taylor showed Lacey into the parlor. "My housekeeper is away for the day, but I'm sure I can rustle us up some refreshments from the kitchen."

They were alone in the house. Why did that bother her? "Don't trouble yourself. I won't be staying long."

"At least sit down." Lacey perched on the edge of the sofa. "What's wrong, my dear? You appear nervous." He sat down beside her. Close, too close. "Obviously you have something on your mind."

Lacey cleared her throat. "It's about Sam."

"He's been shot," Taylor said, much too quickly.

Lacey regarded him narrowly. Did Taylor seem too knowledgeable? "How did you know?"

Taylor shrugged. "I heard some of your cattle were rustled, and that someone was . . . hurt. I just assumed—"

"You assumed correctly. Sam was shot while chasing rustlers."

"He's dead," Taylor said with startling joviality. "You mustn't grieve, my dear. He's not worth it. He abandoned you years ago and won't be missed."

"You misunderstand," Lacey said. "Sam wasn't seriously wounded and is very much alive. The bullet left quite a groove in the side of his head, but he'll recover. A fraction of an inch more and he'd be dead."

"I'm sorry to hear that," Taylor muttered.

"What do you mean by that statement?"

"You didn't let me finish. I'm sorry to hear that he was wounded. I'm not a violent man, Lacey. You ought to know that by now."

"Sam thinks he was targeted for death," Lacey blurted out before she could stop herself.

"A man of his caliber must have countless enemies," Taylor said silkily.

"Sam believes you were behind the rustling. If you could call it rustling, for the stolen cows were found abandoned not far from the main herd."

"Me?" Taylor said in feigned shock. "What a ridiculous notion." He sidled closer, placing an arm around Lacey's shoulders. "You don't believe that, do you, my dear?"

Lacey stiffened. "I don't know what to believe. I don't know Sam anymore. I hardly knew him when we were married. I don't know if he's lying or if he really holds you responsible for his shooting. I don't know what he's capable of."

Taylor's arm tightened. His body felt threatening against hers.

"Believe me, Lacey," he said blandly, "I wouldn't lie to you."

Lacey wanted to believe him, but when she looked into his eyes she saw something she hadn't noticed before. There was no warmth in their icy blue depths. No, she must be mistaken. Taylor had treated her with nothing but kindness since the day they first met. When Uncle Hob died, he'd been like a rock, helping with all the details too painful for her to handle.

"Lacey, you do you believe me, don't you?"

"I . . . want to."

"Gentry is a bastard!" Taylor bit out. "It's obvious he wants to hurt you and is determined to stop our marriage from taking place. You haven't told me everything, Lacey, have you?"

No, and she wasn't going to. "What happened between me and Sam a long time ago doesn't involve you. You're right in thinking he wants to hurt me, but I won't let him."

Taylor sent her a smug smile. "Good, very good. I know a perfect way to get him out of your life without resorting to violence."

Lacey's breath hitched. "I never considered violence an option, and I hope you don't either."

"Not at all, my dear, not at all. I thought about offering him money, but I'm convinced he wouldn't accept it. What I'm going to suggest might shock you, but it's the only way to send Gentry packing. If we make a child together, I suspect he'll be more than eager to let you divorce him."

The shock of Taylor's indecent suggestion rendered her speechless. Taylor took advantage of her momentary lapse by pulling her against him and capturing her lips in a brutally demanding kiss. Disgusted and repelled, Lacey broke free and shoved him away.

"I'm not going to do it, Taylor. I'm not going to sleep with you until after the wedding. Sam isn't going to back down on this either."

"We'll see about that," Taylor said. "Where there's a will there's a way."

Lacey stood abruptly. "I should leave. I left Andy with Rita, and there's no telling what mischief he'll get into without proper supervision."

"You won't have to worry about Andy once we're married," Taylor promised. "We'll send him off to the best school in the country."

"That's out of the question," Lacey retorted. "He's much too young to be sent away."

"Whatever you say, my dear," Taylor said obsequiously. "But in time you'll come to see the wisdom of my words. You and I will have children together one day; you won't even miss Andy."

Not miss Andy? Lacey's eyes glared defiance. "You're wrong, Taylor. No matter how many children we have, Andy will always be a part of me. I really must go."

"Very well. I hope I eased your mind about Gentry. He's trying to poison you against me; that's why he accused me of wrongdoing."

At that point Lacey wasn't sure about anything. She didn't agree with everything he said, but Taylor sounded sincere. Should she believe the man who professed to love her and had helped her after Uncle Hob's death, or the man who hated and mistrusted her? Suddenly her placid life was mired in conflict. Nothing was the same since Sam Gentry showed up on her doorstep.

"I have a lot to contend with right now, Taylor. Forgive me for accusing you unjustly."

Taylor gave her a smile that belied the anger seething inside him. "I'll come out to the ranch tomorrow."

"No. Please don't. Not until things are resolved between me and Sam. There is too much animosity between the two of you."

Cramer had assumed his men had taken care of that saddle tramp for good. He'd been stunned to learn that Gentry had only been wounded. He paid his men top wages and expected results. Now he'd have to approach this in a different way. Another attempt on Gentry's life would throw more suspicion on him, and that was something he couldn't afford if he was to win Lacey and her land.

"Very well, my dear, but I'm not going to let Gentry get away with this. He doesn't frighten me. I won't let him keep us from being together."

In silent fury Taylor watched Lacey ride away. His last words had been produced nothing but a nod from her. She was becoming too involved with her husband, and it didn't bode well for him and his plans.

Lacey marched directly to Sam's room the moment she returned home. She found him sitting up in bed, eating the lunch Rita had prepared for him.

"Where were you?" Sam asked sourly. "You were gone a long time."

"I went to call on Taylor Cramer."

"You what? After I told you to keep away from him?" His eyes narrowed. "Did you consult with him on the ways to bring about my demise? The last attempt didn't work. What have you two devised next for me?"

"I had nothing to do with your shooting, and neither did Taylor," Lacey defended.

"Likely story," Sam muttered.

Lacey blanched. "You must hate me a great deal. Do you truly think I'm capable of murder?"

"My murder," he said beneath his breath.

Lacey's cheeks flamed. She wasn't really surprised at Sam's refusal to trust her. He'd refused to believe she hadn't betrayed him, so why should he believe her now? "Put your mind at ease, Sam. I don't want you dead. I just want you to leave me and Andy alone."

"So you can marry Cramer and live happily ever after," Sam shot back.

His outburst must have caused him pain, for he grasped his head and moaned. Lacey was immediately contrite. "You're in pain."

"I've had a headache since that blasted bullet plowed a groove in my head."

"Let me take a look," Lacey offered. "That bandage should be changed."

"Leave it," Sam growled when she reached over to loosen the bandage.

"Nonsense," Lacey said crisply. "Don't be such a baby. I'm not going to hurt you."

Deftly she removed the blood-soaked bandage and inspected the wound. "The bleeding has stopped. I'll spread more salve on it and replace the soiled bandage with another. I'll be right back with salve and clean cloths."

Sam watched Lacey leave with less than charitable thoughts. Despite her protests of innocence, he didn't know what to believe. Lacey would certainly benefit from his death. It would free her to marry Taylor Cramer. But did he actually think her capable of conspiring with Cramer to murder him? Despite his earlier words, he couldn't quite bring himself to believe that Lacey would resort to murder.

Hearing a noise at the door, Sam turned his head carefully in that direction. Andy stood in the doorway, staring at him uncertainly.

"Mama said I shouldn't bother you."

Sam waved him forward "It's all right, Andy. You're not bothering me. Is there something on your mind?"

Andy hesitated a moment, then sidled forward. "You're not going to die, are you? My real papa died, and I don't want you to die, too."

An unexpected emotion clogged Sam's throat. He'd never been around children much and knew little about them, but this bright little lad had somehow wormed his way into his affection. He couldn't blame Andy for his mother's sins.

Sam cleared his throat. "I'm not gonna die, Andy. My wound isn't even serious. I'll be fit as a fiddle in a day or two."

"Promise?" Andy asked tremulously.

"Promise."

A grin spread across the child's face. "That's all I wanted to know."

"What did you want to know?" Lacey asked from the doorway. "I thought I told you not to bother Sam."

"Papa said it was all right," Andy said. "I didn't bother him. I just wanted to make sure he wasn't going to die."

"He's going to be just fine," Lacey said. "Run along now, I need to tend to Sam's wound."

Andy skipped off. Lacey waited until he was gone before rounding on Sam. "You shouldn't encourage him. You'll never be his father. It will be hard on him when you leave."

"Who says I'm gonna leave?"

"I do," Lacey said with conviction. "Turn your head so I can spread salve on your wound."

A grimace contorted Sam's face as he moved his head to comply. "When will this aching stop?"

"I brought laudanum for the pain. I'll give you some as soon as I'm finished with the bandaging."

"No laudanum. I prefer to keep my wits about me. Perhaps a mild headache powder, if you have it."

"Men," Lacey said with a hint of disgust. "Must you always be in control?"

"I don't like not knowing what's going on around me."

"Very well, I'll get you a headache powder when I finish here. Tomorrow you should be recovered enough to return to the bunkhouse."

Sam folded his arms across his chest and regarded her with amusement. "I'm not going back to the bunkhouse, Lacey."

Lacey went still. "Of course you are. What will the hands think?"

"They won't think anything after I tell them we're married, that we have been husband and wife for six years."

"You can't do that! They believe I'm going to marry Taylor Cramer."

"Not any longer. I'll explain everything to them, if that's what's bothering you. I'll tell them we lost track of one another during the war and that you mistakenly thought I was dead."

Lacey squared her shoulders. "I'll not be a wife to you, Sam Gentry."

"We'll see about that, Mrs. Gentry," Sam replied through gritted teeth. His head hurt so badly he could barely see. He didn't want to argue with Lacey right now. But once he was recovered, he fully intended to make damn sure she didn't get what she wanted. She was going to pay for betraying him.

The next day Sam felt well enough to get out of bed and stroll down to the bunkhouse. His head still ached but with less severity, and his wound was healing nicely. He hoped hair would grow over the scar in time, rendering it all but invisible.

The hands had just returned from the range. Sam opened the door and walked into the bunkhouse amid a boisterous welcome.

"Sam, you old son of a gun!" Rusty greeted. "I was just gonna go up to the house and see how you were doing. Are you ready to move back to the bunkhouse?"

Sam smiled. "As you can see, I'm fine, but I'm not returning to the bunkhouse, Rusty."

The other men heard what Sam had said and stopped what they were doing to listen.

Rusty scratched his head. "You ain't coming back? You ain't leaving, are you? Did that shooter scare you off?"

"Nothing like that. I'm glad everyone is here. There's something I want to tell you."

Once Sam had everyone's attention, he cleared his throat and said, "I haven't been exactly truthful with you boys. You see, I had no idea Lacey Gentry was the owner of the B&G when Rusty brought me here. In fact, I lost track of Lacey after the war and had no idea she was in Texas."

"What are you getting at, Sam?" Rusty asked.

"I don't know how else to break this to you so I'll just come right out and say it. Lacey and I are husband and wife. My full name is Sam Gentry. Lacey believed I was dead all these years, until I showed up here recently."

"Well I'll be a lop-eared jackass," Rusty said. "Why didn't you return to your wife after the war? It don't hardly seem right to let her believe you were dead. Why, I'll bet you never even knew you had a son."

Sam winced but said nothing. He couldn't bring himself to name Lacey a whore for having a child with a lover. Or label Andy a bastard. "That's right. I knew nothing about Andy. But I intend to make it up to Lacey and Andy. That's why I'm moving into the ranch house. I want everyone to know we're married."

"What about Taylor Cramer?" Rusty blurted out. "He ain't gonna like this."

"That's for sure," Barney ventured. That must have been the general consensus, for the other hands nodded their heads in vigorous agreement.

"I don't give a damn about Taylor Cramer," Sam said. "Lacey is my wife, and that's not going to change."

Grinning, Rusty slapped Sam's back. "I don't pretend to understand any of this, but I'm glad Miz Lacey ain't gonna marry that bastard. Andy don't like Cramer, and that's good enough for me. It does my heart good to know he ain't gonna get his hands on old Hob's land."

Sam walked over to his bunk and gathered up his few belongings. "I'll be fit enough to ride again in a day or two," he said as he stuffed clothing into his saddlebags.

"I reckon we'll be taking orders from you from now on," Rusty ventured.

Sam stopped what he was doing to answer Rusty. "I'm going to bow to your knowledge, Rusty. I'm not a rancher but I'm willing to learn. We'll decide what needs to be done together. How does that sound?"

Rusty grinned. "Sounds just fine . . . boss. Will you join us for supper?"

"Another time. I'm going to take supper with Lacey and Andy tonight."

"Don't blame you none," Rusty replied. "Six years is a long time to be away from your wife. You and Miz Lacey have a lot of catching up to do."

Sam merely grunted. He and Lacey weren't the lovers Rusty imagined them, but he wasn't about to admit it. Neither he nor Lacey wanted that kind of relationship. There was too much ill-will between them to forget and forgive. His only reason for sticking around was to punish Lacey. Becoming romantically involved with his betrayer was asking for trouble, and Sam had enough to contend with right now.

Sam returned to the house and stowed his gear in the spare bedroom. Then he went downstairs to find Lacey. Sam knew she wasn't going to be happy about his new living arrangements, but he wasn't going to let that bother him. Lacey wasn't in the house. Rita told him she'd gone to the barn.

"Tell her supper is almost ready, Señor Sam," Rita said. "Will you be joining her and Andy?"

"I'm moving into the house, so I'll be taking my meals here from now on."

Sam found Lacey in the barn, currying her horse. She wasn't aware of his presence until his shadow fell over her. She whirled to face him.

"Sam! You scared the daylights out of me. Must you sneak around?"

"I wasn't sneaking around. You were so engrossed in your thoughts you didn't hear me. Were you thinking about Cramer?"

"My thoughts are none of your business. Why aren't you in the cookhouse with the hands? I heard the supper bell ring a few minutes ago."

"I told them, Lacey. The hands know I'm your husband."

Lacey's cheeks flamed. "You had no right!"

"I have every right in the world. I expected more questions, but evidently the boys accepted my word and let it go at that. I moved my things up to the house. Rita said to tell you supper is almost ready. I'll be joining you and Andy."

"Your audacity is appalling," Lacey hissed as she led her horse back into the stall and closed the gate.

"It got me through some tough places. You used to like that about me. Among other things," he added with daunting boldness. "Or have you forgotten already?"

"I've forgotten everything about you, Sam Gentry," she sniffed.

Her dismissive tone raised Sam's ire. That was a nasty put-down if he ever heard one. Had she forgotten *everything* about him? A slow smile curved his lips. He'd bet his last dollar there was *something* she remembered about him.

She started to walk away. He grasped her arm and swung her around to face him. "Everything? You've forgotten everything?"

She stared at him. "A long time ago."

"Prove it."

She blanched. "Prove it? I don't know what you're talking about."

"Kiss me."

She stepped away from him. "I'll do no such thing."

"You're afraid you'll discover something about yourself if you kiss me," Sam charged. "Kiss me, Lacey. I dare you. I never thought you were a coward."

Lacey had never been called a coward before. At one time she had dared much for Sam. She had hidden him from Yankee soldiers, had risked everything for him. She would have done anything to prevent her father from betraying him, but all that happened a long time ago. Kissing him shouldn't prove a problem, for she felt none of the emotion they had once shared. She had been so young then, so inexperienced. But she was a grown woman now, with nothing but contempt for the man who had let her believe he was dead all these years.

"Well," Sam prodded. "Are you a coward?"

"I'm not afraid to kiss you, Sam Gentry. You're nothing to me but a nuisance. If kissing you will prove that, then I'd be most happy to oblige."

She stood on tiptoes, pursed her lips and pressed them against his.

"Not good enough, Lacey," Sam murmured into her mouth.

Catching her about the waist, he pulled her hard

against him. Lacey inhaled sharply. His body was a solid weight against hers, his scent intoxicating. She wanted to scream in outrage when he nudged her lips apart with his tongue and deepened the innocent kiss she had given him. She felt herself melting against him and fought it, to no avail. Even if she wanted to forget, her body remembered, and reacted.

He groaned her name into her mouth. She shook her head as if to deny her response, but long-repressed emotion ignited and exploded inside her. Betrayed, she cried out in silent supplication. Betrayed by her own wayward body. A cry of denial began deep in her throat. The moment it reached her lips it was swallowed by Sam, whose kisses sucked the air from her lungs, leaving her breathless and gasping.

Lacey felt unbalanced, as if she were floating. She cried out in alarm when she realized she was being pressed down into the soft hay. But Sam's kisses were so spellbinding she couldn't find it within herself to protest. His hard body was pressed into the vee of her legs, his sex a solid ridge between them. She felt a cooling breeze on her bare breasts and wondered when and how he had bared them.

Then he was lifting her skirts, his hand skimming up her inner thigh. When he cupped her, she arched into his hand and screamed. He caught the sound in his mouth. She heard him groan out a curse.

"Damn you," Sam growled. "What are you doing to me? This shouldn't be happening. Your touch has set me afire, and now you have to douse it."

He freed his manhood. A drop of moisture warmed her thigh. She felt his fingers opening her, felt her own dampness. He entered her with his fingers. She sobbed out a denial, which Sam all but ignored. He was guiding himself to her opening when she heard voices and approaching footsteps.

"Sam! Stop! Someone is coming."

Sam seemed to come slowly to his senses. He shook his head as if to clear it, then lifted himself away from her. Lacey leaped to her feet, struggling with buttons and bows. A glance at Sam told her he was setting his own clothing to rights. She was smoothing down her skirts when Barney and Amos entered the barn.

"There you are," Barney said, regarding them with undisguised curiosity. "Andy is looking for you two. Rita has supper ready."

"We were just leaving," Sam said with a hint of humor.

Gathering her dignity, Lacey strode purposefully toward the door. Sam followed close behind, but she didn't dare glance back at him, for she knew without a single doubt that he'd have a smug smile on his face.

Andy met them at the door. "Supper is ready but I couldn't find you."

"I'm here now," Lacey said. "We'll eat as soon as I wash up."

"Are you gonna eat with us?" Andy asked, regarding Sam hopefully.

"Reckon so," Sam said. "I'll wash up at the pump and join you and your mother in a few minutes."

Sam couldn't stop smiling as he washed his hands and face. Lacey could deny their mutual attraction till doomsday, but her body had betrayed her. She would have let him take her right there in the sweet-smelling hay if someone had not come along to disturb them.

Abruptly his smile turned into a frown. What in the

hell was he thinking? Intimacy with Lacey was the last thing he wanted, wasn't it? Making love to Lacey would serve no purpose, except perhaps give them both what they wanted. He remembered how hot she'd been for him while he was recuperating in her home during the war. They couldn't keep their hands off one another.

Maybe moving in with Lacey wasn't a good idea, Sam reflected. He hadn't had a woman in a while, and Lacey was too convenient. Telling everyone about his relationship to Lacey had seemed a good idea at the time. But now he wasn't so sure. How long could he keep from taking from her what his body demanded? Judging from the hard ridge straining his denims, not long.

Andy and Lacey were already seated at the table when Sam entered the dining room.

"Can Papa sit next to me, Mama?" Andy asked with an eagerness that put all Sam's thoughts regarding Lacey to shame.

"He can sit wherever he wants," Lacey said, slanting Sam a disgruntled look.

Sam seated himself beside Andy.

"Rita said you moved your things into the house today," Andy said.

"You ask too many questions, Andy," Lacey chided.

"I don't mind answering," Sam was quick to reply. "I did indeed move into the house today, Andy. But it's all right. I'm your mother's husband, remember?"

"I remember. I just wondered why you moved your things into the spare room. Aren't you and Mama supposed to sleep in the same bed?"

Sam nearly choked on a piece of meat. He swallowed with difficulty and said, "Andy shouldn't be hanging around the hands so much. He's far too precocious for his age. Stable talk isn't for tender ears."

"I couldn't agree more," Lacey said. "From now on you'll be spending more time at lessons, Andy."

"What did I say?" Andy complained.

"Never mind. Eat your supper."

Andy finished his supper, wolfed down his dessert and asked to be excused. Lacey nodded, and Andy scampered out the door.

A smile hovered on Sam's lips as Lacey devoted all her attention to her plate.

Suddenly she glared up at him. "You can wipe that smile off your face, Sam Gentry. What occurred in the barn today will never happen again. I don't know what got into me."

Sam grinned. "I know what *almost* got into you. You were hot for me, Lacey. Your nipples were hard, and you were damp between your legs. I could almost taste your passion. You were—"

"Stop!" Lacey lurched to her feet and threw down her napkin. "Don't say another word."

She ran from the room as if the devil were nipping at her heels. Sam watched her a moment, then charged after her. He caught up with her at the top of the staircase and swung her around to face him.

"Are you afraid of the truth?"

"What is the truth?"

"You want me."

"I don't! You abandoned me."

"You betrayed me."

"I didn't! I was devastated when I learned what my father had done. What hurt the most was the knowledge that it gained him nothing. My brother was already dead.

Just go away, Sam. Go away and leave me and Andy alone. I was better off believing you were dead. I have to marry Taylor Cramer to save the ranch. I can't pay the taxes without him."

The grinding pain of truth sparked Sam's anger. He could offer Lacey nothing; Cramer could give her everything.

"Don't you care that marrying Cramer will make your son unhappy? A ranch is only property; your son should come first. My brothers and I lost our farm and had to split up, but we are still bound by family ties. We genuinely care for one another. You and Andy are family; marrying Cramer would betray your son. Cramer cares nothing for Andy's welfare."

"And you do?"

"More so than Cramer."

"Taylor wants to send Andy to the best schools, give him the education he deserves."

Sam made a disparaging sound in his throat. "Cramer will send Andy to a school so far away you'll rarely see him. Is that what you want?"

Lacey blinked away the tears gathering in the corners of her eyes. "You don't know what I want!"

Sam grabbed her shoulders and pulled her roughly against him. "You're wrong. I know exactly what you want."

As if to prove a point, he lowered his head and seized her lips in a soul-destroying kiss. It wasn't what he'd intended, but he couldn't help himself. His body thrummed with suppressed passion, and his shaft became instantly hard, instantly aroused. His loins ached with the need to thrust himself into her soft, melting center, and he groaned into her mouth.

He kissed her until her lips softened and her body melded into his. Until she went limp in his arms. Then he scooped her into his arms and carried her into his bedroom.

He reached out, took her and turned her so that you
could see that she had turned her — like girl! "I
would start you that you . . . you . . . as you're scared of
nothing."

Chapter Six

Lost in a haze of passion, Lacey gazed up at Sam. Why
was this happening? Sam was trying to confuse her. He
didn't want her—he couldn't want her. She'd loved him
once, but he had accused her of betraying him and then
pretended to be dead. She couldn't allow herself to love
him again. She felt the bed give beneath her as Sam's
hard body pressed her into the mattress, and she fought
desperately for sanity.

"Sam! What are you doing? Stop right now."

"Is that what you really want?"

She found it difficult to breathe, much less form an
answer. "I . . . yes, of course."

He searched her face, his hot gaze settling on her kiss-swollen lips. "Liar."

She jerked upward, trying to dislodge him. He groaned in response. She stopped abruptly when she realized her movements were arousing him.

"Has Cramer made love to you yet?" Sam whispered against her mouth.

"That's none of—"

"Of course he has," Sam interrupted. "You've probably had countless lovers in the past six years. I'm surprised Andy doesn't have brothers and sisters."

"Bastard," Lacey hissed. "You're the only lover I've ever had." She didn't add that he was the only lover she'd ever wanted. No man had ever measured up to Sam.

"Then have me again, Lacey. I'm still your husband. That's not going to change anytime soon."

"You lost that privilege when you let me believe you were dead," she replied. "Making love will only complicate matters between us."

He rotated his hips. She felt the solid bulge of his sex against her thigh, and her breath hitched. He was hard all over. His legs, his chest, his back. Her fingers dug into the muscles of his arms, tense now with wanting. This felt so right yet was so very wrong. Sam wanted her for the wrong reasons. And she didn't want him at all.

"You're wrong, Lacey," Sam said. "You *do* want me. Your body is hot and eager for me."

Lacey gasped. Had he read her mind or had she spoken aloud?

"I'm going to make love to you."

He kissed her, and she lost the ability to think. All

she could do was feel—things she hadn't felt in a very long time. Things only Sam could make her feel. He deepened the kiss, his tongue a hot spear against the roof of her mouth. Suddenly his relentless pursuit became too much for her, and long-denied passion exploded inside her.

"Oh, God, yes."

She buried her fingers in his hair, shifting her body to bring him closer. She touched his tongue with hers and felt a bolt of lightning pierce through her. She arched against him, her fingers plucking at the buttons of his vest.

Sam reared up and stared down at her, as if unable to believe her sudden acquiescence. Then he grinned and lifted himself away from her. Sharing her urgency, he quickly tore off his clothes. Then he returned to her. Too fast, Lacey thought, disgruntled. She wanted to look her fill at him. He had changed over the years. There was nothing boyish about him now. He was all man—solid, powerful, fully aroused . . . needy.

"I want you naked," Sam said raggedly.

Lacey was so heated from his kisses that she could only nod. Her fingers fumbled with buttons and ties until he shoved her hands away and rendered her naked in less time than she could have done it herself. Then he sat back on his heels as his glittering gaze mapped a leisurely route over her body.

"My God, you're lovely. I never imagined . . . I hadn't realized . . . The years have been generous to you," he said lamely.

Their gazes locked. Tension sizzled between them. Lacey closed her eyes, refusing to acknowledge her feelings. Her eyes flew open when she felt his hands on her breasts. His expression was taut, dark with long-repressed emotion. Lacey wondered if he was remembering how desperately they had once loved one another. Then the force of his passion hit her like a searing gale as he lowered his head to her breasts and sucked a turgid nipple into his mouth. She cried out and surged against him, driving her body upward against his.

He responded by kissing her eyelids, her nose, her lips, plunging his tongue so deeply into her mouth that she succumbed easily to his drugging sensuality. Her hips surged upward, asking for what she wanted without words. Her breath caught as his fingers found her, opening her, sliding inside, testing her readiness.

"You *are* eager, aren't you," he whispered when his fingers encountered satiny wetness.

She was more than ready for him, though it rankled her to admit it.

His fingers delved deeper. She felt a shudder go through him when he drew them away drenched with her dew. She buried her face in the crook of his neck as he worked his fingers in and out, slowly at first, then with increased vigor. A buzzing began in her head. Her body felt weightless, her legs trembled. She hovered so close to the edge that she feared she'd burst. Abruptly his fingers left her, and she cried out in dismay. Then she felt his knees pressing her legs apart and his sex prodding against her slick opening.

"Put me inside you," he rasped.

Lacey touched him. Tentatively at first, then more firmly, her hand glided over him.

"You're killing me!" Sam cried. Taking matters into his own hands, he flexed his hips and plunged deep into her core. She stiffened against the initial jolt of pain. It had been so long. Then the storm within her body raged out of control, quickly banishing the slight discomfort as he began to move.

She arched upward, back bowed, groaning out his name as she surged against him urgently, her hips rising to meet every forceful thrust. Her hands dug into his shoulders as she lifted her legs, wrapping them tightly around his waist, locking him against her. The room was silent but for the harsh rasping of their breath, the thudding of their hearts beating in unison. Broken sounds of passion mingled with protesting bedsprings beneath them as their motions became more frenzied, more abandoned. Tension built tighter and tighter, almost too acute to bear, until Lacey thought she'd die of it.

The peak came in a rush of throbbing spasms, unraveling the tangled threads of her composure. Pleasure radiated outward from inside her as the walls of her sex clenched his engorged shaft again and again.

Sam gave a hoarse shout, his head thrown back, his fists tangling in the bed linens. His knuckles turned white as his own climax slammed through him. His hips pistoned convulsively, pushing him deeper, heightening her contractions as their loins met with scalding bursts of liquid heat.

Lacey clamped down hard on her tongue to keep from screaming. She could feel his hot seed spurting inside her, triggering another round of spasms.

Then suddenly it was over. Sam collapsed on top of her. Lacey sank into the mattress, incapable of moving or speaking. After what seemed like hours but was only mere minutes, Sam moved off her. He was quiet, too quiet. She glanced over at him. He was lying on his back, one arm bent over his eyes, his lips turned downward into a scowl.

Suddenly he reared up on his elbow and glared at her. "What in God's name did you do to me? It wasn't my intention to feel anything . . . to feel so strongly. Dammit! Our relationship has enough problems without creating more."

Lacey's lips thinned. "I did nothing. You've been working up to this moment since you arrived. I wanted nothing to do with you, but you persisted. I asked you to leave and you refused. Whatever happened in this bed is of your own making."

"Rest assured it won't happen again," Sam groused. "You have a way of making a man forget his own name. I don't want to pick up where we left off six years ago. You lost the chance to be my wife when you betrayed me."

"You lost the chance to be a husband to me when you abandoned me," Lacey shot back. "Let's pretend this never happened."

"Agreed."

"Does that mean you're going to move back to the bunkhouse?" Lacey asked hopefully. "Or better yet, leave?"

"You'd like that, wouldn't you?" Sam sneered.

"It's the best for all concerned. We can both get on with our lives."

Sam couldn't believe what had just happened. Not only had he made love to Lacey but it had been the best sex he had ever had. Even better than those furtive stolen moments in the barn where Lacey had lost her virginity to him. How many times had they made love before today? he wondered, thinking back to those hectic days when the war raged around them. He could count them on one hand and have a finger or two left over. Obviously Lacey had learned a lot over the years.

Dimly he recalled her tightness when he'd first thrust into her, and he frowned. She told him he had been her only lover. Could she be telling the truth? If so, that would mean that Andy . . . Denial rose inside him. No. Were Andy his son, Lacey would have told him. She never once said that he was Andy's father.

As if Sam's thoughts had conjured up his image, Andy chose that moment to barge into the room.

"I can't find Mama, Papa. She said she'd tuck me in bed."

Lacey gave a squawk of dismay and dove under the covers. Sam grasped the sheet and pulled it up to cover them.

"Is that you, Mama?" Andy asked as he approached the bed.

Sam made his expression deliberately stern for Andy's benefit. "You're going to have to learn to knock, Andy. Married couples like their privacy. Can you remember that?"

Andy nodded, his face solemn. "I'll remember, Papa. Rusty said you and Mama would sleep in one bed, but I didn't believe him."

Lacey groaned again. "You were discussing me and Sam with Rusty?"

"Rusty and I talk about everything. But I didn't ask him anything about you and Sam. I just listened when Rusty and the hands were talking. I don't think they knew I was there."

"What did they say?" Lacey asked in a hushed voice.

Andy cocked his head, as if trying to recall the conversation. "The hands thought it mighty strange that Papa didn't say anything about being married to you when he first showed up at the ranch."

"Is that all?" Sam coaxed gently.

"Rusty said it was none of their business. Then Lefty said that Rita told him you and Mama kept separate rooms. Rusty told them they shouldn't spec-u-late, that you and Mama might have separate rooms, but he'd bet his right arm that you used only one bed."

Sam cleared his throat. "As you can see, Rusty was right. But our sleeping arrangement is not a subject for discussion. Run along now, son. Your mama will come to tuck you in bed in a few minutes."

Andy scampered off. Sam glanced at Lacey and saw that her face had lost all color.

"Damn you, Sam Gentry," she hissed. "I've lost the respect of my foreman and hands, and my own son is asking questions about our relationship."

"We're legally married, Lacey. There's nothing to be embarrassed about."

He rose, walked over to the washbasin and filled it with water from the pitcher. Lacey didn't wait around to watch him wash. With a cry of dismay, she leaped from the bed, threw on her shift and stalked from the room.

Sam tried his best to ignore Lacey during the following days. He deliberately left the house early each morning and devoted his full attention to the ranch. Learning about ranching was no easy task, but he was beginning to feel right at home. He usually ate lunch with the hands, and sometimes he joined them for supper. Eating with friendly faces sure beat those sour looks Lacey threw him across the table. If he had any doubt that

Lacey's punishment was working, he had only to look at her to realize how effective it was.

Bedtime was the worst time of day for Sam. Each night he fought his inclination to stalk into Lacey's room and make violent love to her. She would resist, he realized, but he was also aware that it wouldn't take too much coaxing to rouse her to passion. Lacey's mind might be unwilling, but he was experienced enough to know that her body wanted him. Fortunately, he knew better than to surrender to his lust. He tried to tell himself that his purpose for remaining at the ranch was to punish Lacey, but his almost constant arousal belied his own intent.

One day Sam was repairing a fence in the yard when he saw Cramer ride up to the house. His face hardened and his fists clenched at his sides, but he forced himself to wait to see if Lacey would welcome Cramer before reacting.

Shading his eyes against the glare of the sun, Sam watched as Cramer dismounted at the hitching post and walked toward the house. Suddenly a shot rang out. Sam drew his gun and looked for the shooter. Another shot followed the first. The dirt at Cramer's feet scattered as the bullet struck the ground, missing him by scant inches. Sam saw a movement at the corner of the barn. He spun, ducked low and got off two shots before the shooter ducked out of sight.

Sam's gun was still smoking when several hands ran up to investigate.

"What happened?" Barney asked.

"I'll tell you what happened," Cramer said, striding over to Sam. "Gentry tried to shoot me in the back."

Sam's eyes narrowed. "You're wrong, Cramer. I don't shoot men in the back."

Cramer glanced pointedly at Sam's gun. "The barrel of your weapon is still smoking. There are witnesses, Gentry. My eyes didn't deceive me. I saw you deliberately aim and fire at me."

Lacey ran from the house and forced her way through the circle of men surrounding Sam and Cramer. "What's going on?"

"Your *husband* tried to kill me," Cramer charged.

Disbelief marched across Lacey's face. "I heard the shots, but . . . surely you're mistaken, Taylor. Sam has a temper, but I'm sure he wouldn't shoot you without provocation."

"That's exactly what he did," Cramer insisted. "He's a back shooter, and he won't get away with it."

Cramer grasped his horse's reins and swung himself into the saddle. "You haven't heard the last of this, Gentry." Spurring his mount, he rode away.

"What *really* happened, Sam?" Rusty asked when the hands began drifting away.

"Someone took a shot at Cramer, but it wasn't me."

"Did you fire your gun?"

"I saw a movement near the barn and got off a couple of shots when I realized what had happened."

"Cramer's got clout in this town, son. I wouldn't take his threats lightly."

"Cramer doesn't frighten me," Sam claimed. But that wasn't exactly the truth. Sam had plenty to worry about. He couldn't afford to tangle with the law. He was a wanted man.

"Watch your back," Rusty warned before he turned and walked away.

"Did you do it, Sam?" Lacey asked.

"Don't put me in the same category as your lover," Sam growled. "I've never shot a man in the back and don't intend to start now. I wouldn't waste a bullet on Cramer."

Sam could tell by the look on Lacey's face that she wasn't convinced of his innocence. That shouldn't have surprised him, though it did hurt.

"I hope you're telling the truth, Sam," Lacey whispered. She spun on her heel and strode back to the house.

Sam stared at her departing back, admiring the sway of her hips and remembering the way they looked unclothed. Her body was perfection, without a blemish to mar her beauty. He hadn't been too lost in passion to store every lush curve, enticing hill and mysterious valley in his memory.

Sam shook his wayward thoughts from his head and returned to the work he'd abandoned before Cramer had appeared.

Sam had almost forgotten the altercation with Cramer and was heading to the house for supper when two men rode into the yard. He stopped and waited for them. Then he saw the sun reflecting off the badges on the men's vests and he cursed beneath his breath. The sheriff's visit could mean only one thing.

"Howdy, Sheriff. What can I do for you?"

"I think you know," Sheriff Hale said as he drew rein beside Sam.

"I can think of nothing that would bring you here. Why don't you fill me in?"

"Taylor Cramer filed charges against you today."

Sam remained outwardly calm despite the fury seething inside him. He never thought Cramer would go this far.

"What, may I ask, are the charges?"

"Attempted murder. He said you tried to shoot him in the back, that there are witnesses who will verify that your gun was in your hand and smoking."

"I'll admit I fired my gun, but it wasn't at Cramer. I shot at the man who tried to kill Cramer."

Hale and his deputy exchanged skeptical glances. "Did anyone besides yourself see the man you supposedly shot at?"

Sam frowned. "I don't believe so. No. But that doesn't mean he wasn't there."

"One more question, Mr. Gentry. Did you and Mr. Cramer have an altercation recently?"

"It's common knowledge that Cramer and me don't see eye to eye on certain things, but that doesn't prove I tried to kill him."

"In my books that's damning evidence," Hale said. "That and Mr. Cramer's insistence that he saw you pull the trigger are all the proof I require. You're under arrest, Gentry. Hand over your guns."

Sam's mind went blank. Jail was the one place he'd been hoping to avoid, but now it looked like that's where he was going to end up. How long before Sheriff Hale recognized him from a Wanted poster? Since fleeing was out of the question, Sam unbuckled his gun belt and handed it to the sheriff.

"Can I speak to my wife and son first?" Sam asked.

"I was surprised to learn you were Mrs. Gentry's husband," Hale said. "I knew you bore the same last names but assumed it was coincidence. I heard that Mrs. Gentry's husband had died in the war. She must have been real shocked when you turned up alive."

"You could say that," Sam muttered.

"I reckon it's all right to speak to your wife before I take you in, as long as you don't try to escape. You'll be given a fair trial. The jury might even believe your story, but I wouldn't count on it."

Sam glanced toward the house and saw Lacey watching him from the front porch. He was glad Andy wasn't with her, for he didn't want the boy to think the worst of him. "I won't be long, Sheriff," he said grimly.

Would Lacey be happy to see him behind bars? Sam wondered. Was this but one more attempt on Cramer's part to get rid of him? Did Lacey have anything to do with it? Did Cramer hire someone to shoot at him and miss so he could blame Sam?

"What does the sheriff want?" Lacey asked when he reached her.

"Me," Sam snarled. "Your lover filed charges against me. He claimed I tried to kill him. I'm going to be carted off to jail."

Lacey gasped. "But you didn't do it."

"That's what I told the sheriff, but he doesn't believe me. Cramer is a respected citizen. I'm a drifter, a nobody without a penny to call my own."

"What can I do?" Lacey asked.

"Call your lover off."

"He's not—"

The sheriff must have grown impatient, for he walked his horse up to the porch, cutting off Lacey in mid-sentence. "Sorry, ma'am, but I've got to take your husband in now."

"Is that necessary, Sheriff?" Lacey asked.

"It is if your man is a killer. Maybe he can convince the jury of his innocence."

Sam hadn't slept a wink his first night in jail. He'd neither seen nor heard anything to indicate that the sheriff knew he was a wanted man, and for that he was grateful. His meager breakfast finished, he paced the length of the small cell like a caged animal. How in the hell was he going to prove his innocence without a lawyer?

Sam was still pacing when Sheriff Hale ushered an unwelcome visitor to his cell.

"You have a visitor, Gentry," Hale said. "Mr. Cramer wants to make sure you're the man he saw shooting at him. Damn considerate of him, I'd say. He doesn't want to condemn an innocent man."

"That's right," Cramer insisted. "Might I have a word alone with Gentry, Sheriff?"

Hale hesitated a moment, then said, "I'll be nearby should you need me."

"What do you want?" Sam barked when they were alone.

"I have a proposition for you."

"I'll bet you do," Sam spat. "Out with it, Cramer. What the hell do you want from me?"

Cramer whipped a document from his pocket and thrust it at Sam.

"What's that?"

"A divorce document. Lacey is charging you with desertion and child abandonment. I had my lawyer draw up the papers last night."

Sam stared at the document, then gave a shout of laughter. "There's no way I'm going to sign that."

"What if I tell the sheriff you're not the man who shot

at me? I'll say I was mistaken, that it happened just the way you said. Do you understand?"

"Perfectly. My signature on the divorce document will guarantee my release."

"I knew you'd see reason." He chuckled. "The man who tried to kill me, whether or not it was you, did me a favor. Now I have the leverage to force you to comply with my wishes. Think about it, Gentry. You have a choice. You could spend years behind bars or leave here a free man. All that is required of you is your signature. Once the divorce is final, Lacey and I will marry."

Sam stared at the document as if he expected it to bite him. "Does Lacey know about this? Did she ask you to help her obtain a divorce? Does she know you're blackmailing me?"

"Of course. Lacey and I both want this. We're in total agreement."

Sam let his breath out slowly. It was just as he had suspected. Lacey had conspired with Cramer in order to get him to agree to a divorce. He couldn't count the times she'd asked him to leave her alone. He hoped she was happy now that she was getting what she wanted.

Faced with years in jail, Sam had few choices. He didn't want to sign the document. He didn't want to leave Lacey and Andy to Cramer, but what choice did he have?

"There is one stipulation," Cramer added.

"Of course," Sam said dryly.

"Once you're out of jail, you're to leave town immediately. I'll tell Lacey what she needs to know. You abandoned her once; no one will think it unusual that you left her a second time. You can ride away with the knowledge that I'll be looking after her welfare once we're married."

"That's what I'm afraid of," Sam muttered.

"You don't have much time, Gentry. A few years in prison or freedom. Make up your mind now, for I won't offer the choice again."

Sam sat on the horns of a dilemma. Wanted posters for his arrest could arrive at any time. Or someone might recognize him from posters they'd seen elsewhere. All it would take to send him to prison was a telegram to Dodge City. Returning to Dodge in irons was not a pleasant thought. All things considered, what Cramer offered was a way out of a potentially dangerous situation. Damn! He wasn't ready to leave yet.

"Well, Gentry, what will it be?" Cramer prodded.

"Free me first and I'll sign your damn paper," Sam shot back.

Cramer sent him an assessing look. "How do I know you won't refuse to sign after you're freed?"

"How do I know you won't refuse to have me freed if I sign first?"

Cramer's eyes narrowed. "It seems we're at an impasse."

"I'm a man of my word, Cramer. If I say I'll sign your damn paper, then I'll do it."

"I have the ability to put you back in jail if you refuse to sign," Cramer advised. "I can always change my mind and say you were the man who tried to kill me."

"Don't worry, Cramer. I said I'd sign and I will."

"And leave town immediately afterward."

"What choice do I have?" Sam bit out.

Cramer grinned. "None that I can see. I'll go get Sheriff Hale."

"Bastard," Sam spat.

Cramer returned a few minutes later with the sheriff.

"What's this all about, Mr. Cramer?" Sheriff Hale asked.

"I fear I was mistaken. It wasn't Mr. Gentry who tried to kill me after all. He explained how he had discharged two bullets at the man who tried to kill me, and I believe him. I'm sorry about the misunderstanding."

"Are you sure, Mr. Cramer?" Hale queried. "You seemed convinced that Gentry was your assailant."

Cramer smiled obsequiously. "It was an honest mistake, but fortunately I've discovered my error before an innocent man was brought to trial. Set Gentry free, Sheriff. I'm dropping the charges."

"Are you sure this is what you want?" Hale repeated.

Sam held his breath and let it out slowly when Cramer said, "I know what I'm doing, Sheriff."

Hale fumbled with the ring of keys on his belt, removed one and fit it into the lock. The cell door swung open and Sam stepped out.

"Am I free to go?"

Hale nodded brusquely. "I don't want to see you in my jail again, Gentry. I don't know what's going on here, but I'm giving you fair warning. Stay out of trouble."

"Mr. Gentry is leaving town," Cramer said.

Hale seemed surprised. "What about the ranch? Is Miz Lacey planning on selling out?"

Sam said nothing until Cramer nudged him. "My wife won't be joining me. She and Andy are remaining behind."

"Now that that's settled," Cramer said before Hale

could ask any more questions, "we'll take our leave. Good-bye, Sheriff."

"My lawyer is waiting for us," Cramer said after they exited the jailhouse. "You can sign the document in his office."

Sam nodded grimly and followed Cramer. The sooner he got this over with, the sooner he could get on with his life.

The moment Sam met Lawyer Oakley, he knew the man was cut from the same cloth as Cramer. Both were men who would stop at nothing to get what they wanted. But what exactly did Cramer want? He didn't appear to be in love with Lacey, nor did he like Andy. Sam was inclined to think it was Lacey's land that Cramer coveted, though he had no idea why. During his short stay he had seen nothing special about Lacey's land to set it apart from other spreads in the area.

"You both know, however, that the document requires Mrs. Gentry's signature to make it legal," Oakley said after Sam affixed his signature. "Nor can I guarantee the divorce will be granted in a timely fashion."

"Yes, yes," Cramer said impatiently. "Mrs. Gentry will sign, no problem there. And I'm sure you'll do your best to expedite things. I'm paying you plenty to push it through without undue delays."

Sam had heard enough. "I'm leaving. You two can hammer out the details in private."

"Don't forget the conditions of your release, Gentry," Cramer cautioned. "You're to leave town immediately."

"Don't worry, Cramer," Sam growled. "I have no desire to see Lacey. I wish you joy of her. She's a hot little piece, but I suspect you already know that."

Sam slammed out the door with more force than was

warranted. He was angry. Angry enough to spit nails. He hadn't asked to encounter Lacey again after all these years, and wouldn't have done so deliberately. But their meeting had proved something to him. Though he had fought it for six years, he could not deny the fact that Lacey still provoked strong feelings in him, feelings other than hostility.

Making love to Lacey had been a revelation. She had wanted him as badly as he wanted her. She might want to marry Cramer, but it was Sam who aroused her passion, Sam's name she called out during the heat of climax. God, that had been a sweet moment.

Sam got his horse from the livery and rode out of town. He headed west, away from Denison and away from the ranch. He had little money and nothing of value. The few items in his saddlebags could be described as worthless. But he rode away with the memory of one night of unspeakable bliss with a woman who cared nothing for him.

Chapter Seven

Lacey spent a fretful night. The thought that Sam might have attempted to shoot Taylor in the back disturbed her; she had questioned Rusty and some of the hands and learned that Sam's gun had indeed been smoking. Even more damning was the fact that no one had seen the man Sam said had fired the shots at Taylor.

Deliberately Lacey had kept word of the shooting from Andy. Andy had been napping and apparently had missed the commotion. Lacey had warned the hands not to discuss the incident in front of the boy. She wasn't going to tell him anything until she learned the truth about the incident.

When Andy looked for Sam at the supper table the day of his arrest, Lacey told him that Sam had business out of town and would be away for several days. If worse came to worst, she supposed she'd have to tell Andy the truth. But for now, the less he knew, the less upset he'd be.

Lacey had already eaten breakfast and was now preparing to ride to town to see Sam. She had to know whether he had anything to do with the attempt on Taylor's life. Except for a small, lingering doubt, she was almost convinced that Sam wouldn't shoot a man in the back.

"Where are you going, Mama?" Andy asked as he skipped into the room.

"To town, honey. I won't be long."

"Can I come?"

"Not today. Don't give Rita any trouble while I'm gone."

"Are you gonna see Papa? Tell him I miss him."

Lacey hesitated. How much did Andy know? Or had he merely surmised that something was amiss? "I'm not sure," she hedged. "I should be home for lunch. Meanwhile, why don't you go out to the barn and look for Fluffy's new kittens?"

Andy's eyes lit up. "Can I pick out one to bring into the house?"

"I suppose."

Andy gave a whoop of joy and took off at a run.

Lacey jammed her hat down on her head and headed out the door. She had just led her horse out of the barn when she saw Taylor Cramer ride into the yard. Her heart plummeted when she noted the smug expression on Taylor's face. He appeared inordinately pleased about

116

something, and she wondered if it had anything to do with Sam. Her gut told her it did.

"Taylor, what brings you here? I hope this won't take long, I'm on my way to town."

Taylor dismounted and grasped Lacey's arm, pulling her back toward the house.

"What are you doing?" Lacey snapped.

"If you're going to town with the intention of visiting Gentry, don't bother. He's not there."

Lacey dug in her heels. "What do you mean? Of course Sam is in town. You're the one who had him dragged off to jail."

"Gentry's been released," Cramer revealed. "I'll tell you all about it inside the house."

"Released?" Lacey gasped. "I don't understand."

"You will in a moment." He opened the front door and all but pushed her inside.

Lacey walked into the parlor and whirled to confront Cramer. His superior grin set her teeth on edge. "Well," she said, tapping her foot impatiently. "Kindly explain."

Instead of explaining, Cramer removed a document from his inside pocket and handed it to Lacey. "This will explain a great deal."

Disbelief marched across Lacey's face as she scanned the document. When she saw Sam's signature on the bottom of the page, the breath exploded from her lungs.

"This is a divorce document! How did you get Sam to sign it? Where is Sam now?"

"One question at a time, my dear. First, you are indeed holding a divorce document. My lawyer drew it up, and I presented it to Gentry yesterday. Second, Gentry signed the document quite willingly after I presented it to him.

And third, I have no idea where he is at present. He left town shortly after his release from jail."

"Left town?" Lacey repeated dully. "That doesn't sound at all like Sam. What did he have to do to get himself released from jail? Did you drop the charges?"

"Rather decent of me, don't you think? Sheriff Hale agreed that the evidence against Gentry was flimsy. I'm the only one who saw him with the gun, *after* the shots had been fired," he added. "Even though I was certain he was the shooter, there was a reasonable doubt. Sheriff Hale decided there wasn't enough evidence to bring him to trial."

"Let me get this straight," Lacey said slowly. "Sam was released, signed the divorce papers, and lit out of town without a word to me or Andy."

"That's correct, my dear."

"That doesn't sound like Sam."

"The man's a no-good drifter without a sense of responsibility," Cramer spat. "He abandoned you once; his leaving a second time will surprise no one." His gaze settled on the divorce document in Lacey's hand. "You have pen and ink, I assume? Sign it now and I'll take it back to my lawyer so it can be filed immediately. I understand these things take time, but we will be married the moment the divorce is final."

Lacey stared at the document as if she expected it to bite her. She carried it to the writing table and placed it in a drawer. "I'll sign it later."

Cramer frowned. "Is there a problem? I went to a lot of trouble and expense to obtain this as quickly as I did. Sign it now, Lacey."

Lacey stared at him. His voice had changed subtly— from gentle coaxing to demanding. Her jaw firmed. She wasn't going to be coerced into signing until she read the document and studied all the ramifications. Something wasn't right, but she didn't know what. She might not want to remain married to Sam, and she needed Taylor's money, but she found this whole affair puzzling. Taylor had something up his sleeve.

"I told you," Lacey persisted. "I'll sign the document after I've had time to read it."

Cramer's face turned an ugly shade of red. "I thought you wanted out of your farce of a marriage."

"I do."

"Then sign the document now."

"I will, in my own good time."

"Damn you," Cramer cursed.

It was the first time he'd cursed at her, and a prickle of uneasiness slid down Lacey's spine. Had he kept his true nature hidden from her? If she had not needed him so desperately, she might have been tempted to tell him their marriage was off. But what would she and Andy do when the bank foreclosed on the ranch? Where would they go without money? The thought of no roof over their heads or food in their stomachs was an unpleasant one. Few jobs were available to a woman with a child.

Cramer must have realized that Lacey had no intention of following his dictates, for he said, "I can see you're being difficult today. I'll return when you're in a better mood. Perhaps later today. I can see no reason why you shouldn't sign. Apparently, Gentry is as glad to be rid of you as you are of him."

"I'm sorry, Taylor. I don't mean to be difficult. By all means, come back later this evening. After Andy is in bed," she advised. "I don't want him to know about any of this. He's grown fond of Sam. I want to tell him about the divorce in my own way."

"I understand, my dear," he said coolly. "Until tonight, then." Without warning, he pulled Lacey into his arms and kissed her. Lacey didn't resist, nor did she participate. She merely endured.

Sam rode away from Denison, away from Lacey and away from Andy, certain that what he was doing was right. He could give Lacey and Andy nothing in the way of monetary support. They needed money to save the ranch, and he had none. He was a wanted man. He could spend years in prison if convicted of bank robbery. Rafe and Jess could already be in jail, for all he knew. He wouldn't learn their fate until he met them in Denver for their reunion one year from the day they had parted.

Sam drew rein at a creek about five miles from town to allow his horse to drink and rest. He dismounted, knelt at the stream and drank his fill. Then he sat back on his heels and stared into the blue water. He blinked repeatedly at the reflection peering back at him. His wasn't the only face he saw. Andy's accusing blue eyes stared back at him. His gut clenched. He shouldn't care what the boy thought of him, but he did.

Muttering an oath, he plunged his hands into the water, scattering the reflection. But Andy's image was still with him, imprinted upon his brain. As was the image of Andy's mother. Lovely, deceitful Lacey. He would have loved her forever had she not betrayed him to the Yankees. Part of him wanted to forgive her. Making love to Lacey had opened his eyes to many things. Her response to him had been very real. Either that or she was a very good actress. Sam was experienced enough to know when a woman wanted him, and Lacey had definitely wanted him.

Sitting there thinking of Lacey and Andy wasn't doing him a damn bit of good, Sam decided as he mounted and continued on his way.

"It's just you and me now, Galahad," Sam said, patting his horse's neck. "No wife to complicate my life. No kid calling me Papa. I kinda liked it, even though I knew Andy wasn't mine. Dammit, Galahad, leaving them without a word leaves a bad taste in my mouth."

Of course Galahad didn't answer, but he did turn his head and roll his eyes at Sam.

Several hours later, Sam did something he knew he would regret. Cursing himself for a fool, he jerked on the reins and spun Galahad around in the opposite direction. He didn't give a damn about Cramer's threats. He'd never backed down from a fight and he wasn't about to now. He wanted the chance to tell Andy goodbye. And Rusty. And . . . damn his soul to hell . . . he wanted to convince Lacey that he wasn't a back shooter before he disappeared from their lives.

Lacey pushed her food around her plate with her fork. She wasn't hungry. She still hadn't signed the divorce papers and was puzzled by her hesitation. It was what she wanted, wasn't it? Obviously it was what Sam wanted.

"When will Papa be home, Mama?" Andy asked, disturbing her troubled thoughts.

"He's only been gone one day, honey."

"I miss him. I asked the hands where he had gone, but Rusty said I should ask you. None of the hands would tell me anything. Is something wrong, Mama?"

Despite his few years, Andy was no fool, Lacey thought. He sensed something, and she knew from experience that he wouldn't let it rest until he had the truth.

"I don't have time for explanations now," Lacey hedged. "I'm expecting Mr. Cramer tonight and I want to get you settled in bed first."

Andy made a face. "Why is he still coming around? You already have a husband."

"We'll talk about this tomorrow. Have you finished your supper?"

Andy pushed his plate away. "I'm not hungry."

"Run along then. Put on your nightclothes, and I'll be up in a moment to tuck you in and read you a story."

Andy slid from his chair, his expression troubled. "Don't be long, Mama."

Lacey scraped back her chair and walked to her writing table in the next room. She pulled out the drawer and removed the divorce document. She even picked up the pen and dipped it into the inkwell. Her hand shook. A blob of ink fell onto the paper. She set the pen down, blotted the ink and placed the document back in the drawer without signing it. She slammed the drawer shut and walked upstairs to tuck Andy into bed. She would sign the paper later.

It was late. Andy had been asleep for hours and Rita had gone home, but still Taylor hadn't arrived. Lacey decided not to wait up for him. She wasn't all that anxious to sign the divorce document anyway, she thought as she locked the doors and downstairs windows, doused the lamp in the parlor and made her way up the stairs. A lamp in the upstairs hallway, left burning for Andy's benefit, provided sufficient light for Lacey to undress and find her bed. Crawling between the sheets, she drifted into an uneasy sleep.

Sam rode up to the barn and dismounted. The house was dark but for a dim light visible through an upstairs window. A glance at the darkened bunkhouse told Sam that everyone inside was sleeping.

Sam led Galahad inside the barn, removed his saddle and rubbed him down. He planned to bed down for the night in the loft, but a compelling inner voice drew him outside. He glanced up at Lacey's room. The leafy branches of the elm tree growing beside the house swayed in the breeze, nearly obscuring the window, but he could tell that it was open and the room beyond dark. He fought a battle with himself; the devil inside him won.

Sam placed one foot in the crook of the elm tree and hoisted himself into the branches. He climbed steadily until he was even with the window. Then he crawled onto the sill and dropped silently into the room. The light in the hall cast a golden glow through the open door, revealing a bed and the slight figure huddled beneath the blanket.

Sam removed his boots so he wouldn't awaken Lacey and crept toward the bed. He wasn't certain what had driven him to enter through the window—his mind was hazy about that—but some driving force inside him commanded his actions. Lacey was a temptation he couldn't resist. Abruptly his mood darkened when it occurred to him that she might have plotted with Cramer to get rid of him. Suddenly Lacey stirred, and he stepped back into the shadows.

*   *   *

Lacey awoke to the tingling sensation that she wasn't alone. She sucked in a shallow breath, afraid to move or open her eyes. She knew the intruder wasn't Andy, for he would have climbed into bed with her. Lacey had enough wits about her to know that whoever had come uninvited to her room could only have entered through an open upstairs window. Her window.

She heard a slight movement and cranked one eye open. A slash of moonlight fell across a large figure hovering in the shadows beside the window. Panic shuddered through her. The intruder was big and threatening. She opened her other eye so she could take in all of him. He stood in his stocking feet, tall and intimidating. His legs were long, and even in the poor light she could see the bold ridge of his aroused sex beneath his tight denims.

Had the intruder come with rape on his mind? Was he a drifter who had found his way to the B&G by accident? Lacey didn't want to believe that one of her own hands had broken into her house, but she couldn't discount anything. Her legs shifted nervously beneath the covers. Then she froze, wondering if he had noticed her sudden movement.

"Lacey? Are you awake?"

That voice!

"Sam? Is that you? How dare you break into my room! You scared ten years off my life."

Sam stepped out of the shadow. Lacey sat up and pulled the covers up to her neck. "What are you doing here? I thought you'd be miles away by now."

Sam approached the bed. "We need to talk. I couldn't leave without explaining what had happened."

"Taylor explained everything quite satisfactorily," Lacey said. "Please leave."

Sam grasped her shoulders, his hard fingers digging into her tender flesh. She tried to free herself, and in the struggle the sheet fell away. One shoulder of her nightdress had slid down her arm, revealing the pert tip of a creamy breast. When Lacey noted the direction of Sam's intense gaze, she glanced down at her exposed flesh and blanched.

"Oh, God, Lacey . . ."

His gaze singed her. She didn't stop him when he pulled down the other shoulder, baring both taut breasts. Nor did she protest when he dropped to his knees on the bed and stripped the sheet and blanket from her nerveless fingers. All she could do was stare at his lips, and into his eyes, dark now with desire. A gnawing hunger for this man spiraled through her. It didn't matter what had brought him here, or why. She wanted him.

He bent to kiss her, cradling her head in his hands as he slanted his mouth over hers. His lips moved urgently, tasting, nudging her lips apart as he buried his tongue in the waiting warmth of her mouth. Abruptly his kisses became wildly demanding, ruthlessly possessive, until she was clinging to him, desperately seeking to escalate the pace.

"Wait." Sam grasped her hands, removing them from the buttons of his shirt. Uncoiling himself from her arms, he helped her to remove her nightdress. Then he tore off his own clothing. Before he returned to the bed, he struck a match to the wick of the bedside lamp, closed the bedroom door and turned the key in the lock.

"Why did you do that?"

"I want to see you . . . all of you. And I don't want Andy bursting in on us."

Air spilled from her lungs as she looked her fill at him. He was fully erect, his sex thrusting upward from a nest of dark hair. She wanted him inside her, was almost desperate to feel his strength piercing her, and was disappointed when Sam didn't oblige immediately. She gave a startled yelp when he lowered himself beside her and kissed a trail of fire between her breasts and over her stomach. She went still. Was he headed where she thought he was? His mouth moved lower. She cried out his name. He had never attempted so bold a caress either before or after their hasty marriage.

Sam glanced up at her and ran his fingers over her breasts. She met his smoldering gaze and found the breath to ask, "What are you going to do?"

"Very soon I'm going to taste you. Am I the first to make love to you like that?"

"You mean . . . ?" She shuddered at the thought of his mouth *there*. "You're the *only* man to make love to me in any manner."

If Sam heard her, he gave no indication as he cupped both her breasts and slid his thumbs over the puckered tips. Then he lowered his head and suckled her. Lacey's wits fled as he licked, sucked and nipped each hardened nipple in turn.

When he'd tasted his fill, he slid down her body and pressed her legs apart with his knees. She could feel her face flaming as he spread the petals of her sex apart and stared at her. The intimacy of the act was appalling, frightening . . . wildly erotic. When he tucked his head between her legs and touched her with his tongue, a jolt of pure ecstasy shot through her.

Lacey gasped at the first wanton stroke of his tongue. The overwhelming sensation stunned her. His mouth was disappointingly elusive as he came close to, yet never quite touched, her aching center. She lurched against him, a wordless plea for him to end this torture.

Finally . . . finally, he sought that place where she wept for him. He lashed it with his tongue—a blatantly erotic sensation against her swollen core. Then he breached her with a determined thrust of his tongue, and throbbing pleasure carried her to the stars.

She was still moaning when he braced himself above her, his muscles taut as he filled his hands with the smooth rounds of her buttocks. He came inside her, hot, hard, thick, their flesh melding together as one.

"Lacey, Lacey, Lacey . . ." He whispered her name over and over, his thrusts frenzied, torrid.

There was no holding back for either of them. They kissed ravenously, endlessly. Lacey tasted the hunger in him and responded by writhing in tempo with his lunging hips. Heat uncoiled deep inside her, spreading throughout her body.

She looked up and saw Sam watching her, his eyes dark and heavy-lidded with some unguarded emotion. Then all thought ceased. She was drowning in sensation, her insides clenching around Sam's engorged sex. The urgency was building again, that overwhelming need for release, and she caught his head between her hands, urging his mouth down to hers. He made love to her with his mouth as his body moved below. She bucked beneath him, sending him deeper. Pleasure spread through her, stripped to its rawest form, pulsing so fiercely she couldn't keep it bottled up inside. She screamed.

Sam covered her mouth with his, swallowing her

screams, thrusting until her violent thrashing was replaced by gentle tremors. In the dim recesses of her mind, Lacey heard Sam's shout of completion as his own climax overtook him.

Lacey's wits returned, along with unanswered questions. "Why did you come back? I never thought to see you again after you signed the divorce papers."

"I wanted to explain why I agreed to the divorce. There are things about me you don't know."

Lacey slid away from him and pulled the sheet up to her neck. "I know all I need to know."

"No, you don't. But before I explain, I want you to tell me again why you betrayed me to the Yankees."

Lacey heaved an exasperated sigh. "How many times must I repeat that I had nothing to do with my father's decision to surrender you to the Yankees? If you recall, I wasn't even there when they came for you. Papa had sent me on an errand to keep me from interfering, but he didn't do it out of malice."

Sam snorted. "So you say."

"It's true. We learned that my brother was being held in a Southern prison. Father went to the authorities to try to get him released and was told that the Rebels would only release a prisoner if an exchange was offered. Father told them about you, and they promised to work out a deal for an exchange."

Lacey sighed, recalling the sad day they learned her brother had died of his wounds at Andersonville. Sam had already been taken away; her father's machinations had gained them nothing.

"I tried to trace you, but no one seemed to know what had happened to you. I even wrote to the President. I was told you had died on the prison ship. Crowded conditions and disease on the ship added to the confusion. After a year of brick walls, I accepted that you were dead."

"You didn't take a year to turn to another man," Sam charged irrationally. "Andy is proof of that."

Lacey said nothing. What could she say to a man determined to think the worst about her? He would never believe that Andy was his son. Too much between them remained unresolved.

Sam mulled over Lacey's words. Perhaps he had judged her too harshly. Perhaps he should have returned to Lacey after the war and gotten the truth from her. But it was too late for regrets. After the war he had tried to forget Lacey, refusing to mention her name or tell his brothers about her. He truly thought he had banished her from his mind for good, but seeing her again had brought a resurgence of those long-forgotten memories . . . and feelings he thought had died years ago.

"Do you believe me, Sam?" Lacey asked.

Sam searched her face. "I'm . . . not sure."

"What has this to do with what you were going to tell me? What don't I know about you?"

Sam fought a battle within himself. If he believed Lacey, that meant he should trust her. Could he trust her with the knowledge that he was a wanted man? Telling her would be a dangerous way to prove whether or not she could be trusted. But revealing his secret to Lacey was the only way he could explain his reason for agreeing to the divorce.

"I didn't show up in Texas by chance," Sam began slowly.

"I never thought you did."

"Something happened in Kansas that forced my brothers and me to flee. Our farm was on the brink of foreclosure. We applied to the bank for a loan and were promptly turned down. Then the banker offered us a deal. If one of us married his pregnant daughter, he'd allow the loan. Needless to say, neither Rafe, Jess nor myself were willing to accept those terms. We left the bank in a huff.

"The banker became enraged and set off an alarm, claiming we had robbed the bank. We panicked and ran, though I realize now we should have remained and fought the charges. We hightailed it back to the farm, took what we could carry in our saddlebags and rode away with a posse breathing down our necks. We split up outside of town. Rafe rode west, Jess headed north, and I rode south."

"Why are you telling me this?"

"So you understand why remaining in jail presented a danger to me. There are Wanted posters out for my arrest. I didn't want to be under the sheriff's nose when and if the posters arrived in Denison. However, if I refused to sign the divorce document, Cramer wouldn't have dropped the charges against me. Sooner or later the law would learn I was a wanted man. Spending the rest of my life behind bars doesn't appeal to me."

"So you signed the document and took off," Lacey said. "I can't say I blame you. Why are you telling me this now?"

"Because of Andy. I don't want him to think the worst of me. He may not be mine, but I've grown fond of him. And I wanted you to know I didn't try to kill Cramer. I don't operate that way."

"You've told me. Now you can go."

Sam gnashed his teeth. "Has nothing I've said gotten through to you?"

"Not much. You abandoned me and let me believe you were dead. You didn't care what happened to me during the years we were apart, so why should your confession affect me? It's far too late for us, Sam. I'm losing the ranch. What can you do for me but give me more grief? You rejected me; now it's my turn to reject you."

"Money-hungry little bitch," Sam bit out.

Lacey stiffened. "I'm merely doing what's best for myself and my son."

Sam knew that what he'd done to Lacey was wrong, but at the time he couldn't think beyond her betrayal, and he'd truly never wanted to see her again. It had taken this honesty between them to show him her side of the story. He still didn't trust her completely, but he now believed he might have jumped to conclusions.

Sam stared down at her, suddenly aware that he was growing hard again. He caressed her breast, smiling when her nipple hardened beneath his fingertips. "Your body still wants me."

"I can't help what my body wants, I only know what my mind tells me is right for me."

He willed his erection away. "What is your mind telling you now?"

"That's it's over." She shrugged. "Perhaps there never was anything lasting between us. I need more than you can offer, Sam. I have a son whom I love very much, and a ranch to save. I have no energy left to deal with you."

"What about Cramer? You can't love that bastard."

"Taylor is aware of my feelings. I've had one grand passion; I'm not looking for another. Taylor and I will deal well with one another on an unemotional level."

Sam reared up from bed and began pulling on his clothes. "Did you ever consider that Cramer wants your land more than he wants you?"

Her chin rose. "Of course I have. How could I not? But, for the life of me, I can't see why he should want the B&G. There is nothing particularly valuable about it. Besides," she argued, "Taylor might not love me but he is fond of me. And he respects me."

"Then I'll be leaving you in good hands," Sam taunted. "You deserve one another. It's time I took off. I promised Cramer I'd leave town if he'd drop the charges. I must have been out of my mind to come back here and try to explain. I don't know what the hell got into me."

Sam strapped on his gun belt, shoved his hat on his head and turned to leave. He unlocked the door, then paused with his hand on the knob. "Tell Andy good-bye for me." Then he was gone.

Sam headed to the barn for his horse. He was just reaching for the saddle he'd thrown over the railing when someone called out to him.

"Sam, is that you? I thought I heard someone ride in a while ago. I heard that Cramer dropped the charges against you, and that you'd left town. I knew you'd come back. You wouldn't leave Miz Lacey in a lurch."

A light flared. Sam squinted into its pale glow and saw Rusty, holding a lamp aloft.

"I'm not staying," Sam said curtly. "I came back because . . . oh, hell, you may as well know everything."

Rusty set the lamp down on a bundle of hay. "What is it, Sam?"

Deciding that he trusted Rusty more than he trusted

Lacey, Sam told the foreman everything. About being wanted in Kansas, his reasons for allowing Lacey to believe he was dead, and his fear of going to prison for crimes he hadn't committed.

"I signed the divorce document Cramer presented under duress," he explained. "I'm not proud of the fact that the only reason I told everyone about our marriage and remained here was to punish Lacey for what I'd perceived as her betrayal. Now I'm not so sure she *did* betray me, but it's too late to make amends."

Rusty remained silent a long time, then said, "What about your son? Andy thinks the world of you."

"Andy isn't really my son," Sam said. "But don't get me wrong. He's a youngster any father would be proud to claim."

Rusty gaped at him in shock. "You're a damn fool, Sam Gentry, if you think Andy isn't your son. All I had to do was see you two together to know he's your flesh and blood. He may not have your coloring, but everything else about him is pure Gentry."

Sam felt as if he'd just taken a blow to his gut. What Rusty said couldn't be true. Lacey would have told him if Andy was his, wouldn't she? His first reaction was elation. Then his face hardened. "Lacey must hate me a great deal to keep the truth about Andy's parentage from me."

"Only you can answer that question, son," Rusty said.

"No," Sam growled. "Lacey can answer it better than I. I'm going up to the house and demand the truth."

Neither Rusty nor Sam saw the stealthy figure huddling just inside the barn door, close enough to hear them but far enough away so as to remain outside the ring of lamplight. Taylor Cramer had arrived late at the ranch. His horse had thrown a shoe and he'd had to walk nearly the entire distance. He hadn't considered turning back, for he wanted the signed divorce document too badly.

Cramer had seen the light in the barn and had investigated out of curiosity. He'd heard the entire conversation between Gentry and the B&G foreman, and what he'd learned made him want to shout with glee. But he restrained himself. Moments later the lamp was doused. Rusty returned to the bunkhouse, and Sam strode with grim purpose to the house for another confrontation with Lacey.

Once the coast was clear, Cramer sneaked into the barn and exchanged his horse for one of the B&G horses. Then he rode hell for leather back to town.

Chapter Eight

Sam kicked open the front door, stormed into the house and up the stairs. Lacey reared up in bed as he burst through the bedroom door. The lamp had burned low, but Sam thought he saw a shimmer of tears in her eyes. He brushed his concern aside and charged into the room. He'd come for the truth, and nothing was going to stop him from getting it.

"I thought you left," Lacey gasped. "Haven't you tormented me enough?"

"Who is Andy's father?" Sam bit out.

"What? Why would you ask that now?"

Sam grasped her shoulders and pulled her up until

they were nose to nose. "Who, Lacey? No lies this time. I want the truth."

"Andy is *your* son!" Lacey all but shouted. "If you had half a brain you'd know."

He released her. "Why did you lie to me?"

Lacey scrambled to her knees. "You don't deserve a son like Andy."

Sam snorted derisively. "I suppose Cramer does."

"You chose to believe what you wanted," Lacey said, skirting Sam's question. "I would have told you about Andy if you had been the least bit interested in claiming him."

"What about those other men, the ones you had after me? What makes you so certain Andy is mine?"

Lacey aimed a fist at Sam's face, but his reflexes were too keenly honed. He caught her wrist before her blow landed, pinning it behind her.

"Bastard!" Lacey hissed. "Look at Andy. Really look at him. He's the image of you, despite his fairness. What made you decide Andy was your son all of a sudden?"

Sam noted with chagrin that Lacey hadn't denied having had other men. He vaguely recalled hearing her defend herself while he was making love to her, but couldn't be sure. Her lack of denial now confirmed his belief that there had been other men after him, just as there had been countless women during those years he'd sought to banish Lacey from his memory.

"Rusty made me see the light."

"Rusty, of course. I should have known. Everyone except you assumed Andy was yours. I'm surprised you believed him."

"Rusty said things that made me stop and think. He said Andy was much like me, and when I thought about it, I decided he was right. I accept that Andy is my son," Sam allowed, "and I freely admit I felt a bond between us the moment we met, but I chalked it up to the boy's innocent appeal. He's really something," Sam bragged, unable to suppress the grin spreading across his face. "I'm glad he's mine."

Suddenly Sam's face hardened and he glared down at Lacey with renewed venom. "If you think I'm going to allow Cramer to raise my boy, you're loco, lady."

Lacey glared back at him. "There's nothing you can do about it. You've ignored me and Andy too long for your wishes to be considered. Can you give Andy the life he deserves? Think about it, Sam. You're an outlaw. Andy is better off without you."

Sam gritted his teeth, frustrated beyond endurance. "I didn't rob that bank. I admit I should have stayed and fought the false charges, but my brothers and I were desperate to escape the posse. Dodge City is a lawless town, and justice is swift. We would have been condemned and hung before we were brought to trial."

"I see we're at an impasse," Lacey said. "You're still on the run. You'd be doing Andy a favor by quietly disappearing."

"And leave my son to Cramer? Not on your life. Andy hates Cramer, and I believe the feeling is mutual."

"Andy is jealous. In time he'd come to regard Taylor as his father."

"Don't delude yourself. Andy isn't jealous of me. If you divorce me and marry Cramer, I'll take Andy from you. Remember that, Lacey."

Lacey exploded in fury. "Damn you! I'll tell the sheriff you're a wanted man if you attempt such a thing. I can use the reward," she added.

Sam's eyes narrowed. "I believe you would. What a fool I was to trust you. I won't let you betray me twice."

"You can't stop me."

"Perhaps not, but I can give you something to think about before you turn me in for the reward." He lowered himself to the bed.

"What are you doing?"

"I want you to remember that no matter how many times you betray me, I'm the one who taught you passion. I'm the man who can bring you to shuddering ecstasy even though you profess to hate me."

"You think highly of yourself," Lacey sniffed. "What makes you think you're the only man with the power to move me?"

Sam's smile did not reach his eyes. "Do you think I don't know when a woman wants me? When she enjoys me? I've seen you with Cramer enough times to know he does little for you sexually. Have your other lovers left you as cold as Cramer?"

"My 'other lovers' are none of your business."

"You're still my wife. Of course they matter. Have you signed the divorce document yet?"

"I . . . no, it's still in the drawer, but I certainly intend to sign it. I can't, I won't lose this ranch. It's all Andy and I have."

"Don't sign the divorce, Lacey," Sam said with feeling. It was the closest Sam had ever come to begging, and he didn't like it.

"Sam . . . I . . . don't . . ."

"If my words won't convince you, then maybe this will."

His mouth swooped down over hers, not soft and giving but hot and ravishing. It was a savage kiss, one of fierce possession. His breath came in swift, panting outbursts, as his heated gaze raked over her.

"Don't do this," she whispered raggedly.

He blurted out the truth before thinking. "I can't help myself."

He kissed her again, cupped her breasts, teased her nipples. Lacey fought the feeling spiraling through her and lost the battle. A sound escaped her throat. A soft, tortured whimper. Scorching heat burned through her. Hard, callused hands stroked her body, seeking the damp folds of her sex. A long finger slipped inside her. Moisture scalded her . . . her own moisture, she realized. She wanted to scream out in frustration, curse him for his ability to seduce her, but her weakness for this man made a shambles of her good intentions.

She braced her hands against his chest. She wanted to push him and was shocked when she realized she was dragging him closer. His hands left her. She heard his gun belt drop to the floor. He returned moments later and grasped the full rounds of her buttocks. He shoved her legs apart with his knees and she felt his sex, smooth, hot, hard, prodding her entrance. Holding her steady, he sheathed himself to the hilt. He stilled for a moment, a shudder racking his body. Then he began to move, filling her, filling her so deeply she felt as if he were a part of her.

"Feel me inside you, Lacey," he murmured. He flattened his hand low on her belly, pressed against it with the heel of his hand. The sensation sent her spiraling out of control as she writhed, panted, gyrated wildly beneath him. "Can you feel the pressure? It's good, isn't it?" he whispered hoarsely.

Speech deserted her. She flung back her head and arched upward, taking him deeper. A climactic throbbing began deep within her. Then she was soaring, straining, moaning, peaking. She heard his harsh moan. Felt his final thrust that ended with the spewing of his seed inside her.

Sam rose immediately. He straightened his clothes and strapped on his gun belt.

"Are you still going to tell the sheriff about me?" he asked with an insolence that set Lacey's teeth on edge. Was he so sure she wouldn't?

Lacey wanted to lash out at him, to hurt him for making her want him. For thinking he could dictate her life when he had wanted no part of it.

"You're a threat to Andy and the kind of life I want for him. You couldn't corrupt him if you were behind bars."

Rage seethed through Sam. "I expected no less from you. I should have known better than to confide in you, but I foolishly believed your story naming your father as my betrayer. I won't make the mistake of trusting you again, Lacey. I plan to be well away from here before the sheriff comes looking for me." His eyes narrowed. "Will you betray me again, Lacey?"

Lacey bit her lip. Though she wanted Sam to leave, she had no intention of alerting the law. "Sam, I—"

"No, don't say it. I already know the answer. I'm going to tell Andy good-bye before I leave," Sam warned. "Don't try to stop me."

Lacey leaped from the bed and placed herself in front of him. "No! Leave him alone. He's going to be hurt enough when he learns you won't be coming back."

"He's my son," Sam said grimly as he set her away

from him. "There are things I need to tell him." He picked up the lamp and strode from the room.

Lacey was hard on his heels, fearing the damage Sam could do. Andy was at a vulnerable age; she didn't know how he would handle this. She hovered behind Sam as he set the lamp down, knelt beside Andy's bed and gently shook him awake. Andy blinked groggily, saw Sam and came awake instantly. Sam caught him as he launched himself into his arms.

"Papa! I knew you'd come back!"

"I'm here now, son, but I can't stay. I needed to see you before I left."

Andy's face puckered as if he wanted to cry. "Why do you have to go away again?" He turned pleading eyes on Lacey. "Make Papa stay, Mama. I don't want to lose another papa."

"Andy, there's something I want to tell you before I leave."

"Sam, no! Andy can't deal with this now."

"He's old enough to understand," Sam shot back.

"What is it, Papa?"

"I wanted you to know that I'm your real father. I didn't die in the war. Your mother thought I was dead and I let her believe it. You see, I didn't know about you. Had I known I had a son, I wouldn't have stayed away so long. Do you understand what I'm trying to tell you?"

Andy stared at Sam a long time, then gave a solemn nod. "You're my real papa but you're going to leave me again. Don't you like me?"

Tears clogged Lacey's throat. "I told you he wouldn't understand. You've only complicated matters."

Sam swallowed the lump in his throat. Hurting Andy

hadn't been his intention. He just wanted to hold his son before bidding him a final good-bye. He hugged Andy tight against him, burying his face in the sweet hollow of his neck. He smelled of sleep and innocence.

"I love you, Andy, very much."

"Then why do you have to leave?"

"It's a long story, son, and very complex. But I'm going to make you a promise. One day I'll return for you. I'm not abandoning you forever."

"Don't make promises you have no intention of keeping," Lacey admonished.

Sam ignored her. "This is one promise I'm going to keep, son. I *will* return for you."

"For Mama, too?" Andy asked.

Sam's hard gaze raked Lacey. "We'll talk about that when the time comes."

"Don't stay away too long, Papa."

"I'll try not to. You'd best get some sleep now."

He tried to set Andy away, but the boy clung to him with a tenacity that tugged at Sam's heart.

"Stay with me tonight, Papa. Just tonight. Please."

Sam didn't have the heart to refuse. "Just until you go to sleep. In bed with you now."

Andy snuggled down beneath the covers, gripping Sam's hand tightly. Sam sat on the bed, watching his son fall asleep and wondering if he'd be able to keep his promise. He heard Lacey leave the room and refused to think about her. They had already said their farewells and had nothing more to say to one another. Despite her threat, he really didn't believe she'd go to the sheriff.

An hour before dawn, Sam kissed Andy's forehead and crept from his room. He paused before Lacey's bedroom door, then forced himself to continue down the stairs. The sky was growing light, but there was still something he had to do before he left. He entered Lacey's small office and rummaged through drawers, not finding what he was looking for. Then he crept into the parlor and began opening drawers, until he found what he'd been searching for in the writing desk. Smiling grimly, he tucked the sheath of papers into his pocket and left the house.

The hands were beginning to stir. Sam saw Luke leave the bunkhouse and head over to the cookhouse to prepare breakfast. Sam's mouth watered for a cup of strong coffee and his stomach rumbled with hunger, but lingering at the B&G could be dangerous to his health should Lacey take it into her head to fetch the sheriff.

No one saw Sam mount Galahad and ride away.

While Sam was riding away from the B&G, the sheriff was rousing the telegraph operator from his bed to send a telegram to Dodge City. Taylor Cramer had ridden into town late last night with a wild tale about Sam Gentry being wanted for bank robbery in Dodge. Whether he believed it or not, Sheriff Hale felt duty bound to investigate, so he wired the sheriff in Dodge City, requesting an immediate reply.

The reply arrived late that morning. The Gentry brothers, Sam, Rafe and Jess, were outlaws, wanted for bank robbery. There was a five-hundred-dollar reward on each of their heads. Hale notified Cramer and a posse was formed. The B&G was their first stop.

Lacey arose late, pretending that nothing had happened last night. Unfortunately, the soreness between her legs

143

was an achey reminder that Sam had made love to her twice that night.

"Is something wrong, señora?" Rita asked as Lacey pushed around the food on her plate without tasting it. "Will Señor Sam be down soon? I heard he has been released from jail. I'm glad. Señor Sam wouldn't have shot at Señor Cramer."

"I agree, but Sam isn't here, Rita. I don't want you mentioning him in front of Andy."

Rita sent Lacey a curious glance. When she would have said something further, Andy bounded into the room.

"When did Papa leave? He was gone when I woke up."

Rita quietly left the room.

"You knew Sam was going to leave," Lacey said gently.

Andy's lower lip trembled. "I know, but I hoped . . ."

"We can always hope, honey, but sometimes our wishes don't come true."

"Don't you want Papa to come back, Mama?"

Lacey weighed her words carefully. "I want what's best for all of us, honey." She tried to draw him into her arms, but he pulled away from her.

"No! You're lying! You don't want Papa to come back." Turning on his heel, he ran from the room.

Lacey started to follow but decided to let Andy work out his frustrations before trying to console him. He was in no mood to listen to anything she had to say.

Lacey walked through the kitchen to the back porch, where she picked up the egg basket and continued on to the chicken coop to gather eggs. Rain threatened. It was a dreary, dark day, perfectly matching Lacey's dour mood. She hurried through the gloom and stepped into the chicken coop. The earthy smell of feathers and manure greeted her inside the long, low building. Her mind skittered in all directions as she shooed hens from their nests and plucked the fruit of their labors from beneath them. She had just extracted eggs from the last nest when she heard riders approaching. Many riders. She set the basket on the floor and ran outside. She recognized Taylor Cramer, the sheriff and some men from town.

The riders drew rein when they saw her. "Good morning, ma'am," Sheriff Hale said.

Lacey glanced nervously at the riders, and it suddenly dawned on her who and what they were. A posse from town! Why had they come here? Surely they weren't after Sam, were they? Taylor told her the charges had been dropped.

Lacey's heart began to pound. "What can I do for you, Sheriff?"

"Where's Gentry?" Hale asked without preamble.

"You're looking for Sam? I thought the charges against him were dropped and he was released from jail."

Lacey felt Rusty's comforting presence beside her, lending his support.

"Yep, he was released, all right," Hale admitted, "but that was before we knew he was wanted for bank robbery in Dodge City. I telegraphed Dodge City and formed a posse when I received the reply. Is Gentry here or isn't he?"

Lacey's heart sank. How did they know? Her gaze flew to Cramer. "What's this all about, Taylor?"

Cramer shrugged. "It's like the sheriff said, Lacey. Gentry is an outlaw, a wanted man."

Lacey's gaze returned to the sheriff. "What made you wire Dodge City? Did you see a Wanted poster?"

Hale's eyes shifted away from her. "It doesn't matter how I learned about Gentry's criminal record. What's important is that we bring him to justice. The bastard fooled me, and I don't like that. I had him in my jail and let him loose."

"Sam isn't a criminal," Lacey defended. "There must be some mistake."

"Lacey," Cramer cautioned, "you don't really know the man, or what he's capable of. Is he here?"

"No. He was here last night but left hours ago."

Cramer cursed. "He was supposed to leave town without contacting you."

"How long ago did he leave?" Hale asked.

Lacey shrugged. "I'm not sure."

Hale turned his attention to Rusty and the hands. "What about you, Ramsey? Did you or any of the hands see Gentry leave?"

"I ain't seen hide nor hair of him," Rusty lied. "None of the boys mentioned seeing him, either. Ain't that right, boys?"

Since none of the hands had seen Sam, all agreed with Rusty.

"He can't be too far ahead of us," Cramer said.

"It hasn't rained yet; we have a good chance of picking up his trail," Hale said. "Let's ride, boys."

Lacey's fear escalated as she watched the posse ride away. She had no idea how long Sam had stayed with Andy last night but she hoped it had only been a few minutes, and that he was far enough away from Denison to elude the posse.

Lacey turned back to the house. Rusty stopped her with a hand on her arm.

"You don't believe Sam is guilty, do you?"

"Sam is capable of many things, but I can't believe bank robbery is one of them. He told me all about it before he left. It's all a big mistake."

A grin spread across the foreman's craggy features. "I thought as much. I'm a pretty good judge of character."

"Do you think the posse will catch up with him?"

"There's always that chance," Rusty allowed. "A lot depends on how big a start he has on the posse."

"I know you spoke with Sam last night."

"Yep, right after he rode in. I found him in the barn." Rusty fidgeted nervously. "I know I had no right, but I set Sam straight about something he should have recognized before now. It wasn't my place, but I couldn't let him ride off believing Andy wasn't his son. I don't know a thing about the trouble between you and Sam, or why you chose to let him believe Andy wasn't his, but I felt he should know the truth. Any fool can see the resemblance between Sam and Andy."

"Any fool but Sam," Lacey muttered.

"Are you mad at me, Miz Lacey?"

Lacey sighed. "Not really. In fact, I expected Sam to realize it long before now. Not only is he stubborn, but blind about a lot of things concerning me and Andy."

"I sure as hell hope Sam outruns the posse. How do you reckon the sheriff learned about him?"

"From a Wanted poster, I suppose," Lacey ventured. "Thanks for your support, Rusty. Have you seen Andy? He took off before breakfast and I haven't seen him since."

"I saw him running into the barn when I was coming

out of the cookhouse. You want I should get him for you?"

"Thanks, I'll find him myself."

Lacey strode off toward the barn. Though the doors were open, the inside was dark and murky.

"Andy, are you in there?"

Andy stepped out from behind an old plow. He was so close, Lacey gave a squeal of surprise and stepped back, her hand flying to her heart. "Andy, you frightened me."

"I heard riders and peeked out the door to see who they were. Was that the sheriff, Mama? Who were those men with him?"

Lacey saw no help for it. She had to tell Andy the truth, as much of it as he could understand.

"Those men with the sheriff were the posse," she began.

Andy thought about that for a moment, then said, "A posse chases after bad men."

"That's right, honey."

"Why did they come here? There are no bad men on the B&G."

Lacey stifled a groan. It was now or never, and Andy was bound to figure it out sooner or later. He hung around the hands too much to remain in the dark for long.

"They came for Sam, honey."

Andy frowned. "Papa? Why did they want Papa? He's not a bad man."

"It's all a big mistake, Andy. I'm sure your father will get it all straightened out in time."

Immediately Andy's face cleared. "Don't worry. Papa

will tell them they made a mistake and it will be all right."

Lacey wished she had Andy's blind faith.

Andy grasped Lacey's hand. "I'm hungry, Mama. Can I have my breakfast now?"

Hand in hand they walked back to the house, but Lacey's thoughts were on the posse, and the man wanted for bank robbery.

Sam wasn't in any big hurry. Lacey was bluffing. He didn't really believe she would sic the law on him. Meanwhile, he had nowhere to go, nothing to do but ride to some distant location and hope no one knew that Sam Gentry was wanted for bank robbery. Perhaps he should change his last name. He chewed on that for a while and decided he'd drop his last name altogether. In Texas, no one questioned a man who offered no last name.

Sam's stomach rumbled. He was hungry. Unfortunately, he carried few if any provisions with him. He decided to make a quick stop in Denison to sell his mother's cameo, the one memento he had brought with him, to purchase rations. He had no money, and until he found work, none would be forthcoming.

Sam rode down the town's main street. He remembered seeing a goldsmith on his last trip to Denison and headed for it. Ten minutes later he had parted with the last tie to his family, but with enough money to feed him for a month or two. Though the goldsmith eyed him strangely and appeared nervous, Sam was grateful the man had recognized the value of the piece he'd purchased.

Sam headed over to the grocery store, where he

bought tinned food, flour, sugar, salt, bacon, coffee and other mainstay items. Sam thought the clerk acted mighty strange when he'd placed his order, and he seemed relieved when Sam paid in cash. Puzzled at the man's skittishness, Sam left Denison.

An hour later the posse arrived, having tracked Sam back to town. The grocery clerk ran out to meet them, his arms churning excitedly.

"He was here, Sheriff," the clerk shouted. "The outlaw you're looking for. He can't be more than an hour ahead of you."

"Are you sure?" Hale asked.

"Yep, it was him, all right. I recognized him from his last trip to town. He bought trail food. I can even tell you in what direction he went."

"Don't keep us in suspense," Cramer ground out. "We're wasting time."

"West. He rode west."

"Let's go, boys," Hale said, kneeing his mount.

Sam's stomach felt as if it were touching his backbone, and he stopped beside a creek a few miles outside of town to eat. What he really needed was coffee. Thick, black and a lot of it. He gathered wood and started a fire, hoping it wouldn't rain before the coffee was made. Using water from the creek, Sam filled his battered pot, measured out the coffee and set it on the fire to boil. Then he decided that bacon would taste mighty good, so he cut a few slices and placed them in a skillet he'd retrieved from his saddlebags. Sam's mouth watered as the smell of bacon and coffee wafted through the damp air.

After his breakfast was cooked, Sam fished in his saddlebags for hardtack and sat down to enjoy his meal. He chewed slowly and thoughtfully, his mind returning to those blissfully satisfying hours he'd spent in Lacey's bed. She moved him a way he'd never been moved before. She was the mother of his son.

His son.

A smile stretched his lips. He was proud as hell to claim a son like Andy. And mad as hell at Lacey's lack of conscience. She should have told him immediately instead of letting him believe that Andy was the illegitimate product of an affair with another man. That a child would result from their infrequent couplings had never entered Sam's mind. He wasn't stupid; he should have realized that it only took one time to make a baby. He supposed he just wanted to think the worst of Lacey.

Sam finished his meal and gathered up his gear. He scoured out the frying pan and coffeepot with sand and rinsed them in the creek. Then he packed everything away and mounted Galahad. The sound of pounding hooves caught his attention. Moments later riders appeared in the distance. He had no idea who they were or what they wanted, but they looked to be in a big hurry . . . and headed in his direction.

Sam was torn. His gut told him the riders meant trouble. Trouble he laid at Lacey's door. Lacey had made good her threat and summoned the sheriff. What a damn fool he'd been to divulge his secret to her. She'd proved untrustworthy once; what made him think she could be trusted now? It appeared that he had made the biggest mistake of his life, for if he wasn't mistaken, he was being pursued by a posse.

Seconds before he dug his spurs into Galahad's hide, shots rang out. The posse was hard on his heels and coming fast. Sam hung low in the saddle as bullets whizzed by him. He saw an outcropping of boulders off to the right and swung around in that direction.

Sam didn't shoot back or defend himself. He didn't want killing added to his record. His only hope was to lose himself amidst the boulders and trees before the posse reached him. Then the unexpected happened. A determined bullet found Sam. It lodged in his right shoulder and nearly sent him toppling from the saddle. Pure tenacity kept him from falling.

His heart raced as he approached the boulders and reined Galahad sharply into the maze of huge rocks. Pain speared through him. He was losing blood and beginning to feel light-headed. He didn't believe his wound was life-threatening, but the loss of blood could kill him if it wasn't stemmed. He dashed away the sweat pouring from beneath his hat and concentrated on losing the posse.

Through a haze of red, Sam spied a narrow opening between two boulders. The posse was behind him; for the moment he was out of their sight, but not for long. Sam's mind was fuzzy but still working. The narrow cave was a long shot, but it offered a slim chance of escape if he acted quickly. Sam jerked on the reins, urging Galahad into the dark crevice. Galahad leaped through, and then they were inside. Sam yanked Galahad to a stop and slid from the saddle, barely conscious.

Sam heard the thunder of hooves and placed a hand over Galahad's muzzle. The posse rode past the boulders without giving the cave a second glance. Unable to stand, Sam dropped down to the ground to wait. Either they'd return to look for him or plunge into the forest beyond the boulders, thinking he was still ahead of them.

Sam rested his head against a rock. It was dark and cool inside the cave. He wanted to close his eyes, to let blessed sleep take away the pain. But he had to stay alert. The posse could return at any minute. During his flight he had glanced over his shoulder a time or two at his pursuers and had recognized Cramer. If Cramer was part of the posse, Sam knew he wouldn't stand a chance if he was caught. He'd be hanged from the nearest tree before he could prove his innocence.

Weak from loss of blood, Sam's intentions to remain alert dissolved as he slid effortlessly into unconsciousness.

Chapter Nine

Lacey was a nervous wreck. By early evening she'd had no news about Sam from either the sheriff or Taylor Cramer. For all she knew, they had found Sam and strung him up without a trial. She was sure that was what Taylor would be urging the sheriff to do.

Lacey had lost count of the times Andy had asked if she thought Sam had been captured by the posse. Throughout the day, Andy had maintained his confidence that Sam would be able to explain the mistake to the sheriff's satisfaction. Lacey wasn't so sure. What if Sam had been lying to her about his innocence? It was all so confusing.

Lacey and Andy finished their supper that night and spent time together before Lacey tucked her son in bed. She read him a story and returned to the parlor. Rita had already left for the night, so Lacey settled down with a book and tried to read. But she couldn't concentrate. Her book lay in her lap forgotten as her thoughts returned to the previous night, when she had awakened and found Sam in her bedroom.

Sam had appeared to accept her explanation of what had happened six years ago. He had even confided his secret to her. Then he had made love to her, and for a time everything was forgotten but her love for this man and how he made her feel. It was true, she realized. She *did* love Sam, had never stopped loving him. But whether or not he had committed a crime, he was still an outlaw and could offer her and Andy nothing in the way of security.

Lacey had been willing to marry Taylor to gain security for her son—that was why she hadn't told Sam that he was Andy's father. Besides, Sam had shown no interest in her for six long years. He had let her believe he was dead, which was a despicable thing to do. She still wouldn't have known he was alive had fate not taken a hand and brought them together.

A knock on the door released Lacey from her ruminations. She stared at the door a moment, then rose to answer it. For caution's sake, she called through the door before opening it.

"Who's there?"

"Taylor Cramer. Open up, Lacey."

Taylor! Had the posse returned? She flung open the door, and Cramer stepped inside. "What happened? Did you find Sam?"

Cramer walked to the parlor and flung himself down into a chair. His clothing was dusty, and he looked out of sorts. "The bastard got away. Don't know how we missed him. Had him in our sights for all but a few minutes. He just up and disappeared." Suddenly Cramer grinned. "One of our bullets got him, though."

"Sam is wounded?" Lacey choked out.

"Didn't you hear a word I said?"

"Of course. Sam got away. He could be hurt badly."

"I hope so. The posse is still out there. They're going to search one more day before giving up. But I've had enough. I had more important matters to take care of. Have you signed the divorce document?"

"Not yet. I haven't even taken it out of the drawer."

"Get it. I'll take it back to town with me after you sign it."

Lacey dragged her feet to the writing table. She had no idea why she had put this off. She and Andy needed Taylor to survive. But she couldn't forget Sam's last words to her. He threatened to take Andy away from her if she divorced him. But Lacey was smart enough to know that wasn't about to happen. Sam was on the run. He didn't dare show up in Denison or anywhere near the ranch if he wanted to remain free.

"The document is right here," Lacey said as she opened the drawer and felt inside for it. Her hand came away empty. "It's gone!"

Cramer leaped from his chair so quickly it nearly overturned. "What do you mean, it's gone?"

"Just that. The document is not where I left it."

"You must have moved it."

"No, I haven't touched it." Her brow wrinkled. "You don't suppose Sam . . ."

Nothing more was needed for Cramer to grasp her meaning. "Gentry!" His curses turned the air blue. "Did you mention the divorce document to him?"

Lacey bit her lip, thinking back to their encounter. "I . . . might have mentioned it."

"He took it! Everything I've worked so hard for is gone. The only thing I can hope for now is that Gentry is dead. Unless," he added with sly innuendo, "you change your mind and sell the ranch to me."

Lacey stiffened. She had no intention of selling. She'd promised Uncle Hob on his deathbed that she wouldn't sell out, that she would make every effort to keep the ranch for Andy. She hadn't run out of ways to save it yet.

"No, I can't sell the ranch to you, Taylor. I promised Uncle Hob I'd keep it for Andy. If we can't marry, perhaps I'll reapply for a loan. If the Bank of Denison refuses, I'll go to Fort Worth and apply."

Cramer scowled; then a slow smile curved his lips, as if something had just occurred to him. "Maybe all is not lost. Gentry deserted you. That in itself is grounds for annulment. Never fear, my dear, I won't be defeated. We *will* marry."

He bade her good-bye and made a hasty exit.

Lacey stared at the closed door long after he left. She knew instinctively that Sam had taken the divorce document. He'd said he wouldn't let her divorce him, and she should have realized he'd find a way to stop her, or at the very least slow down the process. Lacey didn't know whether to laugh or cry. Perhaps she would lose the ranch, and that was sad, but on the other hand, maybe Sam had done her a favor by stealing the divorce document, and that made her smile. Once, she had been convinced that marrying Taylor was the best thing for her and Andy; now she wasn't sure. If worse came to worst, she could always sell out to Taylor.

Sam came to his senses slowly. His body was racked with pain, his head was spinning, and his eyes blurred. And he was so thirsty his tongue was attached to the roof of his mouth. For a moment he didn't know where he was. It was dark and cool, and he felt no urgency to leave, but something he couldn't quite grasp dangled just out of his reach. He tried to concentrate, but the pain was too intense. A movement nearby caught his attention, and he turned his head. He saw Galahad with his reins dragging and immediately recalled where he was and why. The posse, a shot, pain. He'd been wounded trying to outrun the posse and had sought refuge . . . where?

It was dark. Too dark to see, but memory was slowly returning. He remembered riding into a crevice between two boulders and sitting on the ground to wait for fate to decide his future. He must have passed out. He moved and was immediately sorry. Dizziness assailed him, but he forced himself to concentrate. Grasping Galahad's reins, he crawled to the opening and peered out. He saw the moon and stars and nothing else. The soulful baying of a wolf was the only sound he heard. Either the posse had given up or they were still out there somewhere, waiting for him to expose himself.

Sam realized he could die if he didn't leave his hiding place and seek help for his wound, and he had too much to live for. He had just discovered he had a son, and he wanted to watch Andy grow up. Sam knew the odds were stacked against him, but miracles did happen.

Grasping Galahad's reins, Sam crawled out of the shallow cave into the black night. He tried to stand. His legs buckled beneath him and he grabbed the saddle to keep from falling. After a moment the world stopped spinning, and Sam managed to drag himself onto Galahad's back. He dropped the reins, but the effort to retrieve them was beyond him. He managed to wrap his arms around Galahad's thick neck before sliding into oblivion.

Galahad walked at a sedate pace, as if mindful of his master's sorry state. Mauve streaks were turning the sky from black to gray when the stouthearted animal stopped. Sam slid from the saddle and lay unmoving on the dusty ground.

A crowd gathered around Sam's limp form. He was poked and prodded, but nothing stirred him. A young woman pushed through the crowd and stared down at him.

"Is he dead?" the woman asked in a language Sam wouldn't have understood had he been awake.

"He lives, Yellow Bird, but his wounds are grave. Do you wish to cure the white-eyes? He has been shot and left unattended too long. He may be beyond your help."

Yellow Bird stared at the white man. He looked to be a fine warrior, even more impressive than her brother, Chief Running Buffalo. It would be a great shame to let him die when she had the skill to save him. Despite her youth, Yellow Bird was a skilled medicine woman, highly respected by her people.

"We are a peaceful people, brother," Yellow Bird said. "We have lived in peace with the white-eyes many years, unlike our warlike Apache brothers. We trade them furs for cooking pots and blankets. I will heal the white-eyes. Carry him to my tipi."

Running Buffalo and another brave carried Sam to Yellow Bird's tipi. They placed him on a sleeping mat and left. Yellow Bird set to work immediately. Thirty minutes later she had skillfully removed the bullet from Sam's shoulder, packed the wound with a mixture of wet moss and herbs to draw out infection, and placed a bandage over it. Then she sat back on her heels to wait.

Throughout the day and the long night she spooned into his mouth an infusion of special herbs known to replenish the body after a substantial loss of blood and to fight fever. She wiped the sweat from his brow and bathed his body with cool water.

Sam regained his wits two days after arriving at Running Buffalo's camp. The first thing he saw when he opened his eyes was the golden brown face and dark, enigmatic eyes of a lovely young Indian woman.

"How do you feel?" the woman asked in halting English.

"Where am I? Who are you?"

"I am Yellow Bird. Your horse carried you to the camp of Running Buffalo."

"You saved my life," Sam rasped in a voice he scarcely recognized.

"I removed the bullet and treated you with a poultice of herbs. You are still feverish and far from well. Many suns will pass before you are strong enough to leave your mat."

"I sincerely thank you, Yellow Bird. Is Running Buffalo your husband?"

"He is my brother. I have no husband."

Sam thought it best not to pursue the subject. "Then

I must thank Running Buffalo for allowing you to treat me. Not many Indian tribes are friendly with white men these days."

Yellow Bird smiled. "We are a peaceful tribe, and go about our business of eking out a living from the forest and the earth. We have no wish to join our militant brothers to the north."

"Thank God for that," Sam said, sighing wearily.

"What are you called?" Yellow Bird asked.

"My name is Sam. Sam Gentry."

"Sam," Yellow Bird said, rolling his name around on her tongue experimentally. "Rest now, Sam. Later you will be given food and drink."

Sam didn't respond. He had already fallen asleep.

Back at the ranch, Laccy waited anxiously for word of Sam. Had he escaped? Did he lie wounded or dead somewhere in a desolate area where no one could find him? All kinds of horrible scenarios passed before her eyes.

A week after the posse lost Sam in the Texas wilderness, Taylor Cramer arrived at the ranch with the news that Sam Gentry had probably died from his wound and the buzzards had claimed his body.

Lacey stared at Cramer in disbelief. "Not again. Oh, no. I was too quick in believing Sam dead once, and it won't happen again. I won't accept Sam's death until I see his body."

Cramer muttered something beneath his breath that Lacey couldn't hear. "What did you say?"

Cramer gave her a fawning smile. "I expected no less from you. I've solved one of our problems, however. I've asked my lawyer to draw up annulment papers to present to the judge. I'll bring them out for your signature soon. Don't worry about the judge not granting the annulment. I know Judge Anderson personally and I guarantee his compliance."

"Taylor . . . perhaps we should wait. This doesn't seem the right time to—"

"It's the perfect time, my dear," Cramer cut in. "Dead or alive, I doubt that Sam Gentry will bother you again. If he does, he'll find a jail cell awaiting him."

"Andy is dead set against our marriage," Lacey hedged. "I thought marrying you was the right thing to do, but now I'm not so sure. I . . . don't love you like I should."

Cramer gave a bark of laughter. "I know you're marrying me to save the ranch. I've known that all along."

"And that's all right with you?"

"Of course." He gave her a smile. "I care for you enough for both of us."

The way he said it made Lacey more doubtful than ever. "Sometimes I think you care about my land more than you care about me."

"Are you questioning my feelings?" Cramer challenged.

"No, I . . . there's still Andy to deal with."

"Leave Andy to me. He'll come around once we're married. You're too soft on the boy."

Suddenly Lacey realized that Sam had been right about Taylor. He would be a terrible father to Andy. She loved her son too much to condemn him to spending his formative years with a stepfather who couldn't stand him.

"Let me think about it, Taylor. Perhaps the best way to handle my situation is to sell the B&G to the highest bidder. I need to get top dollar for the spread. Enough to support Andy and me until I can find work. The next time I go to town, I'll speak with the land agent."

Cramer's eyes lit with greedy pleasure. "That won't be necessary. I'll buy the B&G. If you're sure that's what you want," he added in an ingratiating tone.

Lacey thought his answer came quickly—too quickly—confirming her belief that Taylor did indeed want the ranch. But why? It was a mystery she was determined to solve before she signed away her inheritance from Uncle Hob.

"I don't know, Taylor," she hedged. "Perhaps I'm being a little too hasty. I'm sure you and Andy will come to terms with one another in time. Maybe I'm being too protective. Go ahead with the annulment. As for selling, I just can't bring myself to part with Uncle Hob's dream. Perhaps marriage is the best solution, if you still want me."

Lacey thought she heard his teeth grinding.

"Of course I still want you, my dear. Leave everything to me."

Cramer left shortly afterward. Lacey suffered through his good-bye kiss with stoic acceptance. Rather than alert him to her suspicions, she didn't object when he pulled her into his arms and kissed her with the possessiveness of a man who had just won a victory.

Lacey's emotions were mixed regarding Taylor Cramer. Since Sam had reentered her life, Taylor Cramer and his motives for wanting her had become suspect. Apparently, Sam had seen through him before she had.

Sam. Was he really dead? Her heart told her he was alive, that one day he would return for his son, even if he cared nothing for her.

Lacey left the house after Cramer's departure to talk to Rusty about bringing the cattle in closer to the house in preparation for colder weather. It snowed often in northern Texas, and blizzards and ice storms weren't unheard of. It was always best to plan in advance for adverse weather.

Lacey found Rusty near the corral.

"Something on your mind, Miz Lacey?" he asked when Lacey hailed him.

"I just wanted to make sure plans are in place to move the cattle closer to the house when cold weather arrives."

"Everything's taken care of," Rusty assured her. "Was that Mr. Cramer I just saw leaving?"

Lacey knew that Rusty didn't approve of Taylor and realized she'd have to tread carefully, for she intended to lead Taylor on until she had the truth from him.

"Yes, that was Taylor."

"Did he say anything about Sam?"

"They think he's dead. Taylor said Sheriff Hale was positive that he'd taken at least one bullet."

"You don't believe he's dead, do you?"

Lacey's eyes filled with tears. "I don't know what to believe." Her hand splayed over her heart. "I think I'd know here, in my heart, if Sam were dead, but I feel nothing except a strange ache."

"I don't believe anything Cramer says," Rusty groused. "And you shouldn't either. I hope he'll stop coming around now that he knows you're married."

"My marriage to Sam was never a real marriage," Lacey said with a hint of sadness. "Sam doesn't want me. Taylor offered to obtain an annulment and I'm . . . I'm convinced that marrying him will be best for me and Andy."

Lacey almost choked on the words. She no longer believed marrying Taylor was the solution to her problems, but that information had to remain private for the time being.

Rusty wagged his head. "I sure hope you know what you're doing, Miz Lacey."

"I do, Rusty. Trust me."

Lacey wished she were as confident as she made herself sound. She had to find out what made her land valuable to Taylor before her marriage to Sam was dissolved. *Sam, where are you?* she silently entreated. *Are you dead? Wounded? Will you ever return?* Something deep inside her refused to believe that Sam was dead. One day he would find a way to clear his name and return, and when he did, she wanted to be his wife, not the wife of another man.

Another week passed. Two weeks since Sam had dropped from the face of the earth. Taylor told Lacey that the sheriff was still looking for Sam or his body, but hadn't found either. It was as if Sam had disappeared into thin air. The news that no body was found gave Lacey hope that Sam was alive and holed up somewhere.

Unfortunately, Lacey had gained little insight into Taylor's reason for wanting the ranch. She'd gone to the land office but learned nothing of value. Taylor was very good at maintaining secrecy, and her subtle questions about his business affairs had gotten her nowhere. To keep Taylor from suspecting that anything was amiss, Lacey had signed the annulment document his lawyer had prepared.

It was all very puzzling. Lacey's grief over Uncle Hob's death had blinded her to all but the way Taylor had stepped in to help her. She couldn't have managed without him. He had ingratiated himself to the point that she had come to depend on him. When he had asked her to marry him, she'd been flattered. And when she'd learned the pitiful state of her finances, she'd accepted his proposal as a way out of a deep hole. Then Sam had arrived and made her realize that Taylor had a hidden motive, one that might involve her land.

Another week passed. The weather turned cool. Taylor had arrived with the news that the sheriff had finally given up the search for Sam. Lacey began to worry in earnest that Sam really was dead, but still she clung to hope like a shipwrecked sailor clinging to a raft in the middle of the ocean.

One cool evening Lacey and Cramer were sitting across from one another in the parlor. The cheery fire in the hearth gave off a welcome warmth but did little to remove the chill from Lacey's heart as she contemplated Sam's well-being.

"I have a piece of good news for you," Cramer beamed. "My lawyer informed me that a judge will take your annulment under consideration within the next few weeks. As soon as it's granted, we'll plan our wedding. I've even looked into boarding schools willing to take boys Andy's age."

Lacey bit her tongue to keep from lashing out at Taylor. It would be a cold day in hell before she'd let anyone take Andy from her.

Lacey's thoughts were echoed by a small, angry voice that came from the doorway. "You can't send me away! I won't go. If Papa were here, he wouldn't let you send me away."

Lacey groaned inwardly. She'd tried to keep Andy

occupied elsewhere during Taylor's visits. "Andy, I thought you were playing in the barn with the kittens."

Andy ran to Lacey, glaring up at her. "I saw mean old Cramer ride up and wondered what he was doing here."

Cramer lunged for Andy, but he hid behind Lacey. "You're going to have to learn some manners after your mother and I are married, boy. Sending you away will make a man of you."

Andy's chin rose stubbornly. "But I'm not a man. I'm a little boy." He regarded his mother through big blue eyes brimming with tears. His mouth trembled. "What about Papa? You're still married to him, aren't you?"

Lacey felt the staggering weight of Andy's disapproval. "We'll talk about this later, honey."

"Tell him now, Lacey," Cramer urged. "Tell the boy you're having your marriage to Gentry annulled just in case he's still alive."

Andy blinked away his tears. "What does that mean, Mama?"

While Lacey mulled over her answer, Cramer jumped into the void. "It means that your mother's marriage to Gentry, if he's still alive, will soon be over. She's going to marry me. Isn't that right, my dear?"

"I hate you!" Andy screamed. "I hate you both!"

"Andy!" Lacey cried as Andy dashed from the room. She started to follow.

"Let him go," Cramer said, grasping her arm. "You baby him. He has to learn you can't cater to his every whim."

Lacey would have gone after Andy despite Taylor's words, but decided that the boy was too distraught to make sense of her explanation. She'd tell him she had no intention of marrying Taylor once he'd cooled off enough to listen to reason.

Sam's strength returned slowly. Yellow Bird was a talented healer, and he was grateful for her fine care. Still, his wound had gone unattended too long, and infection resulted. And with it came fever. He recalled the passage of time in bits and pieces. He remembered Yellow Bird spooning liquid into his mouth, cleaning his wound, taking care of his needs, and he knew he'd never be able to repay her. Life was precious; he was lucky he still had his.

During his illness, Sam's fevered thoughts turned often to his son. And to Andy's mother, the woman who had betrayed him not once but twice. Apparently, she had gone to the sheriff right after he'd left the ranch. Hatred welled up inside him. How could he have been taken in so easily by her pleas of innocence? This last betrayal had reinforced his belief that he'd been right about her six years ago. Leopards didn't change their spots.

The more Sam thought about it, the more he became convinced that Lacey wasn't the kind of mother he wanted to bring up his son. He could do a better job himself. That thought led to another. *Why not?* Why not take Andy with him? He'd head west, to California, where no one gave a hoot whether or not Sam Gentry was an outlaw. He and Andy could start over in a new place. The boy might miss his mother at first, but Sam swore to do his best to make a happy life for his son.

Three weeks after Sam arrived at the Indian camp, he felt as good as new and was eager to get on with his life. He told Yellow Bird he was leaving that evening while she prepared their food over the fire pit inside the tipi.

Yellow Bird was crouched down beside the fire, stirring a pot of venison stew. When Sam told her it was time for him to go, she set the wooden spoon aside and settled down beside him.

"Are you not happy here, Sam?"

"I'm grateful to you and your people," he hedged, "but I don't belong here. There is much you don't know about me."

"Tell me. Make me understand why you must leave. Who are the enemies that wish you dead?" Her voice trembled, and she lowered her eyes. "I want to be your woman. Until you arrived, there was no man I wished as a mate."

Sam was stunned. He had no idea Yellow Bird felt that way about him. "I'm married, Yellow Bird. I have a wife and son."

"I know. La-cey and An-dy. You called for them in your delirium. Many of our braves have more than one wife."

"White men have only one wife. I'm sorry, Yellow Bird. You saved my life, and I don't want to hurt you. I do owe you an explanation, however, and you shall have one. I was shot trying to escape a posse. I'm an outlaw, charged with a crime I didn't commit."

"You are innocent?"

"I am no outlaw. Apparently, my wife didn't believe me. She ran straight to the law, and I was forced to flee for my life. I took a bullet, but luck was with me. I found a hiding place and stayed there until the posse gave up and returned to town."

"Your wife, this La-cey, she is a bad person," Yellow

Bird said with conviction. "Tell me about your son."

A smile spread across Sam's face. "Andy is a wonderful boy. I want him, Yellow Bird, and I fully intend to take him away from his mother."

Yellow Bird placed a fluttery hand against his chest, and he felt his muscles jump.

"Can you do that?" she asked.

"I can take Andy away without his mother knowing, and that's exactly what I intend to do."

"You are a strong man, Sam," Yellow Bird said, "and I am a strong woman. We will be good together. Bring your son to me. We will raise him together."

She leaned against him, her fingers roaming over his chest. She had his shirt unbuttoned before Sam realized what she was about. She was so lovely that for a moment he was tempted. It would be good to lose himself in another woman, one who actually cared for him. He knew that making love to Yellow Bird would give him pleasure, but something prevented him from accepting her offer.

Gently, he removed her hands. "I'm sorry, Yellow Bird, but I can't take you like this. I admire you greatly, but it wouldn't be right to take advantage of you."

"White men are strange," Yellow Bird said. "I am offering myself to you without asking for anything in return. Why do you refuse what I offer? You are the only man to whom I have offered so much."

"That's exactly why I can't accept. You are a maiden still. You deserve a man who will be a proper husband to you. I can't give you what you need."

Yellow Bird drew away and stared into the fire. "You are a foolish man, Sam. I could make you happy. Bring your son to me and I will care for him."

Sam took her face between his hands and placed a tender kiss upon her lips. "You are very special, Yellow Bird. One day you will meet someone you can give your heart to. I thank you sincerely for offering yourself to me, but I must return to the ranch and see what has transpired in my absence."

"Will that not be dangerous for you?"

"I can't return openly, but I have a friend at the B&G who will tell me what's going on. I'll decide what to do about Andy after I speak with him."

"Will you return to me?"

"Perhaps," Sam said thoughtfully. "This might be a good place to lie low for a while if I succeed with Andy. No one would think to look for us in an Indian village."

"I will be waiting for you, Sam," Yellow Bird said. "May the Great Spirit aid you in your quest."

Sam left that evening for the B&G. He traveled by night, slept during the day and reached the ranch the following evening. The hands were in the cookhouse eating supper as he crept into the barn, turned Galahad into a stall and sat down to wait for Rusty to make his nightly rounds.

He couldn't wait to find out what had happened during his absence. Then he'd search his heart for what was best for Andy.

Chapter Ten

Shadows lengthened. Sam grew anxious. He wouldn't do anything until he spoke with Rusty. Rusty was the only man he trusted to tell the truth. As for Lacey, he told himself he didn't want to see her, but his body refused to listen. Just the thought of her made him grow hard. Making love with another woman would never be the same.

Sam's thoughts terminated abruptly when he saw a flicker of light at the entrance of the barn. Rusty's face appeared in the circle of lamplight, and Sam stepped out from the shelter of an empty stall.

"Hello, Rusty."

Rusty started violently. The lamp swayed in his hand. "Tarnation, Sam, you scared the daylights out of me. What in hell are you doing here? Are you all right?" he asked anxiously.

"I'm fine, Rusty."

"Miz Lacey said you'd been shot. Everyone thinks you're dead."

Sam's mouth thinned. "Does Lacey believe I'm dead?"

Rusty grinned. "She said she wouldn't believe it until she saw your body."

"I was wounded. Fortunately, I was found by . . . friends. It took a long time for my wound to heal."

"Friends?" Rusty asked. "What friends?"

"Galahad took me to an Indian camp. Running Buffalo took me in and his sister healed my wounds."

"What are you doing back here? Ain't you in enough trouble?"

"You're the only one I trust, Rusty. What's been going on in my absence? How is Andy?"

Rusty shrugged. "Andy is right enough, I reckon, but . . ."

"But what? Tell me, Rusty. Is it Andy?"

"I don't know how to say this, Sam, except to tell you right out. Miz Lacey signed annulment papers that Cramer's lawyer prepared. Nothing is final yet, but I suspect it won't be long."

"Damn! Damn! Damn!" Sam cursed. He knew a divorce required his signature but he wasn't sure about an annulment. Apparently Lacey wanted out of this marriage badly.

"What about Andy? How does he feel about this?"

Rusty's shoulders slumped. "Poor little fella. He took

off and hid in the barn after Cramer left last evening, that's how upset he was. He told me Cramer and his mother intended to send him away. Miz Lacey found him asleep in the barn. Today he refused to listen to anything his mother said. He ran off every time she tried to talk to him. I reckon she decided to let him cool off a mite before explaining her plans, whatever they might be."

"So that's how it's going to be," Sam bit out. "Lacey is sacrificing her son's happiness for the tenuous security Cramer offered. Cramer wants something all right, but it's not Lacey."

"Andy knows that Cramer can't stand him underfoot, but I can't believe Miz Lacey would send her son away to please Cramer. She loves Andy. Until you came along, Andy and Hob were all she had. Andy is everything to her."

"Apparently that is no longer true," Sam said dryly.

"I know it's none of my business, Sam, but I can't help thinking that you and Miz Lacey belong together."

Sam snorted. "You're dead wrong, Rusty. I had good reason for abandoning Lacey six years ago and you know it. I never wanted to see her again after I escaped from the Yankees. I might have felt differently if I'd known I had a son."

"Maybe you misjudged Miz Lacey. Maybe it happened just like she said."

"I was beginning to think so too. Then I made the mistake of telling her I was wanted for bank robbery. You were the only one who knew about it besides Lacey. She saw a way to get rid of me and took it."

"If that's the way you feel, why did you come back? It ain't healthy for you around here. Cramer is still sniffing around Miz Lacey. I never know when he's gonna show up."

"I'm not sticking around long, Rusty. I came back to see Andy. I can't leave until I do. Will you help me?"

"Maybe, maybe not," Rusty hedged. "Andy has been lonesome. I've been sitting with him on the back porch after supper to ease his loneliness. I reckon he'll be there tonight, same as last night. I kinda enjoy lending Andy a sympathetic ear."

"Is Andy there now?"

"I don't know. I was headed that way when I decided to have a look-see around the barn first, like I do every night about this time."

Sam strode to the door and peered outside. The ranch house basked beneath a full moon. He could see the back porch clearly, and the forlorn little boy sitting on the steps.

"Andy is there now, waiting for you."

"What do you want me to do?"

"Bring him to the barn, then leave. I don't want you mixed up in this."

Rusty's eyes narrowed. "In what? What you planning to do, Sam?"

"Right now, nothing. I just want to talk to Andy. The boy needs to know I'm alive, and that I love him."

"Yeah, I reckon a boy needs to know his pa loves him. I'll bring Andy, but if you keep him too long, his mother will come looking for him."

"Thanks, Rusty, I won't forget this."

Rusty shuffled from the barn. Sam watched from the doorway as Rusty spoke to Andy. He pulled back into the shadows when Andy glanced toward the barn. Then Andy rose obediently and followed Rusty.

"Why are we going to the barn?" Sam heard Andy ask as he and Rusty entered the barn.

"There's someone who wants to see you," Rusty answered.

"Who?" Andy asked.

Sam stepped out from the shadows. "Me, son. Rusty brought you to talk to me."

Joy suffused Andy's face. "Papa! You've come back!"

He broke into a run, and Sam scooped him up into his arms. "I couldn't go away without seeing you one last time."

"I'll leave you two alone," Rusty said as he moved toward the door. "Don't keep Andy out too long." Then he was gone, leaving Sam and Andy alone.

"Do you have to leave again, Papa?"

"I don't want to, son, but I have to. I just wanted you to know I didn't rob that bank. I'm not an outlaw."

"I never thought you were. It's all mean old Cramer's fault. Mama is gonna marry him and send me away to school. I don't want to leave Mama, but she doesn't love me anymore." Suddenly his face crumbled. "Take me with you, Papa," he sobbed. "If you loved me, you'd take me with you."

Sam felt as if his heart were breaking. How could Lacey do this to her son? She didn't deserve a son like Andy.

"Please, Papa, don't leave me here. Take me with you."

"Are you sure it's what you want, Andy? You might not see your mother for a very long time." Probably never, but he didn't tell that to Andy.

"Mama won't care. She doesn't love me anymore. She's gonna have babies with Mr. Cramer."

Sam felt a band tighten around his heart. "Did she tell you that?"

"No, but I heard mean old Cramer tell her that she didn't need me 'cause she'd have his sons to spoil."

"I need you, son. I'll always need you. If I take you with me, we'd have to leave now. You can't take anything with you."

"Can I tell Mama good-bye?"

"No, I'm sorry. But if you have any doubts, let me know now. You see, I had every intention of taking you away with me tonight—that's why I returned. But I don't think I could have actually done it if you really didn't want to go."

Tears flowed down Andy's cheeks. "Mama doesn't want me. Neither does mean old Cramer." His shoulders straightened. "I'm ready, Papa. I want to go with you. Maybe someday we can come back to see Mama."

Sam didn't think so but he'd never admit it to Andy. "We'll see, son, we'll see. Galahad is in his stall. Let's go get him."

Sam took Andy's small hand and led him to the stall. Then he lifted the boy into the saddle and led Galahad out of the barn. Mounting behind Andy, Sam dug his heels into Galahad's hide. Moments later they disappeared into the moon-drenched night.

"Where are we going, Papa?"

"Eventually we're going to California. But for now, I'm taking you to meet some friends of mine. I think you'll like them. Have you ever met any Indians?"

Andy's eyes grew round. "Indians! Will they scalp me?"

"These Indians are friendly; no harm will come to you. They saved my life. You'll be welcome there."

Sam's answer seemed to satisfy Andy, for he snuggled down against Sam and drifted off to sleep.

It was past Andy's bedtime, and Lacey began to get anxious when he hadn't returned to the house. It wasn't like Rusty to keep the boy out this late. Because Rusty had been like a surrogate father to the boy, she had allowed Andy to stay up beyond his bedtime as long as he was with him. This was the night she intended to tell Andy that she had no intention of marrying Taylor or sending him away. Somehow she would make her son understand that she was playing a game with Taylor in order to gain vital information.

Lacey opened the back door and found the porch empty. She wasn't really worried, since Andy and Rusty sometimes walked to the barn together in the evening. Grabbing a sweater from the hook beside the door, Lacey walked out into the cool air, glad she'd made Andy put on a jacket before he went outside. She strolled to the barn, smiling when she noted the light inside. No doubt she'd find Rusty and Andy seated on a bale of hay, solving the world's problems.

The barn was empty save for the animals. A shiver of panic crept up Lacey's spine, but she brushed it aside. What reason did she have for panic? Andy was with Rusty. Rusty would let no harm come to her son.

Picking up the lamp, Lacey made a quick tour of the corral and paddock before returning to the barn and searching every stall in case Andy had decided to bed down in the hay. Every stall was empty. Lacey panicked. Glancing toward the bunkhouse, she noted that all was dark inside. Had Rusty let Andy bed down with the hands without telling her? It wasn't like Rusty, but the alternative was unthinkable.

Lacey marched to the bunkhouse and pounded on the door. She heard a shuffling sound inside. A few minutes later the door was flung open. Rusty stood in the opening, his chest bare, his trousers gaping at the waist. When he saw Lacey he quickly did up the buttons.

"Miz Lacey! Is something wrong?"

"I hope not," Lacey said, frowning. "Will you send Andy out, please? I'm disappointed in you, Rusty. It's not like you to keep Andy without informing me. I've been worried sick."

Rusty paled. "Andy ain't in his bed?"

Lacey's heart thumped erratically. "He's not with you?"

Rusty gulped nervously. "No, ma'am."

Lacey's legs threatened to give way beneath her, and she made a grab for the doorjamb. "Where could he be? Did you see him at all tonight?"

"I met him on the back porch earlier."

"Then what?" Pressure built inside Lacey. Did she have to drag everything from him?

"I didn't think it would do any harm, Miz Lacey," Rusty said. "He just wanted to see his son. I never thought he would . . ."

"Rusty, please, tell me what happened. Surely you don't mean that Sam . . . She paused as Rusty's words registered. "Sam's alive?"

"He's alive, Miz Lacey. I found him in the barn earlier. He'd been shot by the posse and dropped out of sight while he recovered from his wound. He said he wanted to see Andy before he left, and I agreed to bring the boy to him, but I told him not to keep Andy out long. I knew you'd be worried and come looking for him."

Lacey's voice rose on a note of panic. "Why didn't you return Andy to the house yourself after Sam saw him? What could you have been thinking of?"

Rusty looked properly abashed. "Sam asked to speak with his son alone, and I saw no harm in it." He swallowed with difficulty. "You don't suppose Sam took Andy, do you?"

Lacey knew that Sam would dare anything, even take Andy away if he thought she was going to marry Taylor. He'd threatened to do so on more than one occasion. "Did you tell Sam that Taylor Cramer and I were planning to marry?"

"He asked, and I told him the truth."

Frustration pounded through Lacey. No one knew the truth but herself. And now Sam had her son.

"I'm sorry, Miz Lacey. I never suspected Sam would take the boy. I like Sam, but he had no right taking Andy away from his mother."

"Do you have any idea where Sam has taken Andy? He can't have had much of a head start."

"I purely don't know," Rusty said sadly. "Somehow I got the idea that Sam was heading west, California maybe, to escape the bank robbery charges."

"Rouse the hands from bed," Lacey ordered. "I want Sam found immediately." Her lips thinned. "He can't have Andy. He's mine."

"Won't do no good," Rusty allowed. "We can't follow a trail in the dark. Wait until morning. I'll have the boys out bright and early."

"*Now*, Rusty. There's a bright moon tonight. Waiting

till morning could give Sam the edge he needs to escape."

Without waiting for Rusty's reply, Lacey turned and strode away. She returned to the barn and saddled her horse. Within a few minutes the sleepy-eyed hands straggled into the barn for their mounts. Less than thirty minutes later every available man on the B&G had gathered in the yard for instructions. Lacey spoke to them before sending them off.

"Sam Gentry has taken Andy. I don't know where he's headed, but he doesn't have that much of a head start. Spread out and see if you can pick up a trail."

"Shouldn't we wait for daylight, ma'am?" Barney asked. "It's kinda hard tracking in the dark."

Hysteria rose up inside Lacey, nearly strangling her. "We can't wait! I can't lose Andy." Kneeing her mount, horse and rider shot forward. The hands had no choice but to follow.

"Damn you, Sam Gentry!" Lacey shouted into the wind racing by her face. "Damn you to hell!"

As he raced through the night, Sam began to have second thoughts. Not about taking Andy, never that. But he did regret the anguish Lacey would suffer when she realized he had taken Andy. He tried to tell himself she deserved it. Any woman who would send away her own son to please her new husband didn't deserve his pity. *Hard-hearted bitch*. No son of his was going to be mistreated by a bastard like Cramer.

Sam maintained a steady pace throughout the night as Andy slept against his chest. He stopped briefly to let Galahad drink from a stream but allowed himself no respite. He knew that Lacey would have men on his trail the moment she realized Andy was missing. Rusty would tell her about his visit, and she would put two and two together and come up with the right answer. She might even bring the law with her. The law was one of the reasons Sam was returning to Running Buffalo's camp. Not only was the camp difficult to find, but no one would think to look for him and Andy there.

Andy stirred and awakened just as the sun began to rise.

"I'm hungry, Papa," he said, squirming in Sam's arms.

"We'll be at Running Buffalo's camp soon," Sam said. "I'm sure Yellow Bird will find something for us to eat. Would you like to stop and stretch your legs? We can't delay too long. It looks like rain, and I'd like to reach the camp before we get drenched."

Andy nodded. "I have to . . . you know."

Sam drew rein and set Andy down on the ground. "Go ahead, son."

Andy returned a few minutes later, and Sam lifted him into the saddle in front of him. "I hope Yellow Bird is a good cook," Andy said, rubbing his stomach. His brow furrowed. "Who is Yellow Bird?"

"Yellow Bird is the woman who saved my life. She's known as a healer among her people. You'll like her."

Andy remained thoughtful. Suddenly he said, "Do you think Mama is crying?"

"Perhaps," Sam allowed. "Do you regret coming away with me?"

"Mama was going to send me away and marry mean old Cramer. I'd rather be with you."

Sam gave Andy a quick hug. "There's no one I'd rather have with me, son."

They reached the Indian camp shortly before noon.

Clouds hung low overhead, and the scent of rain filled the air. Running Buffalo came over to greet Sam as he dismounted and lifted Andy down.

"Welcome back, Sam Gentry," Running Buffalo said. "Yellow Bird has missed you. Who do you bring to us?"

Sam pushed Andy forward. Chest swelling with pride, he said, "This is Andy, my son. Andy, this is Chief Running Buffalo."

"Pleased to meet you," Andy said somewhat skittishly.

He appeared frightened of the bare-chested warrior, and Sam sought to soothe his fears. "Running Buffalo's tribe is friendly to whites. You will like him. He has a son your age who you can play with."

Andy seemed only marginally appeased, but he put on a brave front as he held out his hand to Running Buffalo. The chief grinned and solemnly shook Andy's small hand.

"My son is called Sitting Bear. He will be your friend. But first things first. You must be hungry. I will summon Yellow Bird."

"I am here," Yellow Bird said as she cleared a path through the crowd surrounding them. She stopped before Sam, smiling as she gazed down at Andy. "Your son is much like his father."

Andy grinned. "Papa said you saved his life."

"An-dy," Yellow Bird said softly. "Welcome. Are you hungry?"

Andy nodded vigorously. "I haven't had anything to eat since supper last night."

She offered her hand. "Come with me and I will fill your stomach." She glanced at Sam. "Bring your father."

Andy placed his hand in Yellow Bird's and followed

her to her tipi. "Are you coming, Papa?" he called over his shoulder.

"I sure am, son. I'm as hungry as you are."

Sam thought the smile Yellow Bird gave him promised more than food should he desire it, and after what he'd learned at the B&G last evening, he'd be foolish to reject her. Lacey had betrayed him, disregarded her son's feelings and turned to a man who cared nothing for her or Andy. Taking Yellow Bird to his bed would be no hardship . . . if he could forget Lacey.

Moments after they ducked inside Yellow Bird's tipi, the sky opened up and rain poured down from the heavens.

Rain put a quick end to the search. Lacey and the hands drifted back to the ranch. Drenching rains that began around noon had killed all hope of tracking Sam. Lacey's spirits were about as low as they could get as the boys headed to the bunkhouse for dry clothes before going to the cookhouse for their first meal since the previous evening.

Soaked to the skin, Lacey dragged her steps as she entered the house through the kitchen door. Rita met her, clicking her tongue sympathetically.

"Get out of those wet clothes, señora, before you catch your death. There is plenty of hot water on the stove. I'll fill the tub so you can soak the chill from your bones."

"Thank you, Rita," Lacey said despondently. "I don't suppose Sam sent word back to the ranch while we were out looking for him."

"No, señora, I have heard nothing. Señora Sam will not hurt the boy; he loves him."

"I know, Rita," Lacey said wearily. "That still doesn't excuse what he did. As soon as the rain lets up we'll be out looking for him again." A sob escaped her throat. "I hope he knows enough to keep Andy dry and warm." She headed up the stairs before she broke down completely.

Taylor Cramer was just leaving the barbershop in Denison when he bumped into Sheriff Hale.

"You're just the man I wanted to see," Hale said in greeting. "I received news yesterday I think you'll be interested in hearing."

"If you don't mind, Sheriff, I'm in a bit of a hurry. Can we discuss this another time? I'm on my way to the B&G to see my fiancée."

"Fiancée? Are you talking about Mrs. Gentry?"

"Soon to be ex-Mrs. Gentry," Cramer crowed. "We're going to marry as soon as her annulment is final."

"My news is for both of you," Hale said. "I received a telegram from Sheriff Diller in Dodge City yesterday. The situation with the Gentry brothers has changed since I last contacted him. All three Gentry brothers have been exonerated. They are no longer wanted for bank robbery. The charges have been dropped and their names cleared."

Cramer felt as if the bottom had just fallen out of his world. This could be disastrous for his plans to gain control of Lacey's land. Once Lacey learned her husband was not wanted by the law, she might change her mind about going through with the annulment of her marriage to Gentry.

"I was going to ride out to the ranch and tell Mrs. Gentry myself," Hale continued, "but as long as you're headed out there, you can save me the trip."

"I'll give Lacey the news, Sheriff," Cramer lied. "Though I doubt it will affect Lacey one way or the other. She doesn't really care what happens to Gentry."

"Still, she has a right to know that her husband, if he's still alive, is a free man."

"Sure thing, Sheriff. Now if you'll excuse me, I'll be on my way."

Cramer fumed in impotent rage all the way out to the ranch. The cold drizzle did nothing to improve his mood. By the time he rode into the yard, he knew precisely what he was going to do. Or rather, what he *wasn't* going to do. There was no way in hell he was going to tell Lacey that Sam Gentry was not an outlaw. He'd let her go on believing the law was after Gentry until he had a ring on her finger and the marriage license in his pocket.

Lacey managed a couple hours of sleep before Rita, following instructions to awaken her when the rain ceased, shook her awake.

"The rain has stopped, señora. But you must eat first. You cannot go out without hot food in your stomach."

Lacey nodded groggily. "You're right as usual, Rita. I'll be down directly. Fix me something to carry in my saddlebags for later. No telling when I'll return."

Lacey hadn't realized she was hungry until she sat down to the meal of hot soup, a thick beef sandwich and apple pie. When she finished, she felt ready to face anything, even the man who had taken her son.

Lacey was striding out the door when Cramer rode into the yard. She waited on the porch for him to dismount, impatient at the delay. But she supposed there was no help for it.

Cramer must have guessed from her distraught expression that something was wrong. "Lacey, what is it? Has something happened?"

"Andy is gone," Lacey said on a sob. "He disappeared last night. I'm so worried."

"Gone? Where would he go?"

"Sam took him," Lacey blurted out. "He threatened to take Andy from me if I married you, but I didn't believe him."

"Gentry is alive?"

"Alive and well enough to ride to the ranch and kidnap my son."

Cramer thought that was dismal news indeed—not that he cared about Andy. He'd hoped Gentry had succumbed to his wounds. Then a thought occurred to him, and he smiled inwardly while outwardly commiserating with Lacey. A way for him to ingratiate himself with Lacey had just presented itself. If he returned Andy to her, Lacey would be indebted to him.

"I'll join the search," Cramer said. "I'm a pretty good tracker."

"The rain last night all but obliterated Sam's tracks. We don't have much to go on."

"Did anyone see or speak to Gentry last night?"

"Just Rusty." Lacey decided it was best not to tell Taylor that Rusty had left Andy and Sam alone.

"I'll have a word with him. Go saddle your horse; we'll leave when I return."

Cramer found Rusty by the corral, doling out chores to the hands who were to remain behind. "Can I have a word with you, Ramsey?"

Rusty sent Cramer a sour look. "What are you doing here?"

"I came by to see Lacey, and it's a good thing. I'll take charge from here on out. I understand you spoke with Gentry last night."

"Yeah, we talked."

"Did he give any indication he intended to kidnap Andy?"

Rusty shook his head. "No, he didn't say a word to me about it."

"Did he tell you where he'd been holed up these past weeks?"

Rusty gave him a mutinous glare. "He was wounded. It took him several weeks to recover."

Cramer gave an exasperated snort. "Let's not beat around the bush. Did Gentry say exactly where he went to recover? Does he have friends in the area who might offer him shelter?"

"No friends that I know of, except . . ."

Cramer immediately picked up on Rusty's hesitation. "Except what? Gentry does have friends in the area, doesn't he? Could he have taken the boy there?"

For whatever reason, Rusty turned mulish. "I told you, Sam didn't have nobody he could count on in Texas. All he had was Lacey and Andy."

"You're lying, Ramsey. I suggest you tell the truth."

"What truth?" Lacey asked, looking from Rusty to Cramer as she walked up to join them. "I got tired of waiting. What's this all about?"

"I'm trying to get the truth from your foreman," Cramer spat. "He knows where Gentry took Andy, but I can't get it out of him."

Lacey rounded on Rusty. "Is that true, Rusty? Is there something you haven't told me?"

"I told you the truth, Miz Lacey. Then I got to thinking back on the conversation I had with Sam. He mentioned something about Indians. I was gonna tell you but haven't had the chance. I didn't think it was any of Mr. Cramer's business."

"You're going to be the first to go, Ramsey, after Lacey and I are married," Cramer bit out. "Tell Lacey what you know or I'll beat it out of you."

"Taylor, please," Lacey intervened. "Leave Rusty alone. He's loyal to me." She sent Rusty a tremulous smile. "Do you have any idea where Lacey has taken Andy?"

"I wouldn't lie to you, Miz Lacey. I don't know where Sam took Andy. He did mention an Indian camp, but I can't swear you'll find them there. Sam said an Indian healer saved his life, and that's the sum of all I know."

Cramer lunged for him. "You're lying!"

Lacey placed herself between Cramer and Rusty. "Rusty wouldn't lie to me, Taylor. We're wasting time. We'll spread out and search in every direction. The sooner we find the Indian camp, the sooner Andy will be returned to me."

The search began. One day, three days, a week. Lacey grew thin and haggard, and the hands were grumpy and weary. The ranch was being neglected while the search continued. After two weeks, Lacey came to the sad conclusion that she had to call a halt and let the hands do what they were paid to do.

Cramer, though, for reasons of his own, refused to give up.

"This is draining you, Lacey," he said on the day Lacey sent the hands back to their jobs. "I want Gentry caught as badly as you do. Tell you what. I'll continue the search on my own. An Indian camp can't be that difficult to find."

"I don't want Andy hurt," Lacey warned.

"Trust me," Cramer said. "Once Andy is back where he belongs and Gentry charged with kidnapping, you'll realize how much I care for you."

Lacey stared at Cramer. Had she misjudged him? Time would tell, she decided. "Just bring Andy back to me, Taylor. Then we'll go from there."

"Indeed we will, my dear, indeed we will."

Lacey dragged herself up to bed after Cramer left. She was so angry at Sam that she would have flayed him alive if he were here. How could he do this to her? He knew how much Andy meant to her. Did he have no heart, no compassion?

"Damn you, Sam Gentry!"

Chapter Eleven

Several days passed before Taylor Cramer reported back to Lacey at the B&G. He'd had no more luck than her own men at locating the Indian camp, but he refused to give up.

"Once I locate the camp, I'll hire drifters and out-of-work cowboys to return with me to rescue Andy," Cramer informed her. "There are plenty of men hereabouts eager to use Indians for target practice."

Lacey didn't care who he hired as long as Andy was returned to her, but she didn't want bloodshed. "I want Andy, but not at the expense of innocent Indians. No killing, please."

"Of course not. You know I didn't mean it the way it sounded."

Lacey wasn't so sure.

Sam was grateful to Yellow Bird for welcoming Andy, and for her care of him. Sitting Bear and Andy had hit it off immediately, and Running Buffalo had invited Andy to share a sleeping mat with Sitting Bear. Sam wouldn't have minded, except that the arrangement left him alone at night with Yellow Bird. He wanted to ask for other sleeping arrangements, but realized that all the tipis were occupied. When Yellow Bird invited Sam to share her mat, he moved outside to sleep under the stars. But that wasn't always feasible. Rain and cool weather often sent him back inside the tent.

Sam's days passed pleasantly enough. He joined the men on hunting expeditions and honed his skills in mock battles, but the nights were becoming more and more uncomfortable. Yellow Bird thought nothing of baring her body to him before sliding naked into her sleeping mat, and Sam had been without a woman for a very long time. He didn't know what kept him from availing himself of Yellow Bird's body, unless it was the knowledge that she wasn't Lacey. No matter how many times Lacey had betrayed him, he still wanted her.

Sam was pleased that Andy seemed to be adjusting to being without his mother. The first week, Andy had asked about Lacey nearly every day. Though Andy's bottom lip trembled whenever Sam asked if he wanted to return, he always answered in the negative.

After an extended length of time, Sam decided it was best to leave Running Buffalo's camp. The longer he remained, the harder it would be to resist Yellow Bird.

GET YOUR 4 FREE* BOOKS NOW— A $21.96 VALUE!

Mail the Free* Book
Certificate
Today!

4 FREE* BOOKS 🎀 A $21.96 VALUE

Free *Books* *Certificate*

YES! I want to subscribe to the Leisure Historical Romance Book Club. Please send me my 4 FREE* BOOKS. Then each month I'll receive the four newest Leisure Historical Romance selections to Preview for 10 days. If I decide to keep them, I will pay the Special Member's Only discounted price of just $4.24 each, a total of $16.96 ($17.75 US in Canada). This is a SAVINGS OF AT LEAST $5.00 off the bookstore price. There are no shipping, handling, or other charges*. There is no minimum number of books I must buy and I may cancel the program at any time. In any case, the 4 FREE* BOOKS are mine to keep—A BIG $21.96 Value!

*In Canada, add $5.00 shipping and handling per order for first shipment. For all subsequent shipments to Canada, the cost of membership is $17.75 US, which includes $7.75 shipping and handling per month.[All payments must be made in US dollars]

Name _____

Address _____

City _____

State _____ *Country* _____ *Zip* _____

Telephone _____

Signature _____

If under 18, Parent or Guardian must sign. Terms, prices and conditions subject to change. Subscription subject to acceptance. Leisure Books reserves the right to reject any order or cancel any subscription.

(Tear Here and Mail Your FREE* Book Card Today!)

Get Four Books Totally
F R E E* —
A $21.96 Value!

(Tear Here and Mail Your FREE* Book Card Today!)

PLEASE RUSH
MY FOUR FREE*
BOOKS TO ME
RIGHT AWAY!

Leisure Historical Romance Book Club

P.O. Box 6613
Edison, NJ 08818-6613

AFFIX
STAMP
HERE

Using her would be a mistake, for Sam couldn't be the mate she wanted. He didn't belong in her world anymore than she belonged in his. Had she not been untouched, he might have been tempted. Even though Yellow Bird told him she wanted him no matter how short a time he would be with her, Sam couldn't bring himself to bed her.

Sam spied Andy playing tag with some children and caught his attention. Andy ran over to him immediately.

"Did you want me, Papa?"

"I've been thinking, son," Sam began, "that it's time for us to move on. I'd like to be in California before the first snowfall. We could ride down to Fort Worth and take the stagecoach the rest of the way. I have just enough money left to get us there. Work shouldn't be hard to find in California."

"I rode in a stagecoach once. Me and Mama went from Pennsylvania to Texas in one. I was little and don't remember much about it. I wish Sitting Bear could come with us."

"Sitting Bear belongs with his people."

"Can we write Mama a letter from California?"

"If you'd like. Did I tell you we'll be meeting your uncles in Denver in the spring? Uncle Rafe and Uncle Jess. They'll be surprised to learn I have a son your age, and happy to make your acquaintance." Sam gazed off into space. "It will be good to see them again."

"Do they have children I can play with?"

"Unfortunately, no. I doubt that Rafe will ever marry, and Jess is too caught up in his profession as a doctor to find a woman to his liking. Go back and play with your friends, son. We'll speak of this again after my plans are in place."

Sam had no idea that he and Andy were being observed from the forest of trees that protected the camp from unwanted visitors. Taylor Cramer had finally stumbled upon the Indian camp he'd been searching for these past few weeks. And to his delight, he had spotted both Sam Gentry and Andy.

Cramer's mind worked in devious ways. The camp was a small one by Indian standards, and it shouldn't be too difficult to take what he wanted from it and destroy the rest. An evil smile curved Cramer's thin lips. Perhaps Gentry would die during the attack. That shouldn't be too difficult to arrange. Yes, Cramer thought gleefully; getting rid of Gentry would be a pleasure. Then another thought occurred. Why not rid himself of Andy at the same time? It would certainly make his life a lot easier if Andy wasn't around to distract his mother after he and Lacey were married.

Crawling back into the cover of trees, Cramer found his horse and rode hell for leather back to town. There was much to be done before he could return and destroy the man who'd been a thorn in his side since the day he'd appeared at the B&G ranch.

Lacey went through the motions of living since the day Andy had disappeared, but her heart wasn't in it. She missed Andy dreadfully and would never forgive Sam for taking him. Even the ranch hands worked with listless energy, as if something vibrant were missing from their lives.

Then one morning Taylor Cramer rode into the yard accompanied by a dozen men. From the jubilant look on his face, Lacey knew immediately that he'd found the

Indian camp. Her face lit with excitement as she ran out to meet him.

"You've found him! You've found Andy!" Lacey exclaimed. "I can be ready to ride in a few minutes."

"You're not going anywhere, Lacey," Cramer argued. "I hired men to do the dirty work. You're to wait here for us to return with your son."

Lacey took a good look at the men riding with Taylor and didn't like what she saw. They appeared to be hardened criminal types who would do anything for money. Even kill.

"Rusty said the Indians who gave Sam shelter were friendly. You promised there would be no bloodshed."

Cramer's lips thinned. "You want Andy, don't you?"

"Of course, but killing isn't the way to go about it." She lowered her voice. "I don't trust these men to keep their guns holstered. Look at them. They're the dregs of society."

"I picked these men for the very traits you mentioned," Cramer said. "One look at them will discourage the Indians from defending Gentry. I've seen the camp. It's small and loosely defended."

"They're friendly—they have no need for caution. Promise me there will be no killing."

Cramer shot her an offended look. "I can't promise anything, Lacey. If the Indians resist, my men have orders to defend themselves."

"Shoot to kill, you mean."

"Do you or don't you want your son?"

"You know I do."

"Then leave the particulars to me."

"Just where is this camp located?" Lacey asked.

"Why do you want to know?"

"I was just wondering why it took so long to find it."

"It's well hidden in a clearing surrounded by forest. I was a good fifteen miles from town, following the south fork of the river, when I found it. I had almost decided to turn back when something told me to see what was around the bend."

"What are your plans?"

"My men and I will hide in the forest until dark. Then we'll attack."

Attack! Lacey didn't like the sound of that. Andy could be hurt in an attack, and innocent people killed. She couldn't allow that to happen.

"Thank you for stopping by and telling me," Lacey said, anxious for Taylor and his mercenaries to leave. "I'll wait here for you to bring Andy to me."

"I knew you would see things my way," Cramer smirked. "Look for us tomorrow."

Lacey waited as long as it took for Cramer and his henchmen to disappear in a cloud of dust before hurrying to her room to change into a split riding skirt and buckskin jacket. She retrieved the gun Uncle Hob had given her from the bureau drawer, loaded it and stuffed a handful of bullets into her pocket. Then she went the barn to saddle her mare. Rusty hurried in after her.

"What was that all about, Miz Lacey? Those were some rough-and-tumble men with Mr. Cramer. Are you going somewhere?"

"I don't have time now to talk, Rusty. Taylor found the Indian camp."

"I figured as much. Why didn't he wait for you?"

"He didn't want me along. I'm worried, Rusty. There's going to be bloodshed, and I don't like it. You saw his hirelings. They're a trigger-happy bunch if I ever saw one. Andy could get hurt."

"What are you planning?"

"Taylor intends to attack after dark. I think I can find it on my own. I need to get there first and warn them. Once I speak with Andy, I know he'll want to return to the ranch. Sam will have to let him go."

"Sam might have different ideas about that."

Lacey's chin notched upward. "I'll cross that bridge when I come to it."

"I'm going with you."

"No. Someone has to stay here and look after things. Everything will be fine, I promise." She patted her pocket. "I have my gun." Lacey pulled herself into the saddle. "Tell Rita not to worry, but I'm not leaving the Indian camp without Andy."

Lacey rode away and didn't look back. She knew she wasn't far behind Taylor and his henchmen; she could see their trail of dust ahead of her. She rode steadily, following the south fork of the river, stopping when they stopped to water their horses, remaining a safe distance away. It was early evening when the forest Taylor spoke of loomed ahead. She drew rein and waited until the riders entered the forest.

Lacey dismounted and followed, making a wide circle in order to skirt around them. The men were trying to be quiet, but Lacey still heard their hushed voices and the horses' restless movements. She realized, however, that unless the Indians were expecting trouble, they would suspect nothing. She recalled what Taylor had said about the camp being loosely guarded.

Moving cautiously, Lacey led her mare through the woods. It was growing darker, and she feared that time was running out. How much time did she have before Taylor and his men would launch their attack?

The trees thinned. Lacey peered through the twilight at the camp. All appeared peaceful. The glow of cooking fires illuminated the area. She saw children playing. Her heart began thumping. Was Andy with them? Should an attack occur, the children would be the first to be cut down. She hurried forward, unwilling to let that happen.

She saw them before they saw her—Sam and an Indian woman sitting side by side outside a tipi. The woman leaned into Sam, offering him a tidbit from her fingers. Sam smiled at the woman and accepted her offering. Their easy manner suggested an intimate relationship.

The thought of Sam bedding another woman was painful for Lacey, though she knew it shouldn't be. He'd probably bedded more women than he could count during their six-year separation. Lacey knew she shouldn't feel betrayed, but she did. Tearing her eyes from Sam and the Indian woman, Lacey looked for Andy. She breathed a sigh of relief when she saw him playing tag with another child. Pulling herself together, Lacey realized she had to act fast if she wanted to prevent a massacre.

Suddenly a child spied her and shouted a warning. A tall, imposing Indian brave stood up and strode toward her just as Andy saw her and called to her.

"Mama!"

Lacey spun around, dropping to her knees and opening her arms as Andy ran into them. She hugged him tightly, fearing to let him go lest she lose him again. Lacey would have stayed like that forever if a harsh voice hadn't asked, "What are you doing here?"

Lacey gazed up into Sam's piercing dark eyes. "I came for my son."

"Did you bring the law with you?"

"No, of course not."

"Why should I trust you?"

"Because I'm telling the truth." She rose slowly, holding tightly to Andy's hand.

"How did you know where to find me?"

Suddenly Lacey recalled why she had come. "Never mind that now. You're in danger. The whole camp is in danger. I came to warn you."

"Andy, go with Yellow Bird. Your mother and I need to talk in private."

"Do I have to go? You won't send Mama away, will you?"

"We'll discuss it later. Please do as I say."

Yellow Bird, Lacey thought. So that was his squaw's name.

"Come, An-dy," Yellow Bird said. "We will find Sitting Bear. Perhaps he will share his meal with you so your papa and the bad woman can talk."

"Bad woman!" Lacey huffed indignantly. "Is that what you told her?"

"Why did Yellow Bird call Mama a bad woman, Papa?"

"Please, Andy, not now. Go find Sitting Bear."

Andy left with Yellow Bird, though Lacey could tell he wasn't happy about it.

"What did you tell your squaw about me?"

"The truth. And she's not my squaw. Yellow Bird is a healer. She saved my life." He grasped her arm and pulled her into his tipi. "Enough of this. What makes

199

you think Chief Running Buffalo and his tribe are in danger?"

"Rusty mentioned that Indians had saved your life. Taylor suspected that you'd taken Andy to their village and he set out to find it. I organized my own search too, but sent the hands back to work when we turned up no trace of you or Andy. But Taylor continued on alone. He promised to return Andy to me. He finally found the village and hired thugs to ride with him. They're waiting for darkness to launch their attack."

Sam searched her face. "Why are you telling me this?"

She grasped his shirt front, desperate to make him understand. "To prevent bloodshed, damn you! Why won't you believe me? Do you think I want to see my son harmed? Or innocents die? You have to do something, Sam. Their attack could come at any moment."

Sam must have believed her, for he freed her hands and shoved her away. He left the tipi. Lacey ran after him. He marched determinedly toward the tall Indian who Lacey assumed was the chief. The two men spoke together in hushed, urgent tones. Then the chief whirled about and disappeared into his tipi. He returned moments later carrying a rifle, which he raised in the air and shook vigorously. Sam strode back to her while men dropped whatever they were doing to attend their chief.

"What's happening? Where's Andy? I'm worried."

Sam didn't answer. He motioned to Yellow Bird, and she hurried over with Andy and another young boy in tow.

"Take the women and children to safety, Yellow Bird. Lacey says bad men will attack the camp." He turned to Lacey. "Go with them."

"I'm staying. Taylor won't harm me."

"I don't have time to argue, Lacey. Go!"

"No, I'm staying."

"Dammit, have it your way. At least keep out of sight."

Lacey didn't know why she had insisted on staying. Andy was safe—that was all that mattered, wasn't it? Who was she trying to fool? She knew that Taylor hated Sam and wouldn't hesitate to use this attack as an excuse to kill him. She didn't stop to wonder why she should care; she just knew she did. Sam had hurt her so many times in so many ways—why couldn't she just forget him?

Because you haven't been able to forget him in six years, a voice inside her said. When she believed Sam was dead, she'd been able to go on with her life, but when he turned up on her doorstep alive, all those suppressed feelings came rushing back to swamp her.

Lacey had so many reasons to hate Sam. He had abandoned her. Taken Andy. Turned to another woman. The list went on and on. Why couldn't she make her heart believe she hated Sam? Why did her body thrum with awareness in his presence?

Lacey's thoughts skidded to a halt when she noticed that the Indians were now all armed and appeared to be moving about the camp according to some plan. The women and children had quietly disappeared, and the campfires had been extinguished. It was so dark she could see nothing but shadows moving into position. In the distance she heard the haunting call of an owl.

She started violently when Sam came up behind her and whispered in her ear. "They're coming. That owl was Painted Horse. It was the signal telling us that Cra-

mer and his men are on the move. Stay inside the tipi."
Then he was gone.

Lacey didn't argue. She returned to the tipi but remained where she could peer out the tent flap. Suddenly there was dead silence; not even a dog barked. Then she saw them, limned in misty moonlight. They crept into camp, guns drawn. It suddenly occurred to Lacey that Taylor's henchmen had probably been given orders to shoot indiscriminately at whatever moved, with little concern for Andy's life.

Hatred for the man she'd thought of as a friend and future husband welled up inside of her. Sam had taken Andy but would not have hurt him, but she knew that Taylor would prefer not to have Andy around to complicate his life. She was so angry she left the tent against Sam's wishes and might have given the ambush away if Sam had not snagged her around the waist and dragged her back inside.

"What in hell do you think you're doing?"

"Look at them," she whispered. "They're mercenaries. They don't care who they shoot. They would have killed Andy along with the Indians if I hadn't arrived in time to warn you. I wanted to march out there and tell Taylor exactly what I think of him."

Sam sent her a sharp look. "Save it. Taylor's men aren't going to kill anyone. They're walking into a trap."

Even as Sam spoke, savage war cries cut through the stillness. Biting off a curse, he exited the tipi and melted into the darkness. Peering out the tent flap, Lacey saw a scene straight out of hell. Gunfire erupted; bodies clashed. Lacey couldn't tell who was who as men engaged in hand-to-hand combat. The din of battle and cries of the wounded pierced through her heart. Had Yellow Bird gotten the women and children to safety in time?

It was over as suddenly as it had begun. Taylor's men retreated, dragging their wounded with them. The Indians didn't give chase. They let their attackers go, attesting to their desire for peace. Lacey stepped out of the tipi as campfires were rekindled and the women and children began drifting back to camp.

Suddenly a man in full retreat halted at the edge of the camp, staring at Lacey in disbelief. "Lacey, is that you?"

Lacey swung around to confront Cramer.

"My God, it is you!" Cramer exclaimed. "What are you doing here? I thought I told you to stay home."

"I followed you, Taylor. I didn't trust your men not to hurt Andy, and I was right. If I hadn't arrived in time, innocent people would have been cut down without a chance to defend themselves. And Andy with them. You care nothing for my son."

"Those are harsh words, Lacey. I continued looking for your son when everyone else had given up. I wanted to restore Andy to you."

Sam appeared at her side, his body tense. "You'd be a fool to believe him," he hissed.

"I'm not stupid, Sam."

"Get Andy and leave with me now," Taylor ordered. "Gentry can't hold you against your will."

Lacey glanced at Sam, saw his fierce expression and wasn't so sure about that. "I'm getting Andy and leaving," she said. "He doesn't belong here. Please, Sam. I want to go home."

"With Cramer? After what he did?"

"Taylor has nothing to do with how I feel. Andy belongs back on the ranch. He's happy there. What can you offer him?"

"Unconditional love," Sam bit out.

"At one time I thought that was what we had, but I learned differently. Andy is a child; he won't understand if you suddenly decide you don't want a son and leave us."

An angry flush crept up Sam's neck. "I'll always want Andy."

"Lacey, I can't stand here forever," Taylor called out. "Are you and Andy coming or aren't you?"

"Lacey can leave, but Andy stays with me," Sam asserted.

A cry of distress slipped past Lacey's lips. "You wouldn't!"

"I would dare anything for my son. Tell me, Lacey, have you signed the annulment?"

"I . . . yes, I had to," she continued in a quiet voice so Taylor couldn't hear her. "You see, I'm convinced Taylor wants my land for some devious reason, and I'm determined to find out what it is. I thought that signing the annulment would make him trust me. I no longer trust him, Sam. You were right about him, and I was wrong."

"I see," Sam said evenly. "So we're no longer married—"

"I'm not sure. The judge hasn't granted my petition yet."

"Once the petition is granted, we'll no longer be married," Sam contended, "which means you'll be free to remarry. If not Taylor, then some other man with enough money to save your ranch. No other man can be a real father to Andy. Andy doesn't want to be sent away to school. He needs at least one of his parents with him. I gave him a choice, and he chose to come with me. I didn't take him against his will.

"You know I can't return to Denison," Sam continued. "I'm a wanted man. I need to go far away, where no one cares that Sam Gentry is an outlaw."

"Not with my son! Are you forgetting that I saved your skin tonight? I could have stayed home and let you and your Indian friends be slaughtered."

"I'm grateful, and so is Running Buffalo. But if I'm not mistaken, you were the one who sent the law after me in the first place."

"I did no such thing!" Lacey said, affronted.

"I didn't imagine that posse. The bullet in my hide was very real. How do you explain the posse when you were the only one who knew about me?"

"I assumed the Wanted posters had caught up with you. I told no one about you—I would never do that. My threat was an empty one. The sheriff showed up at my door the day you left, demanding to know where you were. I told them nothing."

"Am I supposed to believe that?"

Lacey felt as if her heart were being ripped apart. She couldn't bear Sam's animosity. Was there nothing she could do to prove she hadn't betrayed him? The answer was obvious. Sam hadn't believed her six years ago and didn't believe her now.

"Lacey, why are you standing there? Get Andy. I'm growing impatient."

"Go with Cramer, Lacey," Sam said through clenched teeth. "Andy and I don't need you."

"Mama! Papa! I was worried about you." Andy ran into Lacey's outstretched arms. "Did the bad men go away? I hid in a cave with Yellow Bird and the others, but I didn't want to. I wanted to help Papa fight the bad men."

"Hurry!" Taylor called when he saw Andy.

"Are you leaving, Mama?"

"You and I are both leaving," Lacey said, casting a sidelong glance at Sam.

Andy squinted through the darkness at the figure standing near the camp's perimeter. "Is that mean old Cramer?"

"Sure is, son," Sam answered. "He led the attack on our friends."

Andy sent his mother an aggrieved look. "Are you going with him, Mama?"

"Well . . . yes, but not—"

"I'm staying with Papa," Andy said staunchly.

"Andy, it's not as if I'm going to—"

"I don't care. I'm staying. You can stay, too, Mama, if you want to." He gazed up at Sam. "Mama can stay, can't she, Papa?"

"I think it would be better if she left."

"I'm not going anywhere without Andy," Lacey declared.

"Suit yourself, but Andy isn't leaving my protection."

"Are you coming, Lacey?" Cramer's voice held a note of desperation. "It's not safe here for me."

"You'd better answer," Sam advised.

"Go ahead and leave, Taylor. I'm not going with you."

"You're what? Are you mad?"

"Perhaps I am. Tell Rusty to take care of things in my absence. And, Taylor, don't come back with the intention of attacking these innocent people again. And leave the sheriff out of this."

"You prefer that outlaw to me?" Taylor spat. "Unappreciative bitch. I tried to restore your son to you, and now you tell me to leave and not come back? I can't believe it of you."

"You'd better leave, Taylor. Sam's friends are getting nervous."

Cramer cast a nervous glance at Running Buffalo, who was looking at Sam for directions. Then Cramer turned and disappeared into the forest.

Lacey didn't know if her decision had been a wise one, but she did know she couldn't, wouldn't, let Andy out of her sight again. The ranch could fall to ruin or be sold from under her before she'd give up her son.

Sam wasn't sure how he felt about Lacey's decision to stay. In a way, he'd expected it of her, and would have been disappointed if she had abandoned her son. But he didn't delude himself into thinking she had stayed because she held any strong feelings for him.

"If you're remaining here in hopes of taking Andy away, forget it. You won't succeed. You are free to leave any time you wish, but Andy remains with me. We'll be leaving for California soon."

"How do you expect to support Andy? California is far away, and you'll need money to get there."

"Let me worry about that. It's late. You can share Yellow Bird's tipi."

"I wouldn't think of keeping you from Yellow Bird's bed. I'll sleep with Andy."

"Andy sleeps in the chief's tipi with Sitting Bear."

"How convenient for you."

Sam sighed. "Lacey, I'm in no mood to exchange barbs."

Lacey seemed to collapse inward. "Neither am I. I'll share Yellow Bird's tent . . . for now."

Running Buffalo chose that moment to join them. Sam introduced him to Lacey.

"This is your woman?" Running Buffalo asked.

Sam nodded before thinking. Lacey wasn't his woman. He wasn't sure she had ever been his woman.

"On behalf of my people, I thank you, La-cey, for warning us about the unprovoked attack. I have spoken with Yellow Bird," the chief continued. "She will share my tipi so that you can be with your mate."

"Yellow Bird agreed to that?" Lacey asked, apparently stunned by Yellow Bird's offer.

"I am chief. Yellow Bird must do as I say." Without another word, he turned and strode away.

"Where is Andy?" Lacey asked.

"Probably sleeping. I saw Running Buffalo's wife herding him and Sitting Bear inside her tipi while we were talking. It's very late." He grasped her arm. "Come along. Running Buffalo will set out guards to make sure Cramer doesn't return, but for now there is nothing more for us to do."

Lacey dug in her heels. "I want Andy with me."

Firming his jaw, Sam swept Lacey into his arms and carried her into the tipi, ducking beneath the entrance flap before setting her on her feet. "I won't have you disrupting the entire camp after what they've been put through."

"I'm not going to sleep with you, Sam Gentry. I don't want anything to do with you."

Ignoring Lacey, Sam stared into the dying embers of

the fire burning in the center of the tipi, watching pensively as a finger of smoke curled upward through the smoke hole. Her words bit deeply into his heart when he knew they shouldn't. Yet he couldn't deny the fact that he wanted her. Making love to Lacey had been one of the greatest pleasures he'd ever experienced. He remembered how she looked—her lovely face suffused with ecstasy, her lush body arched against him as she exploded around him. The image made him grow hard, and it was with great difficulty that he jerked his thoughts back to the present.

"The sleeping mats are rolled up at the back of the tent," he growled. "Get undressed and go to bed." He turned to leave.

"Where are you going?"

Sam whirled around. "I thought you didn't care."

Her chin rose. "I don't. It's a warm night. I suppose you and Yellow Bird will find someplace to . . . to—"

"Damn you!" Sam hissed. Teeth clenched, hands fisted, he ducked through the opening and disappeared into the shadows.

Chapter Twelve

Lacey undressed down to her shift and drawers and crawled into the sleeping mat she had unrolled and placed near the back of the tipi. It was surprisingly comfortable, and she was exhausted. With a sigh on her lips, she closed her eyes and prayed for sleep. Disturbing thoughts spinning around in her mind chased away the respite she so desperately sought. She wondered if Sam and Yellow Bird had gotten together, and if they were enjoying themselves. She wished fiercely for rain, then silently chided herself for acting the jealous wife.

Weariness ended her mental musings as sleep finally claimed her. But it wasn't a deep sleep, for she awoke abruptly to the sure knowledge that she was being watched. Her heart pounded in erratic rhythm and her spine tingled with awareness as she slowly opened her eyes. She saw him standing in a patch of moonlight filtering down through the smoke hole.

Her gaze started at his booted feet, then glided slowly upward over muscular legs, powerful thighs, to his . . . She gasped. He was fully aroused. The hardened ridge in his trousers provided ample proof that he hadn't bedded Yellow Bird. Elation speared through her, but she quickly subdued it. Why should she care who Sam did or did not bed?

Raising her eyes above the blatant proof of his desire, Lacey was startled to see that his chest was bare. Moonlight turned his torso to molten gold, gilding each rippling muscle and corded tendon. His face was shadowed, but she knew that if it were visible, his eyes would be mesmerizing pools of pure seduction. She averted her gaze. She couldn't succumb to Sam's sexual allure—not now, not after what he'd done to her. He had stolen her son and would have taken him far away forever.

"Lacey."

She squeezed her eyes tightly shut.

"I know you're awake."

A resigned sigh slipped past her lips. "What do you want? Didn't Yellow Bird satisfy you?"

He dropped to his knees beside her. "Yellow Bird is not now nor has she ever been my lover."

Another sigh. "Why should that matter to me?"

He found her hand in the dark and placed it on his arousal. "After everything that's happened between us, I still want you."

She tried to jerk her hand away, but he held it in place.

211

"Go away, Sam. I can't forgive you. You took my son away."

"You gave me up to the Yankees."

"You abandoned me for six long years."

"You sent a posse after me."

Anger suffused her words. "I didn't! I swear it."

Sam's soft whisper pierced the charged darkness. "I wouldn't have taken Andy to California without giving you a chance to join us," he confessed. "I thought I could take him away, but at the last minute I had a change of heart. I planned to return to the B&G and ask you to join us. It would have been your choice. You had but to choose me and your son over Cramer and the ranch."

"You're lying."

"No, it's true. I hadn't even told Andy yet. It was something I just recently decided."

"You . . . you wanted me with you? I thought you didn't trust me."

"I don't, but we could make the best of it for Andy's sake. I never thought much about children until I met Andy. Fatherhood was not an option for me. I already had a wife, albeit one I had no interest in seeing again, and there was no other woman I was close to."

"How long would you have let me go on thinking you were dead?"

"I honestly don't know. Forever is a long time. For all I knew, you had remarried."

"Go away, Sam. I don't want to listen to this. My emotions are too fragile where you're concerned."

"I want you, Lacey. When I saw you again, I realized that time had changed nothing. You're a fire in my blood. I can be angry with you one minute and want you fiercely the next. Let me love you."

He stretched out on the sleeping mat, gently pulling her against his hard length. Lacey bit her tongue to stifle a moan of pleasure.

"When I left the tipi tonight, I had no intention of returning," Sam revealed, "but something compelled me to return."

His hands slid down her back; they were so hot that Lacey's skin caught fire. She moistened her lips, felt them trembling as his hands found the mounds of her buttocks. Then his mouth came down hard over hers. Not soft and gentle but hot and ravishing. It was a deep, almost brutal kiss, one of savage need. Lacey couldn't stop her response as she kissed him back, her hands clutching desperately at his shoulders. His breathing was erratic, coming hard and fast, when he broke away.

He began pulling off his boots, his motions frantic.

"What are you doing?"

"Taking off my clothes."

"Making love will solve none of our problems."

"Maybe not, but it sure as hell will make us feel better."

His boots hit the ground. He lifted his hips and skimmed his denims down his legs, kicking them away. Then he was beside her, bringing her hard against him, holding her tightly, kissing her thoroughly, slanting his mouth over hers, molding their lips together. When he nudged her lips apart, taking her deeply with his tongue, Lacey sighed into his mouth.

A scalding moistness seeped from between her legs. She felt as if she'd just jumped into an inferno. His kisses grew more ardent. He cupped her breasts, plucked the tips into hard buds with his fingers through the material of her shift. Lacey felt her body softening, preparing for his entrance, and she moaned.

Suddenly he grasped her shift in both hands and tugged upward. "This has to go," he breathed raggedly.

With little effort he pulled the shift over her head and off. "And these are definitely in the way." With one quick motion he stripped off her drawers.

Lacey barely had time to register the fact that their nude bodies were molded together before Sam's hands began seeking out all those places that gave her the most pleasure. He caressed her breasts until they felt heavy and swollen, suckled her nipples into hard nubs, driving her nearly insane with need. Another moan slipped past her lips. She wanted this, needed this, but feared the consequences of her submission.

Sex without the elements of trust and love was just an act. Was that what Sam wanted, to perform an act that meant little to him save for a moment of ecstasy? Oh, God, if only she felt like that, willing to sacrifice love and trust for pleasure. But Lacey wanted what Sam obviously wasn't willing to give her. She struggled for sanity.

"Sam, stop and think about what we're doing. Is it in Andy's best interests? Is it in *our* best interests?"

"You talk too much," Sam growled around the plump nipple he was suckling.

Lacey tried, truly she did, but her body seemed to have a mind of its own. She felt hot all over, as if her nerve endings were on fire. Then Sam's mouth started a downward trek and all semblance of control fled. Her stomach contracted beneath the wet heat of his mouth. She grasped his head as he aimed lower, bringing him closer as his tongue slid along satiny smooth petals.

When he spread her open with his thumbs and tasted her deeply, she nearly arched off the mat. She gave a ragged cry and tugged his hair, urging him upward. She wanted him inside her . . . now.

Sam raised his head and chuckled. "Easy, love. Pace yourself. I want to watch your face when you fly apart." Then he returned to his succulent feast, his mouth and tongue driving her to insane heights.

Lacey gasped, her body straining upward into his intimate caress while one of his hands charted the smooth roundness of her bottom and the other fondled her breasts. The taut feeling inside her grew tighter and tighter, tension built until she felt as if she would explode.

Then she was there, poised on the brink. One final thrust of his tongue and she tumbled over, breaking into a thousand tiny pieces. Half sobbing, she clung to his shoulders. When the waves of shimmering pleasure finally receded, she opened her eyes and gazed up at him through a shimmering haze. He was smiling at her, his dark eyes glowing. She barely had time to recover before he crawled upward and impaled her.

"Put your arms around me," he whispered in her ear. She obeyed without hesitation, her hands sliding over his damp skin as he began to move forcefully between her legs, his body lifting and thrusting with strong, relentless strokes.

He kissed her again, roughly, his mouth fiercely possessive as he thrust and withdrew, and she cried out at the sweet, hot ecstasy of it.

Her response stunned her. She was sure she had already given everything she had to give, but her body suddenly thrummed back to life. She gave herself up to it, to that feeling of flying without wings. She heard Sam's harsh breathing, felt his hands lift her bottom as his hips pumped, plunging in and out of her. Thunder burst in her head. No, it was Sam's voice crying out in the dark silence.

"Lacey . . . God!"

It was enough to send Lacey over the edge. She followed Sam into oblivion seconds after he exploded inside her.

Lacey's wits returned slowly. She felt drained, utterly depleted. Apparently, Sam suffered from the same malady, for he rolled away and collapsed beside her, his chest rising and falling as he took in great gulps of air.

Lacey couldn't speak, the effort was too great, but she could still think. Her response to Sam's loving overwhelmed her. Against her better judgment, her love for Sam had been rekindled. She had recognized the danger but had refused to heed the warning. She knew that Sam was wanted by the law, that their painful past prevented a future together, but love was blind.

She could still dream, Lacey thought wistfully. The reality was that Sam was an outlaw. How long could they be together before the law caught up with him? Oh, God, she was so confused, and a little bit crazy to want Sam as desperately as she did.

To love Sam.

Sam stared into the darkness, seeing nothing, hearing nothing but his own harsh breathing. What the hell was wrong with him? When he'd entered the tipi tonight, he had no intention of making love to Lacey. He'd waited to return until he figured she'd fallen asleep. But the moment he'd entered the tent, awareness of her struck

him like a physical blow. He'd tried to control his reaction; he'd even spread out his sleeping mat and taken
off his shirt, fully intending to lie down and turn his
back on Lacey.

Then he made the mistake of watching Lacey sleep,
and all his good intentions fled. He had stepped closer
to her mat, staring at her with unquenchable longing.

What happened next had been destined by fate. He
had grown hard just looking at her, and when he realized
she was awake, nothing could have stopped destiny.

God, would he never learn? Would he still want her
after she betrayed him a third time? And he knew she
would, given another opportunity. Unfortunately, that
didn't stop him from wanting Lacey. Fate had played a
dirty trick on him when it arranged their meeting after
years spent in convincing himself he cared nothing for
her. After tonight, forgetting Lacey was going to be difficult . . . no, impossible. He rolled to his side and found
Lacey staring at him.

"That was . . . words can't describe how I feel," he
said on a gusty sigh. "I can't say I'm sorry it happened,
but it wasn't what I intended when I returned to the tipi
tonight."

"What was your intention? To humiliate me?"

Sam reared up on his elbows. "Is that what you
think?"

"I don't know what to think anymore. I don't know
you, Sam. I loved you once, and mourned your 'death'
deeply. I knew I would never love again and was content
to go through life lavishing all my love on Andy. Why
did you have to come back into my life now, when my
life had finally gotten back on track? All I ever wanted
was security for Andy."

"You call promising yourself to Cramer getting your life back on track?"

Lacey refused to meet his eyes. "I was wrong, I'll admit that much. Taylor wants something besides me. I just haven't figured out what."

Her gaze flew upward to meet his. "What happens now, Sam? We've already proved we want one another, but that's beside the point."

"What is the point?"

"Andy. We both want what's best for him. Whether or not you committed a crime, the law says you're an outlaw. You'll need to travel far and fast to escape jail. Is that what you want for Andy, a life of running from the law?"

"I can't think that far ahead. Not with your body pressed against mine and your lips so close I can almost taste them."

"Don't do this, Sam. You are my weakness; don't take advantage of me."

"Put your arms around me," he rasped.

"No, I—"

"Kiss me."

She sucked in a shuddering breath, blinked repeatedly, then let the air out of her lungs in surrender. Her arms went around him as their lips met and clung. Arms and legs entwined, they kissed and caressed until passion demanded that they join their bodies.

Sam rolled on his back and pulled Lacey on top of him. "Ride me, sweetheart. Take me deep inside you. Forget the past. Think only of now."

"I want to forget. Oh, God, make me forget," Lacey pleaded in a strangled voice.

Grasping her buttocks, Sam lifted and spread her. He

slid deep inside, groaning in pleasure as she contracted snugly around him. Then she began to move, undulating against his loins in an erotic rhythm that made Sam forget his own name. It didn't take long. Completion burst upon them simultaneously. Sam's last thought before he succumbed to ecstasy was that he never wanted this to end. Lacey was his. She'd always be his.

Entwined in each other's arms, Lacey and Sam were unaware that morning had crept up on them as they slept. Nor did they know that Yellow Bird had ducked into the tent to bring them food and saw them intimately entwined upon the sleeping mat. She said nothing, but her expression held a wealth of emotions. Anger, hurt, disappointment. She regarded them through narrowed eyes, then set the bowl down on the floor and spun away.

Sam awakened first. He disentangled himself from Lacey's arms and pulled on his clothes. The morning was cool, so he built up the fire in the center of the tipi before he left to bathe in the river. On the way out he stumbled over the bowl of food that had been left near the tent flap. He frowned. It hadn't been there last night, which meant someone had left it this morning. Yellow Bird. He glanced over at Lacey, remembering how he and Lacey had been intimately entwined in sleep and wondering if Yellow Bird had seen them. He shrugged off the thought and ducked outside.

As if his thoughts had conjured her up, Yellow Bird appeared beside him. "Where are you going, Sam?"

"To the river," Sam said. "Soon it will be too cold to bathe in the river. I intend to enjoy it while I can."

"I will walk with you." A moment of silence ensued

before she asked, "Did you enjoy your woman last night? Your anger must be easily appeased. I thought you did not like La-cey."

"I figured it was you who left food in the tipi this morning. There are things you don't understand about me and Lacey, Yellow Bird. There are things I don't understand myself."

"Will she return to her home?"

"I don't know. There are issues between us that need resolving before anything can be decided. Lacey refuses to leave without Andy."

"An-dy wishes to remain with you," Yellow Bird said fiercely. "You are safe here, Sam. The men who attacked us are cowards; they will not return. Besides, Running Buffalo will soon take our people south to our winter campground."

"I don't know if I really want to take Andy from La-cey," Sam said after lengthy consideration. "On the other hand, I don't see how I can let her have him, knowing she will end up marrying Taylor Cramer or some man just like him. Andy deserves better than that."

"Send the bad woman home," Yellow Bird advised. "Come with us to our winter camp. I will take care of you, Sam Gentry."

They had reached the river, but Yellow Bird seemed in no hurry to leave. "Go back to camp, Yellow Bird. I'm going to bathe now."

"I have seen all of you, Sam Gentry."

She edged closer, so close their bodies were nearly touching. She twined her arms around Sam's neck. She swayed toward him, and he placed his arms around her waist to steady her.

"I will treat you like a man should be treated," Yellow Bird promised. "Send the bad woman home."

Neither Sam nor Yellow Bird saw Lacey standing behind them. She had awakened moments after Sam left the tipi and had risen immediately. She had stepped out of the tipi just as Sam and Yellow Bird disappeared down the well-trod path leading to the river. She had followed close on their heels, stopping abruptly when she saw Yellow Bird and Sam embrace. Stifling a cry, she spun around and fled. Sam must have heard her, for he glanced up, catching a fleeting glimpse of her as she ran off.

Sam spit out a curse and removed Yellow Bird's arms from his neck, giving her a gentle shove. "Go back to camp, Yellow Bird, I don't want to hurt you, but there is no future for us."

Yellow Bird stared at him for the space of a heartbeat. Her voice intense with emotion, she said, "La-cey will leave you, Sam. She is not the woman you need." Then she pivoted on her heel and hurried off.

Sam stripped and plunged into the cold water. How in the hell did he get himself into these predicaments? he wondered. His brothers had always teased him about his penchant for getting into trouble, and he supposed it was well deserved. Of the three brothers, he was the most unpredictable.

Yellow Bird had saved his life. He was indebted to her, but not enough to bed her. After loving Lacey last night, he couldn't imagine going through life without her. But without trust, how long could their relationship survive? Would having a son together compensate for the lack of trust?

Sam ducked beneath the water and came up sputtering. Then he waded ashore and pulled on his clothes, his mind whirling with options and choices that were painfully limited. He was still a wanted man . . . an outlaw. A man in his position had no business dragging a woman and innocent child all over hell while trying to evade the law. But he couldn't give up Andy—not now, not after growing to love the boy.

By the time Sam returned to camp, he had come to a decision of sorts. He was keeping Andy. If Lacey refused to leave without her son, that was her problem. When he and Andy left for California, she could accompany them or not; it was her choice.

Sam found Lacey inside the tipi with Andy and Yellow Bird. They were seated together, eating the food Yellow Bird had provided. Sam sat down beside Lacey. She stiffened and leaned away from him. He accepted a bowl from Yellow Bird and began to eat.

"Isn't it nice to have Mama with us, Papa?" Andy piped up. "She said she's not ready to go home yet. I don't want to return home unless we all go together."

"Is your mother prepared to travel to California with us?"

Andy looked hopefully at Lacey. "Are you, Mama?"

"We'll talk about it later, honey," Lacey replied, looking pointedly at Yellow Bird. "When we're alone."

"Can I go play with Sitting Bear now? Running Buffalo made me a bow and he's going to show me how to use it."

"A bow? I don't know—"

"Let him go, Lacey. Running Buffalo won't let any harm come to him."

"Very well. Be careful, honey."

Andy darted off. Silence reigned until Yellow Bird

picked up the dirty bowls and left the tipi. Her manner toward Lacey was decidedly unfriendly, but Sam let it pass. The moment Yellow Bird was gone, Sam turned his full attention to Lacey.

"It's not what you think, Lacey. What you saw meant nothing."

Lacey bristled indignantly. "What makes you think I care?"

"Perhaps you don't, but I want to set the record straight. What you saw at the river was simply a display of Yellow Bird's affection. It wasn't reciprocated."

Lacey gazed down at her hands. "After last night I thought . . ." Her voice trailed off.

"What did you think?"

She lifted her eyes to his. "That you agreed to let Andy go home with me."

Sam's expression hardened. "Is that what you were doing last night when you surrendered to me? Were you taking advantage of my weakness for you to get your way in this? It won't work, Lacey. I won't deny that I want you, but I want my son more."

"No! It wasn't like that at all," Lacey insisted. "What happened between us was spontaneous. I couldn't have stopped it; we both know that."

"So what are we going to do about it?" Sam asked softly.

Her chin rose defiantly. "I'm taking Andy home. You can have your Indian squaw. Yellow Bird hates me. There might not be anything sexual between the two of you now, but it's bound to happen."

"Yellow Bird wouldn't hurt you. She's a healer. She values life. Like I said before, you're free to leave whenever you please, but Andy stays with me." He hoped

223

she'd agree to accompany him but would not stop her from leaving without Andy.

There was a flash of fire in her hazel eyes, and Sam waited for her outburst.

"Damn you, Sam Gentry! I'm not leaving without my son. You and Yellow Bird can cavort all you please; just don't expect me to surrender to you again. Next time I'll be on my guard."

"Can I assume that to mean you're coming to California with us?"

"Assume anything you like, but know this. One way or another I'm leaving, and it won't be without Andy." Rising abruptly, she grabbed a water skin from the back of the tipi and stormed off.

Sam stared after her, a frown wrinkling his brow. He knew he was being obstinate, but he wasn't going to let Lacey win this time. If she wanted Andy, she could join them on their trek to California.

Lacey watched from afar as Andy and Sitting Bear played with their tiny bows. Their arrows didn't go far, and Lacey was relieved to discover she had nothing to worry about. She wandered down the path to the river to fill the water skin. She needed a good wash and wanted to bathe in private. Unlike Sam, she was protective of her modesty.

Sam was gone when she returned to the tipi, much to Lacey's relief. She found an iron kettle and set water to heat over the fire. She heard a noise behind her and pivoted, not surprised to see Yellow Bird. This was her tipi, after all.

Yellow Bird wasted no time on preliminaries. "Why are you still here? You are no good for Sam."

224

Lacey minced no words. "I'm not leaving without Andy, and Sam refuses to let me take him away."

"You have hurt Sam," Yellow Bird charged. "He does not care for you."

Anger surged through Lacey. "What did Sam tell you about me?"

"Very little, but I know he is not happy with you. I can take away his sadness. You will bring him nothing but trouble."

"You're welcome to Sam," Lacey retorted. "I've lived without him the six years I thought him dead, and I don't need him now. Andy is all I require to make my life complete."

"You have another man," Yellow Bird charged. "One An-dy does not like."

"That man is no longer in my life or my future—not that it's any of your business. Look, Yellow Bird, I don't want you for an enemy. Take Sam, if he'll have you, but Andy is mine. Please leave now so I may bathe in private."

Yellow Bird searched Lacey's face as if trying to decide the veracity of her words; then she nodded and made a hasty exit.

Lacey truly didn't know what to make of Yellow Bird. She appeared sincerely fond of Andy, and it wasn't difficult to tell she was enamored of Sam. But, strangely, Lacey perceived no real harm in the woman. Nothing threatening. She couldn't help feeling uneasy, however. She was, after all, an interloper in a world far different from her own. She feared that the Indians' goodwill toward her depended largely upon Sam's regard.

* * *

The following days passed with nothing resolved between Lacey and Sam. Lacey refused to allow Andy out of her sight. Though she worried about the ranch, she made no attempt to leave, for Sam would stop her if she tried to take Andy away. She lived for the day when Sam would let his guard down, and when he did, she'd seize the moment.

Lacey's greatest fear was that Taylor would return with the law. She couldn't forget that Sam was a wanted man, and that Taylor wasn't above using stealth or violence to get what he wanted, and he wanted her ranch. Why?

When neither Taylor nor the law showed up, Lacey began to breathe easier. She knew Running Buffalo hadn't let down his guard, for each night he sent men into the forest to watch for intruders. Lacey was growing accustomed to daily life in the Indian camp. She'd even taken over cooking the food Sam provided for them.

But she hadn't allowed Sam into her bed since that first night. They slept in the same tipi whenever Sam chose to make an appearance, but that was as far as it went. She never questioned him when he failed to return, and had no idea where or with whom he slept. Sam had offered no argument when Lacey insisted that Andy sleep beside her each night. He didn't need to say anything. His lowering looks said it all.

Lacey stirred the beans and prepared the rabbits Sam had bagged that morning. The heat from the fire felt good, for the evenings had turned downright cold. Lacey hoped that she and Andy would be safely home before the first snowfall.

"Something smells good."

Lacey pretended indifference, but her heart thudded

wildly as Sam walked up behind her. His hair was still wet from his wash in the river, and the thought of a cold dip in the river on these chilly evenings made her shiver.

"Supper will be ready as soon as I make the bread." Yellow Bird had grudgingly shown her how to prepare Indian bread, and she'd become quite good at it.

Sam plopped down on the ground beside the fire. His manner was surly as he stared into the fire. "Running Buffalo will take his tribe south for the winter in a few days," he began. "It's time for me and Andy to leave."

Lacey dropped the spoon she was holding and stared at him.

"You knew all along I planned to leave," Sam said. "You have to make up your mind about what you're going to do. You can come along, but it won't be an easy journey. I don't have enough money for three fares, so we'll have to forgo the stagecoach." He shot her a guarded look. "You can always return to the ranch and become Cramer's wife. Lord knows you haven't been much of a wife to me."

Lacey sent him a barbed look. "Allowing you to make love to me was a mistake. There's no love between us. Without love, sleeping together is pointless."

"Are you so sure there's no love between us? There's *something* between us, Lacey. Something neither of us is willing to acknowledge."

His words stunned her. Her legs went rubbery beneath her as she plopped down beside him. "Are you saying you care for me, Sam?"

"It wouldn't be difficult to care, Lacey. You're the mother of my child. We loved each other deeply once. I don't know if that depth of feeling will ever return, or if I want it to, but I'm not indifferent to you. I've demonstrated that to you on numerous occasions."

"Does that mean you're willing to believe I didn't betray you to the Yankees, or send the posse after you?"

Sam looked away. "Perhaps. My mind still isn't clear on some things."

Lacey stiffened. "You're contradicting yourself, Sam. You can't care for me if you don't trust me. I'll go with you and Andy to California, but not as your wife. What you feel for me is lust; I'm not sure you ever loved me."

Her words lingered in the air like autumn smoke, thick and choking.

Chapter Thirteen

Sam did not return to the tipi to sleep after their charged conversation. Lacey had no idea where he spent his nights but she suspected it was with Yellow Bird. The Indian squaw appeared far too smug of late, as if she had much to be pleased about. Lacey had no intention of asking Sam about his sleeping arrangements. She feared she already knew.

The entire camp was preparing for their move south. Everyone had a job, including Lacey. Among her chores was helping to gather late berries, then laying them in the sun to dry. To her regret, Andy was never allowed to accompany her and the other women, so that avenue of escape was closed to her.

One day Yellow Bird managed to lure her away for a private word. "We leave for our winter camp in three suns," Yellow Bird said. "I know you do not wish to go to California with Sam, so I will help you leave."

Immediately Lacey's suspicions were aroused. "Why would you help me? You don't even like me."

"Sam Gentry and I are lovers," she lied. "We were lovers before you came to our camp. You know I do not lie, for he has left your sleeping mat for mine. He does not want you."

"I won't leave without Andy, and Sam refuses to let me have him."

Yellow Bird leaned closer. "You do wish to leave, do you not?"

"I told you, not without—"

"You can take An-dy with you. I will give Sam sons, many sons. He does not need yours."

Lacey searched Yellow Bird's face. She seemed sincere, but could she trust the healer? "How can you help me? Andy and I are rarely left alone. We need horses and—"

"I will see to everything, trust me. Tomorrow the men leave on a hunting expedition. Sam is to accompany them. He asked me to watch over you and Andy while he is gone."

Excitement gripped Lacey. This was the chance she'd been waiting for. "How long will Sam be gone?"

"The men will range far afield in search of game. They will be gone two suns. You could be home long before they return."

Lacey still wasn't convinced. "Helping me and Andy

will surely invite Sam's anger. I'm surprised you're willing to risk his animosity."

"I am not stupid. I will arrange things so that he will not hold me responsible. Once you are gone, he will turn to me for all his needs."

"You're wrong. Sam is going to California."

Yellow Bird smiled. "He will stay. Running Buffalo is fond of Sam. Together we will convince him to stay with our people. White man's law cannot reach him while he is with us."

Despite her inclination to suspect Yellow Bird, Lacey felt she had no other choice. "Tell me what I must do."

Lacey listened carefully, then nodded acquiescence. If all went as planned, she and Andy would soon be home. And she'd never see Sam again. That thought sent her reeling. She'd been slowly falling in love again with Sam. It had started soon after he'd turned up on her doorstep, alive and well. She wanted to hate him, had reminded herself time and again of all his faults, but it hadn't done a bit of good. He was still the same Sam she had fallen in love with six years ago, and nothing could change that.

Oh, he had changed, in countless ways, but the Sam she had once loved was still there. He had become more distrustful, harder, more eager to condemn without justification, but her heart refused to listen to her arguments. Making love with Sam was like grasping a little bit of heaven for herself. But she couldn't let her love for Sam interfere. She had to do what was best for Andy. Traipsing over the countryside one step ahead of the law definitely wasn't in Andy's best interests. Suppose Sam was caught and sent to jail? What would become of Andy?

What would become of her?

It suddenly occurred to Lacey that she had one more night with Sam. One more night . . .

Sam was anxious to be on his way to California. He'd reluctantly delayed his leaving because Running Buffalo had asked him to join a hunting party the next day. He knew Lacey would consider his absence an opportunity to flee with Andy, so he'd asked Yellow Bird to keep Lacey and Andy apart and under observation at all times. Yellow Bird had readily agreed, but an unexplained anxiety tugged at him. Sam knew that Lacey was looking for an opportunity to flee with Andy, but he trusted Yellow Bird, and he didn't want to insult Running Buffalo by refusing to join the hunt after the Indian chief had befriended him.

That evening Sam returned to the tipi to take supper with Lacey. They had spoken only briefly these past few days, and he felt a compelling need to soothe things between them. He was conflicted where Lacey was concerned. Trusting her again would be difficult, given their troubled past, but loving her would be so easy.

He found Lacey alone. "May I share your meal tonight?"

"If you like. I always cook," Lacey said, "even though you prefer to take your meals elsewhere."

"Where's Andy?"

"Sitting Bear asked Andy to spend the night with him, and I didn't have the heart to deny him." She dished up a bowl of venison stew and handed it to him along with a piece of Indian bread.

Sam accepted the food and sat across from her. "This is very good," he said around a mouthful of savory stew.

Lacey gazed at him across the fire. "Is there something in particular you wished to discuss with me?"

"I'm joining the hunting party tomorrow. Will you promise to be here when I return?"

"I said I'd go to California with you," Lacey hedged.

"I know what you *said*," Sam said pointedly. "I want to know if I can trust you not to flee with Andy while I'm gone."

"That doesn't deserve an answer," Lacey returned shortly.

"I'm taking that to mean I can trust you this time," Sam said, aware that he was placing more trust in Lacey than she deserved. If they were to travel to California together, the distrust between them had to end, and if she was willing to give her word, he would rely on her to keep it.

Lacey gnawed the underside of her lip as she pondered the answer to Sam's question. Should she refuse to give her promise, Sam might decide not to join the hunting party, ruining a good chance to escape. On the other hand, if she did give her word and broke it, the lie would destroy all hopes for a future relationship. Damned if she did and damned if she didn't. Whatever she did, Sam would have one more reason to hate her. In the end, Lacey did what she had to do. She lied.

"I'll be here when you return, Sam."

Sam seemed to relax visibly, but guilt made Lacey lower her gaze to her bowl. She couldn't look him in the eye for fear he'd know that she was lying. To her relief, Sam merely nodded and continued eating.

Lacey's gaze returned to Sam, aware that this was probably the last time she'd ever see him, the last time they would be together. Her eyes lingered on his face, memorizing every unforgettable feature and storing it where she could bring it back during those long, lonely days and nights to come.

Sam's face had character. Strong and ruggedly handsome, it held the strength of conviction and the stubbornness of a man who rarely backed down once he made a decision.

Six years ago Sam's body merely gave hint of the strength he would one day command, and the promise had become reality. Sam's toned body and rippling muscles provided ample proof of his vigor and virility. The thought of Sam's virility made Lacey's mouth go dry. Sam was the only man who had made love to her, but she knew intuitively that no other man would please her like Sam.

She wanted him. Denying that truth would be lying. If only . . . An outrageous thought suddenly occurred. Why not? She and Sam were alone, and the night stretched before them. If she could experience his loving one more time, she could hold the memory in her heart forever. It would be a wonderfully erotic reminiscence to draw upon in the years to come.

Sam set down his bowl. His eyes were shuttered as he searched her face. Could he sense her need? Lacey wondered.

"I don't like this coldness between us, Lacey," Sam whispered. "We have a son in common. We're still married until the annulment is granted. I wish . . ."

A treacherous warmth began to spread through her. "Tell me, Sam. Perhaps we wish for the same thing."

A tentative smile stretched his lips. "Perhaps we do." He stared at her lips. Lacey licked moisture onto their suddenly dry surface, unaware of the provocative nature of her innocent act. No words came to mind as her lips parted in blatant invitation. Sam seemed to harbor the same need as he stood and pulled her up into his arms.

"Whatever else stands between us, love, we'll always have this," he whispered raggedly. "Our bodies know what they want, whether or not our minds agree. Will you let me love you tonight? I've missed you."

Let him? She'd die if he didn't. "Love me, Sam, oh, please, love me."

His hands tightened on her shoulders, his body already hardening as his mouth tilted over hers, hard, demanding, his tongue nudging her lips apart with a heated thrust. Laccy heard him groan, felt her knees quaking, her heart pounding. Sam had but to touch her and she went up in flame.

She breathed in his scent. His hand closed around her breast, and he whispered another groan of pleasure into her mouth, a sound that pulsed feeling clear down to the center of her womanhood. The breath caught in her throat when her bodice parted beneath his fingertips and his warm, rough palm cupped her breast. Driven by need for this man, she threaded her fingers through his hair, caressed his cheek. She could feel the abrasive stubble of his day-old growth of beard, feel the warmth of his skin, the strength of his hard jaw.

Her hands slid downward, thrilling to the strong beat of his heart. Then she was lost in the fierce rhythm of his deep kiss, scarcely aware when he drew her down with him to her sleeping mat. His hands were shaking slightly when he removed her skirt and drew her drawers down her legs. She gasped his name when his fingers found the heart of her, touching, stroking, playing amid the slick folds until her body wept dewy tears.

His hand left her briefly to tear open his trousers. "You're ready for me, love. I'm coming inside you now."

In one fluid motion, Sam pulled her onto his lap so that she straddled him. A strangled cry left her throat when he thrust hard and deep inside her.

Grasping her buttocks with both hands, he rocked back and forth, the thick fullness of him sliding in and out of her tight sheath. She closed around him as if they had been made solely for one another. Her eyes drifted shut, and she gave herself up to the seductive rhythm of their joining, knowing this was the ultimate memory she would carry with her forever and beyond.

Sensations built one atop the other until the tension could no longer be contained. A ragged cry was torn from her as his forceful thrusts released her. Stars burst, thunder roared, pleasure exploded. Sam cried out her name and climaxed moments later.

The fire turned to ash in the firepit. A howling wind arose outside the tipi, rain lashed down from the heavens, but the lovers felt no cold, heard nothing but the beat of their hearts. After their first bout of lovemaking, Sam had stripped off his clothing and lain down beside her. He awakened her during the night and they made love again, and once again near dawn, shortly before Sam left her to join the hunting party.

Savoring the memories of Sam's loving, Lacey turned over and went back to sleep.

A cold, damp dawn greeted Sam as he saddled Galahad. He had left the tipi early in order to have a private moment with Yellow Bird before riding off. He saw her speaking with her brother. When she saw Sam, she made her way over to him.

"I have prepared food for you," Yellow Bird said shyly.

Sam accepted the hide bag of trail food and stuffed it into his saddlebags. "Thank you, Yellow Bird. I'm glad you're awake. I wanted a word with you before I left."

"Do not worry, Sam. I will look after An-dy and La-cey."

"Lacey has promised to be here when I return. It won't be necessary for you to guard her during my absence."

Yellow Bird's eyes narrowed. "La-cey told you this? Do you trust her?"

After a brief hesitation, Sam said, "I might live to regret it, but this time I'm giving her the benefit of the doubt."

"I hope you are not making a mistake, Sam," Yellow Bird said, allowing none of her elation to show.

Sam searched her face, then nodded curtly and rode off to join Running Buffalo.

A short time later Yellow Bird strode purposefully toward Lacey's tipi, not bothering to announce herself as she threw back the flap and ducked inside. "Why are you still sleeping? Do you not wish to leave? Why did you promise Sam you would be here when he returned?"

Lacey stretched languidly beneath the blanket. She hadn't excepted Yellow Bird to arrive before she had time to wash and dress. "Is it time?" She rose up on her elbows. "I told Sam what he wanted to hear. I regret lying, but I had no choice."

Yellow Bird sniffed the air, her nose wrinkling in distaste. Her voice was rife with recrimination. "You and

Sam shared a mat last night. The proof of your joining lingers in the air. Perhaps you did not lie to Sam. Perhaps you no longer wish to leave."

Lacey glared at Yellow Bird. "Sam is my husband. What we do is none of your concern," she said defensively. "I lied to Sam for Andy's sake. Andy would be miserable if Sam took him away from Texas. He's too young for the life Sam has planned for him. Sam will always be on the run, looking over his shoulder for the law. Andy needs stability."

"You have made a wise choice," Yellow Bird said complacently. "I will fetch your horse and bring Andy to you."

"How will you handle Sam's anger?"

"Do not worry about Sam. I will ease his sorrow. I will see that he does not miss you or his son."

Turning abruptly, Yellow Bird left the tipi, her words lingering behind to taunt Lacey. Was Yellow Bird right? she wondered. Probably. Why would Sam miss her when Yellow Bird was more than eager to offer comfort?

Dismissing her painful thoughts, Lacey dressed hurriedly and left the tipi. There was nothing to take; everything she owned was on her back.

Andy stood beside Yellow Bird, a puzzled expression on his little face.

"Mama, Yellow Bird said we're leaving. Where are we going? Why can't we wait for Papa?"

Lacey opened her arms and Andy ran into them. "We can't wait for your papa, honey. We have to leave now."

"Where are we going?"

"Home."

"To the ranch? Without Papa?"

"I'll explain later," Lacey said as she lifted him into the saddle.

"But . . . but, Mama, what about Papa?"

Lacey mounted behind Andy. "It's too complicated to explain right now."

Ever astute, Andy said, "Papa doesn't know we're leaving, does he? Do I have to leave Sitting Bear? I don't have any friends to play with at the ranch."

"What about Rusty and the hands? They're all your friends."

"It's not the same," Andy said sullenly. "You go without me. I'll wait here for Papa."

Lacey sighed. "Don't be difficult, Andy. There are reasons we must leave now."

"There are provisions in your saddlebags," Yellow Bird said. "Take care of Andy. He is a good boy and I have grown fond of him."

Lacey kneed her mare and they shot forward, leaving the Indian village and memories of loving Sam behind. She might even be carrying his child. It wasn't something she'd regret, for then she'd have another part of Sam to love.

Darkness had descended by the time Lacey and a weary Andy reached the ranch. No one was about; it was suppertime and the cookhouse was ablaze with light. Lacey debated whether to make her presence known immediately or wait until the hands finished their dinner. The choice was taken from her when the cookhouse door opened and Rusty stepped outside. He headed toward the barn, saw Lacey and stopped dead in his tracks.

"Miz Lacey, is that you? Praise God, you're home."

He hurried over, lifted Andy from the saddle and

helped her to dismount. "Are you all right?"

"We're both fine, Rusty. Come into the house and tell me what's been going on in my absence."

"I'll carry the boy," Rusty said, scooping Andy into his arms. "The poor mite looks plumb tuckered out."

"I have a friend named Sitting Bear, Rusty," Andy said. "He's my age. I've never had a friend my age before."

"Sounds like you had a grand time, Andy," Rusty replied.

They had just reached the porch when the door flew open and Rita rushed out. "Señora! Andy! *Por Dios*, you are home."

"Rita, what are you doing here this late?"

"Rita's been staying at the house since you left," Rusty explained. "She wanted to be here when you returned. We're all powerful happy to have you home again, Miz Lacey."

"Sí, señora," Rita agreed. "It is true. Are you hungry? I can have something ready pronto."

"Take Andy to the kitchen and feed him, Rita. I'll have something later. Rusty is going to catch me up on what's happened on the ranch during my absence."

"Sí, Señora." Rita looked past Lacey, a frown disturbing her brow. "Is Señor Sam with you?"

Lacey flushed and looked away. "No. Sam won't be returning to the ranch."

Andy picked up on her answer immediately. "That's not true, Mama. Papa wouldn't let you take me away if he thought he'd never see me again."

"That's enough, Andy," Lacey said crossly. When Andy's face puckered up as if he were on the verge of tears, Lacey realized she'd spoke too harshly and immediately regretted it.

"I'm sorry, honey, Mama is tired. I need to talk to Rusty first; then I'll explain why we had to return home without your papa. Go along with Rita. I know you're hungry."

"All right, Mama," Andy sniffed as he allowed Rita to take his hand and lead him away.

"Come into my office, Rusty. I imagine a lot has happened in my absence."

Lacey seated herself behind the desk. Rusty plopped down in the chair Lacey indicated. "Start with the cattle, Rusty. How do they fare? Any more attempts to rustle them?"

"The herd is just fine. They've been moved down from the pastures for the winter," Rusty answered. "They'll be ready to drive to the market come spring. I know you need the money."

"Unfortunately, the money from the sale of the herd won't be enough. My only hope is that the bank will accept my anticipated profits from the sale as collateral for a loan to pay my back taxes. Has Taylor Cramer been around?"

"He came out once, after his aborted attack on the Indian village. He told us Sam wouldn't let Andy leave and that you wouldn't leave without Andy. He said Sam told you to leave but you refused. We haven't seen hide nor hair of him since. I can understand why you wouldn't want to leave Andy, and I knew Sam wouldn't hurt either of you, but Cramer was powerful angry."

"I can imagine," Lacey said dryly. "I arrived at the Indian camp in the nick of time, Rusty. Taylor and his ruffians launched a surprise attack shortly after my arrival, only it wasn't a surprise since Sam had heeded my warning. I'm sure Taylor's men would have killed indiscriminately, without a care for Andy's welfare. Had I not arrived when I did, innocent people would have been cut down without warning and I could have lost Andy and . . . Sam."

"I'm surprised Cramer didn't return to the Indian village for another try. I wonder why he didn't appeal to the sheriff for help. Sam *is* wanted by the law."

"That is a puzzle," Lacey said. "I can understand why hired ruffians wouldn't want to go up against Indians, but that doesn't explain why Taylor didn't bring the law into it. The Indian village is small, and a sheriff's posse could have easily overrun the camp."

"Maybe Cramer never reported the incident to the sheriff," Rusty ventured.

"I'll ride into town in a day or two and see if I can learn what Taylor is up to. For some unknown reason, he wants the B&G badly enough to marry me."

"The grazing is good when we have enough rain, but not any better than Cramer's land," Rusty offered. "Water might be a consideration, but the same river runs through both your land and Cramer's. It's a pure puzzle to me, Miz Lacey."

"I'm puzzled, too," Lacey said on a sigh. "I wonder if my marriage to Sam has been annulled yet."

"I don't know, but I'll be sad to see it happen. How did you convince Sam to let you take Andy?"

Lacey took a sudden interest in her fingernails. "I didn't convince him. He went off with a hunting party. I promised I wouldn't leave while he was gone."

"You lied?" Rusty said on a note of disbelief. "That ain't like you, Miz Lacey."

"I did it for Andy's sake," Lacey defended. "Sam is a wanted man. Andy's future was at stake. What kind of life would my son have with a man on the run?"

"I reckon you did the right thing," Rusty reluctantly admitted, "but I ain't so sure Sam will agree. He might show up at the ranch mad as a hornet."

In her mind, Lacey pictured Sam and Yellow Bird intimately entwined on a sleeping mat. "That won't happen. Sam appreciates his freedom too much to return. Showing his face around these parts would be dangerous."

"What about Cramer. You ain't gonna marry him, are you?"

Lacey's face hardened. "No, but perhaps I'll let him think I will. Taylor is up to something, Rusty, I'm just not sure what. Don't worry, I'd give up the ranch before marrying Taylor. He would have let his hirelings kill Andy had I not intervened. I couldn't marry a man like that."

"Them words warm my heart, Miz Lacey. I appreciate your confiding in me." He searched her face. "You look worn out. Go get yourself something to eat and go to bed."

"I will, Rusty. You've been a good friend to me and Andy."

"Hob asked me to look after you before he died, and that's what I aim to do." He rose to leave. "Just don't start getting too curious about Taylor. It might be dangerous."

"I'll take care, Rusty."

Lacey went to the kitchen after Rusty left, intending to collect her son and tuck him into bed. She found Rita there alone.

"Where's Andy?"

Rita smiled. "The poor kid fell asleep before he finished his meal. You were with Rusty, so I carried him up to bed myself. Sit down, señora. I kept your food hot. Eat; then it's up to bed with you."

Lacey appreciated Rita for more reasons than she could count, just as she did Rusty and the hands. Not only were they protective of her and Andy but they had made allowances for her lack of ranching skills. But she was learning, and God willing, she'd not lose the ranch she so loved.

Lacey ate sparingly of the food Rita placed before her, then trudged up to bed, more weary than she had imagined. She'd gotten little sleep the night before and had ridden hard to reach the ranch by nightfall. Without bothering to undress, she flopped across the bed and fell immediately asleep.

Sam and the hunting party returned to camp triumphant. The game had been plentiful and the women had set to work immediately, dressing the meat and setting it out over the fire to dry in preparation for their trek south. Sam looked for Lacey among the women and failed to find her. When he saw Yellow Bird hurrying over to greet him, a terrible premonition set his heart to pounding.

The expression on Yellow Bird's face was contrite, and Sam's fears escalated. "I am sorry, Sam."

Sam dismounted, gripping Yellow Bird's shoulders hard enough to elicit a groan of pain. Immediately his hands fell away.

"What is it, Yellow Bird? Tell me. Has something happened to Lacey or Andy?"

"You told me La-cey would not leave, that she promised to be here when you returned."

Sam's mind raced. "Lacey's gone? Are you sure? Did Andy go with her?"

Yellow Bird nodded. "La-cey took An-dy with her."

Sam cursed fluently. "She promised! I trusted her! Damn her to hell! She lied. She looked me in the eye and deliberately lied."

Sam set his foot in the stirrups and started to mount.

"Where are you going?"

"After my son."

Yellow Bird tugged urgently at Sam's leg. "You arc not thinking clearly, Sam. Do you wish to spend your life in prison? That is what will happen if you return for your son. Let them both go."

"You don't understand, Yellow Bird. I didn't know I had a son until a few months ago. I love that boy, and I don't want to spend my life without him."

"You have no choice, Sam. La-cey lied to you. She cannot be trusted. She told me she does not want you. She is going to marry another man."

Sam released his foot from the stirrup. "Lacey told you that? When?"

"Many times. She made no attempt to hide her scorn for you when we spoke together. I saw her shortly before she left. I asked her to walk to the river with me to fetch water. She declined. If I'd had any idea she planned to leave, I would not have left her. She and Andy were gone when I returned."

A wealth of emotions coursed through Sam, but he couldn't say precisely which one hurt the most. Once again he had trusted unwisely, and once again Lacey had betrayed him. After the passionate night they'd spent together, he'd been so sure that things would work out for them. He wouldn't make that mistake again.

Sam had been anxious to return to camp and tell Lacey that he believed her about everything, that he trusted her. He'd already accepted that she hadn't betrayed him to the Yankees, and that the sheriff had learned about the bank robbery from another source, but he had trusted in vain. He'd become so enthralled with Lacey that he believed all her lies. How could he have been so gullible?

Yellow Bird tugged on Sam's arm. "Come with me. I have food prepared. You are tired and not thinking clearly. When you've had time to think, you will realize that La-cey's leaving is for the best. I can be everything she was not to you, Sam."

Sam shrugged her aside. Nothing Yellow Bird said registered above the sounds of anger roaring through his head. He valued her friendship, but she couldn't reach him on a personal level. Not like Lacey, who had reached him on every level possible between a man and woman. What a fool he'd been, he thought as he strode angrily toward the beckoning silence of the forest.

"Sam, where are you going?"

"Somewhere to think."

"I will come with you."

"Suit yourself, but I warn you, I won't be fit company."

"La-cey is a bad woman," Yellow Bird said, running to keep up with him. "Let me comfort you."

Sam stormed into the darkest part of the forest, then abruptly dropped down beneath a lofty elm. He paid little heed to Yellow Bird as she sat down beside him. Sam's thoughts ran amok. If he went to California, he'd never see Andy again. If he stuck around here, however, he could end up in jail. What a mess he'd gotten himself into. He would have been better off if he'd never encountered Lacey again or learned he had a son. But he did have a son—one he couldn't abandon.

"What are you thinking, Sam?"

"About the cruel jests life plays on unsuspecting fools."

"I would not be cruel to you, Sam. Do not leave. Come with me to our winter camping grounds. Let me be the woman you need."

Sam stared at her, seeing the woman who had saved his life, a woman who would never betray him, a woman who freely offered the love Lacey withheld. Could Yellow Bird provide the solace he craved?

Grasping her slender shoulders, he pulled her against him, molding her soft body to his. No time like the present to find out, he thought as he lowered his head and pressed a kiss to her eager lips.

Chapter Fourteen

Kissing Yellow Bird was a mistake. There was no fire, no uncontrollable passion, no sensation except a pleasant feeling of soft lips opening beneath his. Even as her body moved sensually against him, his mind began to reject her. His sex was limp, not even close to arousal. Perhaps he was tired.

He tried again, pulling Yellow Bird beneath him, touching her breasts, cupping her between her legs. Still nothing. What the hell was wrong with him? He'd never had a problem bedding a woman before, no matter how exhausted he was. Damn Lacey! What had she done to him? He rolled away and lay on his back, one arm flung over his eyes.

"Sam, please do not stop."

"It's no good, Yellow Bird. I can't do this. Any man would be proud to make you his. It's not you; it's me."

"I won't give up, Sam. I can wait. One day you will come to me. I do not want you to go to California."

Sam sat up, gazing absently into the distance. After a long pause, he said, "I can't go to California and leave Andy behind. Perhaps I *will* go with your people to their winter camp. It's not nearly as far away as California."

"Running Buffalo will be pleased. You make me very happy, Sam Gentry."

"Don't hold any false hopes, Yellow Bird. I can't give you what you want."

"One day I will change your mind, Sam. I will never give up on you."

Sam felt nothing but pity for Yellow Bird. He wasn't capable of loving her, either emotionally or physically. He'd suspected it for a long time and now he was certain. And he knew the reason why. He'd never stopped loving Lacey despite her many betrayals, despite his efforts to forget her over the years.

"Go find your bed," Sam said gruffly. "The hour grows late."

There was a dull sameness to her days since Lacey returned to the ranch. She immersed herself in bookwork, trying to balance the losses against the meager profits, but nothing had changed since the last time she'd gone over the figures. She still owed five years back taxes, which were due the last day of the month, only three weeks away. If Uncle Hob had told her about his financial woes before he died, she wouldn't have been so shocked when she learned the truth.

Andy moped around as if he'd lost his best friend, and nothing Lacey said or did seemed to lighten his mood. He asked about Sam so often that Lacey was forced to tell him that Sam had to leave Texas to keep from going to prison. To Andy's credit, he steadfastly refused to believe that Sam was capable of committing a crime.

Lacey chose a mild, sunny day to ride to town to reapply for a loan. The first time she'd asked she'd been turned down, but this time she had a healthy herd waiting to go to market. She considered it a good bargaining point, but would the bank? After the spring drive, she'd have hard cash in her hand as proof that the ranch was profitable. But that was spring and this was now.

Lacey went to the barn for her horse. Andy skipped up to join her. "Are you going somewhere, Mama?"

"I have business in town, honey. I won't be long."

"Can I come?"

"Not this time. Rita will keep an eye on you."

"What if Papa comes and wants me to go with him again?"

Lacey dropped to one knee, her hands lightly grasping Andy's slender shoulders. "I explained why Sam won't be returning to the ranch, Andy. You're getting your hopes up for nothing."

"Papa isn't an outlaw," Andy said belligerently.

"I don't believe he is, either, but the law thinks so. Why don't you see if Rita has taken the cookies she was baking out of the oven? I'll bet she has some nice fresh milk to go with them."

"You think?" Andy said, his eyes alight with pleasure. "I hope the cookies have chocolate in them."

"I wouldn't be surprised," Lacey said as Andy ran off. She wished she could be so easily distracted. There seemed to be no end to her worries. If it wasn't the ranch, it was Sam.

Sam. Did he hate her for lying to him? Had he turned to Yellow Bird for comfort? Lacey had been torn between her son's welfare and her love for a man who didn't deserve it. In the end, her son had come first. She'd had to deny her own feelings to keep Andy from being hurt. That was what a mother did, even if it broke her heart.

Lacey rode at a leisurely pace, planning to reach the bank about the time it opened. The shade on the bank door was just being raised when Lacey drew rein at the front entrance. Dismounting, she draped the reins over the hitching post and waited for the clerk to unlock the door.

"Lacey! Is that you? Thank God you've returned!"

Lacey spun around, stiffening when she saw Taylor Cramer hailing her from across the street. He was standing in front of the saloon, talking to some unsavory-looking cowboys. She kept her distaste under control as he hurried over to join her.

"Lacey, I'm so glad you're safe! I've been worried sick about you and decided to hire men for another rescue attempt." He gestured toward the cowboys milling around him. "We were just discussing strategy." There was a biting edge to his voice when he said, "I'm surprised Gentry let you go."

"I'm here—that's all that matters," Lacey said. "You

251

no longer need those men. Pay them off and let them go."

"What about Andy? Is he still with Gentry?"

"No. Andy is home with me."

"Wonderful," Cramer said with little enthusiasm. "I have good news for you. That's why I was anxious to get you away from Gentry. Your annulment has been granted. You're a free woman, Lacey. We can marry immediately. Today, if you like."

A buzzing began in Lacey's head. She was no longer married to Sam. After six years she really was free. Why did that make her feel so sad?

"I can't marry you, Taylor."

Cramer's eyes narrowed. "Of course you can."

"No, I can't. Not after the way you and your hirelings charged into the Indian camp. Andy could have been killed."

Cramer's fists clenched at his sides. "I would have watched out for Andy. I was very angry with you for warning Gentry, but I've forgiven you."

"You forgave *me?"*

His voice lowered. "I still want you, Lacey."

"Why?" Lacey asked. "It's my land you want, isn't it, Taylor? What's so special about the B&G?"

"Nothing. Nothing at all. It's always been you."

"Liar."

Cramer had the decency to flush. "Look, Lacey, if you can't come up with the back taxes by the end of the month, you and Andy will be turned out of your home. You'll have nothing. Winter is coming. Where will you go? What will you do? Marrying me is a simple solution. I can pay your taxes."

"I haven't given up on a bank loan," Lacey insisted.

"I'm going to reapply for one today. Beef is in demand back East after the lean war years, and my herd should bring a good price come spring. I'm hoping that will influence Mr. Markle to change his mind about the loan."

"Don't count on it," Cramer said. "When you come to me for help, you'll find that my offer won't be as generous as it is now." He tipped his hat. "Good day, Lacey."

Lacey's fondest hope was that she'd never have to rely on Taylor Cramer for help. With that thought in mind, she squared her shoulders and marched into the bank. She asked for Mr. Markle, and after a slight wait was ushered into the banker's office.

Markle stood politely. "What can I do for you, Mrs. Gentry?"

Lacey cleared her throat. "You've turned down my loan once, Mr. Markle, but I'm hoping you will reconsider."

Markle sighed. "Please sit down, Mrs. Gentry, and tell me why I should change my mind."

"I have over five hundred head of cattle waiting to go to market in the spring. I'm expecting at least fifteen dollars a head, maybe more. The market is good right now. But the money will be too little, too late, and it won't be enough to cover the five years of back taxes Uncle Hob owed. The money is due in full by the end of the year."

"I'm aware of your circumstances," Markle said.

"Yes, well, I'm hoping the sale of my herd in the spring will be sufficient collateral for a loan."

"How much do you require?"

"Thirty-five hundred dollars. Enough to pay the loan,

meet the payroll and satisfy my creditors."

Markle cleared his throat. "Not an inconsiderable sum."

"I stand to lose my home if the bank doesn't come through for me."

"You have to understand the bank's position on this," Markle intoned dryly. "The risk is too much for the bank to bear. Many things could keep your herd from reaching the railhead. Jayhawkers are active in Kansas. Can you pay the forfeit they demand for letting your cattle pass through? Weather is another factor. There are stampedes and river crossings to deal with. You're bound to lose a portion of your herd, which is rather small by Texas standards."

"Our herd is small because it was decimated by drought and disease. Uncle Hob was unable to buy more stock due to lack of funds."

"I understand your husband recently showed up after a lengthy period of estrangement," Markle ventured. "Perhaps if he applied for a loan in his name, the board of directors might be inclined to grant it. The bank is reluctant to loan money to a woman. They have done so a time or two in the past and suffered severe losses."

Lacey studied her fingernails. "Mr. Gentry and I are no longer married. Our marriage has been annulled."

"I see. Weren't you supposed to marry Taylor Cramer before your husband showed up? Once you wed Cramer, you won't need a bank loan. Mr. Cramer is a wealthy man."

"At present, I have no plans to remarry. Is that your final decision, Mr. Markle?"

"I'm sorry, Mrs. Gentry, but there is nothing more I can do for you. Perhaps a larger bank in a different city might be willing to bear the loss should you be unable to repay the loan."

Lacey rose with dignity despite her bitter disappointment. "I won't waste anymore of your time, Mr. Markle. Good day."

Lacey left the bank in a daze. She felt as if her life were falling apart. Sam was gone, there was no hope of saving her ranch, and Andy blamed her for taking him away from his father. Matters couldn't get any worse.

Of one thing Lacey was certain. She wasn't going to marry Taylor or sell him the ranch. She'd have to make plans for the future after she and Andy were evicted, but those plans didn't include Taylor Cramer. If he wanted the ranch so badly, let him bid for it on the courthouse steps when it was sold for back taxes.

Lacey had one more stop to make before she returned home. She wanted to visit the land office. There had to be some reason Taylor wanted her land. She was leading her mare toward the land office when the sheriff hailed her.

"Mrs. Gentry, can you spare a minute?"

Lacey waited for the sheriff to catch up to her. "Did you wish to speak with me, Sheriff?"

"That I did, Mrs. Gentry. I'll bet you were happy to hear your husband has been cleared of charges stemming from that bank robbery in Dodge. I wanted to apologize in person for the law's mistake. Have you seen him? I hope he wasn't seriously wounded. It was a terrible mistake."

Lacey stared at him. "I . . . I don't understand. Are you saying that Sam is no longer wanted by the law? How long have you known?"

Hale's brow furrowed. "Some weeks now. I received

a telegram from Sheriff Diller in Dodge stating that the Gentry brothers have been exonerated. He thought I should know since Denison was the last place Sam Gentry was seen. Your husband has nothing to fear from the law."

"Why didn't you tell me?" Her voice shook with barely suppressed anger. "You had no right to keep something as important as that from me."

Hale looked properly abashed. "I'm sorry, Mrs. Gentry, but I thought you knew."

"How could I know? You never told me."

"I intended to ride out to your place to give you the news as soon as I heard. Then I happened to bump into Mr. Cramer. He said he was riding out to the B&G and would tell you himself. I figured it would save me a trip out there, so I agreed. I had no reason to believe Mr. Cramer would deliberately withhold the information from you."

Lacey's first thought was that this was something Sam needed to know. It could change the course of his life. Of their lives.

"Thank you, Sheriff. I'll see that Sam receives the good news."

"Tell him he's welcome back in Denison, and that I hope he bears no grudge against me or the posse. We were only doing our job."

His words barely registered as Lacey swung into the saddle and rode off. Instead of heading straight home, she made a slight detour to Taylor Cramer's spread. She drew rein in a cloud of dust and flying hooves and leaped from the saddle. Mindless of the curious stares following her, she walked up the front steps and pounded vigorously on the door.

Cramer opened the door himself. A slow smile stretched his lips. "Lacey, I see you've come to your senses. Which will it be? Are we to marry or will you sell me the ranch?"

Lacey shoved open the door and strode past him. She halted in the foyer and spun around to confront him, her face a mask of fury. "Damn you, Taylor Cramer! Why didn't you tell me Sam had been exonerated?"

Cramer's expression immediately turned wary. "Where did you hear that?"

"I ran into the sheriff in town. He said you were supposed to deliver that information to me. But that didn't meet with your plans, did it? You wanted me to believe Sam was still wanted by the law. Do you know what your omission cost me? Cost Sam? You'll never have my ranch, Taylor. I'll beg, borrow or steal the money to keep you from having my property."

"Simmer down, Lacey," Cramer cajoled. "You're well rid of Gentry. The man cares nothing for you. If he did, he wouldn't have abandoned you."

"What happened between me and Sam a long time ago has nothing to do with this—with us. What did you expect to gain by letting us believe Sam was still wanted by the law?"

"You know damn well what I wanted," Cramer snarled. "I wanted Sam Gentry out of your life. He was a complication I hadn't counted on. It seems I succeeded. Gentry is gone, and you are no longer married to him."

He moved closer, his demeanor abruptly changing. "Let's put all this behind us, my dear. I really do want you, Lacey. It's more than the land."

"I doubt that," Lacey spat. "I'll never forgive you,

Taylor. If you want the B&G, you'll have to bid for it on the courthouse steps. Get out of my way."

Lacey shoved him aside and charged out the door. "Stay away from me, Taylor. My hands have instructions to shoot trespassers."

Lacey fumed all the way home. She couldn't begin to count what Taylor had cost her. Because of him, her marriage to Sam had been annulled. If Sam had known he was no longer a wanted man, there would have been no reason for him to go into hiding. He'd been hunted and wounded like a dog for a crime he didn't commit, and Taylor had known all along that Sam was guiltless. How could she have ever thought Taylor Cramer was interested in her welfare? What a fool she'd been to believe he cared for her.

Lacey rode into the yard and dismounted. Lefty ran up to take the reins.

"Is Rusty around, Lefty?"

"He's in the tack room, Miz Lacey."

"Thank you." Lacey hurried off. She needed to talk to someone, and Rusty was the only one who would understand.

Lacey entered the tack room. The scent of leather and horses was overpowering, but it wasn't an unpleasant smell. Lacey knew she would miss everything about the ranch after she was forced from her home.

Rusty saw her immediately. "Did you get the loan, Miz Lacey?"

"I need someone to talk to, Rusty."

Concern colored his words. "What is it? Did something happen in town?"

"Yes. Something good. I spoke with the sheriff. The charges against Sam and his brothers were dropped some time go. Sam is no longer wanted by the law."

A smile lit up Rusty's craggy features. "Glory be! Is this something Sheriff Hale just learned?"

"No, and that's the problem. He's known for a long time. Taylor Cramer was supposed to tell me but conveniently forgot to mention it. Everything that's happened since needn't have happened at all."

Rusty spit out an oath. "Do I have your permission to shoot Cramer if he shows up here again?"

"You can run him off my land, but shooting him will only get you in trouble."

"What are you gonna do? Sam needs to know the charges against him have been dropped."

"My sentiments exactly. I'm going to return to the Indian village and tell him. He might not welcome me, but he'll surely welcome the news I bring."

"I'll ride along with you."

"No need for that. I can find the camp on my own."

"You ain't going alone, Miz Lacey, and that's final. How soon do you want to leave?"

"First thing in the morning. It's too late to start out now. I hope and pray Sam is still there. He might be on his way to California by now, and the Indians may have left for their winter grounds."

"I'll saddle the horses and be ready to leave first thing tomorrow morning," Rusty said.

Lacey headed out the door. "I'll be ready."

"Miz Lacey, before you go, did you learn anything in town about your land, or why Cramer might want it?"

"I never got to the land office. I did get to the bank, though—not that it did me any good. Mr. Markle turned down my request for a loan. Then I learned about Sam and was anxious to come home and make plans. When

I return, the first thing I'll do is find out why Taylor is so eager to get his hands on my land."

Lacey went to the house, anxious to talk to Andy. She found him in the kitchen with a big piece of cake in front of him. His eyes lit up when he saw her.

"Mama! You're home. Did you take care of your business?"

"Yes, honey, I did. I also learned something that should make you happy."

"You saw Papa!"

"No, son, but I did learn that Sam is no longer wanted by the law. The charges have been dropped."

Andy squinted, as if trying to digest what Lacey had just told him. Apparently, it was too much for his five-year-old mind. "What does that mean, Mama?"

"It means that your papa can come home without fear of being sent to prison. The law doesn't want him anymore. He's a free man."

Andy let out a yelp of delight. "Can we go to Running Buffalo's camp and tell him?"

"Rusty and I are leaving first thing in the morning. I can't take you with me this time."

"Aw, Mama, I want to be the one to tell Papa he can come home."

"Sorry, honey, but I'll tell him for you. I'm sure he'll want to see you as soon as he knows he's free to return."

"Promise?" Andy said.

"Promise."

Lacey prayed she wouldn't have to break her promise. What if Sam decided not to return? What if he had already left for California, believing he was still wanted by the law? What if he loved Yellow Bird?

After supper that night, Lacey tucked Andy in bed and

sought her own bed. She wanted to be well rested when she started out for the Indian camp in the morning. And she had to prepare herself for disappointment if Sam had already left for California.

Lacey and Rusty left early the following morning. They reached the Indian village at sundown. Lacey's heart plummeted when she saw that nothing remained of the camp except cold fire pits.

"This is the place, I'm sure of it," Lacey cried.

"They were here, all right," Rusty concurred as he hunkered beside one of the fire pits and examined the contents. "I'd say they left three, maybe four days ago. The women and children will be walking. I could easily catch up with them."

Tears of remorse dampened Lacey's cheeks. "For what purpose? Sam won't be with them."

"Maybe, maybe not. If Sam's not with them, they can at least tell me if he rode west like he planned."

Lacey shook her head. "It's too late. We'll stay here for the night and return home tomorrow. I hope I can find the words to explain to Andy why his papa won't be coming home."

The farther Sam rode away from the B&G, the more he regretted leaving. Nothing was right in his world. He wasn't an outlaw, and he shouldn't have to be on the run, worrying about when the law would catch up to him. He should be with Andy, teaching his son how to ride and all the other things a son learns from his father.

Sam tried to blame Lacey for the problems he'd encountered in Texas, but his heart knew it wasn't true. The Wanted posters would have caught up to him sooner or later. The more he thought about Lacey lying to him and taking Andy away, the more he realized that she'd been acting in Andy's best interests. Sam was angry, but he understood. He'd taken Andy away without Lacey's permission, and that was just as bad. Of course, he'd had a good reason. Taylor Cramer would make Andy's life miserable, and he didn't want that for his son.

Sam glanced over his shoulder at the long line of women and children trudging after the packhorses. Three days on the trail had left them weary and haggard. The life of an Indian woman was hard, Sam reflected. They were expected to raise and dismantle the tipis each night and morning and prepare food for their men. All the manual labor associated with everyday living, except for hunting, fell on their shoulders. He admired them a great deal. But he also admired Lacey for carrying on without him after she gave birth to Andy. It couldn't have been easy for her.

"Your mind is far away, friend," Running Buffalo observed as he rode up beside Sam. "Your woman and son are gone, and you are bitter."

"Lacey will take good care of Andy," Sam replied, "but I will miss him. I would go to him now if I dared."

"You are right to fear the white man's justice," Running Buffalo said sagely. "Will you remain with us? Yellow Bird is fond of you. She would accept you for her mate if you would have her."

"Yellow Bird deserves a man who will be around to provide for her," Sam said. "I am not that man."

"Your honesty speaks well for you, Sam. I value your friendship, but I believe as you do. My sister should choose a mate from among our people. Many braves have asked for her, but she has refused them. I have not forced her to accept one of them, for I respect her wishes to choose her own mate."

"Don't worry, Running Buffalo, I agree wholeheartedly. Your sister is lucky to have you for a brother."

"My sister is strong-willed. She will not easily give up on you."

"I don't want to cause any trouble, Running Buffalo. I have tried to discourage Yellow Bird, but I fear you are right. She is as determined as she is strong-willed. I've noticed some of the young braves aren't as friendly to me as they once were. They look upon me as a contender for Yellow Bird's affections. I don't want to cause dissention among your people. Perhaps I will go to California like I originally intended."

"It is your choice, Sam Gentry."

Though the chief hadn't asked him to leave, the conversation left little doubt in Sam's mind that Running Buffalo thought his sister's infatuation with Sam was damaging to the tribe. Sam was beginning to think the same thing. But he'd been too hurt to think clearly after Lacey had taken Andy away. The knowledge that Lacey had looked him in the eye and deliberately lied had plunged him into despondency.

Suddenly Sam's choice became clear. "Time has come for me to leave," he told Running Buffalo. "After I'm gone, tell Yellow Bird I left because I am not the right man for her."

"I will tell her. Will you go to California? Is it very far?"

"California is farther away than I want to be," Sam said, "but it will be a safe haven for me. In a few months I will travel to Denver, in Colorado, to meet my brothers. I pray all is well with them."

"Family is a good thing," Running Buffalo maintained. He searched Sam's face. "My heart tells me you do not wish to go to California."

"You must be a mind reader. You're right. I don't want to leave Andy behind. I might never see him again."

"I think it is your woman you do not wish to leave. Go to her, Sam. Your heart will not be at rest until you have made peace with her."

Sam thought about Running Buffalo's words the rest of the day. He was still deep in thought when he found a secluded spot away from the main camp that night and crawled into his bedroll. A sleepless hour later, Sam knew exactly what he was going to do. He wasn't going to California. He was going to Dodge City and try to clear his name. He didn't like being an outlaw. He and his brothers were innocent, and he was determined to prove it. Somehow he intended to make banker Wingate admit that the robbery was all a hoax.

Sam was nearly asleep when he heard a rustling noise in the grass. His hand curled around the hilt of his gun. But a weapon wasn't necessary, for moments later he heard a soft voice call out to him.

"Sam, I wish to speak to you. Are you awake?"

Sam cursed beneath his breath. "Dammit, Yellow Bird, you know better than to sneak up on a body in the middle of the night. Can't it wait till morning?"

"You are leaving." It was a statement, not a question.

"It's inevitable, Yellow Bird. Did Running Buffalo tell you?"

"No. It was something I sensed in my heart."

Sam smiled at Yellow Bird through darkness relieved only by diffused moonlight filtering through the canopy of trees above him. "I'll always remember you kindly, Yellow Bird."

"You're going back to *her*."

"I don't know," Sam said truthfully. "I do know I'm not going to California. I need to clear my name, and I can't do it in California. I'm not an outlaw and don't like being one."

"I am afraid for you, Sam."

He touched her cheek. "I'll survive."

"What you intend to do is dangerous."

"I want my son to be proud of me. I don't want him going through life thinking his father is an outlaw."

"What about La-cey? I think you care for her more than you care for me."

"It's really strange, Yellow Bird. For years I made myself forget that Lacey even existed. But seeing her again opened a floodgate of emotions. I wanted to hate her and almost succeeded. Maybe she did betray me to the Yankees and maybe she didn't. Maybe she did send a posse after me and maybe she didn't. She lied to me, and I can understand that. She wanted what was best for Andy."

"La-cey will marry a man your son hates."

"I'm not so sure about that," Sam said thoughtfully. "Lacey isn't a fool. She warned us about Cramer's attack because she knew there would be bloodshed. The bastard wanted me and Andy dead, and she'd never marry a man like that."

"I would have done anything for you, Sam, but I know now that I can never have you."

"You are better off without me, Yellow Bird. There are many fine braves eager to join with you."

"Perhaps one day," Yellow Bird said without conviction. "It is with much sorrow that I must tell you what I have done."

Sam tensed. "What are you talking about? What did you do?"

"I helped your woman and your son leave the village. I told La-cey that you and I were lovers, and that you did not want her."

Sam jerked upright. "That was a lie! We had reconciled the night before I joined the hunting party. I had hoped . . ." He sighed regretfully. "What's done is done. It's too late for recriminations."

"Forgive me, Sam," the Indian maiden choked out. "It was wrong of me."

"I forgive you, Yellow Bird. If Lacey hadn't wanted to leave, she wouldn't have gone."

"Good-bye, Sam. I will never forget you."

"Good-bye, Yellow Bird. I will always be grateful to you. You gave me life when I would have died, and your people sheltered me."

Yellow Bird was gone as silently as she had appeared. Sam closed his eyes. He thought of Lacey and what he had lost. He had no idea what the future held for them, or if they even had a future together, but he did know he couldn't go through life as an outlaw.

Chapter Fifteen

Lacey and Rusty returned to the ranch in a somber mood. Their sober expressions were enough to discourage questions, much to Lacey's relief. She was too distraught to discuss the situation with anyone. Unfortunately, she still had to face Andy.

As luck would have it, Andy was playing in the yard when she and Rusty arrived. His face lit up, and he raced over to meet them. Lacey dismounted and waited for him.

"Where's Papa?"

"You talk to the lad," Rusty said as he took charge of their horses.

Lacey's heart sank. She hated to dash Andy's hopes but she had no choice in the matter. Sam was never coming back, and the sooner he faced reality, the better off he'd be.

"Where's Papa?" Andy repeated.

"We'll discuss it inside, son," Lacey said.

Andy trotted along beside her, but she could tell by his expression that he'd already begun to suspect that something was amiss. Lacey went directly to the parlor, sat on the sofa and drew Andy onto her lap.

"This isn't easy for me, honey," Lacey began, "because I know it's going to hurt you."

Andy's lips trembled. "Didn't Papa want to come home?"

"We never found him. He already left for California."

"Won't I ever see him again?"

"I wouldn't go so far as to say that," Lacey hedged. "Sam could turn up when we least expect it."

A tear slipped from the corner of Andy's eye. "Can we go to California and look for Papa?"

"I'm afraid not."

"I'm never going to see Papa again," he said on a sob. "You lied to me."

"I'm sorry, Andy. I shouldn't have promised something I wasn't sure I could deliver. You got along without a father until Sam showed up; you can do it again."

Andy jumped off Lacey's lap, his expression belligerent. "I don't want to talk about it anymore. You lied to me!"

Whirling around, he ran off.

"Andy, wait!"

She heard the front door slam and started after him. By the time she reached the door, he was already out of sight. She stared out into the encroaching darkness, trying to decide whether or not to go after him. She realized he was in no mood to talk or listen to her and ultimately decided to leave him alone to work out his anger by himself. Andy was hurting, and not ready yet to listen to reason. As much as she wanted to take him in her arms and hold him, she knew he wouldn't be receptive.

Sighing despondently, she silently cursed Taylor Cramer for this turmoil in her life. She decided to wait until suppertime, and if Andy hadn't shown up by then, she'd go after him.

Andy returned to the house when Lacey called him in for supper two hours later. To her immense relief, he didn't mention their previous conversation as he washed up on the back porch and took his seat at the table. He remained strangely detached and uncommunicative throughout the meal, which worried Lacey. He merely nodded when spoken to and kept his eyes on his plate.

"I'm done, Mama. Can I please leave the table?" Andy asked in a small voice.

"We need to talk, honey."

"Not now, Mama. I'm tired."

"I'll come up and tuck you in later. We'll talk tomorrow, if you'd rather."

She watched Andy trudge up the stairs, her heart breaking for him as well as for herself.

Andy didn't go to bed immediately. With grim purpose, much like his father's, he stripped the case from his pillow and stuffed it with clothes and his favorite toys. Then he hid it under the bed and climbed beneath the covers. When Lacey came up to tuck him in, he pretended sleep. He waited until Lacey left and the house was dark before crawling from bed, retrieving his pillowcase and creeping down the stairs. Before he left the house, he made a detour to the kitchen in search of food.

He found two apples, half a loaf of bread, a hunk of cheese and a handful of cookies, which he stuffed into the pillowcase with his clothing. He knew California was a long way off, but he figured he'd be able to reach it in a couple of days. Dawn was still several hours away when he quietly let himself out of the house.

Andy remembered hearing that California was west of Texas, and he wandered aimlessly until sunrise. Then he turned west, away from the rising sun, recalling that the sun rose in the east.

Andy walked for hours before he felt the first pangs of thirst. He'd completely forgotten to bring water, but he wasn't too worried yet. There were plenty of creeks and streams in Texas, and even a river or two. He was bound to run into water soon.

Luck was with him. He did indeed find a stream. The pillowcase was heavy, and he set it down on the bank as he knelt and quenched his thirst. Once his thirst was quenched, he sat down to rest, leaning against a sturdy tree trunk. He was tired. Surely he must be close to California by now. Pleased at his progress, he closed his eyes and dozed off.

Andy's sleep was deep and peaceful. He didn't hear riders approaching, nor was he aware that one of the riders had dismounted and stood over him, a contemplative look on his face.

"Ain't that Lacey Gentry's son, boss?"

Taylor Cramer glanced at his foreman and nodded. "It is indeed, Harper. I wonder what he's doing out here all by himself."

"Wake him up and ask him," Harper suggested.

"Good idea," Cramer said as he nudged Andy with his toe.

Andy awoke with a start. He blinked, rubbed his eyes, and scrambled to his feet when he saw Cramer and his foreman.

"What are you doing out here, boy?" Cramer asked.

"I'm going to California to find my papa. Are you going to California, too?"

"Why would you think that?"

"This is the way to California, isn't it?"

Harper snickered.

Cramer ignored Andy's question. "Did you run away from home, boy?"

Andy's bottom lip quivered. "I wanted to find my papa."

Cramer stared at Andy through narrowed lids. Suddenly he smiled. "How would you like me to take you to California?"

"Why would you do that?" Andy asked suspiciously.

"Because I'm fond of you."

Andy grasped his pillowcase and backed away. "You don't like me and I don't like you. I can get to California on my own."

"I doubt that. Get him, Harper."

Though only five years old, Andy was astute enough to realize he was in trouble. Dropping his heavy bundle, he turned and ran. Harper kneed his horse and scooped Andy up, dangling the squirming bundle beneath his arm like a sack of potatoes.

"What should I do with him, boss?"

"Take him back to the house and lock him in the spare bedroom. Keep him out of sight. I don't want anyone to see him. I've got plans for young Gentry. He couldn't have chosen a better time to run away."

"You ain't gonna hurt him, are you?" Harper asked. "You know I'd do anything for you, but I draw the line at harming a lad barely out of diapers."

"Let me go!" Andy screeched at the top of his lungs. "I ain't no baby. I wanna go home."

"Don't worry, Harper. Young Master Gentry will come to no harm."

Harper rode off, apparently satisfied with Cramer's answer.

Lacey thought it odd when Andy didn't come down to breakfast, but she figured he was sulking in his room. She decided to let him sulk awhile. When he still hadn't stirred long after the breakfast hour came and went, she began to worry in earnest. A prickling sensation crawled up her spine as she climbed the stairs to Andy's room.

She opened the door, saw the empty bed and experienced a jolt of panic. Andy was gone! Had he risen early and left the house before anyone was stirring? Her heart began to pound, and she raced down the stairs, calling Andy's name. Rita came from the kitchen, wiping her hands on her apron.

"What is it, señora? Is Andy still angry?"

"He's gone, Rita! Do you suppose he's with Rusty? Or one of the hands?"

"Sí. Where else could he have gone?"

Andy wasn't with Rusty. Nor was he with any of the hands. They searched the barn, cookhouse, bunkhouse and tack room. Lacey even went down to the storm cellar and up to the attic, while Rita searched Andy's room for clues.

While in the attic, Lacey heard Rita call her name and came rushing down the rickety stairs. "What is it, Rita?"

"Andy's clothing is missing. And the pillowcase is gone from his bed. *Madre de Dios,* the niño ran away!"

Lacey grasped the wall to steady herself, her face drained of all color. The thought of Andy lost in the Texas wilderness nearly brought her to her knees.

"No! Andy wouldn't do such a thing."

Rita's dark eyes softened with pity. "He wanted his papa. He never knew a father's love until Señor Sam came along."

"Oh, God!" Lacey sobbed. "Andy wanted to go to California to find Sam. He can't have gotten far. I'll have Rusty and the hands out searching for him in no time. Our Andy will be back with us soon, Rita, I promise."

Lacey prayed she was right as she rushed off to alert Rusty and the hands. She found them gathered in front of the barn, awaiting the outcome of her search inside the house.

"Did you find Andy, Miz Lacey?" Rusty asked.

"No, Rusty, we didn't find him, but I think I know what happened."

"You don't suppose Sam took him, do you?"

"No, not this time. Sam's gone for good. Some of Andy's clothing is missing; so is the pillowcase from his bed. I think he ran away. He wanted to go to California to find his father. He's just a child; distance has no meaning for him. He's out there somewhere, lost and afraid. We've got to find him."

"Saddle up, boys," Rusty ordered. "Let's bring the lad back to his mother."

"I'm going with you," Lacey said.

*   *   *

It was late afternoon when Rusty came upon the pillow-case with Andy's belongings. Elated, he continued on, hopeful of finding Andy nearby. Near dusk, he crossed paths with Lacey and showed her the pillowcase stuffed with Andy's belongings.

"Where could he be?" Lacey wailed. "It's getting dark. He'll be frightened."

"Why don't you go home, Miz Lacey? Maybe Andy got cold and hungry and returned to the house. Me and the boys will keep searching. All night, if we have to."

"I don't know, Rusty—"

"Please, Miz Lacey. You ain't doing your son any good wearing yourself out."

Lacey gave a shaky sigh. "Perhaps you're right. Maybe Andy is home waiting for me now."

Lacey's hopes soared as she rode back to the ranch. Andy might have headed home as soon as it started to get dark. She'd probably find him in the kitchen with Rita, stuffing himself after going without breakfast and lunch. She even managed a smile as she rode into the yard and led her mare into the barn.

"Sorry, girl," she said, patting the mare on the rump. "No time for a rubdown tonight." She spared a moment to remove the saddle, then all but ran to the house.

"Rita!" she called as she flung open the door. "Has Andy returned?"

Rita appeared immediately, wringing her hands. "No, señora, didn't you find him?"

Lacey's shoulders slumped. "I thought . . . I hoped . . . No, we didn't find him. We found the pillowcase with his belongings, but not Andy."

Rita's face crumbled. "Poor little boy."

"The men will keep searching. They're bound to find

him soon. How far could a little boy on foot have gotten?"

"Go to bed, señora. I will wake you when they return."

"I couldn't sleep a wink. I'll wait in the parlor."

"I will be in the kitchen, if you need me."

"It's OK, Rita. There is nothing you can do right now."

"I will be there, señora. Would you like something to eat? How about some coffee?"

"Nothing, Rita, thank you."

Lacey sank down onto the sofa and rested her head against the back, listening to the ominous silence. The house seemed so empty without Andy's boundless energy. Knowing that Andy was lost in the vast darkness made her want to retch. He was so small, so young; any number of things could happen to him out there. He was defenseless in a dangerous world. A sob gathered in her throat; she closed her eyes and began to pray.

When Rita checked on Lacey a short time later, she found her sleeping soundly. Clucking her tongue, Rita pulled an afghan over her and tiptoed from the room.

The sound of voices lured Lacey from sleep. She opened her eyes, surprised to see sunlight flooding the room. Her gaze found Rusty, who was speaking in hushed tones to Rita. She leaped to her feet.

"Rusty! Did you find Andy?"

Rusty's expression was guarded as he answered Lacey's question. "I'm sorry, Miz Lacey. If Andy was out there we would have found him."

"What are you saying?"

"The boys and I scoured the area. Like you said, Andy couldn't have gone very far. It wasn't until this morning that I returned to the place where Andy had dropped the pillowcase. Daylight revealed signs I missed in the dark."

"What signs?"

"Hoofprints. At least two riders had been there before me. I studied on it a long time and came to the conclusion that someone found Andy and carried him off. The boys and I returned to report to you."

Hope soared within Lacey. "Thank God! The only explanation is that a neighbor found Andy. He'll be with us soon, Rusty."

"That's what I figured," Rusty agreed.

"After the hands eat breakfast, tell them to go to bed. You, too, Rusty. You were out all night. Tell the hands I appreciate their effort. I'm sure Andy is just fine."

"If you're sure, Miz Lacey."

"Very sure. Go get some rest."

"You have plenty of time to wash up and change before breakfast," Rita said after she let Rusty out.

"Yes, perhaps that would be best," Lacey agreed. "Call me if Andy returns while I'm upstairs."

"Sí, señora."

Lacey washed and changed clothes in short order, anxious to return downstairs to wait for Andy. She wouldn't rest easy until he was safe within her arms. A niggling fear persisted, and she tried without success to put it from her mind. What if Andy hadn't been found by a neighbor? What if he'd run into outlaws?

Sighing despondently, Lacey tied her long blond hair back with a ribbon and hurried downstairs. She had just reached the middle of the staircase when she heard a commotion at the front door. A smile stretched her lips and her eyes lit up as she rushed down the remaining steps and flung the door open.

"Andy . . ."

Her smile dissolved. "What are you doing here? I thought I told you never to darken my door again." She started to close the door.

Taylor Cramer held the panel open and shoved past Lacey. "I think you'll want to hear what I have to say," he said, whirling to confront her.

"I doubt that."

"Shall we talk about Andy?"

Color leached from Lacey's face and the breath left her lungs in a whoosh. Speech was impossible, though she had countless questions to ask.

"Andy *is* missing, isn't he?" Cramer asked smugly.

Her voice restored, Lacey whispered shakily, "What do you know about Andy?"

"He's safe," Cramer said.

Relief shuddered through Lacey, but another worry took its place. "Where is he?"

"Where he won't interfere with our plans."

"Plans? Damn you, Taylor Cramer! What have you done with my son?"

"Let's go into the parlor, my dear. We have our future to discuss."

Cramer strode into the parlor. Lacey followed as if in a trance.

"We have no future together, Taylor."

He sat down on the sofa and patted the place beside him. "Sit here, Lacey."

"Not until you tell me what you've done with my son."

"I told you, he's safe. A lot safer than he'd be wandering the countryside in the dark. What did you do to him to make him run away?"

"He told you he was running away?"

"He said he was going to California. That bastard Gentry doesn't deserve that kind of devotion."

"If you have any compassion at all, you'll bring Andy home. Now. I'll bring the law into this if I have to."

"No, you won't, my dear. You can't prove I took Andy. The boy ran away. He could be anywhere. He could have met up with a coyote, a bear, or even a wolf. All manner of wild animals prowl at night."

"And you're the worst of the lot," Lacey spat. "What do you want from me, Taylor? What will it take to get Andy back?"

"Ah, now we come to the heart of the matter."

"You win, Taylor. I'll sell you the ranch. All I require is enough money to tide me and Andy over until I can find work."

"Why should I pay you anything when I hold all the cards?" Cramer said nastily. "The taxes—which aren't inconsiderable, I might add—will be paid from my own pocket. No, Lacey, I'm not going to buy the ranch."

"You expect me to give it to you?" Lacey gasped.

"In a way. Once we marry, it will be mine."

"The thought of marriage to you revolts me."

"At one time you were damn eager to marry me."

"That was before . . ."

"Before Gentry?"

"Before you showed your true colors. You never liked my son. You wanted to send him away."

"Andy was an inconvenience. But you have no choice now, Lacey. We will marry, and quickly. Before . . ." His sentence ended abruptly.

Lacey was instantly alert. "Before what? Does your haste to wed have anything to do with my land?"

"You ask too many questions. You do love your son, don't you?"

"You know I do."

"Good. We'll marry on Saturday. That's three days from now. Leave the arrangements to me. I'll come for you in my buggy Saturday morning."

Lacey's chin quivered but her voice was firm. "I'm not going to marry you, Taylor, so you might as well bring Andy home."

Taylor sent her a superior smile. "You'll marry me. Otherwise you'll never see your son again. Expect me on Saturday, my dear, around ten o'clock. You know," he mused as he rose to leave, "I'm quite looking forward to bedding you." His eyes settled on her breasts. "I spoke the truth when I said I wanted you as much as I want your land. Taming you should prove interesting."

Lacey bristled. "You've never told the truth. Forget about marriage. I'll deed the ranch to you. Just bring Andy home."

His eyes glittered with dark desire. "I want more than that. I need the land, but you're the bonus. Three days, Lacey. Resign yourself to it. I want a flesh-and-blood woman in my bed, not a marble statue. Don't bother to see me to the door, I'll let myself out."

"Bastard!"

His laughter lingered long after he was gone.

Lacey waited until Cramer rode away before leaping into action. She wasn't afraid of him. She was going to go to the sheriff despite Taylor's threats.

Lacey saddled her horse and rode to town. She didn't tell anyone where she was going. Rusty and the hands were still sleeping, and Rita would only worry. When she reached town she rode directly to the sheriff's office. She found Sheriff Hale sitting behind his desk, browsing through Wanted posters. He lifted his head and greeted her with a smile.

"What can I do for you, Miz Gentry? Has Sam Gentry returned yet?"

"Unfortunately, no. Andy is missing, Sheriff," she blurted out. "He's been gone all night."

Hale's brow furrowed. "Missing, you say?"

"Kidnapped. He went out last night and failed to return."

"What makes you think the boy's been kidnapped? He's probably lost and can't find his way back home."

"Andy ran away," Lacey revealed. "He wanted to go to California to find his father."

"There you have it," the sheriff said complacently. "The lad can't be far away. Send your hands out to look for him. If he's been out all night, he's probably more than ready to return home."

"The search began yesterday and continued all night. I just found out this morning what happened to him."

"Then getting him back should be a simple matter," Hale said, clearly annoyed.

"You're not listening, Sheriff. I said Andy was kidnaped. Taylor Cramer took him without my permission."

"That's a pretty harsh accusation, Mrs. Gentry. Do you have proof?"

"Only my word. Mr. Cramer came out to the ranch this morning and told me he had my son. I asked Taylor to bring Andy home, but he refused."

"Why would he refuse?"

"He's holding Andy hostage until I agree to marry him."

Hale stared at her. "Now, don't that beat all. I never heard of such a thing."

"It's the truth. I need your help, Sheriff. Taylor will have to release Andy if you ride out there with me and demand his return."

"I'd feel mighty foolish if you're mistaken," Hale said. "Taylor Cramer is a respected citizen of this community. I don't think we should go off half cocked."

"Please, Sheriff, don't let me down. You were elected to uphold the law."

Lacey's state of panic must have gotten through to him, for he rose and strapped on his guns. "You win, Mrs. Gentry. I'll ride out to the Taylor spread with you, but I don't expect anything to come of it."

Lacey's fear escalated as she and the sheriff ate up the distance to Taylor's ranch. Had Taylor hurt Andy? Was her son hungry? Andy was a growing boy; he required nourishing food and adequate sleep.

Lacey rode into the yard ahead of the sheriff and drew rein at Cramer's front door. She leaped from the saddle and was up the porch stairs before Hale had even dismounted. With a fervor born of desperation, she pounded on the door, calling out Andy's name.

"Lacey, Sheriff Hale. What brings you out here?"

Lacey spun around at the sound of Cramer's voice. He stood behind them, hands on hips, his most charming smile stretching his lips.

"I was in the barn. One of my hands informed me I had visitors. What can I do for you?"

"You know good and well what you can do for me,"

281

Lacey said through clenched teeth. "Release Andy. I'm taking him home."

Taylor sent Sheriff Hale a puzzled look. "What is my fiancée talking about, Sheriff?"

Sheriff Hale removed his hat and wiped his brow on his sleeve. "Mrs. Gentry says you kidnapped her son. What do you have to say about it?"

Lacey quelled the urge to strike Cramer when he gave a bark of laughter. "I fear my fiancée is delusional, Sheriff. What makes her think I kidnapped her son?"

"Because you told me!" Lacey all but shouted. "You're holding him hostage."

"What a perfectly ridiculous idea. Are you feeling well, my dear?"

"Do something, Sheriff! Search the house. I know Andy is in there."

Cramer sighed. "Go ahead, Sheriff. Lacey won't be happy until you search the house. After you finish, you're welcome to search the outbuildings."

Hale gave a reluctant nod. "I hope you don't hold this against me, Mr. Cramer, but you can see how distraught Mrs. Gentry is. I hope marriage to you will have a calming effect on her."

Cramer's smile did not reach his eyes. "You can depend on it."

Lacey personally searched every nook and cranny of Cramer's house. But she refused to yield when Sheriff Hale suggested that they leave. She vehemently insisted that the outbuildings be searched and the hands questioned. Hours later, she finally conceded that Andy wasn't on the premises, and that none of the hands questioned knew anything about her son. But that didn't prove that Taylor hadn't hidden Andy where he couldn't be found. And that frightened her. Taylor now held the winning hand.

He had convinced the sheriff that Lacey was delusional, but the fact remained that Andy was missing. The best Hale could do was promise that he and his deputy would look for Andy. Then he took his leave.

"Are you satisfied, my dear?" Cramer said after the sheriff rode away.

"Where is he?"

"He's being well taken care of. If you don't cause me any more problems, I may take you to see him after we're wed."

"Bastard!"

"Now, now, that's not the kind of talk I want to hear from my future wife. Shall I see you home?"

"I can get there on my own," Lacey hissed. "If you hurt Andy, I swear I'll kill you."

Cramer's fingers dug into her shoulders as he dragged her against him. "You'll change your tune once you're in my bed. I'll conquer you, Lacey, mark my words. One day I'll have you purring."

"Not in this life," Lacey bit out.

Lacey gasped as his mouth came down hard on hers. His kiss was brutal, possessive, without a lick of warmth. When she realized her struggles were exciting him, she went limp in his arms. With an oath, he thrust her away.

"I'll teach you how to respond properly once you're mine," he spat, giving her a rough shove. "Go home and prepare yourself for our wedding."

Her chin firm, shoulders stiff, Lacey walked away before the urge to kill Taylor got her in trouble. She might be forced to marry him, but she vowed that he'd regret it. He could have her land—it was no longer important, as long as Andy was safely returned to her.

Lacey rode home bearing the weight of the world on her shoulders. If Sam were here he wouldn't allow this travesty, she reflected. Suddenly she was glad Sam wasn't here. He'd go after Taylor with a vengeance, even if it meant breaking the law. And she didn't want that for Sam. He'd just been declared a free man; she couldn't have stood by and let him throw that away. No, it was good that he was gone. She'd had to rely on herself before and she could do it again. Taylor might marry her, but he'd never own her.

Rusty ran over to join her when he saw her ride into the yard. "Where have you been, Miz Lacey? Where's Andy?"

"Andy won't be returning just yet." The words nearly choked her, but Rusty deserved to know.

"How come?"

Lacey ignored his question. "I'm marrying Taylor Cramer on Saturday. Andy will come home after the wedding."

Comprehension dawned slowly, but when it did, Rusty howled in outrage. "Cramer's got Andy! The son of a bitch! Let me take care of him for you, Miz Lacey."

"No, Rusty. You're to do nothing, say nothing, not even to the hands. I want this kept between you and me."

"But—"

"Please, Rusty, I want your promise. No one is to know."

"No one, Miz Lacey?"

"No one."

"If that's what you want."

"It's exactly what I want. I'll handle Taylor in my own way. And believe me, he's not going to like it."

Chapter Sixteen

Sam was cold, tired and hungry. He'd intended to bypass the B&G and ride directly to Dodge City, but Galahad kept pulling at the reins, as if aware that a warm barn and food were close at hand. When Sam had left the Indians, he'd decided not to see Lacey or Andy until his name was cleared, but the closer he got to the ranch, the more he realized how impossible that would be.

Something stronger than Sam's will compelled him to rein Galahad toward the ranch. If he was lucky, he'd find a meal of leftovers in the cookhouse and Galahad could spend the night in a warm barn.

Light streamed from the cookhouse as Sam rode Galahad into the barn and dismounted. Ignoring the hunger pangs clenching his gut, he unsaddled Galahad, rubbed him down and made sure he had plenty of feed, including a measure of oats. Then he strode to the cookhouse, uncertain of his welcome. Sam needn't have worried. Only three men were inside—Luke, the cook, Rusty and Lefty. All three were huddled over steaming cups of coffee.

"Could a hungry man get a bite to eat?" Sam asked from the doorway. Three heads swiveled in his direction.

Rusty was on his feet instantly. "Sam! You old dog. You're a sight for sore eyes. We all thought you'd be halfway to California by now."

"Changed my mind," Sam grunted.

"Sit down," Luke said, already on the way to the stove. "You're in luck. There's leftover beefsteak and a pot of beans on the stove." He reached for the coffeepot. "Drink up. It'll warm your bones."

"Just what I need, Luke, thanks."

Sam warmed his hands on the hot cup before raising it to his lips. The strong brew slid down his throat and hit his empty stomach with a satisfying jolt.

"Tastes good. I intended to bypass the ranch, but now I'm glad I didn't."

Rusty's brow wrinkled. "Bypass the ranch? You mean you weren't gonna return?"

"I'm headed north, to Dodge City. I'm determined to clear my name. I'm not an outlaw and hoped to prove it before returning to the B&G."

"Dodge!" Lefty blurted out. "I thought you came back 'cause you heard that Miz Lacey was gonna marry Taylor Cramer."

"What!" Sam set his cup down on the table so hard

it shattered. "We'll see about that." He leaped to his feet. His chair hit the floor as he stormed out the door.

"I thought you were hungry!" Luke called after him.

"Wait, Sam, there's something you should know first!" Rusty exclaimed, bounding after him.

"Let him go," Lefty advised. "Let Miz Lacey tell him."

"I hope to God she tells him everything," Rusty muttered.

Sam paid little heed to the buzz of voices behind him. His head spun with the crushing blow he'd been dealt. How could she? How could Lacey marry Cramer when she knew the kind of man he was?

Each step Sam took added another dimension to his anger. Had Lacey lost her mind? What kind of woman was she to disregard her son . . . *his* son's welfare? He marched up to the door, found it locked and pounded on it so hard he could feel the panel bow inward beneath his fury.

He hadn't been pounding long when the door suddenly opened. Dressed in a nightgown and robe, Lacey stepped back as Sam charged inside.

"Sam! Oh, my God! You didn't go to California. You've come back."

"And not a moment too soon," Sam gritted out as he slammed the door shut with his boot heel.

Lacey paled. "You've seen Rusty. What did he tell you?"

"I almost rode on without stopping," Sam spat. "I changed my mind about California. I didn't like being an outlaw. I intended to ride straight to Dodge and force banker Wingate to tell the truth about the bank robbery. I wanted to return to you and Andy a free man."

287

"Rusty didn't tell you?"

"Tell me what?"

"You *are* a free man. The charges against you and your brothers have been dropped."

Sam staggered backward. "Who told you that?"

"Sheriff Hale. He received a telegram from Sheriff Diller in Dodge. Sheriff Hale doesn't know all the details; the telegram said only that the Gentry brothers were no longer wanted for bank robbery. You're a free man, Sam."

Sam felt as if the weight of the world had just been lifted from his shoulders. He was a man his son could be proud of. Elation made him forget his anger, forget why he was angry. He only knew he had reason to rejoice, and that Lacey was here to rejoice with him. Never had he wanted her more.

"God, Lacey, all I can think of now is how badly I want to make love to you."

He held out his arms. Like a sleepwalker, she walked into them. His arms closed around her. He bent to kiss her, cradling her head in his hands as he made slow love to her mouth. His lips moved fervently against hers, circling, tasting, nudging them apart for the bold thrust of his tongue.

Lacey couldn't deny she wanted Sam, for she did, desperately. Tomorrow, after she married Taylor, he'd hate her. She needed this, wanted this, for in all likelihood she'd never experience Sam's loving again. She clung desperately to him as he kissed her, praying that his passion was stronger than his anger, for she knew he had burst into the house because Rusty had told him she was going to marry Taylor.

The last thing Lacey wanted Sam to learn was that

Andy was being held hostage, that she was marrying Taylor to save their son. The longer she kept his passions engaged, the less likely he was to question her. Lacey was well aware of Sam's volatile temper. The truth would send him gunning after Taylor.

Her thoughts were shattered when Sam scooped her into his arms and mounted the steps two at a time. The door to her room was ajar. He opened it fully, strode inside and pushed it shut with his foot.

"I can't wait," he gasped as he sat on the bed and positioned her on his lap with her legs straddling him. She pulled her knees close around his hips. "Lift up a minute."

She raised slightly and felt his deft fingers unfasten his trousers. Then she felt the long, hard heat of him searching for her center while his hands opened her robe and nightgown, baring her breasts for his mouth. He suckled her greedily, pulling her gown and robe away in his eagerness to touch more of her flesh. Her fingers bit into his shoulders when he found the opening he was seeking and thrust upward.

She moaned, her body bowed backwards as he filled her.

He bucked beneath her, thrusting deeper, touching something vulnerable in the center of her being. She pushed up, then slid down again. He cupped her buttocks, helping her achieve the motion that gave them the most pleasure. She swiveled her hips; he reacted to this new sensation with a guttural groan. She cried out softly as he slammed her against his loins, driving himself deeper. She rose and sank against him again and again, until raw rapture thrummed through her veins.

She wanted it to go on forever but knew she would

die if he didn't release her soon. It was too much and not enough. It was both glorious and frightening.

It was love. Pure and simple and terrifying.

Drowning in sensation, Lacey cried out, her muscles clenching as Sam's forceful thrusts escalated. The urgency was building, tension heightening. Sam's lips burned an open-mouthed path down her neck, her throat. He kissed her shoulders, the tender spot where her pulse was racing, nuzzled the full curves of her breasts. His warm breath teased her nipples into aching points, drawing them one at a time into his mouth, tugging and releasing, then lashing his tongue across the hardened tips.

Lacey's cries grew frantic, her insides clenching with every tug of Sam's lips. Awash in pleasure honed to exquisite sharpness, the storm inside her unleashed its fury. Her senses fragmented beneath his sensual onslaught. Sam soon joined her in that delicious upheaval. Too quickly it was over.

Sam buried his head between her breasts. She barely heard him say, "I'm sorry. I didn't intend to take you so quickly. I'll go more slowly next time."

His eyes were dark pools of renewed desire as he lifted her and gently placed her on the bed. His piercing gaze mesmerized her; she couldn't look away. Without him inside her she felt hollow. It was a feeling she knew she'd have to live with the rest of her life. He undressed her quickly, shed his own clothes in record time, and joined her.

"I've missed you," he whispered against her lips.

"What about Yellow Bird? She said—"

"She lied. We were never lovers. Before I left, she confessed that she'd lied to you and asked to be forgiven. I think she finally realized that she would never be more than a friend to me."

"Did you forgive her?"

Distracted by the sudden rise and fall of her breasts, Sam didn't answer right away.

"Sam, did you forgive her?" Lacey repeated.

"Hmmm?" He lifted his glittering gaze from her breasts. "Oh, that. She saved my life. Despite the anguish her lie caused, I couldn't find it in my heart to withhold forgiveness."

Lacey lost her train of thought as his hands began a slow journey over the contours of her body.

He kissed the tip of her nose, then brushed his lips over her mouth. "I almost didn't stop at the ranch before heading up to Dodge. I can't believe it's over at last, that my brothers and I are free men. Now I can be the kind of father Andy can be proud of."

Lacey went still. Andy was the last person she wanted to discuss with Sam. Telling Sam the truth would not be in Andy's best interests. As long as Andy was Taylor's prisoner, it was imperative that she keep Sam away from Taylor. The only way to do that was to keep Sam too occupied to ask questions.

"You talk too much, Sam," Lacey said.

She started to rise. "Where are you going?" Sam asked.

"You'll see."

She went as far as the washstand. She felt his eyes on her as she poured water into the bowl and dipped a cloth into it. Then she proceeded to wash all traces of Sam's seed from her body. She rinsed the cloth and carried it back to the bed. She felt Sam go rigid when she gently applied the cloth to his sex. After cleansing him thoroughly, she lay back on the bed and smiled.

291

She raised her knee invitingly. He gently cupped it and slid his fingers down the inside of her thigh, "See what your teasing has done?"

His fingers found her, spread her, pierced her. He bent to taste her mouth. There was no urgency to the kiss as his lips moved slowly, teasingly over hers. He seemed in no hurry to end the sweet torment as he found another, more intimate place for his mouth and tongue. He continued to ply his magic upon her vulnerable body until she was twisting on the sheets and saying his name in harsh, broken gasps. In desperation she caught his head between her hands and tugged him upward, urging him over her. If he didn't fill her now, this instant, she'd die.

He shifted upward and pushed himself inside her. Her hips arched to meet his driving thrusts, matching her movements to his until they moved together in perfect harmony.

Everything was right in her world now, but she dared not think about tomorrow, not with Sam holding her so fiercely close. Tomorrow he would hate her. Even if he'd forgiven her for leaving the Indian camp after promising not to, she knew he would never forgive her for marrying Taylor.

Her thoughts halted as Sam's movements increased, and suddenly she was flying. Then dimly, as if from a great distance, she heard Sam's harsh cry, felt him stiffen and then slowly relax on top of her.

Lacey lay quietly as her heart gradually slowed to a normal beat. She felt bereft when Sam softened and slid out of her. The feeling increased when he rolled away and settled beside her. She thought he'd fallen asleep until he rose up on his elbow and stared down at her. Her gut clenched, anticipating his next words.

"Rusty must have been mistaken."

Lacey pretended not to understand. "He should have told you immediately that the charges against the Gentry brothers had been dropped."

The accusation in his eyes pierced through to her soul. "That's not what I meant, Lacey. Rusty said you were going to marry Taylor Cramer. I rushed up to the house in a rage, ready to wring your beautiful neck. The good news you gave me, combined with the urgent need to make love to you, made me forget my anger. I could think of nothing except finding the nearest bed and putting myself inside you. But that's not the point I'm trying to make here. Why did Rusty think you were going to marry Cramer?"

Thank God he didn't know she was getting married *tomorrow*. "Because it's true. Can we talk about this later? You're exhausted. I can see it in your face."

"So you had been prepared to marry that bastard? I'm glad you changed your mind. You're not going to marry Cramer. But make no mistake. *If* you disregard my wishes and marry Cramer, I'm taking Andy away from you. Andy is my son. The law will be on my side."

Lacey hadn't changed her mind. She bit her lip to keep from blurting out the terrible secret that was eating her alive. Only Rusty and Rita knew the truth. The hands had been told that Andy was safe and would return home soon. Lacey knew they had questions, but Rusty had warned them against prying.

"Lacey, has our marriage been annulled?"

After a lengthy pause, Lacey said, "We're no longer married, Sam."

"You care about me, I know you do. How could you

still want to marry Cramer, knowing the kind of man he is?"

"Please, Sam, try to understand. I thought you were gone for good," she hedged. "I'm about to lose my home. Andy and I would be out in the cold with nowhere to go and no money for food or shelter. I was desperate."

"I'm here now," Sam said. "Don't worry, I'll find a way to save the ranch. We'll remarry tomorrow and apply for a loan together. You'll get your loan, and Andy will have his father back. A boy needs both parents."

I'd never see Andy again if that were to happen, Lacey silently lamented. "Is that the reason you want to marry me? Because of Andy?"

"Dammit, Lacey, don't put words in my mouth. Haven't you realized by now that I care for you? I never thought I'd say those words, but I've never meant anything more."

"Please, Sam, don't say anything else." She couldn't bear to have him bare his soul when she had no intention of abandoning her plans to marry Taylor. Andy's life was at stake. And perhaps Sam's, if he learned why she must do this thing.

Sam frowned. "Something is wrong, I can feel it. You can't still hate me. You couldn't make love with such feeling if you didn't care for me. I know I've wronged you in the past, but I'm hoping you will forgive me. Now that I'm a free man, we can plan a future, we can be a family." He stared at her. "Do you love me, Lacey?"

Under any other circumstances Lacey would have shouted her love to the heavens, but what Sam wanted was impossible now. Turning away, she refused to meet his gaze. Undaunted, he grasped her face between his hands and forced her to look at him.

"Tell me you *don't* love me."

A sob burst from her throat. "I love you, dammit. Are you happy now?"

Sam nodded. "It's settled, then. No more talk about marrying Cramer. I'll go out to his place tomorrow and put an end to it. By nightfall tomorrow you'll be my wife, and Andy will have two parents who love him."

Lacey said nothing. Let him think what he wanted. At least he didn't insist on seeing Andy tonight.

As if his decision solved everything, Sam snuggled Lacey into the curve of his body. "Go to sleep, love. I'm so tired I could sleep the clock around, so be sure and awaken me at dawn. We've got a busy day ahead of us."

Lacey had other ideas. She'd be gone long before Sam awakened. Gone before the hands stirred from the bunkhouse. In order to avoid a confrontation between Sam and Taylor, she knew she couldn't wait until Taylor came to the house for her in his buggy. She made a hasty decision to ride out to Taylor's place before his scheduled arrival. She couldn't defy Taylor as long as he had Andy.

Lacey scarcely slept a wink for fear of oversleeping. Sam was still sleeping soundly when she carefully disentangled herself from his arms and eased out of bed. He didn't move a muscle as she washed and dressed and let herself out of the room and closed the door silently behind her. The bunkhouse was silent as she crept past it to the barn. Moments later she rode her mare away from the B&G, to a future not of her choosing.

The sun was peeping from behind a cloud when she reached the Cramer spread. She dismounted before the house and rapped sharply on the door. It took a few minutes to rouse Cramer, and when he finally appeared, his chest was bare and he was tugging on his trousers. His surprise was genuine.

"Lacey! What are you doing here at this hour? I wasn't to pick you up for hours yet."

"I . . . I couldn't sleep, so thought I'd save you the trip."

An arrogant grin curved his thin lips. "An eager bride—how refreshing. I'm pleased you've resigned yourself to our marriage. Come in, come in. My housekeeper will cook breakfast for us. Wait for me in the parlor while I speak to her. Breakfast will be ready by the time I finish dressing."

Lacey waited until Taylor had spoken to the housekeeper and disappeared up the staircase before heading to the kitchen for a private word with the woman. She found the housekeeper busy over the stove. She had met Mrs. Beaver before and addressed her by name.

"Good morning, Mrs. Beaver. I hope I'm not inconveniencing you."

The dour housekeeper banged a skillet on the stove. "Too early for guests. No decent women pay calls on gentlemen this time of morning."

Lacey let her hurtful remark pass. "I wonder if you could answer a question. It would mean a great deal to me."

"You can ask, but I can't promise an answer," she replied in a surly tone.

"You remember my son, don't you?"

"You mean that pesky young'un of yours? What's he done?"

"He hasn't done anything. I was wondering if you've seen him here recently."

Mrs. Beaver sent her a sullen look. "Ain't seen him. Not since the last time he was here with you."

"Are you sure?"

"Are you calling me a liar?"

"Of course not. Thank you. I'll wait in the parlor for Taylor."

"Don't think you're gonna change things around here after you marry Mr. Cramer," Mrs. Beaver called after her. "I'm in charge here, and that ain't gonna change."

Lacey didn't dignify her words with a response. She had no intention of taking over Taylor's household, or becoming the kind of wife he expected.

Cramer appeared in the parlor a short time later, dressed in appropriate wedding attire. Lacey stared at him with disdain.

Though he looked dapper in black suit, string tie and white shirt, she found nothing commendable about him. Her own attire left much to be desired. Since she never wanted this wedding, she hadn't bothered donning wedding finery—not that she had anything fine enough for a wedding.

"Shall we go into the breakfast room?" Taylor said. "I'm sure Mrs. Beaver has prepared a festive breakfast for us."

Lacey accompanied him to the breakfast room, her spine stiff and unforgiving. "I want to see Andy before the wedding."

"I'm afraid that's impossible, my dear. In good time. In good time."

He pulled out a chair for her. Lacey stared at it, then sat down. "Is he well? You haven't hurt him, have you?"

"He's fine. That's all you need to know for now."

Mrs. Beaver entered the room with a platter of eggs

and another of bacon. She placed them before Cramer, then left and returned moments later with biscuits and freshly churned butter.

"A breakfast fit for a king and his queen," Cramer crowed. "I hope the coffee is strong and black, Mrs. Beaver. I don't want my bride falling asleep during the ceremony. Don't bother with a wedding supper. I'm taking my bride to a hotel."

"I wasn't planning on fixing a wedding supper," the dour woman replied.

Cramer chuckled as Mrs. Beaver marched back into the kitchen. "I'm afraid taking a wife has put my housekeeper's nose out of joint. She's become rather possessive of me over the years. I'm sure you can work things out with her, however."

Cramer dug into his food with good appetite while Lacey merely shoved hers around on her plate. She'd had no appetite since Andy had turned up missing—thanks to Taylor Cramer. Unfortunately, there was nothing she could do about it except marry the bastard and hope he'd return Andy unharmed.

Lacey sipped coffee and tried not to think about Sam. She hoped he was still sleeping soundly, for she knew that when he awakened and found her missing he'd go to Rusty for answers. Poor Rusty wouldn't have a chance against Sam's determination. She wanted to be married before all hell broke loose.

"Can we leave for town now?" Lacey asked when Taylor had scraped his plate clean.

"That anxious, are you? You surprise me, Lacey. I thought you'd be a reluctant bride."

"If you think I'm anxious to become your wife, you're badly mistaken. The sooner we get this over with, the sooner you'll return Andy to me." She pushed her chair back.

"Very well. We can leave as soon as the buggy is hitched. But I warn you, don't expect to see your son until after the wedding night."

Taylor's words kept echoing through Lacey's head all the way to town. The wedding night. Sam was the only man she'd ever made love with. How could she let another man touch her? A shiver raced down her spine. Could she do it for Andy? The answer was elusive, for she had no idea what she would do until the time came. The thought of bedding Taylor was abhorrent to her, but losing Andy was unbearable.

God help me, she silently implored.

They reached town all too soon. Taylor drove directly to the church. The hour was early, but Lacey hoped the preacher would accommodate them. She had to be married before Sam arrived. And he *would* arrive—of that Lacey had little doubt. Not only would he arrive—he'd be in a murderous rage.

Sam rolled over in bed and reached for Lacey. His hand closed on emptiness. He cranked his eyes open. Sunlight streamed through the window. My God, how long had he slept? Where was Lacey? A gut-wrenching premonition took hold and refused to let loose.

She didn't . . . She wouldn't . . . Not today . . . Leaping from bed, he dragged on his clothes and raced down the stairs, calling Lacey's name. Rita appeared from the kitchen, her expression mirroring her shock.

"Señor Sam! I didn't know you were here. We all thought you had gone to California."

299

"Yeah, that was my intention," Sam said impatiently. "Is Lacey in the kitchen?"

Rita looked ready to burst into tears. "No, señor. I . . . I'm sorry—"

"I'll find her."

"Would you like something to eat first?"

Sam was already halfway out the door. "No time, Rita."

Sam ran to the barn, expecting to find Lacey inside. She was not there and her mare was missing. He checked the henhouse, tack room and corral. He ran into Rusty outside the cookhouse.

"Sam! You're still here. Were you able to talk some sense into Miz Lacey?"

"You mean about marrying Cramer?" Sam shrugged. "I thought it was all settled last night, but now I'm not so sure. Lacey is missing—so is her mare. When was she supposed to marry Cramer?"

Rusty stared at Sam. "My God, didn't she tell you?"

The foreboding Sam had felt earlier turned into raw panic. "Tell me what?"

Rusty refused to meet Sam's eyes. "I promised I wouldn't say anything."

"Where's Andy? Maybe he'll tell me. What in the hell is going on, Rusty?"

Rusty looked torn, as if he wanted to confide in Sam but feared to do so out of loyalty to Lacey.

"If Lacey is in danger, I want to know. Have you seen Andy this morning? He wasn't in the house, and I don't think he's sleeping."

"Dang it, Sam, you weren't supposed to know."

Icy fingers crawled up Sam's spine. "What's that supposed to mean? Has something happened to Andy? Spit it out, Rusty."

After a lengthy pause, Rusty said, "You're the boy's pa—you got a right to know. Andy turned up missing three days ago. He packed some duds and ran away. He had a few hours' head start, but we shoulda found him. All we found was a pillowcase holding his belongings. Later I discovered signs indicating that he had met up with someone. Hoofprints were all over the place."

Sam's eyes narrowed. "Go on. Met up with who?"

"You ain't gonna like this, Sam. Taylor Cramer has Andy. He told Lacey he wouldn't return the lad unless Lacey married him. The wedding is supposed to take place today."

"Today! Son of a bitch! Lacey didn't tell me the wedding was set for today. Why didn't she go to the law?"

"She did. The sheriff went out to Taylor's place and searched it from top to bottom. Andy wasn't there. Of course, Cramer denied taking the boy, and Sheriff Hale believed him. Lacey felt she had no choice but to marry the bastard."

"Why didn't she tell me this last night?"

"I reckon she knew you'd go gunning for Taylor."

"Damn right I would. He kidnapped my son."

"A confrontation between you and Cramer is what Miz Lacey was trying to avoid. You're a free man, Sam, and I reckon she wanted you to remain that way. Killing Taylor won't bring Andy back. No one knows where Taylor has taken the boy, so killing him will serve no purpose."

His expression grim, Sam turned abruptly and strode to the barn, checking his guns on the way.

"Where you going?"

Connie Mason

"To stop a wedding and force Cramer to tell me where's he's taken Andy."

"I hope you know what you're doing," Rusty said. "Miz Lacey wanted to handle it herself."

"She isn't capable of handling Cramer. I'll kill the bastard before I let Lacey marry him."

Killing wasn't Sam's way of solving problems, but in Cramer's case it would be a pleasure. He prayed he wasn't too late to stop Lacey from making the biggest mistake of her life.

The words stuck in Lacey's throat as she and Taylor stood up before the preacher. Her mouth was so dry she had to swallow several times before she could make herself repeat the two words that would bind her to a man she despised. She paused so long the preacher repeated his question.

"You have to say something, Lacey," Taylor prodded. "You know you're going to do what's best for your son."

That did it. Taylor's thinly veiled threat unclogged her throat and she whispered, "I do."

Moments later the preacher pronounced them man and wife. The kiss that followed was one of mastery and possession, and Lacey did all she could not to gag. They followed the preacher to the vestibule of the church, where they signed the necessary papers.

It was done, Lacey thought as she left the church with Taylor. She was Mrs. Taylor Cramer. It sickened her to think that at one time she had welcomed the title, but that was before Taylor had shown his true colors. At the moment, all Lacey could think of was Andy, and how happy she'd be to have him with her again. Then Taylor's crude words abruptly roused her from her apathy.

"I think we'll go directly to the hotel, my dear. You're mine now. Once I've bedded you, you'll have no doubt about my mastery over you."

Lacey balked. "I want to see Andy."

"All in good time. I'm eager to consummate our wedding vows."

"You promised."

"I promised you'd see him, but I didn't say when. My life will be less complicated without your spoiled brat causing problems."

Rage seethed through Lacey. "The only reason I married you was because you held Andy hostage. I've kept my part of the bargain; now you keep yours."

"When the time is right, I'll bring Andy home. Perhaps I'll wait until your belly swells with my child. I need an heir for the wealth I've accumulated. I'm about to become even wealthier," he bragged, "since adding the B&G to my holdings."

Lacey stopped just short of the waiting buggy. "What did you say?"

"I said I'm about to become wealthier—"

"No, not that. What did you say about Andy?"

"I've decided to let Andy stay where he is for a while."

"Bastard!" Lacey hissed. "You'll tell me where Andy is or I'll—"

A pistol shot cut off Lacey's words. She watched in horror as Taylor clutched his chest and fell to the ground. Blood bloomed on his shirt beneath his hand. Lacey dropped to her knees beside him, fearing that the wound was a fatal one. Panic swept through her.

"Taylor! Don't die! Where's Andy? Oh, God, please don't die. Tell me where you've taken Andy."

Taylor's eyes opened slowly. "Too . . . late . . ." Then his eyes rolled back into his head.

Chapter Seventeen

Sam pushed Galahad to his limits as the stalwart horse closed the distance to town. Sam *had* to stop Lacey from marrying Cramer before it was too late. Each mile he traveled increased his anger. Lacey should have told him that Cramer was holding Andy hostage, and then trusted him to handle the situation instead of making a muddle of things herself.

Splatters of foam flew from Galahad's mouth as the poor animal stretched his legs to match his master's urgency.

Sam pulled back on the reins as he entered the town and guided Galahad down Denison's main street. He knew from previous visits that the church sat at the north end of town, and his heart pounded erratically as the church came into view.

Sam spotted Lacey and Cramer immediately and drew rein a short distance away. They were standing beside a buggy, engaged in heated conversation. Sam had no idea whether they were going into the church or just leaving it. Lacey's back was to him. Cramer was so engrossed in the conversation he hadn't yet noticed Sam. Sam was about to call out to them when he saw something that froze his blood.

The sun's reflection off the barrel of a rifle.

The rifle was pointed directly at Lacey and Cramer. Sam couldn't see the gun's owner, who was concealed by thick bushes alongside the church. What Sam did see was the barrel poking out of the foliage. Fear laced through him. Was the bullet intended for Cramer or Lacey? He didn't wait to find out.

He drew his six-shooter and aimed into the bushes. His gun exploded at the same time as the shooter fired. Sam had no idea if his bullet hit the shooter, for the rifle was instantly withdrawn, but the shooter's bullet had found a target in Cramer's chest. Sam spurred Galahad into the bushes, but the shooter had disappeared.

Then he saw Lacey kneeling before Cramer, screaming words he couldn't hear. Dismounting quickly, he left Galahad's reins dangling and raced toward Lacey and the fallen Cramer. He heard Lacey cry out, "Don't die, Taylor! Please don't die!"

Sam was beside her now, kneeling to examine Cramer, his smoking gun still in his hand. Lacey turned to him, tears streaming down her face. The preacher ran out of the church, stopped a passerby and sent him after the sheriff and the doctor.

"Why did you do it, Sam?" Lacey cried. "Now we'll never find Andy."

Sam looked property stunned. "I didn't shoot him, Lacey."

Lacey's lips trembled. "Is he dead?"

Sam found a weak pulse in Cramer's neck. "No, but he's as near death as a man can get. The assassin's bullet hit damn close to his heart."

"You shouldn't have shot him. That's exactly what I was trying to prevent. I'll never get Andy back now."

Sam gritted his teeth in frustration. "I didn't shoot him, I swear it."

The words had no sooner left his mouth than the sheriff arrived. He looked at Cramer, saw the gun in Sam's hand and drew his own weapon. "You just can't stay out of trouble, can you, Gentry? Move away from the victim and drop your gun."

"I didn't shoot Cramer."

"Your gun, Gentry," Sheriff Hale repeated.

Sam dropped his gun. The sheriff picked it up, sniffed the barrel, then ran his hand over it. "The barrel is still hot and the smell of gunpowder is prominent. Your gun has been fired recently, Mr. Gentry. What have you got to say for yourself?"

"I shot at the man who gunned down Cramer," Sam argued. "He was hiding in the bushes. I'm not sure my bullet hit him, because he was gone when I got there."

"How convenient, but I don't buy it. The first time you shot at Cramer, you missed. This time you got lucky."

"I didn't shoot Cramer now and I didn't shoot at him

before," Sam bit out. "I had no reason to kill him."

"What about jealousy? That's enough reason for me, and I suspect the judge and jury will agree. Crimes of passion are common enough nowadays."

Just then the doctor arrived. He pushed everyone aside and knelt before the victim. "It doesn't look good," the doctor said in a no-nonsense manner.

"Is he alive?" Lacey asked. "Can he talk?"

"What are you to the victim?" the doctor asked curtly.

Lacey started to say "Nothing," when the preacher spoke up.

"She's Mr. Cramer's wife. I married them not a half hour ago."

Sam groaned but said nothing.

"I don't hold out much hope for him, Mrs. Cramer, but I'll do my best. I'll know more after I dig the bullet out. Let's get him to my office," he said to the milling crowd.

Immediately four men stepped forward and lifted Cramer. Lacey followed as they carried him down the street to the doctor's office. Sam started after her but stopped abruptly when Sheriff Hale poked him in the back with his gun.

"You're going to jail, Gentry."

"How many times do I have to tell you? I didn't shoot Cramer."

"Tell that to the judge and jury. Move, Gentry."

"My horse—"

"My deputy will take care of him."

Cursing beneath his breath, Sam walked ahead of the sheriff, anger raging inside him. What rotten luck. Cleared of one crime and accused of another. Rafe and Jess were right. Trouble seemed to follow him. Not only did the sheriff think him guilty of attempted murder, but Lacey thought so, too. Of course, Lacey wasn't thinking clearly; he couldn't blame her for that. If Cramer died, they might never know where he had hidden Andy.

"You've got this all wrong, Sheriff," Sam said in an attempt to make Hale understand. "Another man shot Cramer, and you're letting him get away. He might have my bullet in him. That ought to prove my innocence."

"I've weighed the evidence, and you're the only likely suspect. You belong in jail, where you can't hurt anyone else."

Sam spit out a curse. How could he prove his innocence from a jail cell when no one, including Lacey, believed him? Damn, life wasn't fair.

Lacey waited in the outer office while Dr. Larsen fought to save her husband's life. Taylor had to live long enough to tell her where to find Andy. He just had to!

Minutes turned into hours. Lacey paced the limited confines of the office, her thoughts whirling furiously. She was so angry at Sam she couldn't think straight. What in the world was he thinking when he shot Taylor? Hadn't Rusty told him about Andy? Hadn't he explained why she had to marry Taylor? The last thing she'd wanted was Sam's interference. Now, thanks to Sam, Taylor lay near death and she might never find the answers she sought.

The door opened. Lacey rose expectantly. The doctor walked into the room, wiping his hands on his blood-splattered apron.

"I'm sorry, Mrs. Cramer. I couldn't save him."

Lacey released a long, low wail and sank into the nearest chair.

"I dug the bullet out. It had nicked your husband's heart. He died while I was working on him. He felt nothing."

"Did . . . did he say anything?"

"He never regained consciousness. What do you want done with the body?"

She gave him a blank look. "The body?"

"You're the next of kin. If you'd like, I could have the undertaker pick up the body. You can make arrangements directly with him when you feel up to it."

"Next of kin," Lacey repeated dully. What did that mean? She hadn't wanted to be Taylor's wife, much less his next of kin. "Yes, that would be fine with me, thank you. I'll speak to the undertaker when I'm . . . more myself. I don't have much money, but I'll see that your fee is paid."

"Don't you know? Taylor Cramer was a rich man. You're his heir. You stand to inherit all his wealth. If I were you, I'd get myself to the bank and talk to Mr. Markle about your husband's assets. You do have valid marriage papers, don't you."

"Taylor had them on him," Lacey answered woodenly. She was still reeling from the surprising turn of events. Scant days ago the banker had denied her request for a loan; now she stood to inherit a great deal of money.

"I'll bring out your husband's personal effects. Don't go away."

Lacey couldn't move, much less walk out the door. Everything had happened so fast her head was still spinning. She started pacing in an effort to regain control of her senses. After a short wait, the doctor returned and handed her a bundle wrapped in brown paper.

"I emptied your husband's pockets. He had quite a bit of cash on him. His jewelry is in there, too."

Lacey stared at the bundle, loathing welling up inside her. Then she shook off her aversion and accepted the bundle. "Thank you, Dr. Larsen."

Lacey left the doctor's office in a daze. Married and widowed in the same day. First the wedding she'd never wanted, then the knowledge that Sam had killed Taylor before her husband of fifteen minutes could tell her where to find Andy. She spared a moment to wonder what the next few hours would bring.

Lacey entered the bank and found herself the recipient of sympathetic looks. Apparently, the news of Taylor's death had preceded her. She asked for Mr. Markle and was ushered into his office immediately.

"Let me extend my condolences on behalf of the bank," Markle said solemnly. "Please sit down and tell me what I can do for you, Mrs. Cramer."

"Dr. Larsen suggested that I see you before I return to the ranch," Lacey began. "Taylor and I were married shortly before . . . before his death. I'd like a review of my late husband's assets being held at your bank."

Lacey didn't much care that her request might sound mercenary to the banker. If she didn't have the money to pay her back taxes by the end of the week, she'd be turned out into the cold.

"I usually meet with heirs after the funeral," Markle said with a hint of censure. "But if you insist."

"Just tell me if there's enough money in the bank to pay the back taxes on the B&G."

Markle stared at her. "You have no idea of your late husband's wealth, do you?"

"Not a clue. All I'm interested in now is paying the

taxes and . . ." She almost said "finding my son," but decided to keep that knowledge to herself.

"Excuse me a moment while I get the necessary papers for you to sign. It won't take long to transfer your late husband's assets to your name. I assume you have your marriage papers with you."

"I have them," Lacey said.

"Very well. I'll be right back."

Lacey used the time alone to unwrap the bundle of Cramer's personal effects and scan the contents. The marriage papers were there amid several large-denomination greenbacks and various pieces of jewelry. Lacey removed the marriage papers and all the greenbacks, leaving everything else for a more thorough inspection later.

Lacey placed the marriage document before Markle when he returned. "Everything seems in order, Mrs. Cramer," he said after a cursory glance. "Once you sign these papers, the cash in your late husband's bank account will automatically be transferred to you. Mr. Cramer had other assets besides cash. You should visit his lawyer for a complete accounting of properties and such. He'll handle all the legal work for you."

Lacey had little interest in anything Taylor owned beyond the money to pay her taxes. She signed the papers and returned them to Markle.

"Very good," Markle said. "Is there anything else I can do for you?"

"I'd like a bank draft in the amount of the back taxes I owe and fifteen hundred dollars in cash. I'd like to pay the back taxes on the B&G before I return home."

"On which ranch will you make your home?" Markle asked. "You now own two ranches."

Two ranches? The thought was staggering. What was she going to do with two ranches? Sell one, obviously, and it wasn't going to be the B&G.

"I can't decide anything right now," Lacey said. "I'll be on my way as soon as I have the money I requested."

"Don't you want to know how much money your late husband has in his account?"

"Very well," Lacey said, eager to leave. "How rich am I?"

"Very rich," Markle gloated. "Mr. Cramer's bank account has grown to fifty-five thousand dollars. That's a considerable sum, even in this day and age."

Astonishment rendered Lacey speechless. Several minutes passed before she was able to speak.

"Did I hear you right? How could anyone be that rich?"

"Taylor Cramer was a resourceful man, and a canny one when it came to business. His lawyer can tell you more than I. You will have no financial worries in the future, young lady."

Markle left the room and returned shortly with the money and bank draft Lacey had requested. He counted out fifteen hundred dollars in her palm, and she left the bank in a daze. She was still in a daze when she entered the tax office and produced the bank draft to pay her taxes in full. The clerk handed her a receipt and extended his condolences for her late husband's death. Lacey didn't want condolences; she wanted her son.

Sheriff Hale intercepted Lacey as she left the tax office. "Your buggy is in front of the jailhouse, ma'am. One of my deputies drove it from the church for you."

"Thank you, Sheriff. I'd like to see Sam before I return home. Is that possible?"

313

"It's all right with me. I need to ask you a few questions before you return home anyway."

Lacey followed Hale to the jailhouse. He held the door open for her and she stepped inside. "He's in one of the holding cells," Hale said, directing her down a passageway. "Call out if you need me."

Lacey walked down the passage and ran into a row of cells. Only one was occupied. Sam must have seen her coming, for he clung to the bars, his expression anxious.

"Lacey, thank God you came. How is Cramer?"

"He's dead, just like you intended," Lacey said on a sob. "How could you, Sam? Didn't Rusty tell you that Taylor was holding Andy hostage? Why did you have to take the law into your own hands? Why didn't you let me handle it my way?"

"I admit that I left the ranch in a rage. I was prepared to do anything short of murder to stop the wedding. I don't kill men in cold blood."

"If you didn't kill Taylor, who did?"

"Damned if I know, but I did get off a shot at him. We shot simultaneously; that's why only one report was heard. I wish there was some way to convince Sheriff Hale of my innocence."

Lacey was halfway convinced that Sam was guiltless. But a tiny degree of doubt still lingered.

"Lacey," Sam said earnestly, "you know I'd do nothing to harm my son. Why would I kill Cramer when he was the only one who could tell us where to find Andy?"

"I'm so confused," Lacey whispered. "I don't know where to look for Andy, and I'm at my wits' end. Marrying Taylor was my only hope of seeing my son again."

Sam reached through the bars and cupped her cheek.

"I knew why you'd agreed to marry Cramer the moment I learned he held Andy hostage. I wanted to reach the church before you married the bastard."

"It was already too late when you arrived. I was Taylor's wife at the time of the shooting."

"You're his heir," Sam said thoughtfully. "My God, Lacey, do you know what that means? Your ranch is safe now. You can pay your taxes. And you have money to hire trained detectives to find our son."

Lacey swallowed painfully. "I already thought of that and withdrew money from the bank to pay the taxes. As for Taylor's other assets, I care nothing for them."

"Don't look a gift horse in the mouth, love. Take whatever is coming to you. You deserve it after what that bastard put you through."

"I can't think straight," Lacey said. "So much has happened today."

"I didn't kill him, love. There really was an assassin hiding in the bushes."

"I have to go," Lacey said, backing away. "I don't know what to think. Even if I believed you, you'd still have to convince the sheriff."

"Nothing can keep me here," Sam bit out. "I need to find our son."

"Don't do anything foolish, Sam. If you're really innocent, the truth will come out. I have to go. I'm going to go through Taylor's personal papers. If I'm lucky, I'll find something to lead me to Andy. I'll return tomorrow and let you know what I've found."

"You won't have to go through this alone, love. I swear I'll be out of here soon to help you."

Lacey attempted a smile and failed. She choked out a good-bye and fled. She hoped Sheriff Hale didn't have too many questions, for she was close to the breaking point.

"Did you get the truth from Gentry, Mrs. Cramer?" Hale asked.

That name. She hated it. "Please call me Lacey. I spoke with Sam. He denies shooting Taylor. He swears another man did it."

"Do you believe him?"

Did she? Lacey wanted to. Dear God, she wanted to. "I don't think Sam is capable of cold-blooded murder."

"I reckon that's up to the judge and jury to decide."

"My son is still missing, Sheriff. What are you going to do about it?"

"You still think Mr. Cramer had something to do with your son's disappearance? Now, that's real puzzling, considering you married the man."

"I married Taylor because he held Andy hostage and for no other reason," Lacey retorted. "He said I'd never see my son again if I didn't marry him."

Hale looked unconvinced. "Are you certain?"

"Very certain."

"I'll see what I can do. I'll ask around; maybe someone knows something about your son's disappearance. Go home, Mrs. . . . Lacey. You look done in. That's all the questions for now."

"What about Sam?"

"I'm afraid he'll have to stay here until someone comes up with another killer."

Lacey nodded wearily. "I'll be back tomorrow. Perhaps by then one of us will have learned something about Andy's disappearance."

The buggy was waiting for Lacey on the street outside the sheriff's office. She climbed into the seat and picked up the reins. Seconds later the buggy clattered off down the road.

Rusty and the hands crowded around the buggy when she reached the ranch. Rusty helped her down, his expression grim.

"Is it done, then? Where's your bridegroom?"

Lacey nearly pitched forward when Rusty released her, but caught herself just in time. "What's wrong, Miz Lacey? Did something happen in town? Did you see Sam?"

"Sam's in jail," Lacey said dully. "He . . . he shot and killed Taylor minutes after our marriage, before Taylor could tell me where he'd hidden Andy."

"Gawd almighty," Rusty whispered. "Sam said he'd kill Taylor, but I never thought he'd do it. He ain't the kind to shoot a man in cold blood. Are you sure, Miz Lacey?"

"No, that's the problem. I don't believe he did it. I did at first, but I changed my mind after talking to him. Unfortunately, what I think doesn't matter. There is no other suspect, and the sheriff thinks he did it."

"What can we do, Miz Lacey? I feel so damn helpless."

"I want you and Lefty to ride over to the Cramer spread and explain everything to the hands. I'm Taylor's sole heir; the ranch and all his assets now belong to me. There might be some legalities before the transfer is completed, but I've already taken money out of his bank account to pay my taxes.

"Lefty, I'm appointing you foreman of the Cramer spread until I decide what to do with it. Can you handle it? Rusty can help out if the hands there give you any problems."

Lefty's chest puffed out. "I won't let you down, Miz Lacey. Some of Cramer's hands might leave, but that's all right. With winter coming on, the workload will be light."

"I'll come by tomorrow on my way to town," Lacey said.

"What about Andy?" Rusty asked. "We're gonna get him back, ain't we?"

Lacey recalled the bundle of Taylor's personal effects and retrieved it from the buggy. "I'm hoping there's something in Taylor's belongings that leads us to Andy. If not, I'll turn his house upside down until I find something. Someone has to know where Taylor has taken my son."

"Me and Lefty will leave right away, Miz Lacey."

"As soon as you return, let me know how the men reacted to Taylor's death," Lacey said. "I don't want any trouble."

Lacey strode to the house. It seemed an eternity since she'd left her bed with Sam sleeping in it, but in truth it had been less than twelve hours. The most eventful twelve hours of her life.

Lacey found Rita in the kitchen and had to go through the whole story again.

"Señor Sam did not do it, señora," Rita staunchly defended. "He is not a killer."

"I'm inclined to think the same thing, Rita, but I'm not the judge or jury. I don't know what I can do to help him."

"Señor Sam could find Andy, I know he could," Rita declared. "He loved the boy."

"I wish I had some idea who wanted Taylor dead."

Rita snorted. "A man like Señor Cramer must have many enemies."

"You're right, Rita, and I'll track down every one of them, if I must. But first I'm going to inspect Taylor's belongings for clues to Andy's whereabouts."

She placed the bundle on the kitchen table and slowly unwrapped it. One by one she examined the contents. There was a letter from a man in Washington that she didn't bother to read, and several notes pertaining to business. Nothing to indicate where Taylor had taken Andy.

"Did you find anything?" Rita asked anxiously.

"Nothing," Lacey sighed. "Perhaps I'll have better luck at Taylor's house tomorrow. I'm going upstairs, Rita. Call me when supper is ready. Something light will do, since I don't have much of an appetite."

Lacey picked at her food and finally pushed her plate aside. She moved to the parlor while Rita cleared the table. Rusty arrived from the Cramer ranch to report soon afterward.

"How did it go?" Lacey asked anxiously.

"Pretty good, considering. Two hands quit immediately after hearing that Cramer was dead, but the others seemed to accept Lefty as foreman. It helped that the foreman of the outfit was away on some errand for Cramer. We won't know what it was until he returns. He might give Lefty some trouble, but I reckon he can handle it."

"I'm going out there in the morning and speak with the hands myself. Perhaps I'll send extra men from the B&G to help Lefty."

"Let me know if there's anything else I can do. Good night, Miz Lacey."

"Good night, Rusty."

Lacey flirted with sleep but had difficulty attaining it. She hadn't seen Andy in days and missed him dreadfully. What had Taylor done with him? So many appalling scenarios came to mind that she couldn't bear thinking about them. Instead, she shifted her thoughts to Sam, and the fate that awaited him if he were found guilty of murdering Taylor.

Had it been just last night that she had told Sam she loved him? It seemed like eons ago. Did she still love him? Love wasn't an emotion one could turn on and off at will. She'd never stopped loving Sam, not when he had professed to hate her and not now. Sam might be many things, but he wasn't a cold-blooded killer. If he said someone else had shot Taylor, then she believed him.

Lacey finally drifted into an uneasy sleep, but sometime during the night she awoke from a frightening nightmare. She dreamt that Sam was hanging from a tree, his face horribly contorted in death. She saw herself standing beneath the hanging tree. She was grieving alone, which in itself was even more frightening because Andy wasn't with her. What did it mean?

Sleep was impossible after that. Closing her eyes would only bring more terrifying dreams. She felt as if the weight of the world was balanced on her shoulders and she was faltering beneath the onerous burden.

At first light Lacey dressed in riding clothes and went downstairs. Rita had just arrived to begin her duties.

"No breakfast for me, Rita," Lacey said. "I couldn't

swallow a bite. I have no idea when I'll return; there's so much to do and so little time."

Lacey hurried to the barn to saddle her mare. Rusty was already there.

"I've saddled your mare, Miz Lacey. You want me to go with you? It won't be no trouble."

"No, Rusty. Stay here, I'll be fine."

Lacey mounted and rode off.

The Cramer hands were milling around Lefty when Lacey turned into the yard. She took Lefty off for a private word before addressing the hands.

"You all know what happened in town," Lacey began. "Though our marriage was of short duration, Mr. Cramer and I were indeed married when he was slain. I'm not sure yet what I'm going to do with the ranch, but no one will lose their job because of the tragedy. I placed Lefty in charge and expect everyone to work with him. If anyone wishes to leave, he is free to do so. Your pay will be immediately forthcoming. Any questions?"

Despite some grumbling, no one spoke up. Lacey took that as a good sign and went inside to speak to Mrs. Beaver. She found the housekeeper placing dust sheets over the furniture in the parlor.

"I'm sorry, Mrs. Beaver," Lacey said with feeling. "I know how fond you were of Taylor."

"If it wasn't for you he'd still be alive," Mrs. Beaver spat venomously.

Lacey staggered beneath her vicious barrage. "How can you say that? I had nothing to do with the shooting."

"I heard Mr. Cramer was shot by your former husband. He was jealous of Mr. Cramer and took his life. If that's not your fault, I don't know what is."

Lacey squared her shoulders. "I'm sorry you feel that

way, Mrs. Beaver. For your information, Sam Gentry didn't kill Taylor."

The housekeeper sniffed disdainfully. "That's not what I heard. One of the hands rode into town last night and got the whole story."

Lacey bristled indignantly. "Under the circumstances, I feel it best that you leave."

"Wasn't planning on staying anyway. I'm already packed. I'm going to live with my brother's family in town."

"One of the hands will drive you to town. Follow me into Taylor's office and I'll see that you receive a generous severance pay."

Mrs. Beaver's deep-set dark eyes glittered with hostility as she accompanied Lacey into Cramer's study. Lacey's gaze went immediately to the safe.

"Do you happen to know the combination to Mr. Cramer's safe, Mrs. Beaver?"

"Why would I know a thing like that?"

Lacey said nothing as she dug into her skirt pocket and pulled out a sheath of bills. She peeled off a one-hundred-dollar bill and handed it to the housekeeper. Mrs. Beaver's eyes bugged out. It was probably more cash than she'd ever seen at one time.

"Why are you giving me this?"

"I'm sure you deserve it."

Without so much as a thank you, the housekeeper marched out the door with her nose in the air. Lacey gave scant thought to the woman as she methodically began to search through Cramer's desk. An hour later, after pulling out drawers and scattering papers, she had found nothing that could lead her to Andy. But she did make one discovery.

She found the combination to Taylor's safe taped to the bottom of a drawer.

Chapter Eighteen

Lacey's hands shook as she knelt before the safe and spun the combination dial to match the numbers on the paper. She made a mistake and started over. Her relief was palpable when she pulled on the door and it opened.

One by one she removed the contents of the safe and laid them out on the desk. When the safe was empty, she carefully inspected each item. The land deeds puzzled her. What did Taylor want with property in Texas, New Mexico and Arizona? She set the deeds aside, reminding herself to question Taylor's lawyer about them. Next, she emptied one of the three cloth sacks she discovered inside, and was stunned when gold coins tumbled out.

Setting the sacks aside, Lacey perused the letters she found in the safe. She learned nothing from them and quickly discarded them. They mostly pertained to railroad rights. Perhaps later she would delve more deeply into them. The safe also contained several pieces of jewelry. Once her inspection was completed, Lacey put everything back in the safe and closed the door. She was no closer to finding Andy now than she had been yesterday.

Lacey left the ranch and rode to town. Before visiting Sam, she intended to pay a call on Taylor's lawyer. Someone *had* to know something about Andy. Lacey located the lawyer's office above the barbershop. She climbed the stairs, rapped on the door and stepped inside.

The lawyer looked her over, then greeted her with a lascivious smile. "Come in, don't be bashful. If you are in need of a lawyer, you've come to the right place."

Lacey was instantly alert. Lawyer Oakley didn't impress her, and he seemed more interested in her person than in her business.

"I'm Lacey Gen . . . er . . . Cramer."

"You're Taylor's widow. Terrible thing, that. I wasn't expecting someone as beautiful as you." He indicated a chair. "Please sit down."

Lacey perched on the edge of the chair while Oakley circled her like a bird of prey. "Did my . . . husband leave a will?" she asked when he seemed in no hurry to open the conversation.

Oakley made an impatient gesture. "I advised him

many times to make out a will, but he always put me off. He refused to consider his own demise. He was in his prime and healthy as a horse. He said wills were for the elderly."

"What does that mean to me? Was I wrong to draw funds from Taylor's bank account?"

"No, indeed. You had every right to claim Cramer's money, and everything else he owned. You're his next of kin. With no will to indicate his wishes, you stand to inherit his estate. If you'd like, I'll prepare the necessary papers and present them to the judge next time he comes to town. But since there are no other heirs, his estate is yours to claim. In addition to his money, I helped him acquire certain lands he was interested in. He kept the deeds in his home safe."

"Do you know why he made those land purchases?"

"He didn't confide in me. Taylor Cramer was a very private man. I doubt that anyone knew why he did the things he did."

"One more thing, Mr. Oakley. Did my . . . husband ever mention my son?"

"He might have mentioned him casually a time or two. Why do you ask?"

"This is important, so please think carefully before you answer. Andy is missing. I have reason to believe that Taylor was holding him hostage. Do you know where Taylor hid him?"

"That's a serious accusation, Mrs. Cramer. What proof do you have?"

"Just answer my question, please."

"The answer is no. I haven't spoken to your husband in several weeks."

"Thank you, Mr. Oakley. Go ahead and prepare the

necessary papers. Whatever you charge is fine with me."

"Very well. My fee," he said, lowering his voice to a seductive level, "can be paid . . . in many ways, if you get my meaning. You're a beautiful woman, Mrs. Cramer. I'll enjoy doing . . . business with you. Lonely widows are my specialty."

"I'll pay in hard cash, thank you," Lacey said indignantly. "Now if you'll excuse me, I have business elsewhere."

Rising stiffly, Lacey walked out the door with as much dignity as she could muster. How dare the man! How many unsuspecting widows had he compromised? she wondered as she descended the stairs and headed over to the jailhouse.

Lacey was eager to learn if Sheriff Hale had discovered anything new about Andy's disappearance since she'd last seen him. And she wanted to see Sam. Even if Sam had shot Taylor, he didn't deserve to be punished. Taylor Cramer was a man without scruples, a man who had kidnaped an innocent little boy in order to get what he wanted.

But Sam *hadn't* killed Taylor, of that she was confident. The man she loved wasn't a killer.

The sheriff rose from behind his desk to greet Lacey when she entered.

"Have you learned anything about Andy's disappearance?" Lacey asked without preamble.

"Sorry, Lacey, I wasn't able to turn up a thing. I won't give up, though."

Deflated, Lacey sank into the nearest chair. "Someone has to know something."

"I agree, but I haven't come across that person yet. Don't give up, Lacey."

327

Connie Mason

"I won't. I can't!" she said fiercely. "I want to see Sam. He must be worried sick about Andy. Have you learned anything that could clear Sam of Taylor's murder?"

"No, nothing. I reckon you'll just have to accept the fact that Sam Gentry killed Taylor Cramer."

"Never!" Lacey said ardently. "Sam isn't guilty. I'd stake my life on it."

"Your faith is commendable, Lacey, but unless another suspect comes forward, Gentry will be brought to trial."

Lacey sighed despondently. The whole world was turning against her. She might never see her son again, and the man she loved could spend the rest of his life in prison . . . unless a necktie party got to him first.

"Can I see Sam now, Sheriff?"

"Go right ahead, Lacey. You know where to find him."

Lacey walked down the corridor on wooden legs. What was she going to tell Sam? How could she face him? He must feel helpless—unable to prove his innocence and prevented from searching for Andy. She found Sam sitting on his bunk, looking as thoroughly dejected as she'd ever seen him. He saw her and his face lit up.

"Lacey! Any news of Andy?"

"No," Lacey said morosely. "I searched Taylor's desk and safe and found nothing to link him to Andy's disappearance. I didn't have time to go through Taylor's bedroom, but I doubt I'd have found anything. Taylor was very clever. Oh, Sam, I . . . I'm so frightened. What if I never see Andy again?"

Sam clutched the bars so tightly his knuckled turned

white. "Don't talk like that. It's not like you to give up. Andy *will* be found."

"What about you, Sam? Will Taylor's killer come forward? Will you be convicted of a crime you didn't commit?"

Sam's heart swelled with love. "You *do* believe I didn't kill Cramer. I feared you wouldn't."

Lacey nodded jerkily. "You're not capable of murder, Sam. I meant what I said that night we made love, the night before Taylor was shot. God, it seems so long ago."

"I've been a bastard, haven't I, love? Forgive me. Jail is no place for a declaration of this sort, but it has to be said. I love you, Lacey. I fought it for six years but was never able to completely forget you. I prided myself for having banished you from my memory, but I was only fooling myself. If I had never run into you in Texas, I would have gone to my grave still wanting you. When fate brought us together, I could no longer deny the love I'd refused to acknowledge during our years apart. I love you, Lacey. I'll always love you."

Sam watched the play of emotion on Lacey's lovely features and wished he could dissolve the bars and hold her in his arms.

"You mean it, Sam? Truly?"

"Truly, love. Now dry your eyes and tell me what you found in Cramer's safe."

Lacey gave him a watery smile. "Gold, lots of it. Letters from various people, and deeds to properties in Texas, Arizona and New Mexico."

Sam frowned as he mulled over everything Lacey had told him. "What in the world did he want with all that land?"

"I don't know. It's all so puzzling."

"Did you visit Cramer's lawyer?"

Sam could tell by the look on Lacey's face that something had happened. "What is it? What did Cramer's lawyer tell you? Did Cramer leave a will designating an heir other than yourself?"

"No, I'm Taylor's sole heir. It's . . . well, I don't trust the man. He and Taylor are cut from the same cloth."

Fierce anger welled up inside Sam. "What did he do to you?"

"Nothing. I wouldn't let him. I questioned him about Andy, but he appeared to know nothing about our son's disappearance. He said he hadn't spoken to Taylor in several weeks."

"Damn! Someone has to know something."

"That's what I told Sheriff Hale."

Sam felt so damn helpless. His son was missing and the woman he loved was going through hell, and it tore him apart.

"If only I were free . . ."

Would he ever be free? Unless someone came forward with information, he was likely to hang. Western justice was swift and lethal.

"You *will* be free," Lacey said fiercely. "I just know that something or someone will turn up to clear your name."

Sam wished he were as confident as Lacey. This surely had to be the lowest point in his life. His life had taken many downward turns, but this was by far the worst.

"Don't worry about me, love. I'll beat this somehow." His words held little conviction. "Concentrate on finding Andy."

"We'll get our son back," she said with a determination that further endeared her to Sam. "And we'll be together as a family again. I love you, Sam."

"Those words are all I need to see me through this ordeal," Sam said.

Lacey lifted her face up to the bars, and Sam leaned forward until their lips touched. An aching sweetness stole through him. He pushed his arms between the bars and tried to draw her close, but cold metal prevented the closeness he yearned for. He deepened the kiss, fearing this might be the last kiss they would share. The raspy sound of someone clearing his throat broke them apart.

"Sorry to disturb you," Sheriff Hale said, "but something interesting just turned up."

Lacey's face lit up. "You found Andy!"

"No, but I think you'll welcome this news. Move aside, Lacey, so I can unlock the cell."

Sam sent Hale a wary look. What was going on? Was there a necktie party waiting for him? Was he to have no chance to prove his innocence? It was Dodge City all over again. Lacey stepped away from the bars, and Sheriff Hale unlocked the cell door.

"Follow me," Hale said.

"Where are you taking him?" Lacey asked anxiously.

"There's someone in my office who I'm sure you'd like to thank."

Sam's spirits soared. Had someone stepped forward and confessed to Taylor's murder? Holding tightly to Lacey's hand, he followed Hale down the corridor. He blinked in surprise when he saw Dr. Larsen waiting for them. What kind of trick was this? What could the doctor know about Taylor's killer? He didn't arrive at the scene until the murderer had escaped.

"I assume you both know Dr. Larsen," Hale said. "I want you both to listen to what the good doctor has to say."

Sam's heart pounded erratically. He glanced down at Lacey and saw that her eyes were wide and hopeful. He prayed that whatever information the doctor was about to impart would not disappoint her. As for himself, he feared to raise his hopes too high, for nothing had gone his way thus far.

"Go ahead, Doctor," Hale said. "Tell us what you found."

Dr. Larsen raised his hand, palm up. Sam leaned forward, frowning when he saw the bullet resting in the doctor's palm.

"This is the bullet I dug out of Mr. Cramer," Dr. Larsen explained. "Thought you should see it. Came from a rifle."

"I've already examined the bullet," the sheriff said, addressing Sam, "and sent for the gunsmith to verify my findings. If he agrees with me, you'll be released."

Lacey gasped. "Sam! Did you hear that?"

Sam heard but was too stunned to answer. He picked up the bullet and took a closer look. He knew enough about bullets to know that this one did indeed come from a rifle. He owed the doctor more than he could pay for bringing this to the sheriff's attention.

"I'd heard that Taylor was shot with a .45 caliber pistol and thought it strange that the bullet I'd removed from Mr. Cramer came from a rifle," Dr. Larsen continued. "I didn't want to see an innocent man hang for a crime he didn't commit and decided to come forward with the information."

"I know for a fact that Gentry didn't have a rifle,"

Hale revealed. "The gun in his hand was a .45, and there was no rifle in his saddle boot. That's when I realized there might have been a killer hiding in the bushes, just like Gentry said."

Sam grasped the doctor's hand, pumping it vigorously. "I don't know how to thank you, Doctor."

"Glad I could help, son."

"Ah, here's the gunsmith," Sheriff Hale said. "Come in, Stevens." He retrieved the bullet and handed it to the gunsmith. "Can you name the weapon this bullet came from?"

Stevens held the bullet up to the light and studied it carefully from all angles. "The bullet came from a rifle, Sheriff."

"Are you sure? Could it have come from a .45?"

"This ain't no .45 bullet, Sheriff, I'd stake my life on it."

Lacey made an inarticulate sound, clinging to Sam as if he were a lifeline.

"Thanks, Stevens. You've been a great help."

"Is that all, Sheriff?" Stevens asked.

"Yes, you're free to go now."

"What about me, Sheriff?" Sam asked. "Am I free to go?"

"In a minute. What can you tell me about the man who shot Mr. Cramer? Can you describe him to me? There's a killer on the loose in my town, and I want him behind bars."

"I didn't see the man," Sam recounted. "I saw the rifle barrel protruding from the foliage, realized it was pointed at Cramer and Lacey, and my gut reaction was to shoot into the bushes before he fired. I don't know if my bullet hit him. When I went to look, he was gone.

333

As far as I know, his identity is a mystery. I sure as hell hope you find him."

"So do I. I reckon you can go now."

Sam breathed an audible sigh. Now he and Lacey could get on with their lives. "I'm eternally grateful to you, Dr. Larsen. If there's anything I can do for you, don't hesitate to ask."

"You're welcome, son. I'll remember your offer."

"You'll want your guns," Sheriff Hale said as he opened his drawer and withdrew Sam's gun belt. "I hope this is the last time you're a guest in my jail."

"You can count on it, Sheriff," Sam said as he buckled his gun belt around his hips. "I've got a son to find."

"Rest assured I'll do everything in my power to restore your son to you."

Despite his worry over Andy, Sam felt nothing but elation as he left the jail a free man. He'd had enough dealings with the wrong side of the law to last a lifetime. From here on out his life was going to be a peaceful one. Dull, even.

He glanced at Lacey. She appeared dazed. "Are you all right, love? You look shaken."

"You're free, Sam, truly free. When we find Andy, we can get on with our lives. We'll be a real family."

Her bottom lip was trembling, and Sam wanted to take her into his arms to reassure her. But that would come later. They had something more important to do first. "We'll get Andy back, sweetheart, I guarantee it. But there's something we need to do first."

"Nothing is more important than Andy," Lacey protested.

Sam said nothing as he guided Lacey down the street with a firm hand against the small of her back.

"Where are we going?"

Sam gave her an enigmatic smile. "To see the preacher."

"To make Taylor's funeral arrangements? Why is that important to you?"

"I don't give a hoot about Cramer. We're going to see the preacher for another reason."

Lacey's confusion made him chuckle. But he didn't bother to explain. They had reached the parsonage. Sam opened the gate, grasped her arm and guided her up to the house. Before Lacey could question him further, he rapped sharply on the door. The door was opened by a plump little dumpling of a woman.

"We'd like to see Reverend Garland," Rafe said.

"I'm Mrs. Garland. Please wait in the parlor while I get my husband."

"What are you doing?" Lacey hissed after Mrs. Garland showed them into the parlor and bustled off.

"Patience," Sam said.

Reverend Garland appeared a few minutes later. He stopped abruptly when he saw Sam.

"You! What are you doing out of jail?"

"The sheriff turned me loose when evidence proving I wasn't guilty turned up."

The preacher's skeptical gaze shifted to Lacey. "Is this true, Mrs. Cramer?"

"It's true, Reverend. The sheriff has positive proof that Sam didn't shoot Taylor."

The preacher looked immensely relieved. "I've been expecting you, Mrs. Cramer. I assume you want me to speak words over your husband's grave."

"I . . . I . . . yes. I'm sorry it's taken so long to make

arrangements. I'll let you know the time," Lacey stammered.

"That's not the only reason we're here, Reverend," Sam revealed. "Lacey and I want to get married. Right here. Right now."

"We do?" Lacey gasped.

"You do?" Reverend Garland echoed.

"We do," Sam said firmly.

"But . . . but . . ." the preacher sputtered. "Mrs. Cramer was just married yesterday."

"That was yesterday. Today Lacey is a widow. Is there a legal reason why we can't marry?"

"No, of course not . . . except, well, it doesn't seem proper. There's been no period of mourning. The man isn't even buried yet."

Lacey tugged on Sam's sleeve. "Are you sure this is what you want, Sam?"

His voice was low and ardent. "I've never wanted anything more. I love you, Lacey. You're the mother of my son. For all we know, you might be carrying another child of mine."

Reverend Garland gasped audibly. "Is that true, Mrs. Cramer?"

Lacey blushed and lifted her head proudly. Sam had never admired her more. "Sam is telling the truth, Reverend. I married Taylor Cramer because he held my son hostage. He refused to release Andy until I agreed to become his wife. I've always loved Sam and I still do."

"Well, now, that puts a different face on things. I'm not one to stand in the way of true love. I'll fetch my wife to act as witness."

"Thank you, Reverend," Sam said gratefully.

"You could have asked me first," Lacey hissed after the preacher left the room.

"I was afraid you'd refuse," Sam replied. "I wanted us to return to the ranch as husband and wife."

Reverend Garland returned with his beaming wife. Sam and Lacey stood before him, holding hands and smiling into each other's eyes as he read the vows. The ceremony was blessedly brief. With heartfelt relief, Sam turned to kiss his bride. Lacey lifted her mouth, and he tasted the sweetest kiss he'd ever known.

When the papers were signed and delivered, Sam realized he lacked the funds to pay the preacher. Seeing his dilemma, Lacey promptly pulled a greenback from her pocket and offered it to the reverend. Garland's eyes lit up when he noted the large denomination of the bill, and his gratitude was long and profuse.

Once the parsonage door closed behind them, Sam pulled Lacey into his arms and kissed her properly. They were both breathless by the time he broke off the kiss.

"That's just a prelude to what I'm going to do when I get you alone," Sam promised. "Let's go home, love."

"There's something I have to do first," Lacey said. "I'm not looking forward to it, but he has no one else."

"Arrange for Cramer's burying," Sam guessed.

"I should make arrangements with the undertaker and pay for the burial. You don't have to come with me if you don't want to."

"You're not alone anymore, Lacey. I'm your husband. You have my support in everything you do."

The undertaker appeared relieved to see them. "I was beginning to worry when I didn't hear from you, Mrs. Cramer. The body is ready for viewing. I gave your husband the finest casket I had in stock. I suggest we hold

337

the services as soon as possible. Tomorrow morning, if that meets with your approval."

"There will be no viewing or services," Lacey advised, "but tomorrow will be fine for the burying. Reverend Garland promised to say words over the grave. Will you inform him of the time?"

The undertaker sent her a puzzled look. "What time would be convenient for you?"

"I won't be attending."

"You're not gonna attend your own husband's funeral?"

"That's right." She pulled the remaining greenbacks from her pocket and handed them to the undertaker. "Will this cover everything?"

The undertaker stared at the money. "It's more than enough. That's mighty generous of you, Mrs. Cramer."

"She's Mrs. Gentry now," Sam informed him. "We were married today."

The undertaker appeared shaken. Sam grinned. He and Lacey were going to be the talk of the town. They took their leave a few minutes later, retrieved their horses from the livery and headed back to the ranch. All they needed to make their happiness complete was Andy. To that end, Sam intended to ride out to the Cramer spread in the morning and personally interrogate each and every cowboy who'd been working for Cramer at the time of Andy's disappearance.

Sam's heart swelled with happiness when the B&G came into view. The farm back in Kansas had been the only home he'd ever known, until he and his brothers had lost it. He wasn't by nature a roamer, and had felt like a fish out of water without a place to call home. He didn't know a whole lot about ranching, but he intended to make this spread prosper for Lacey and Andy's sake.

"What are you thinking, Sam?" Lacey asked, disturbing his introspection.

"About you and Andy. I'm going to make the B&G a place you can be proud of."

Lacey's sob tore at his heart. He reined in beside her and lifted her from her mare, settling her before him in the saddle. "Don't worry, love, we're going to find our son."

"I want to believe you, Sam, but Taylor was so secretive I fear we'll never find him."

"Cramer had to have had an accomplice." His jaw firmed, his conviction unshakable. "We'll find Andy."

Sam and Lacey's return to the B&G was greeted with boisterous enthusiasm. Questions came so fast and furious that Sam held up his hand to stop them.

"Whoa, boys, one at a time," he said as he dismounted and handed Lacey down. "Let's start with Rusty."

Rusty stepped forward, grasping Sam's hand and pumping vigorously. "If you don't beat all, Sam. I thought you were in jail. Miz Lacey didn't break you out, did she?"

Sam laughed at the thought of Lacey storming the jail. "The sheriff received proof of my innocence and released me. I owe it all to Doc Larsen. He dug the bullet out of Cramer and realized it came from a rifle, not a .45. All I carried was a .45 so I couldn't be the killer."

Suddenly Rusty sobered. "What about Andy? Any clues to where Cramer hid the boy?"

Sam's arm crept around Lacey's waist, bolstering her with his strength. "No, but we haven't given up. Not by a long shot. I won't give up the search until I find him."

"You'll find him," Rusty concurred.

Connie Mason

"Where are you gonna make your home, Miz Lacey? You own two ranches now," Amos called out.

"That's easy, Amos. I'm not giving up the B&G. My home is here."

"There's something else you should know," Sam said, beaming down at Lacey. "Lacey and I were married today."

"Well, I'll be a flop-eared jackass," Rusty guffawed. "Keeping up with you two is nigh on impossible. Married, not married, married. After all that, I'd say you two belong together. Congratulations. Andy will be tickled pink to have his parents together."

The mention of Andy's name seemed to dampen the enthusiasm. Lacey's smile faltered. "Andy will be thrilled with the way things turned out." She squeezed Sam's hand. "Shall we go up to the house and tell Rita our good news?"

Hand in hand they walked to the house, surprising Rita in the kitchen.

"Señor! *Dios!*" She made the sign of the cross. "I thought—we all thought—you were in jail."

"It was all a misunderstanding, Rita," Sam said, giving the rotund woman a hug. "I'm home now, and I'm not going anywhere, except to find Andy and bring him home." He gave Lacey a wink. "Do you want to tell her or shall I?"

"I'll tell her," Lacey said. She grasped Rita's hand. "Sam and I were remarried today."

A delighted grin spread across Rita's handsome features. "*Dios.* That *is* good news. Now Señor Sam can look after you and Andy. Señor Sam is strong. He will find Andy. I will cook a festive supper tonight to celebrate your marriage."

Sam had other plans. "Thank you, Rita, but I think we'd prefer something on a tray. Lacey is exhausted and clearly in need of rest. Andy's disappearance has taken a toll on her. Don't fix anything fancy. Set the tray outside the door before you leave for the night."

Rita's eyes twinkled. "I understand. Good night, señor, señora."

Lacey didn't argue when Sam scooped her up in his arms and ascended the stairs. With Sam's comforting arms around her, she had no difficulty believing he'd find Andy and they'd live happily ever after. He was so strong, so vital, so indestructible, and she loved him desperately. Neither years nor distance had destroyed that love, and she knew now that Sam felt the same, despite the way he'd fought against loving her when fate reunited them.

This was the man with whom she intended to spend the rest of her life. There would be other children to keep Andy company. She smiled dreamily. Perhaps she was already carrying Sam's child.

Sam carried Lacey to their room and closed the door behind him. He removed his hand from beneath her knees and set her carefully on her feet. Lacey scarcely had time to draw in a breath before his mouth took hers in a deeply sensual kiss that made her toes curl. He kissed her until she couldn't breathe, until her body sang and a heady rush of blood pounded through her veins.

"I want to make love to you, Lacey, but if you'd rather not tonight, I'll understand."

The seductive timbre of his voice stirred her, making her aware of her own mounting desire. "This is our wedding night."

341

Sam nodded slowly. "I want to make it one you'll remember forever."

"I haven't forgotten, not once, any of the times we made love in the past. You've *always* made it memorable, my love. Even when we were too young to appreciate the passion we shared."

A groan rumbled from Sam's chest as he carried her to the bed and followed her down. He kissed her with so much feeling Lacey felt surrounded and protected by his love. She broke off the kiss, wanting, needing more.

"Make love to me, Sam. I've never needed you more than I do now."

Chapter Nineteen

Sam's eyes glowed with mounting desire. "Making you happy will always come first with me," he whispered. "I need you as badly as you need me."

Lacey wound her arms around his neck and pulled him against her. Passion swirled around them, so thick it was impossible to breathe without inhaling it. She moistened her lips, felt them trembling. She heard a low sound rumble from his chest as his mouth came down over hers. His kiss was hard and ravishing; one of fierce possession. His breath scorched her; his mouth tasted of ambrosia.

She couldn't think past her next breath, her next heartbeat as Sam broke the kiss and slowly undressed. Then, with remarkable haste, he released his gun belt and stripped off his own clothing. He stood over her, his body resplendent in its nudity, a powerful figure in full arousal. Her breath caught as her gaze traveled the length of his powerful form. Her wits scattered abruptly as the bed shifted beneath his weight. He kissed her again, cupping her breasts, plucking the ends into ripe buds. A hiss left Lacey's throat. The pads of his thumbs felt rough against her swollen nipples.

Lowering his head, he took the heavy weight of one breast into his mouth. Smoldering fire seared along her skin as hard hands stroked, teased and caressed her body. An eternity later he pressed her down into the soft mattress and spread her legs. She felt the hot, rigid length of him pressing against her opening. But instead of thrusting mindlessly, he kissed her again, and yet again, making her breasts ache and her womanhood throb.

She watched with growing excitement as his dark head moved down. He kissed and sucked her nipples, pausing for a moment on his downward trek to lick her navel before sliding lower. One errant finger sifted through the thatch of blond curls at the base of her thighs, then slipped inside her.

Lacey moaned, thrashing mindlessly. "Now, Sam. Please."

"God, yes," he moaned, moving upward and thrusting forward, sheathing himself to the hilt. Her hips arched to meet his driving loins. She clutched the sheets lest she fly off the bed and moaned his name over and over. With a growl, he plunged his tongue into the waiting warmth of her mouth, clasping her head and burying his fingers in her lush mass of hair to hold her still for his ravishing tongue.

Lacey refused to be restrained as waves of pleasure radiated from her core to every sensitive part of her body. A scream welled up in her throat and burst forth. Ecstasy seized her and carried her away.

"Sweet God," Sam muttered thickly. He flung his head back, his eyes sliding shut. "Not even heaven could taste this sweet."

Sam was like a volcano about to erupt. When he felt Lacey tighten around him, felt the contractions pulsing against him, he could wait no longer. Lifting his head, he shouted out his joy. Unmoving, he lay atop her a blissful moment before lifting himself and rolling away. His eyes were closed, his breathing harsh and heavy. From a great distance he heard Lacey's voice.

"Sam."

With great effort he turned his head toward her. "Hmmm?"

"That was . . ."

"I know, I feel the same way. Words can't describe what I'm feeling right now. I don't deserve you, Lacey. I've hurt you terribly. I was wrong about you from the beginning. How can you love a flawed creature like myself?"

"Don't you know, Sam? Sometimes the things we value most are flawed. That's part of what makes them lovable. Like you, Sam. You're not perfect but you're exactly what I need, what I want."

Sam gave a shaky laugh. He prayed that Lacey would never change her opinion of him. He couldn't survive without her love. While he and his brothers were together as a family, he'd been able to function, but he'd always known that one day his brothers would find wives and have families of their own, leaving him the odd man out.

His brothers had overlooked his reckless ways, laughing at his uncanny ability to get into trouble. He realized now that his recklessness was his way of compensating for what he had left behind in Pennsylvania. God, he'd been such a fool.

"Let's just say we're perfect for one another," Sam said.

He closed his eyes, utterly exhausted. He would have fallen asleep if Lacey hadn't trailed her fingertips over his chest, tormenting him with the promise of another bout of erotic pleasure. She began to kiss down his throat to his shoulders, continuing in a meandering line down his chest.

"Damn!" The curse exploded from his lungs when Lacey's lips tugged at his flat male nipple. Scorching heat lashed him when she ran her tongue down the furrow of dark hair on his chest. Her probing tongue paused to explore his navel, and a shock of raw pleasure shot through him.

Suddenly she rose on her knees and leaned over him, her greedy eyes fastened on that part of him that stood at rigid attention. Shock waves roiled through him when she touched her hot mouth to the tip of him, then swirled her tongue over the tight, aching head.

Sam fought desperately for control as his wife tasted him thoroughly, teasing him beyond human endurance. "Enough!" he roared as he grasped her about the waist, pulled her over him and impaled her. Propelled by urgency, he plunged deep, again and again, groaning as she clenched around him, driving him nearly insane. His pistoning hips drove faster, deeper, reaching for her soul. He released his seed into her shuddering womb moments after she stiffened and cried out.

Sam fell asleep with Lacey lying atop him, his softening sex still embedded inside her. He murmured a protest but didn't stir when Lacey moved off him and settled into the curve of his body.

Pangs of hunger awakened Sam later that night. He padded to the door, opened it and found the tray Rita had left for them. He carried it to the bed and lifted the cover. A delicious aroma reached the sleeping Lacey's twitching nose. She opened her eyes, stretched, then lurched upright when she saw Sam with the tray of food.

"Ummm. I smell fried chicken!" she exclaimed. "I hope you like it cold."

"I could eat it raw right now," Sam assured her.

Rummaging further, Sam found tortillas, baked beans rich with molasses and generous slices of apple pie.

"Rita didn't forget a thing," Lacey said. "Do you want to wash up first?"

"Ladies first," Sam said.

He watched avidly as Lacey walked naked to the washstand, poured water into a bowl and made her ablutions. When she finished, she tossed the water out the open window and refilled the bowl with fresh.

"Your turn."

Sam needed no further encouragement. The sooner he washed, the sooner he could get back to the food. Lacey had already dug in when he returned to the bed. Rita had included plates, glasses and silverware on the tray, along with a pitcher of lemonade.

"Ummm. The chicken is good," Lacey said between mouthfuls.

"So are the beans," Sam added. He leered at her bare breasts. "I'm not sure I can sleep on a full stomach."

Lacey gave him an impish grin. "What *can* you do on a full stomach?"

"I'd be happy to show you after you're through eating."

They finished their meal and made love again, their passion slowly building to a tumultuous explosion.

"I'll never forget our wedding night, Sam," Lacey sighed when they finally settled down to sleep. "Only one thing would make this the happiest day of my life."

Sam knew exactly what she meant, for he felt the same way. He and Lacey would never be truly happy until Andy was restored to them.

Sam arose before Lacey had awakened the following morning. He wanted to speak to Rusty and the hands before he began his search for Andy. He'd promised Lacey he'd find their son and he intended to keep his promise.

The cold wind sucked the breath from Sam as he made his way to the cookhouse, where the hands had gathered for breakfast. The thought of Andy suffering cold and hunger while he was warm and fed made him sick. What if Cramer had turned Andy loose in the wilds of Texas to fend for himself?

"What are you doing up so early?" Rusty teased when Sam entered the cookhouse.

"I can't afford to linger in bed while Andy is missing," Sam answered as he walked over to the cookstove to warm his hands. "I'll need every available hand to join in the search."

"Everything here is pretty much done," Rusty said.

348

"We've been mending fences and repairing some of the outbuildings during the cold spell. You and Miz Lacey will be wanting to add to your herd, and me and the boys were putting things in good repair. But that can wait. We need to bring our Andy back home."

Sam sat down heavily. He hadn't let Lacey see his fear, but it was there nevertheless. Andy was just a small boy, with few or no survival skills. The boy wasn't mature enough to cope with Cramer's evil machinations. What if Andy was already dead? Placing his elbows on the table, Sam dropped his head into his cupped hands and gave in to his despair.

Rusty cleared his throat. "We'll find him, Sam. You gotta keep your spirits up for Miz Lacey's sake."

Sam raised his head. "I'm sorry, Rusty. Crying won't bring my son back. I'm riding out to the Cramer place this morning and questioning the hands myself. Perhaps they'll remember something they forgot when Lacey and the sheriff questioned them."

"There's plenty of food left over from breakfast," Luke said. "Are you hungry?"

"No, but I sure would appreciate a cup of coffee."

Luke poured Sam a cup of steaming coffee and placed it before him. "Hot and black, Sam, just the way you like it."

"Time's a-wasting, boys," Rusty said, rising.

"Stay, Rusty," Sam said as the hands filed out the door. "I want your opinion about—"

Suddenly Lefty burst through the door, pushing the others aside.

Sam shoved away from the table. "Lefty! What the . . . I thought you were at the Cramer spread."

"I was, Sam, but there's something you should know. The foreman just returned."

"Is he giving you trouble?" Rusty asked.

"Not really. When he learned that Cramer was dead, he seemed kind of anxious. He was packing up to leave when I passed the bunkhouse and heard him talking to one of the hands. He knows something about Andy, Sam. I'd stake my life on it."

Sam was already out the door. "Tell Lacey I went over to the Cramer spread," he called back to Rusty. "Don't tell her anything else. I don't want to get her hopes up."

Sam and Lefty reached the Cramer ranch in record time. Sam drew rein outside the bunkhouse, leaped from Galahad's back and strode through the door like a man with a mission. He had arrived just in time. Harper had just turned away from his bunk and was heading out the door, his bulging saddlebags thrown over his shoulder. He stopped in his tracks when Sam burst into the room.

"Are you Cramer's foreman?" Sam barked.

"Yeah, I'm Sid Harper. What's it to you?"

"I understand you've been away on ranch business."

"What of it? I ain't done nothing wrong."

"That's debatable. Tell me, Harper, are you willing to die for a dead man?"

Sam could have sworn he saw sweat popping out on Harper's brow. The man knew something, he was certain of it.

"I know you. You're Sam Gentry. You killed Mr. Cramer."

"You're wrong, Harper. I didn't kill anyone, and the sheriff had sufficient proof to set me free." He stepped forward until he stood nose to nose with Harper. His eyes narrowed into slits and his voice held a note of menace. "What have you done with my son?"

Harper gulped audibly. "I don't know what you're talking about."

Sam's hands flew out to circle Harper's neck. "I mean business, Harper. Andy's a small boy. He couldn't defend himself if he wanted to. Did you kill him?"

Harper's eyes bugged out as Sam's hands tightened. "I couldn't, I wouldn't do that. I swear I—"

"The truth, Harper, or you'll never leave this room alive."

Harper's voice rose on a note of panic. "Honest, Mr. Gentry, I didn't hurt Andy. I ain't a killer and I'd never do anything to harm a child. When I balked at killing the boy, Mr. Cramer paid me to take him where no one would find him."

The pressure on Harper's throat eased. "What exactly did you do with my son?" Sam snarled. "Did you abandon him in the wilderness? Andy had no survival skills; that's the same as killing him."

"No, I swear I didn't abandon him!"

"If you don't tell me where Andy is in the next five seconds, you're a dead man. One . . . two—"

"I took him to Fort Worth," Harper choked out.

Sam maintained unrelenting pressure on Harper's throat. "Where?"

"I need air," Harper gagged.

Sam's fingers eased. "I'm waiting."

"I took Andy to an orphanage and left him in the care of nuns."

"An orphanage!" Sam exploded. "What orphanage?"

"A mission orphanage. Saint Leo's."

Sam shoved Harper away so hard he stumbled and fell. He was so damn angry he could have killed the man, and might have if Lefty hadn't stepped forward to whisper a word of caution in his ear.

"He ain't worth it, Sam."

Sam must have seen reason, for he thrust Harper at Lefty, "Take the bastard to the sheriff. What he did was against the law."

"I didn't hurt the boy," Harper protested hoarsely, rubbing his throat. "Ask him yourself."

"Believe me, I will. Take him away, Lefty."

Harper lifted himself from the floor, dusted off his hat and found himself facing Lefty's six-shooter. "I'm going, I'm going."

Never had Sam felt so emotionally drained. Andy was alive, if Harper could be believed. Before long he'd be home where he belonged, with parents who loved him. Pulling himself together, Sam mounted Galahad and rode home. He wanted Lacey to be the first to know that Andy was alive, so he bypassed the bunkhouse and rode directly to the front door. His steps were light, his mood buoyant as he leaped onto the porch and strode through the door, yelling for Lacey at the top of his lungs.

"Sam, what is it?" Lacey cried, rushing down the stairs. "Is it Andy? Please, God, let him be alive."

Sam opened his arms, and Lacey rushed into them. He lifted her off her feet and swung her around.

"Sam, please, don't keep me in suspense. Is Andy all right?"

"Pack your valise, love, we're taking the next stage to Fort Worth."

Lacey frowned. "Have you lost your mind? Why are we going to Fort Worth?"

"Because that's where Andy is."

"Sam Gentry! If you don't tell me this minute what

you're talking about, I'm going to smash you."

Grasping her hand, Sam dragged her into the parlor and pushed her down onto the sofa. Then he knelt beside her, clasping her hands in his.

"Our son is safe, love. Someone *did* know where he was. Cramer's foreman took him to Fort Worth. He'll be with us again very soon."

"Why Fort Worth?"

"Cramer had Harper take Andy to Saint Leo's orphanage. We need to go there and claim our son."

Sam drew Lacey up into his arms when she began to tremble. "I know, I know. I felt the same way when I heard. But an orphanage is safe, sweetheart. Worse things could have happened to Andy."

"Can we leave now?"

"As soon as you pack a few things. We might have to spend the night in town while we wait for the stage, but at least we know Andy is safe. I'll throw a few things of my own together while you're doing your packing."

They were well on their way to town fifteen minutes later.

As luck would have it, the stage had already departed and they had to wait until the next day. They boarded their horses at the livery and walked to the hotel. Sam rented a room for the night, then ordered a bath and supper sent to their room. They bathed together in the tub, made love afterward and ate their dinner before a cozy fire. Andy's almost certain return allowed them their first peaceful sleep in days.

The stagecoach was only an hour late, which boded well for the journey Sam and Lacey were about to undertake. Two uneventful days and one night in a crowded way station later, the stage pulled into Fort Worth. The trip had been exceedingly monotonous as mile after mile of wild, desolate land, bleak hills and stunted grass and mesquite passed before their eyes. The cold, fierce winds blew dust devils thick enough to choke a steer.

Sam collected their valises while Lacey looked over the town. The usual number of saloons vied for space on both sides of the street with a barbershop, dry goods store, feed and hardware store, greengrocer and various other establishments.

"What now, Sam?" Lacey asked after Sam had collected their bags and joined her on the boardwalk.

"We find the sheriff's office. I'm sure he can direct us to the orphanage."

They walked down the street, then crossed the rutted road when Sam spotted the sheriff's office. The sheriff wasn't in, but his deputy supplied the answers they sought. Saint Leo's orphanage was situated two miles north of town. Sam rented a buggy, and they left immediately.

Saint Leo's rested forlorn and neglected on an arid patch of ground with nary a tree to shade its bleached wooden exterior. Chickens scratched lazily in the dirt near the front porch, whose railing was missing several slats. Lacey felt her heart constrict for the unfortunate children residing within those barren walls.

Sam pulled the buggy to a stop in the front yard. He leaped to the ground and lifted Lacey down. "Shall we?" he said, grasping Lacey's arm and guiding her up the front steps.

Suddenly Lacey balked. "What if Andy isn't here? I'm so frightened, Sam."

"There's only one way to find out, sweetheart," Sam said as he rapped sharply on the door.

Long, suspenseful minutes passed before the door cracked open and a woman in a nun's habit peered through the opening.

"I'm Sister Michael. How may I help you?"

"I'd like to speak to your superior about one of your children," Sam said.

The door opened fully, revealing a small, birdlike woman whose tiny frame was nearly swamped by her voluminous habit. "Please come in. You can wait in Sister Adele's office while I summon her. She handles the adoptions."

"Oh, but we don't—"

"Thank you," Sam said, interrupting Lacey in mid sentence. As soon as the nun turned her back, Sam hissed into Lacey's ear, "We'll cross that bridge when we come to it."

The dun-colored walls were depressing, Lacey thought as she followed Sister Michael. There were few children in sight, and even less evidence of their existence. Lacey shuddered. Were they hidden away somewhere?

They were ushered into a small, sparsely furnished room to wait. Moments later a around woman with red cheeks and twinkling blue eyes bustled into the room. She greeted Sam and Lacey with good humor. "I'm Sister Adele. According to Sister Michael, you were inquiring about one of our children."

"Yes," Sam answered. "We're interested in recent additions to your establishment."

"We've only had two children join us in recent weeks. Little Andy and baby John. How did you hear of them?"

"Oh, God, he's here," Lacey whispered, collapsing into a nearby chair. "Where is he?"

"Are you all right, my dear?" Sister Adele asked kindly. "Would you like a glass of water?"

"No, nothing. Please, I want to see Andy. I want my son."

Sister Adele looked perplexed. "We have only orphans in our home."

"Let me explain," Sam began once he brought his emotions under control. "Andy was taken from us by force and brought to your orphanage. We're his parents."

"But Mr. Harper said Andy's parents were dead, that he had no relatives and no one to care for him."

"Didn't Andy tell you differently? He's usually quite outspoken."

"The poor little tyke has scarcely spoken a word since his arrival. He's made a friend or two but doesn't respond to any of the sisters. We've been worried about him."

"Where is he?" Lacey cried.

"The children are at lessons this time of day. And those too young for lessons usually nap during the afternoon."

"Could you please send for Andy?" Sam requested.

Sister Adele eyed them narrowly. "Are you sure you're Andy's parents? We're very protective of our children. You can see we haven't much, but we do our best with what God has provided."

"Very sure," Sam informed her. "Andy can provide the identification you require."

"Very well. I'll fetch him myself."

Sister Adele left the room in a swish of black skirts.

"What if Andy doesn't remember us?" Lacey asked shakily.

"It hasn't been that long, love."

"Sister Adele said he's been unresponsive since he arrived. You know yourself what a little chatterbox he is. What if . . . what if the terrible experience damaged him in some way?"

"Stop it, Lacey!" Sam said sharply. "You're worrying yourself sick for no reason. Andy may be young but he's a smart little boy. He probably had nothing to talk about, nothing in common with the poor abandoned children here."

Lacey's reply was forestalled when Sister Adele returned with Andy trailing behind her. His head was bowed, his shoulders slumped. A cry of dismay escaped Lacey's throat. The sound brought Andy's head shooting up. Sam was shocked by the vacant look in Andy's eyes. This wasn't the same Andy he knew and loved. This was a boy with empty eyes—a boy without hope.

Neither Sam nor Lacey could move, frozen in place by the lost little boy who stared back at them as if he didn't know them.

"Andy," Sister Adele gently prodded. "Your mama and papa have come to take you home."

Lacey stepped forward, her face suffused with joy. "Andy, Mama and Papa are going to take you home."

Unsmiling, Andy blinked. "Take me home?"

Lacey knelt on the threadbare rug and held out her arms. "Yes, darling. We've finally found you. We're going home. We're going to be a family again."

Sam cursed beneath his breath. The experience had so disturbed Andy that he couldn't grasp what had happened to him. For one uncertain moment Sam feared that

357

Andy would refuse to recognize them. His eyes focused first on Lacey, kneeling with her arms open, and then on Sam. He remained unresponsive, and pain tore through Sam.

"Andy, remember me? I love you, son. I won't let anything bad happen to you again, I swear it."

An eternity passed before Sam saw a change in Andy. Joy chased away hopelessness, illuminating Andy's expressive face. A ragged cry ripped from his throat as he launched himself into Lacey's arms.

"Mama!" He hugged Lacey fiercely. A sound very close to a sob was torn from Sam as he knelt and enclosed them both in his arms.

"Mr. Harper told me you were both dead," Andy said tearfully. "I knew it couldn't be true, but when you didn't come for me, I thought you didn't want me because I was bad and ran away. I know it was wrong, but I didn't want mean old Cramer to be my new papa."

Lacey's voice trembled with emotion. "Oh, Andy. You didn't gave me a chance to explain. I never intended to marry Mr. Cramer. It's over, honey. Your papa and I are going to be together forever, and you're going to be with us."

Andy smiled at Sam through his tears. "Is that true, Papa? Are we going to be together?"

"You have my word on it, son. Are you ready to go home now?"

Andy glanced at Sister Adele, who was beaming at the trio with undisguised pleasure.

"I'll admit I had doubts when you two first arrived," the nun said, "but Andy's response to you was genuine. You are indeed his parents. I don't know how this all came about, and I don't really want to know, but I'm happy your little family is reunited. Andy is a dear little boy. We tried to make him happy, but in his heart he knew he didn't belong here."

Andy smiled at Sister Adele. "I didn't mean to be bad, Sister, but I missed my mama and papa. You were all very good to me."

Suddenly the halls echoed with the laughter of children, transforming the ramshackle dwelling from a dreary abode to one of impoverished happiness.

Sister Adele's face lit up. "Ah, the children have finished their classes for the day. Would you care to come out to the yard and watch them at play? We don't have much, but we try to keep them occupied and well fed, though sometimes the latter is difficult when the townspeople are sluggish with their donations."

"I'd like that," Lacey said, holding tightly to Andy's hand. "Are any of the children ever adopted?"

"We tend to be very careful about adoptions," Sister Adele said. "We don't want the children used as slave labor and we screen prospective parents carefully. Some are genuinely interested in taking a child to love, while others consider it a cheap way to get hired help."

Sam's heart went out to the children who would never know a parent's love. He and Lacey exchanged a speaking look, as if their thoughts ran in the same direction.

"There's Betsy," Andy exclaimed. "Can I say goodbye to her and some of my other friends?"

"Of course," Lacey said as she watched Andy run off.

"Sam and I are eternally grateful for the care you've given Andy," Lacey said, "and we'd like to make a small donation to your institution."

"That's not necessary," Sister Adele protested. "God usually provides, sometimes in ways we don't understand, but we've always managed to put food on the table."

"Perhaps we can help God in a small way," Sam said thoughtfully. "We'd like to arrange a donation of—"

"Five thousand dollars," Lacey blurted out.

Sister Adele teetered on the balls of her feet. Sam reached out to steady her in case she decided to faint. Of course she did no such thing. "Fi . . . five . . . thousand dollars? Oh, my, I don't know what to say. We can spruce up the building, add a dormitory, buy toys and take in more children. The good Lord truly did send you to us."

Andy came trotting back a few minutes later, having made his farewells. "I'm ready to go home now."

Chapter Twenty

Andy sat between Sam and Lacey in the buggy on the ride back to town, chattering like a magpie. He relayed everything that had happened to him since he'd run away, and asked about all his friends at the ranch. He said nothing more about Taylor Cramer, and neither Sam nor Lacey offered information about Cramer's fate at the hands of an assassin.

They boarded the stage the next day and arrived in Denison two days later. Andy was excited to be home again, and skipped beside them as they walked to the livery to get their horses. Suddenly Andy stopped and went very still.

"What is it, son?" Sam asked, instantly alert.

"That man," Andy said, pointing to a cowboy slouched against the saloon wall, rolling a cigarette.

"What about him? Have you seen him before?"

Andy nodded slowly. "I saw him at the ranch the day someone shot at mean old Cramer. I was supposed to be taking a nap but was looking out the window instead. He was hiding behind the barn. I saw his face when he poked his head out and aimed his gun at mean old Cramer. Everyone said *you* tried to kill mean old Cramer, Papa, but I knew better."

"Why didn't you say something before now?" Lacey asked.

"Nobody asked me. I thought it was a secret. But I *did* tell you Papa didn't shoot at mean old Cramer."

"Get the horses, Lacey," Sam said. "I'm going for the sheriff."

"Why is Papa going for the sheriff, Mama?" Andy asked.

"Someone killed Mr. Cramer, honey. It could be that man you pointed out to us. He shot at Mr. Cramer once, so he must have had reason to do it again. This time he didn't miss. Hurry—there might be gunplay when the sheriff arrives to question him, and we shouldn't be on the street."

Lacey hustled Andy inside the livery, then turned and peeked out the door.

"What's happening, Mama?"

"Papa and the sheriff are crossing the street to talk to the cowboy. He doesn't appear apprehensive, so maybe he'll surrender peacefully."

Lacey had spoken too soon. When the cowboy realized that Sam and the sheriff were honing in on him, he bolted. The sheriff drew his gun.

"Halt or I'll shoot!"

The cowboy kept running. The sheriff fired a warning shot over his head. The cowboy whipped out his gun, turned and fired. The shot went wild. Sam reacted swiftly. Drawing his six-shooter, he shot the gun out of the cowboy's hand. The cowboy clutched his hand to his chest and cursed violently. The sheriff collared him while he was still nursing his hand and prodded him toward the jailhouse. Sam followed close on their heels.

Relieved that it had ended without anyone being seriously hurt, Lacey paid the hostler, set Andy atop Galahad and led the horses from the livery.

"Are we going home without Papa, Mama?"

"We're going to the jailhouse, honey. As soon as Papa is through there, we'll all ride home together."

Sam followed the sheriff and the protesting cowboy inside the jailhouse.

"What's this all about, Sheriff?" the cowboy asked. "I ain't done nothing. I was just standing there minding my own business when you came after me. You can't put a man in jail for minding his own business."

"Why did you run?" Sam asked.

"None of your business, Gentry."

"You know me?"

"Yeah, I know you. Your foreman refused to hire me after that bastard Cramer fired me."

"Now we're getting somewhere," Sheriff Hale said. "What's your handle, cowboy?"

"Most everyone calls me Monk."

"Very well, Monk. Did you kill Taylor Cramer?"

"I didn't kill nobody."

"You were seen shooting at Mr. Cramer."

"That's a damn lie! Nobody saw me!" Suddenly realizing what he said, he added hastily, "I never shot anybody."

"Maybe a few days in jail will loosen your tongue," Hale said. "Move, Monk. There's a nice cozy cell waiting for you."

Sam followed the sheriff and his prisoner into the jailhouse and down the corridor. He wasn't going to leave until the killer confessed. As they passed the cell holding Sid Harper, Sam was surprised to hear Harper call out Monk's name.

"If it ain't Monk! I'm not surprised to see you here. It was only a matter of time before the law caught up with you."

"You know this man?" Hale asked.

"Sure. He used to work for Mr. Cramer. He was fired several weeks ago for stealing from the hands."

"He shouldn't have fired me," Monk muttered. "I was gonna pay them back. I lost heavy at poker and had to redeem my IOU's."

"No wonder Rusty wouldn't hire you," Sam said. "He has a canny ability when it comes to judging a man's character."

"Cramer shouldn't have fired me," Monk repeated.

Hale nudged Monk into the cell next to Harper's and closed the door. "Sounds like you had good reason to want Cramer dead, Monk."

"Cramer had enemies," Monk muttered. "Anyone could have shot him. Why pick on me?"

"As I said before, there's a witness."

"You're bluffing."

"Am I?" Hale turned to Sam. "Would you object to bringing Andy here to identify the prisoner?"

Sam hesitated. "Look, the boy's been through hell. Is this necessary?"

"It is if we want to bring Monk to trial."

Sam decided to cooperate with the sheriff. He found Lacey and Andy waiting for him outside.

"Did he confess, Sam?" Lacey asked anxiously.

"Not yet. Are you sure that's the man you saw, Andy?"

"Yes, Papa."

"Would you mind looking at him again and telling the sheriff what you just told me?"

Andy's eyes widened. "Can the bad man hurt me?"

"No, son, he's behind bars. Remember what I said? I won't let anyone hurt you again. You believe me, don't you?"

"Sam," Lacey began, "I don't think Andy should—"

"It's Andy's choice, love. I won't force him to do anything he doesn't want to do."

"I'll do it, Papa. I want you to be proud of me."

"I'm proud of you no matter what you decide. Are you sure?"

Andy nodded solemnly.

"That's my boy," Sam said, lifting Andy from Galahad's back. "Let's get this over with."

Sam took Andy directly to Monk's cell. Lacey trailed behind. Sheriff Hale was waiting for them.

"Do you know this man, Andy?" Sheriff Hale asked, standing aside so Andy could view the prisoner.

Andy clung to Sam's hand as he stared up at Monk. "He's the man who shot at mean old Cramer," he said with unshakable conviction. "I saw him from my bedroom window."

"He's lying!" Monk shouted.

"I don't lie!" Andy retorted. "Do I, Mama?"

"No, honey, you don't lie," Lacey concurred.

Suddenly Andy spotted Harper in the next cell. The boy showed no fear as he marched over to Harper's cell and glared up at him. "You're the mean man who took me to the orphanage. I don't like you."

"I didn't hurt you, kid. Tell them I didn't hurt you."

"You took me far away. That's the same as hurting me."

"Can we leave now, Sheriff?" Sam asked. "I want to take Andy home. He's been through enough today."

"I reckon it's all right. Andy seemed pretty positive about what he saw. Leave Monk to me. I'll have a confession from him before this day is over."

Andy rode home perched in the saddle before Sam. Exhausted from the long journey from Fort Worth, he soon fell asleep, his small body curled trustingly against his father. He didn't stir until they rode into the yard and the whooping and shouting awakened him.

"We're home, son," Sam said.

"Welcome home, scamp," Rusty said, scooping Andy from the saddle and whirling him around. "We sure did miss you."

Rita came rushing from the house, alternately weeping and hugging Andy. The hands' welcome was just as jubilant. At first Andy seemed overwhelmed, but after a while he appeared to thoroughly enjoy being the center of attention.

"Can I go to the barn to see the kittens, Mama?" Andy

asked when he grew tired of being fawned over. "I'll bet they've really grown."

"Aren't you tired?" Lacey asked.

"Not anymore. I slept on Galahad."

"Run along, then."

"I'll fix you something special to eat," Rita promised.

"Something with chocolate?"

Rita laughed. "I wouldn't be surprised."

Andy trotted off to the barn, trailed by several cowboys, each of whom had something new to show him.

"Sure is good to have him home," Rusty said, wiping a tear from the corner of his eye. "He seems no different. Most lads his age would be shaken up by the experience, but not our Andy. How did it go in Fort Worth?"

Lacey and Sam took turns telling Rusty everything that had happened since they left home—how they found Andy at the orphanage, how unresponsive he was at first, then how happy he'd been to see them.

"But that's not all," Sam confided. "The mystery of who shot Cramer has been solved."

"Well, I'll be danged. Did you recognize the killer in town? I thought you said you didn't see his face."

"I wasn't the one who identified the killer. We had just gotten off the stage and were walking to the livery for our horses when Andy spotted a cowboy loitering near the saloon. He suddenly recalled seeing the cowboy on the B&G the day someone took a shot at Cramer. He saw the whole thing from his bedroom window. I fetched the sheriff, and Andy identified the cowboy as the man who shot at Cramer. Since no one asked Andy about it, he never mentioned it to anyone before now."

"Damn! Who is he? Did he confess?"

"I think you'll recognize the name. He calls himself Monk."

"Monk? Is he big and mean-looking? Yeah, I know him. He came here looking for work, but I refused to hire him. Something about him set my teeth on edge. He's not the kind we want on the B&G."

"Seems he had a grudge against Cramer for firing him. The sheriff took him off to jail, and Andy positively identified him as the shooter." Sam's chest puffed out. "He's the smartest five-year-old I've ever seen. I can't wait until my brothers meet him."

"Think a jury will convict Monk?" Rusty asked.

"I wouldn't be surprised. He had a reason, weak as it is, to want Cramer dead. I suspect he'll crack under questioning before he comes to trial."

Sam placed an arm around Lacey's shoulders. "We'll talk tomorrow, Rusty. Lacey and I need some time alone right now."

Sam's blunt words made Lacey's face glow a becoming pink.

"Don't worry about Andy interrupting you," Rusty said, grinning. "I'll keep him occupied till Rita calls him in for supper."

"Much obliged," Sam said, returning Rusty's grin.

"Sam Gentry!" Lacey scolded after Rusty left. "You didn't have to be so obvious."

"We've just been given a couple of uninterrupted hours," he murmured, pulling her against him. Then, to the delight of everyone who happened to be looking, he scooped her up and carried her into the house. He didn't put her down until they reached their bedroom.

"What exactly did you have in mind?" Lacey asked as he set her on her feet.

"We haven't made love in days. The night before we boarded the stagecoach, to be exact. We're still newly-weds, in case you've forgotten."

"Hardly newlyweds. We've been married six years. As far as I'm concerned, neither the annulment nor my brief marriage to Taylor counted."

"I was wrong to let you believe I was dead," Sam said as he began unbuttoning her bodice. "My brothers are gonna be shocked when I turn up in Denver with a wife and a five-year-old son."

"Andy will be six soon."

Her bodice fell away. Lacey tried to concentrate on the conversation, but Sam's hands on her breasts made coherent thought difficult. "Will you take Andy and me to Denver with you?"

"I wouldn't leave you behind for anything in the world. I want to show you and my son off to my brothers."

He pushed her skirt and petticoats down her hips and lifted her out of them. "Enough talk. I can't wait, love. I want you now."

Instead of putting her down, he carried her to the bed and deftly removed her drawers, stockings and shoes. With shaking hands he removed his gun belt and skimmed his trousers down his hips. Lacey gaped at his arousal. His swiftness to respond never failed to surprise her. His trousers were still bunched around his ankles when, with a fulminating groan, he lowered himself on top of her, spread her legs and thrust into her waiting warmth.

Their loving was fierce and frantic. Neither seemed to want a gentle, unhurried coupling. Both were primed and ready for the breathtaking climax that splintered through them much sooner than they would have liked. It seemed like an eternity before Sam found the energy to lift himself off and away.

"Give me a few minutes and we'll do this again, only we'll take our time."

"We have a lifetime to make love," Lacey said, snuggling against him.

"Given the frequency of our loving, it could result in a brother or sister for Andy," Sam warned. "Would you like more children, love?"

"Ummm?" she murmured sleepily.

"Children, Lacey. Shall we have more children?"

Lacey gave an exaggerated yawn. "I'm afraid we don't have any choice in the matter. I've suspected for a long time, but now I'm sure that Andy is going to have a brother of sister whether he wants one or not."

Sam went still. "You mean you're . . . My God, I'm going to be a father again! Why didn't you tell me before now?"

"I wasn't sure until I missed my second cycle."

"You won't have to go through this alone, love. This time I'm going to be with you every step of the way. No more riding, no more heavy work, no more—"

Lacey roused herself to mock anger. "For heaven's sake, Sam, I'm not a china doll. I gave you a healthy son; there's no need to smother me. Trust me to give you another healthy child. Can I go to sleep now?"

"Only if you let me wake you up in an hour. That will give us time to make love again before Andy comes bouncing in on us."

Lacey gave a sleepy laugh. "You're a greedy man, Sam Gentry."

"I'm only greedy for you, love. Always and forever."

370

Chapter Twenty-one

The Reunion

Rafe Gentry stood beneath the crystal chandelier in the lobby of the Antlers Hotel, a worried look on his handsome face as he watched the door. He'd been in Denver two days, waiting for his brothers to show up. The suspense was tormenting him. He had no way of knowing if either of his brothers were alive. For all he knew, one or both could have been captured and sent to prison before they knew the charges against them had been dropped.

A smile touched his lips as he recalled how his Angel

had braved banker Wingate and fought to restore the Gentry brothers' good name. There was no one in the world like his Angel. He wished he had brought her along with him, even though she was due to deliver very soon.

Rafe glanced at his pocket watch. It was nearly two o'clock and he'd been standing beneath the chandelier since noon. The lobby was crowded, but he spied an empty chair positioned where he could keep an eye on the front entrance. But first he made a detour to the front desk.

"Are you sure neither Jess nor Sam Gentry has checked in?" he asked the clerk.

"As I explained this morning, sir, you're the only Gentry registered," the clerk replied.

"Thank you."

Rafe began to worry in earnest. One or both of his brothers should have arrived by now. He turned away and headed for the empty chair, determined to keep watch all day if need be. And the day after that and the day after that.

"Rafe! You're here!"

Rafe whirled, a smile chasing away his gloomy thoughts when he saw Jess hurrying toward him. "Jess! Thank God. I was beginning to worry."

The brothers embraced, then stood back to look at one another.

"You don't look any the worse for wear," Jess said, grinning. "I reckon I have *you* to thank for taking us off the Wanted list."

"Not me. My Angel made it all possible. She refused to give up until Mr. Wingate admitted he'd lied about the bank robbery."

"I heard you were married. Where is this paragon?"

"I had to leave Angel home, and I'm not happy about it. She's due to deliver our child very soon. You should see my Angel, Jess. She not only sings like an angel but looks like one, too. She saved my life. What about you? Are you practicing medicine somewhere?"

Jess beamed. "I have a successful practice in Cheyenne, in Wyoming Territory. Where did you end up?"

"Right here in Colorado. Angel owns a gold mine near Canon City. We lived at the site for a time, until we bought our ranch. How did you learn that the charges were dropped against us?"

"I got tired of running and returned to Dodge, hoping to clear our name. That's how I found out. Do you suppose Sam knows? Is he here yet?"

"Sam hasn't arrived yet, but that doesn't surprise me," Rafe said. "If you recall, we never knew what Sam was going to do from one minute to the next. After he came back from the war, there was something of a mystery about him. I always felt he was keeping something from us."

"He'll show up," Jess predicted.

Suddenly Rafe became aware that Jess wasn't alone. His gaze settled on a lovely green-eyed, dark-haired woman who stood behind Jess. She smiled and held out her hand.

"I'm Meg, Jess's wife."

"Forgive my lapse," Jess apologized. "I was so excited at seeing Rafe that I forgot to introduce you to my brother. Rafe, this is Meg."

Rafe extended his hand. "Welcome to the family, Meg. The past year has been eventful for both of us, brother," Rafe teased, eyeing Meg's bulging stomach.

"Meg and my Angel have a great deal in common. I'm surprised you let Meg travel in her condition."

"Have you forgotten? I'm a doctor."

Rafe glanced at Meg's pale face and said, "Meg looks exhausted, Jess. Why don't you get her settled in. We can talk later. Let's all meet for supper in the dining room."

"I am tired," Meg acknowledged. "A bath and a long nap before supper sound wonderful."

"What about Sam?" Jess asked. "Are you going to stay down here and wait for him?"

"I'll stay awhile longer," Rafe said. "I sure hope nothing has happened to our little brother."

"Sam has had lots of practice getting himself out of scrapes. Don't worry, he'll be here."

The brothers embraced again, then parted. Rafe glanced around the lobby, then seated himself in the chair he had spotted earlier. He was still there when Jess joined him an hour later.

"How's Meg?" Rafe asked.

"She's tired but otherwise fine. I left her sleeping."

"Sit down," Rafe said, indicating the recently vacated chair beside his. "We've lots of catching up to do. For starters, how did you meet Meg?"

Jess chuckled. "Believe it or not, Meg was the best female bounty hunter in Wyoming Territory. We met while she was tracking three outlaw brothers who robbed a bank in Cheyenne and killed the guard. I was camped outside Cheyenne when two of the outlaws stumbled upon my campsite. Meg found us and mistook me for one of the brothers. It was a natural mistake, but Meg bit off more than she could chew. One of the outlaws shot her. I saved her life."

"That must have been Meg's lucky day, you being a doctor and all. I reckon one never knows where one will find love."

"You can say that again, brother. Not only do I have Meg, but the thriving practice I've always wanted."

"Doctoring isn't a lucrative profession," Rafe mused. "Are you getting by all right? Angel and I can help out if you need it. The Golden Angel mine is producing well. We've got more money than we need."

"Thanks, brother, but Meg and I are just fine. Her foster father came into some money and settled a portion on Meg. We've got more than we need and are considering sponsoring an orphanage in Cheyenne. Money never really mattered to me. Medicine and my family are my life."

"What do you suppose Sam has been up to?" Rafe speculated.

"Knowing Sam, I suppose he's brawled and whored in every town he's passed through."

Jess chuckled, then sobered. "Did you encounter trouble after you fled Dodge?"

"If you call sitting beneath a hanging tree with a rope around my neck trouble, then the answer is yes. I was being sought for murder before the Dodge City charges were dropped."

"My God! Who were you supposed to have murdered?"

"The passengers on the stagecoach I was accused of robbing. And after that, Angel's husband of one day."

Jess whistled softly. "My problems were nothing compared to yours. Fortunately, we both came out winners. You appear to adore your Angel every bit as much as I do my Meg."

"What do you think the chances are of Sam showing up with a wife?" Rafe said thoughtfully.

Jess guffawed. "You're kidding! It won't happen. After Sam returned from the war, he vowed he'd never marry. Wonder what happened to evoke those sentiments."

"We may never know."

"It doesn't look like Sam is going to show up today," Rafe said. "I'm going up to my room and get ready for supper. I'll see you later in the dining room. How does six o'clock sound to you?"

As they spoke, a man with a young boy hanging onto his hand and a pregnant woman at his side walked past them. As they headed for the stairs, the brothers paid scant heed to the small family who approached the desk to check in.

Suddenly the man whirled and stared at the brothers. "Rafe! Jess!"

The brothers spun around. Rafe spotted Sam first.

"There's Sam!"

"How did we miss him?" Jess wondered aloud.

"Probably because of the woman and child with him." Rafe grinned. "I can't wait to hear Sam's explanation. It promises to be more interesting than either of ours."

The brothers greeted one another exuberantly, embracing and pounding each other on the back. "I knew you'd both show up," Sam crowed. "Lacey told me not to worry. She said if both my brothers were as resourceful as me, I had nothing to worry about."

Andy tugged at Sam's sleeve. "Papa, are these my uncles?"

Sam beamed down at Andy. "They sure are, son. Rafe, Jess, I'd like you to meet my son Andy." He pulled Lacey forward. "And this is Lacey, my wife."

Greetings were extended all around. "I reckon the Gentry brothers don't let any grass grow under their feet," Rafe said. Our wives are expecting, just like yours."

Sam puffed out his chest. "Lacey is expecting our second child. Andy here is also my son. He'll be six soon."

"Don't you mean stepson?" Rafe said without thinking. He hoped his thoughtless inquiry wouldn't be misconstrued. But it just wasn't possible for Sam to have a five-year-old son, for he'd been fighting a war then.

"I know this is going to come as a shock, but Lacey and I have been married for more than six years. We married in Pennsylvania during the war and became estranged afterward. To make a long story short, Lacey and I met purely by accident in Texas, after I fled Dodge I learned I had a son and . . . well, Lacey and I settled our differences and discovered we still loved each other."

"You married during the war and we never knew about it?" Rafe charged, aghast. "Dammit, Sam, how could you have kept something like that from us? Why did you abandon your wife and child?"

"It's a long story, Rafe, and we've traveled a long way. Let me get Lacey and Andy settled in our room first."

"We're all meeting in the dining room for supper," Jess said. "Since there are so many of us, I'll arrange for a private dining room. Our wives can get to know one another, and we can talk to our hearts' content."

"We're all here except for Angel," Rafe corrected. "I've got a couple of ideas about how you all can meet her. I'll tell you about it at supper tonight."

"Can I tell you about my adventures?" Andy piped

up. "A bad man took me away from Mama and Papa. Far, far away."

Rafe looked askance at Sam. "Is that true?"

Sam's mouth thinned. "All too true, I fear. But it ended well."

"The bad man got killed," Andy announced grandly.

Jess's eyebrows arched upward, and Sam quickly set him straight. "I didn't do it, Jess. Someone else got to him first."

"You can tell us all about it tonight, Andy," Rafe said. "Your mama looks tired. Why don't you and your papa take her to her room?"

The brothers parted, each anticipating their reunion later that evening and the recounting of their adventures.

"I like your brothers," Lacey said once they were settled in their room. "Like you, they must have encountered many adverse situations after they fled Dodge City. They appear to have thrived. And both are happily married."

"That is a surprise," Sam allowed. "I thought all Jess cared about was medicine, and Rafe never seemed interested in taking a wife. They both appear as happy as I am."

"You're all special men, Sam."

Meg was awake when Jess returned to their room. "Sam arrived," Jess said. "He took us both by surprise. Not only did he arrive with a wife, but he has a five-year-old son."

"You mean stepson?"

Jess laughed. "No, I mean son. It seems Sam has kept a secret all the years since the war. He married early in the war and fathered a child."

"And he never told you? Why didn't he bring his wife and child home to Kansas with him after the war?"

"Evidently he abandoned his family because of a misunderstanding. He found them living in Texas. I don't know the whole story, but I'll bet it's a whopper. If Rafe or I had known, we would have made him face up to his responsibilities. Sam always was a maverick. We'll hear everything tonight at supper. I stopped on my way up here and engaged a private dining room."

"I can hardly wait," Meg enthused.

"How are you feeling, love? The trip from Cheyenne must have been grueling for you."

"I'm fine, Jess. Just a few twinges. I doubt we'll make it back home before I deliver, though. We might be stuck here longer than we anticipated."

"I took that into consideration before we left," Jess said. "The new doctor in town is taking over my patients until I return. The town has grown so much, there's plenty of room for another doctor."

He placed his hand on her stomach. "Our babe is active tonight."

"Takes after his father," Meg said with a twinkle. "I can't wait until we can make love again."

"Nor I, love. Did I tell you that Sam's wife is expecting?"

"All the Gentry wives are pregnant? Good heavens, what a crowd we'll have at our family reunions."

"I hope there will be many family reunions," Jess said wistfully. "We've all seemed to settle in different parts of the country. Sam in Texas and Rafe in Colorado."

"I don't think anything could keep the Gentry brothers apart for long," Meg predicted.

*   *   *

Jess and Meg were the last to arrive in the private dining room. Meg was introduced to Sam and his family, then everyone started talking at once. Being the oldest, Rafe acted as moderator while each brother in turn related his adventures, or misadventures, as it turned out. The conversation was temporarily interrupted while the food was being served, but continued long after the meal had been consumed.

After everyone had run out of questions and explanations, Rafe called them all to attention and made an unexpected announcement.

"I'd like to issue you all an invitation to come with me to Canon City to meet my wife. It will mean three nights on the road, but Angel will be thrilled to have you. Having a reunion in a hotel leaves much to be desired. What do you say? I don't like leaving Angel alone so close to her time."

Sam and Lacey agreed immediately. Jess and Meg spoke together in low tones before they, too, agreed to the visit.

"Will tomorrow be too soon for you? There's a noon stage we can take."

"Sounds good to me," Sam said. He turned to Lacey. "Can you abide another three days in a stagecoach?"

"If Meg can do it, so can I," Lacey maintained.

Meg patted her stomach and groaned. "I think this babe can settle down for another ride. But I'm warning you, he's anxious to see the light of day."

"Then it's settled," Rafe enthused. "Let's meet in the lobby at eleven o'clock."

The stagecoach was only an hour late. The Gentrys vied for seat space with two other passengers. Unaccustomed to mountains, Lacey oohed and oohed during most of the trip, while Meg appeared oblivious to the breathtaking scenery. A small smile tugged at Meg's lips as she rested her hands on her burgeoning middle, her thoughts apparently turned inward.

Jess was getting anxious. He'd birthed too many babes not to know that Meg's body was preparing itself for imminent birth. And that worried him. She was still a month away from her due date. He wished he could examine her, but that was impossible in their circumstances. But that still didn't stop him from being concerned.

They arrived in Canon City on a glorious sunny day. Rafe was anxious as he arranged for a pair of buggies and a wagon to carry his guests and their baggage to the ranch. His anxiety had persisted throughout the trip down from Denver. He worried excessively about Angel, alone on the ranch but for Bessie and the hired hands. He knew the ranch wasn't far from town, and that the doctor had promised to keep an eye on Angel, but he'd feel better once he was home.

The family crowded into the buggies while Rafe followed behind with the baggage wagon. The moment the ranch came into sight, his apprehension escalated. Something was wrong. He sensed it the moment he rode through the gate sporting a sign above it proclaiming it Angel Acres. The two buggies had arrived before him, and their occupants were gathered before the front door, waiting for him.

"This is some spread," Sam enthused. "Imagine, both of us ranchers. The only difference is that you raise horses and I raise cattle."

Rafe heard nothing above the pounding of his heart. He reached for the doorknob and flung open the door.

"Angel! Bessie!"

Bessie appeared at the top of the stairs, wringing her hands. "Thank God you're home, Mr. Gentry!"

Rafe paled. "What is it, Bessie? Is it Angel? Is she all right?"

"She's in trouble, and I don't know how to help her. She's having the baby but it won't come out," Bessie wailed.

"Did you send for the doctor?"

"Two days ago, but he had an accident and can't come. I thought I could do this myself, but it's beyond me."

Rafe took the stairs two at a time. Jess was hard on his heels.

"Has Mrs. Gentry been in labor the whole two days?" Jess asked the housekeeper.

Too excited to speak, the woman could do little more than nod.

"If anything happens to Angel, I don't know what I'll do," Rafe exclaimed.

Jess caught up with him. "I'm a doctor, Rafe. Let me handle this. Just show me the way."

Rafe burst into the bedroom, fearful of what he'd find. When he saw Angel lying pale and writhing in pain against a mound of pillows, he rushed to her bedside.

"Forgive me, Angel. I shouldn't have left you," he said, raising her hand to his lips.

"I'll . . . be fine, Rafe. It's just taking longer than I expected. Did you meet your brothers? Are they well?"

"Better yet, I brought them and their wives with me.

Sam has a five-year-old son, and both Jess and Sam's wives are expecting."

Angel cried out as a contraction ravaged her body. Rafe felt a hand on his shoulder and moved aside to make room for Jess.

"This is my brother Jess, sweetheart. He's a doctor. Do you trust him to help you?"

"I'll need to examine you, Angel, but I'll try to be gentle."

Angel appeared too lost in pain to answer, but she did nod.

"Go downstairs and tell the others what's happening," Jess advised his brother. "I'll know more once I examine your wife. You know I'll do my very best, Rafe."

"I know, Jess, it's just that . . . God, why can't anything be simple?"

Angel stifled another cry, and Jess turned back to his patient. "Give me a few minutes alone with Angel before you return, Rafe, and I'd appreciate it if you saw that Meg is made comfortable. I wouldn't be surprised if she delivers early."

Rafe appeared reluctant to leave. "Go on, Rafe," Angel said, giving him a wobbly smile. "Make our guests comfortable. I'm in good hands. You once bragged about Jess's doctoring skills, so trust him to deliver our babe."

Rafe kissed her forehead. "I'll be back shortly."

"Send Bessie up with plenty of hot water, strong lye soap and clean cloths," Jess called after Rafe.

Reluctantly Rafe left his Angel in Jess's capable hands and went downstairs. Sam, Meg and Lacey were gathered in the parlor, waiting for a report on Angel's progress. Bessie was in the room, serving refreshments.

"How is she?" Lacey asked anxiously.

"Jess is examining her now. The baby should have been born by now." Spying Bessie, Rafe said, "Jess wants plenty of hot water, strong lye soap and clean cloths, Bessie."

"Right away, Mr. Gentry," Bessie said, hurrying off.

"I'll help her," Lacey offered. "I've already had a child and know what to do."

"I'll join you," Meg said.

"No, stay here, Meg, unless you want Jess running back and forth between rooms delivering babies," Lacey said. "I know you haven't said anything, but I can tell you're close to delivery."

Rafe gave Meg a startled look. "Is that true, Meg?"

Meg flushed. "I don't know. I've had some pain off and on since last night, but I'm not sure what that means."

"It means you're going to bed . . . now. I'll show you to the room you and Jess will share."

"I'll take Andy to the kitchen and get him something to eat, then lend Bessie a hand," Lacey said as she took Andy's hand and hurried off to the kitchen while Rafe and Sam helped Meg up the staircase.

"Ah, here's the hot water," Jess said as Bessie and Lacey entered the room carrying the items Jess had asked for.

He poured hot water into the basin and scrubbed his hands. "Would you ladies kindly step outside the door for a moment while I examine my patient? I'll call you in when I'm ready for you to assist me with the birth."

Lacey and Bessie went into the hall and closed the door behind them. Rafe joined them a few minutes later.

"What's going on in there?"

"Jess is examining Angel. How's Meg?"

"I think you're right. She may be in the early stages of labor."

"Don't tell Jess," Lacey advised. "Meg has hours to go yet, and Angel needs all his attention."

Suddenly an agonized scream came from behind the closed door. Rafe started violently, an agonized expression contorting his face. "What is that!"

"I'm sure everything is just fine," Lacey said in a tone that suggested just the opposite. There had been no complications when she delivered Andy.

"Hell and damnation! I'm going in," Rafe said as he barged into the room.

Jess looked up and gave him an exasperated look. "Take it easy, Rafe. You look like a man at the end of his tether."

"What's going on in here? I heard Angel scream."

"The babe was turned wrong. The child could not have been born in the position it was in. I turned it. Everything should progress normally now."

Rafe knelt at Angel's side, concern wrinkling his brow. She was too pale; her lovely eyes were deeply shadowed and filled with pain. "Are you all right, love? Jess said it won't be long now." He glanced up at Jess. "What can I do?"

"Exactly what you're doing now. Let her squeeze your hand and brace her when she pushes."

"How can I help?" Lacey asked, stepping forward.

"Prepare a basin of warm water and have blankets ready."

Lacey moved with alacrity while Jess turned back to Angel. "Do you feel like pushing, Angel?"

"Tired, so tired," Angel murmured. Then she stiffened

as a violent contraction ripped through her body.

"Push, Angel!" Jess urged. "You want this babe, don't you?"

"Please, Angel, help Jess," Rafe begged. "It's almost over."

"I'll . . . try . . ."

Jess placed his hand on Angel's stomach. "Another contraction. Come on, Angel, you can do it."

Rafe watched helplessly as Angel's face contorted with the effort, and he braced her back as Jess suggested. Suddenly Jess gave a whoop.

"He's crowning! The babe has blond fuzz on its head. Just one more push, Angel, and you can hold your babe in your arms."

Rafe was astounded at the effort Angel was expending and the pain she was experiencing, and vowed that this would be their last child.

"Here he comes!" Jess shouted as the babe slipped into his waiting hands. "It's a boy, Rafe, and a good-sized one at that."

A son. He had a son.

Jess cleared the mucus from the babe's mouth, held him by the feet and gave him a light slap upon his tiny bottom. Everyone in the room held their breath until the babe filled his lungs with air and gave a healthy cry. Jess handed the babe to Lacey and returned his attention to his patient. A short time later he delivered the afterbirth, and Bessie carried it away in a basin.

"Can I see my baby?" Angel asked weakly. "Is he all right?"

Rafe took the babe from Lacey, opened the blanket and counted the fingers and toes. Then he placed the babe in Angel's arms. "Here he is, love. Every pink and wrinkled inch of him. He has all the right number of fingers and toes."

Angel hugged the babe to her breast, too exhausted to do more than cuddle him close. She fell asleep while Lacey was bathing her. Rafe took the babe from her arms and placed him in the cradle that he had carved with his own hands.

"They'll both sleep for a while," Jess said as he gathered up his things.

"I'll sit with her," Rafe said. "The rest of you go and get some rest. Lacey looks ready to drop, and I don't know what I would have done if you weren't here, Jess. You saved the lives of Angel and my son."

"What are brothers for if they can't help one another when they need it?" Jess said. "I'd best go look in on Meg now."

Jess heard Meg moaning before he opened the door to the room assigned to him and Meg. He began shaking like a leaf as he approached the bed. It was one thing to deliver his sister-in-law's baby, but this was *his* wife, *his* baby.

Meg was sitting on the edge of the bed, her face pale, her pupils dilated. Jess knew immediately that she was in pain. "How long have you been like this?"

"The pains started last night," Meg whispered. "I didn't want to say anything until I was certain." She offered him a wobbly smile. "Jess . . . I'm . . . certain."

Jess bit out a curse and ran to the door. "Bessie! More hot water, soap and cloths. Quick!"

Lacey opened the door to her room and peered out. "Jess, is it Meg?"

"She's in labor," Jess said. "I won't know how far along until I examine her."

"I'll be right there."

"I don't know if Bessie heard me," Jess answered. "I need more water, soap and cloths."

"I'll take care of it," Lacey said.

Sam appeared in the doorway. "What can I do?"

"Keep Andy occupied," Lacey said. "He's feeling somewhat abandoned right now. Take him out to look at the horses."

Jess waited impatiently for the hot water, eager to scrub and examine Meg. When the water arrived, he scrubbed and began the examination while Lacey stood by the door.

"My God, Meg, you're almost there!"

"I knew it was going fast," Meg said, panting.

"Let me help you undress," Lacey offered, moving to assist Jess.

Lacey had no sooner gotten Meg into a nightgown than she announced in a strangled voice, "The babe's coming!"

"Push, sweetheart," Jess urged. "You're doing magnificently. I wish all women delivered as easily as you."

"It's . . . not . . . so easy," Meg gasped as she bore down.

"I have it!" Jess crowed. "It's a boy, love. We have a son."

For the second time that day the wail of a newborn filled the air. It was music to Jess's ears. Two new Gentrys in the same day! He glanced at Lacey, a smile hovering over his lips as he gazed pointedly at her large stomach.

"I hope you're not thinking of making it three in one day."

"Not on your life," Lacey laughed.

All the Gentrys except Angel and Meg gathered in the parlor after supper that evening. Exhausted but jubilant, they toasted the new mothers and their babes.

"I reckon you're going to have me and Meg on your hands longer than you expected, Rafe," Jess ventured. "Meg and our son won't be ready to travel for a month or two."

"That couldn't please me more," Rafe acknowledged. "What have you named your son?"

"We're going to call him Justin. What about your boy? Have you and Angel settled on a name yet?"

"Angel picked out Gabriel, and that suits me just fine. I'll probably call him Gabe."

"I'm going to have a girl," Lacey announced with utter confidence. "And I'm naming her Emily Ann."

"I've got two months to change her mind," Sam laughed. "But all joking aside, if we have a girl, I think Emily Ann is a fine name for our daughter. We'd planned to be back in Texas for the delivery, but we can stick around a couple weeks longer, if it's all right with you, Rafe."

"You're welcome to stay as long as you like," Rafe beamed. "This is going to be a family reunion none of us will ever forget."

Epilogue

Six Weeks Later

"I knew we should have returned home two weeks ago," Sam lamented as he watched his wife struggling through the last stages of labor.

"I'm sorry, Sam. Emily Ann just wouldn't wait," Lacey panted.

"It won't be long now," Jess encouraged. "Support her back, Sam."

Meg and Angel stood beside the bed, offering encouragement, but Lacey was concentrating too hard to pay heed to what was going on in the room as she struggled through each consecutive contraction.

"Now, Lacey," Jess cried. "Bear down with the next one."

Lacey felt a tremendous pressure, then relief as the babe slid into Jess's capable hands.

"She's small," Jess said as he cleared the babe's air passages. Suddenly the tiny mite gave an outraged wail. Sam smiled hugely. "Her lungs certainly are healthy."

"Emily Ann," Sam said, awed by the miracle of birth. "Our daughter is beautiful, Lacey. Nearly as beautiful as her mother."

Meg took the babe and wrapped her in a blanket. "There's a little boy outside the door who can't wait to greet his new sibling."

"Let Andy see his sister, Sam," Jess said. "I'm still busy with Lacey, so he can't come in yet." Meg handed the babe to Sam.

Holding Emily Ann gingerly in his arms, Sam opened the door and stepped into the hallway. Andy and Rafe were waiting just outside the door.

"Do I have a sister or brother?" Andy asked, jumping up and down.

"A sister," Sam said, holding the babe out for Andy's inspection. "Meet Emily Ann."

Andy gave a squeal of delight. "She has dark hair. But she's all wrinkled. That's all right, Papa, I'll love her anyway. Can I see Mama now?"

"Not yet, son, but soon. I'm going to put Emily Ann in her bed now. We'll call you in to see Mama as soon as she's ready for visitors."

Sam reentered the bedroom. Angel took the babe from his arms and carried her to her cradle. Then she and Meg tiptoed from the room.

"She's beautiful," Angel said as she joined Rafe and Andy in the hallway. "I hope we have a daughter next."

"There won't be a next time," Rafe assured her. "I couldn't bear to see you suffer like that again."

"Famous last words," Meg said, grinning. "Besides, look at the easy time Lacey and I had. Each time is different, and Angel isn't likely to have a difficult time next time."

"I said—" Rafe began.

"I know what you said, darling," Angel said archly, "but let's wait and see what happens in a year or two."

The bedroom door opened and Sam and Jess walked out into the hall. "They're both sleeping," Sam said. "How about a toast to the newest Gentry?"

They all trooped down to the parlor. Rafe dug out a bottle of vintage wine and they toasted Emily Ann and Lacey.

A month later, the entire family gathered in the dining room for a celebratory dinner before Sam, Lacey, Andy, Jess, Meg and the babies departed for their separate homes.

Sam raised his glass in a toast. "Lacey and I expect you all at the B&G ranch one year from today."

"And the year after that, you're all invited to Cheyenne. But, please, if any more babies are expected," Jess said with a long-suffering sigh, "plan them so that I won't have to deliver two in one day."

A round of laughter followed as they toasted the next gathering of the clan.

Author's Note

The Outlaws: Sam concludes my Outlaw series. I hope you enjoyed the three irresistible Gentry brothers and the women they loved.

My Medieval fans have been asking for another book like *The Black Knight*, which proved immensely popular with my readers. I'm happy to announce that my next book will be a Medieval set in 1214, the time of King John Lackland.

Dominic Dragon, the landless second son of an earl, earned the name Dragon Lord for his skill and fearlessness in battle. When the king needs a trusted man to protect the Scottish border, he gives Fairwinds Castle

Connie Mason

and the accompanying lands that belonged to an executed traitor to Dominic. In order to keep the lands, Dominic must wed either the mother or daughter of the traitor.

When Dominic arrives at Fairwinds, he finds not only the beautiful, grieving widow, but *twin* daughters, Rose and Lily. The sisters are as different as night from day. Feisty Rose and gentle Lily. Dominic, wanting nothing to do with the quarrelsome, fractious Rose, promptly announces his decision to wed Lily that very day.

But *is* it Lily whom Dominic weds? You'll have to read *The Dragon Lord* to find out. If you like a bit of history in your books, the story ends with King John being forced to sign the Magna Carta by Dominic and the border barons. Look for *The Dragon Lord* in November 2001.

I enjoy hearing from readers. For a newsletter and bookmark, send a self-addressed, stamped envelope to me at P.O. Box 3471, Holiday, FL 34690. My e-mail address is conmason@aol.com, and my website is www.conniemason.com.

Happy Reading,
Connie Mason

The OUTLAWS: Rafe

Connie Mason

He is going to hang. Rafe Gentry has committed plenty of sins, but not the robbery and murder that has landed him in jail. Now, with a lynch mob out for his blood, he is staring death in the face . . . until a blond beauty with the voice of an angel steps in to redeem him.

She is going to wed. There is only one way to rescue the dark and dangerous outlaw from the hanging tree—by claiming him as the fictitious fiancé she is to meet in Pueblo. But Sister Angela Abbot never anticipates that she will have to make good on her claim and actually marry the rogue. Railroaded into a hasty wedding, reeling from the raw, seductive power of Rafe's kiss, she wonders whether she has made the biggest mistake of her life, or the most exciting leap of faith.

___4702-0 $5.99 US/$6.99 CAN

Dorchester Publishing Co., Inc.
P.O. Box 6640
Wayne, PA 19087-8640

Please add $1.75 for shipping and handling for the first book and $.50 for each book thereafter. NY, NYC, and PA residents, please add appropriate sales tax. No cash, stamps, or C.O.D.s. All orders shipped within 6 weeks via postal service book rate. Canadian orders require $2.00 extra postage and must be paid in U.S. dollars through a U.S. banking facility.

Name_____
Address_____
City_____State_____Zip_____
I have enclosed $_____ in payment for the checked book(s).
Payment <u>must</u> accompany all orders. ☐ Please send a free catalog.

Pure Temptation

Connie Mason

Spirits can be so bloody unpredictable, and the specter of Lady Amelia is worst of all. Just when one of her ne'er-do-well descendants thinks he can go astray in peace, the phantom lady always appears to change his wicked ways. A rogue without peer, Jackson Graystoke wants to make gaming and carousing in London society his life's work. And the penniless baronet will gladly damn himself with wine and women—if Lady Amelia gives him the ghost of a chance. Fresh off the boat from Ireland, Moira O'Toole isn't fool enough to believe in legends or naive enough to trust a rake. Yet after an accident lands her in Graystoke Manor, she finds herself haunted, harried, and hopelessly charmed by Black Jack Graystoke and his exquisite promise of . . . Pure Temptation.

___4041-7 $5.99 US/$6.99 CAN

the Black Knight
Connie Mason

He rides into Chirk Castle on his pure black destrier. Clad in black from his gleaming helm to the tips of his toes, he is all battle-honed muscle and rippling tendons. In his stark black armor he looks lethal and sinister, every bit as dangerous as his name implies. He is a man renowned for his courage and strength, for his prowess with women, for his ruthless skill in combat. But when he sees Raven of Chirk, with her long, chestnut tresses and womanly curves, he can barely contain his embroiled emotions. For it was her betrayal twelve years before that turned him from chivalrous youth to hardened knight. It is she who has made him vow to trust no woman— to take women only for his pleasure. But only she can unleash the passion in his body, the goodness in his soul, and the love in his heart.

___4622-9 $5.99 US/$6.99 CAN

Dorchester Publishing Co., Inc.
P.O. Box 6640
Wayne, PA 19087-8640

GUNSLINGER

Connie Mason

He blows into Trouble Creek on a raw April wind, a fast gun for hire to the highest bidder. But when Chloe Sommers offers him a job protecting her herd, she has no idea Desperado Jones has a hidden agenda as deadly as his Colt .45. All she sees is a man packing even more raw sex appeal than firepower. She senses right away that his dark good looks and blatant virility are a threat to her peace of mind. But she never guesses what she will discover after a night of explosive loving: Desperado holds a secret claim on her ranch and a far more binding claim on her wayward heart.

___4532-X $5.99 US/$6.99 CAN